BISECTION

Sheila Jenné

Alnitak Press

Also by Sheila Jenné

Black Sails to Sunward (2023)
The Sea of Clouds (2024)
Invasive (2025)
Under False Colors (2026)

www.sheilajenne.com

to John

without whom this book would still be sitting in a drawer

CREW OF THE GALAJAK

Spacers

Pav – Captain, Liberty sect

Resh – Second in command and medic, Unity sect

Gaj – Engineer, Liberty sect

Talek – Second engineer, Liberty sect

Daz – Navigator, Liberty sect

Zin – Computer specialist, Unity sect

Scientists

Karnath – Biologist, Curiosity sect

Lex – Linguist, Curiosity sect

Jahac – Linguist, Liberty sect

Tazag – Anthropologist, Unity sect

Prazad – Alien tech specialist, Liberty sect

Femat – Sociologist, Liberty sect

CHAPTER ONE

Tria

It was the first full day of our polar biological survey, and already I was arguing with my other half.

I stepped on the heel of the shovel, driving it a handspan into the tundra. *Tell me again why you didn't bring this up before we left home?*

Resa lifted her shoulder and dropped it again. *I didn't know it was going to be like this,* she said. Well, perhaps said is the wrong word. Resa is my left, so we don't communicate aloud. We share a body, and I hear whichever of her thoughts she chooses for me to hear.

I told you the average springtime temperature for the northern tundra is about ten below zero, I said. I had been correct. A wind like a sandblaster tore down from the craggy slopes, making my eye tear up. The tears formed crystals in my eyelashes, which I brushed away with a heavy mitt.

Those numbers mean nothing to me, she said in frustration. *You should have told me I would feel ice in my bones. Or that the dryness would suck the moisture out of our nose.*

That's not how I talk, or how I think. Such poetic nonsense is a left tendency. So while I think in degrees, she seems to expect a metaphor. She might as well ask for... well... a metaphor from a right.

Bending down, I scooped a few crumbs of frozen earth into a vial. Back at the base we'd examine the sample for extremophile bacteria. If there were any, that would tell us something important about whether, and how, life might evolve on a frozen planet. There is one in Kinaru's solar system, always assumed to be lifeless, but if there were organisms here, why not on our nearest neighbor?

No mediator would take my part, anyway, Resa continued. *You were selected for this mission because you are the best person for the job. And it would be equally uncomfortable for anyone.*

You wouldn't need a mediator! I protested, offended. *When have I ever refused you anything important?* But internally I quailed at the thought of turning down this mission. Could I really have made that sacrifice? I had been lucky enough to be assigned exobiology as my career right when it was an emerging field. I was positioned to be one of the first to visit another planet, if we managed to travel to one before my working years were over. But not if I got a reputation as so ruled by my left I would turn down prestigious assignments.

She made a dismissive gesture. *It doesn't matter. I couldn't have really demanded you give this up. I know how important it is to you.* Taking the vial from my hand, she stuffed it into our coat's left pocket. *Maybe I'm not really objecting. Maybe I just want to complain. It's cold as space out here, and you always act like you don't feel it.*

It's true, she feels the cold much more than I do. She feels everything more. As the right, I'm the thinker, the logical one.

"Tria il Resa!" called my team leader, Heda il Trambo, over the screaming of the wind. "Come around this outcropping with me. If we can get out of the wind a little, we'll have a much easier time digging."

I shouldered my shovel and followed my mentor, trudging across the stony permafrost. There was no snow. It is far too dry on the Northern Continent for there to be any; the frozen ground was barely touched with frost. A few icy bits skittered along the ground; that was all the moisture for miles, if you didn't count what we had brought with us.

I was just rounding the outcropping when I almost tripped over Heda il Trambo, who had stopped dead. His stout figure, made even stouter with layers of heavy clothing, blocked me from seeing beyond him. "Is something the matter, Professor?" Without the wind screaming so loudly in my ear, my voice sounded too loud.

He turned, shushing me. "Look! What do you see?"

I followed his pointing finger. "The camp? How have we gotten so turned around?" Then I looked again at the squat buildings, the radio antenna, the solar panels. "That's not our camp. Who else is on the Northern Continent right now? I thought we were the only expedition for a hundred miles!"

"We are," said Heda. "I can't imagine what business anyone else could have here."

"What do you think, Professor?" I asked, pulling my scarf down to speak more clearly. "Could it be smugglers or something?"

He waved a hand dismissively. "Oh, I wouldn't want to leap to conclusions. It's probably something innocent."

"It could be abandoned," I started to say, but just then I saw a figure come out of the door, stomping its way over to the radio antenna to tinker with it. From this distance, and in their heavy clothing, it was impossible to tell anything about them. Their clothes were black, which was a bit odd— ours were all brown leather, with the fur inside. But I admit I don't know what clothing is common in every region of the north.

"Let's go over and introduce ourselves," I said. "I mean, there's no one else for three hundred miles. We should know our neighbors."

"Do you have a weapon?" he asked. "I mean, just in case."

"I have the stunner," I answered. "It's rated up to snow apes so it can surely handle a person if we need it to."

"Keep it under your coat for now, Tria," said Heda. "Don't want to scare them. We're just friendly neighbors saying hello."

Thus prepared, we came out of the shelter of the outcropping and started to walk toward the mysterious base. The figure tinkering with the antenna didn't look up; the wind was far louder than any sound we made, tramping across the frozen earth.

The closer we got, the stranger the shelter looked. What was that gray, smooth material it was built out of? It didn't look like stone or metal. What was that platelike dish near the antenna? A fancy radio receiver? This wasn't a makeshift shelter of smugglers hiding from customs. It looked like a scientific station, like ours, only bigger and more advanced. Yet the Science Ministry would surely have notified us if another scientific expedition was coming to the exact same place as we were. Unless there was some kind of top-secret government research going on we weren't privy to? But that just didn't seem like the placid, paper-pushing Science Ministry I knew.

At last we were within a few yards of the shelter, and Heda let out a loud halloo. Wouldn't want to seem to be sneaking around.

The person at the antenna started wildly, waving their arms. Clearly not expecting company any more than we had been. Then they turned around.

We stopped dead. Heda clutched my arm suddenly in shock. The person working on the antenna...was not Kinaru. Could not possibly be.

All we could see beneath its big black hood was its face, which was gray and scaly. Its eyes were large and yellow, under a heavy green brow ridge. Its nose was thin and flat, but in about the expected place, and its lipless mouth looked...well, *almost* like a Kinaru mouth. But the proportions of everything were wrong; the face was much longer and narrower than ours.

On seeing us, the creature's mouth dropped open and a green crest of quills or scales fluffed up on its head, so that its hood fell off. It spoke, but its words were incomprehensible and not, I thought, really intended for us. Instead it waved its arms about a moment and darted inside the shelter.

We stood there, as if paralyzed. Aliens. Real aliens. Exactly the thing we always dreamed of studying. But we had always thought we'd find them on their own planets, after building spaceships and finding a way to cross the vast distances of space. Not here, on our own Northern Continent.

After a moment Heda grasped my arm. "Quick," he said. "We have to tell the others."

He went back to fetch the rest of the team, while I retreated behind the rocks to watch the camp. This was it: the goal of my life, right before me. So much I could learn from even this one glimpse. Body pattern like ours: was that common in exosapients? Heavy coat: not from the fourth planet then. If it had come from a climate like that one, it ought to be comfortable here. Then did they have lightspeed travel? How, when physicists had claimed it was impossible?

More beings came out from behind an outcropping of rock, moving quickly. One shouted while the others rushed in and out of the buildings carrying boxes.

They're leaving, said Resa suddenly.

I watched them running back and forth. They had to be. Assuming the ship was behind the outcropping of rock beside their camp, they were surely packing it up. As if to prove her point, the largest shelter suddenly collapsed into a mess of cloth and poles, and one of the beings folded it into a tight package.

I am not an emotional person, but at that moment I felt a strong negative reaction. Not leaving, so soon! No chance to record a sample of their language, not a skin sample, nothing. We would be left with the knowledge they were out there, a few tantalizing hints, and nothing else. I could write a paper on this—and I would—but it would have to be half speculation or else fit on a single page.

Heda returned with the others. "They're packing to go," I said. "They must not have wanted to be discovered."

"I would do the same," Heda said, "if I were observing a new life form.

My involvement would contaminate the results."

"If you were studying animals, perhaps!" said one of the others. "We're people, we deserve more than this."

Rez il Tapa, my fellow junior researcher, opened a notebook and started rapidly sketching everything he saw. By the progress they'd made so far, we had a matter of hours before they were completely gone.

"We should confront them," said Beva il Nepo, the number two scientist on our team. "Force them to at least speak with us."

"They clearly don't want to," Heda argued. "How do we know they won't kill us for attempting it?"

"Nepo says it is worth the risk," Beva argued.

"Oh, *Nepo* says," said Rez scornfully. "Has Nepo calculated the odds of success, or is she just following emotion like usual?"

Nobody bothered answering that. Everyone knew the kind of judgments one could get from lefts. I felt Resa stiffen. Rez il Tapa was our intended spouse. Naturally she wouldn't like to hear prejudice like this out of her right-husband. But it hardly seemed like the time.

I will speak to him later, I told her. By the tension I could feel against me, she wasn't mollified.

The others continued discussing the aliens' motives, their biology, their technology. Was that giant dish beside the antenna a radio receiver? Could we circle wide around the camp and try to get a better look at the ship?

Resa reached over and touched my hand, demanding my full attention. *We should try to sneak aboard.*

What? And leave the planet with them? I was shocked, but also intrigued. It would be one way to get the data they meant to deny us. Perhaps there was a place on their ship I could hide and observe them in secret. The only problem then was how to get back home to report my findings. That would depend on too many factors to predict. *We might not be able to return.*

Don't you want to find out? she coaxed. *Aren't you a scientist?*

She had me there. I did want to find out, more than anything. More than publishing a paper, more even than becoming a lead researcher. I had been assigned as a scientist because of my boundless curiosity, my desire to know. And here was a mystery greater than any other I could expect to find.

But you, I ventured. *You'd have to leave everything. Your pets. Our house by the river—you love that house. Tapa.*

I don't care, she said, an odd tone in her mental voice I couldn't interpret. *I want to do this. If I give my consent, why would you argue? Aren't I giving you the exact thing you want?*

I hesitated a moment. This couldn't be right. It was too generous, too much what I wanted, with nothing to recommend it to her. Was she having a silly whim? Would she regret it by the end of the day? I didn't have time, as I usually did, to let her think things over and feel things out. She'd taken a week to decide if she really liked that house by the river.

But could I say no to this opportunity? The only thing that could possibly have stopped me would have been her. And she claimed to want it.

Maybe it was selfish. Maybe it was wrong. But I unslung my pack and set it on my feet. "I'd like everyone's emergency rations, if you don't mind," I said. "Or anything else you have that I could use. I want to try to stow away on that ship."

Heda immediately took off his pack. "That is an amazing suggestion," he said, eyes wide with excitement. "We could learn so much more about them that way."

Rez shook his head in shock. "It's verifiably insane," he said. "We know nothing about these creatures. For all we know, they'd cut us up and put us in jars. We may be no more than animals to them. Did Resa put you up to this? That's just the sort of irrational scheme lefts always dream up."

"Trust me to be in control of my left," I said calmly. For once, Resa did not react to this. "I have her consent, at least."

"Should all of us go?" Heda asked. "I hate to let you do this alone."

"Most of you have spouses or children," I pointed out. "And a larger party would mean a higher risk of discovery."

Rez il Tapa turned and walked stiffly away, back toward our own shelter. I watched him go. He had been looking forward to the wedding, he had always said. The marriage board had assigned us to each other, citing our compatible careers and similar temperaments. I had thought Resa had been fond of Tapa. But perhaps not as much as I had assumed, if she was willing to go.

It was, perhaps, wrong of me to volunteer for this when it meant breaking off our marriage contract. But until the marriage actually took place, it was our right to back out for any reason. They knew this. But one of them was upset with me. Perhaps both. I would have preferred a cordial farewell.

But before I had finished gathering my supplies from the others, he returned with another pack. "I got your things," he said, handing it to me. "More instant food, your tooth cleaner, your hairbrush. Who knows how long you'll be hiding on the ship. I packed water as well, but your priority will have to be obtaining more. I expect it will last you a few days at least."

Resa gave a soft sigh and reached out, lightly touching Tapa's cheek. I saw now that tears were streaking down it, freezing in the frigid air.

"I am sorry to have to leave you," I said for both of us. "Please consider yourself free from our obligation. I can't say when or if we might return."

"I understand," said Rez. "Tapa would like me to urge you to take all due caution."

I met Tapa's eye and nodded sharply. "I promise."

Together, our little party began our wide circle around the alien base. I would have to approach from an unexpected direction to have a hope of not being spotted.

Half an hour ago I had had my life planned out for decades. Now, suddenly, I was on the brink of something no Kinaru had done before.

I didn't regret a thing.

Resa

Too little time. There was too little time to say goodbye.

We were crouched behind a rock, waiting for a moment when all the aliens would be safely engaged somewhere else. I rooted through the bag Rez il Tapa had sent, making sure we had everything I would need. Bless them, they'd remembered my craft bag and Tria's books. If we had to hide out for a long time, we would appreciate that.

I felt the cold frost beneath me, stared at the twilit sky. How could I say goodbye to Kinaru when all I could see of it was this wasteland? If I had only known, when I left on this trip, what a journey I was starting on…

Then what? I would have said goodbye more carefully? I had walked through every room of my house, touched every knickknack, walked one last time along the cobblestone sidewalk along the river. I had caressed every one of my pets. Turned my face to the sky with my eyes closed and drank in the red warmth. It just didn't feel like enough, anymore. I thought I would miss the sun being so bright and hot. I hadn't thought I was saying goodbye to the sun itself.

Tria was running toward something. Me? I was running away. Had always been running away. The north pole had seemed far enough, but even here I felt the cobwebby cling of limitations, expectations, needs. I had to go farther. Even if it killed me.

In the bottom of the bag was a little sketchbook, not mine. I flipped it open. Tapa's sketches. He had loved to draw for me. There was my little house with the orange vines climbing up the porch, blooming in turquoise flowers. My lizard, my sand spider. Me, in profile so you couldn't see Tria at all. Somehow you could see the love in it behind the lines. Tapa had loved me, and I was leaving him. Surely, if he included these drawings, it meant he understood. Or at least that he forgave me. It would have to be enough.

Tria glanced down at what I was doing. *Having second thoughts about leaving Tapa?*

No. I stuffed the sketchbook back in my pack and pulled the string tight. *I was just thinking about everything I'll miss. The taste of fresh fruit. The wind off the desert.*

Are you regretting this? It isn't too late to back out.

I gave a dismissive gesture. *No. I know this is what I want to do.*

Want, such a strange word. Have to, I could have said. But she would have argued with that. This was something she wouldn't—couldn't understand. Couldn't understand why I struggled like a gossamer-winged insect in a net, because she couldn't see the net—it had never been a net to her. It gave her purchase, while beating my wings against it was tearing me apart. And she would have only said: be still. Don't thrash around. To her that would be an answer.

CHAPTER TWO

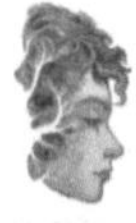

Tria

The low sun cast long streaks of shadow over the frosty landscape—useful for getting into the ship unseen. I still couldn't see the ship itself, but it was obvious where it must be. The aliens always disappeared behind a specific crag with their boxes and bundles. It would be hidden there, in a gap we still couldn't see.

I gave a final wave to the rest of the group, hanging back behind a further rock. They had all wished me the best. Heda had even hugged me, which was a first. He had been my mentor for years, closer in many ways than my own father. He would certainly worry about me until I returned, if I ever did.

I wonder if anyone in the universe is as kind as Kinaru are, Resa said morosely.

You sure you don't want to turn back?

I'm sure. Just homesick in advance.

A part of me thought I should back out on her behalf. She'd never be happy away from home. She wasn't thinking clearly. It was my duty to protect her from impulsive decisions. But I was too excited about the scientific opportunity to be that selfless.

At last the aliens gathered around the last structure, preparing to pull out whatever supports kept it up. No one else was between myself and their ship's hiding place. I would have to hope the ship itself was unguarded. At worst, I told myself, they would catch me, and I would get a closer look. I had to believe they weren't violent if they hadn't shot us on sight. Surely they could have done so.

Still, it was a risk, and I was surprised that Resa showed no sign of fear. Instead she was only crying quietly, tears flowing freely down her cheek and freezing to the spot. I reached across to her side and brushed away the ice with my mitt. I understood her feelings, but this was no place to stand around. *If we want to do this, it has to be now.*

I dashed from behind the rock and ran to the crag as fast as I could. I ducked behind it, only to stand there puzzled.

There was nothing there. Just more cliffs. Yet I knew this was where the aliens had gone. I carefully moved along the rock wall beside me, searching for a gap. There had to be one—the aliens had walked back here easily, with their hands full. They couldn't have meant to climb.

It wouldn't take them long to disassemble their shelter. I grasped the crag to see if there was a hope of climbing up, burdened as I was with two large packs.

Or I tried to. Instead I almost tumbled to the ground. The crag *wasn't there.* I waved my hand through it. The whole thing was an illusion.

I gave a quick look around. I could only see the edge of the building the aliens were working on, and two of the aliens with their backs toward me. All at once the building collapsed and they set to work folding it up. This was my chance.

Holding my breath automatically, as if diving into a pool, I stepped into the crag.

From inside, everything outside the artificial crag looked like a gray fog. But I only glanced that way for a moment. My attention was taken up by the ship.

It was a cylinder of light gray metal, as big around as a small house, stretching as high into the air as a several-storey office building. The top was capped with a blunt cone.

In front of me gaped a doorway, just a gap in the cylinder tall enough for a person to go through with their arms stretched over their head. Within was a ramp, shallow at first but then steeply curving upward till it was vertical.

I could see no other way in, so I walked onto the ramp. Strangely, as I walked, the ramp didn't seem steep at all. It seemed to remain flat, while the ship rotated around me. I stood at the end of the ramp and looked behind me. It still *looked* curved. But the ground was now behind me, while what felt like below me was… sideways?

Artificial gravity, it had to be. Physicists had thought it was impossible. But they had said that about faster-than-light travel, and here this ship was, far from anywhere it could have reasonably come from.

Can you stop being a scientist for one second and find a place to hide?

Resa was right. I looked around the room I was in. It was a long, plain room filled with boxes and crates. The fancy antenna was folded up along one side of the room. That left a large hollow behind the dish, a perfect place for me to hide. I picked my way through the crates and climbed behind the dish, taking off my backpack and stowing it between my knees. Crates blocked my view of the main pathway through the room. I hoped it would also block the aliens' view of me when they came inside to stow their shelter.

Kinaru scientists said the pressures of a rocket takeoff were intense; I wanted to secure myself somehow. But the cupped dish was probably as close to a seat as I could get. I adjusted myself till I felt I was as safe as I could be and prepared to wait.

The heat was intense after the cold of the outdoors, and I quietly wiggled out of my heavy coat. My fingers hurt from the sudden change in temperature. Resa rubbed my hand with hers to ease the itching.

I stayed there for more than an hour, listening to the aliens come and go. They talked to each other in a sibilant language, but their voices sounded friendly. At least when they spoke to each other.

Are you frightened? I asked Resa.

A little, maybe. Are you?

I blinked. She sometimes asked me these questions, and I didn't care for it. What was I even supposed to make of them? *I don't know,* I said at last. *I believe that we made a calculated risk, but I don't yet see any clue as to whether it will go well.*

That isn't what I asked. But there was a note of amusement in her mental voice. I didn't think she was upset with me.

The aliens' voices came closer, and I held my breath. If I couldn't stay concealed until they'd taken off, the whole thing was a waste. They'd probably just toss me off. At best.

A gray-scaled hand with five fingers and two thumbs grasped the edge of the dish, and an alien face peered over. This close, its golden eyes, with slitted pupils, looked even stranger. The crest of green quills on its head fluffed suddenly, like a startled prickle-hog, and it pulled back, calling to the others.

Failure. I got to my feet, peering over the edge of the dish. Three of the aliens were standing there, two with green crests and one with yellow. The one who had found me seemed surprised. The other green one seemed excited. It gesticulated and flapped its hands, almost dancing with energy. Unless that was anger. I couldn't be sure. Reading too much into an alien's body language would be a mistake.

Except that the yellow-crested one *did* seem angry. It was the tallest of the three, and seemed to be shouting. At last it stalked off, up a flight of steep stairs.

The other two stood around, looking at me and talking to each other. They both made eye contact with me, lowering their eyelids in a half-blink. The equivalent of a smile? A threat display?

This was the moment I had dreamed of since I'd begun my career.

Observing aliens, trying to decipher their intentions. Yet it was distracting to do so with the knowledge in the back of my mind that they might kill me at any moment.

The yellow-crested one came back with a large group of aliens—at least a dozen. They were all talking at once, but the yellow one waved them all to silence, giving an order to one of the green ones.

That one took a small black object out of a box and carefully extended it to me, as one might offer a treat to a carnivorous animal. I took it and looked it over. It seemed like a tiny speaker, attached to a flexible hoop or clasp. I looked up at the green-crested alien. It had taken out several more and was distributing them to the others, who put them near the tops of their heads, on what might have been their ears. Cautiously, I inserted mine into my ear, twisting the hoop to keep it in place.

A soft voice in my ear was saying in my language, over the sound of an alien speaking, "If that doesn't work we've got a whole library of languages we can try." A translator! So I wasn't doomed to be chattered at incomprehensibly until they threw me out of the rocket.

The yellow one stepped closer than the others and crouched down slightly to meet my eye level. "We didn't expect to find *humans* here."

That word was left untranslated; I shook my head at it. "I'm sorry, I don't know what that is."

"Earth," it said impatiently. "Earthlings? You came to this planet?"

"I was born on this planet," I said.

The green one interjected. "Does everyone here look like you?"

I glanced down at my body. "More or less."

That one turned to the yellow one. "Convergent evolution," it said. "The shape of humans must have been fit for this environment also. Inside, it may be very different."

I hoped they didn't intend to open me up and find out. "Please," I said. "I would like to come to space with you. You could study me, in exchange for letting me study you."

The yellow one stared at me, crest prickling upward. "We don't interact with primitive races. It's the law."

"We're not primitive," I said, a little defensively. "We might not have your technology level, but we're hardly living in tents."

"The standard of a developed planet," put in the green one, "is one that has space travel, unified planetary government, and a decent standard of living for all sentient residents."

"We have two of those," I said. "We have a centralized planetary government and there is no poverty or hunger. Everyone has access to medical treatment. Everyone is equal."

The yellow one flipped its fingers downward dismissively. "But that doesn't mean we're letting you look around a fold-capable ship when you don't already have one."

"Isn't it a little late to be discussing this?" asked a brown one. "Since we already took off?"

I leaned on the dish, shocked. There had been no sense of motion. The artificial gravity must have canceled it out.

The aliens started arguing with one another, and my translator overlaid all their voices, making it even more confusing.

"We should land again and drop it back off," one alien was arguing. "Even getting spotted was cultural contamination. The government won't be happy when we get back."

Another countered, "If we bring it back, it will contaminate them even worse. It's already seen far too much of our technology."

I tensed. I could see an easy solution to their problem, by killing me. Who knew what their ethical constraints were.

The tall yellow one stared at the ceiling and heaved a sigh. "It would have helped if *certain people* had detected the settlement near us. It was literally under a mile away and none of you were aware."

"They weren't using radio!" protested one stocky one with a green crest. "Their radios don't have the range."

"On the radar, it looked like a settlement of large animals," said a tall brown one.

"Does *anyone* agree we should go back and drop it off?"

I held my breath. Even if they did, I certainly had more information than I had before. But not enough. I wanted to know what they ate, get a look at a cell sample, maybe X-ray one.

The aliens held their many-fingered hands out, palm up or down. Perhaps a signal of which course of action they favored? In any event, the yellow one heaved another sigh. "Fine. Fine! On your heads be it, when we report back to the board."

It turned to me, saying flatly. "Welcome to the Shatakazan ship *Galajak*. I am Expedition Leader Pav 116, of the Liberty sect. As I command this ship, my presence is required elsewhere. I am assigning Underscholar Karnath 371, of the Curiosity sect, to be your liaison. Please make known all of your needs to him." It flattened its crest and walked away without waiting for any answer from me. The other aliens mostly followed her.

The green alien who had handed me the earbud—Karnath—remained. "Please forgive Pav. She can be abrupt. What is your name?"

"Tria il Resa, of Orchard District University."

Karnath flattened his crest at me. A gesture of respect? "Are you a scientist, then, at this university of yours?"

"Yes."

"So am I. I think we might get along very well."

Thus reassured, I clambered over the various crates and into the clear center of the room. "Am I... safe here?"

He blinked. "Of course. We wouldn't be so careful about not contaminating your planet if we didn't care. It's just, we've never taken on a stowaway before. There isn't really a procedure. I suppose we'll have to figure it out on our own, hm? That reminds me." Going back to the box the translator had come out of, he pulled out a bracelet, which he explained would kill any pathogens which might pass between me and them. "Not that it's normal for diseases to cross species, but you wouldn't want to be the first, would you?"

I carefully snapped it on my wrist, using my teeth to hold it still. Karnath looked at me oddly as I did so. Wondering why I didn't simply ask my left for help? But Resa was fidgeting impatiently, pulling at the hem of our shirt. At first I'd assumed she was upset, but I realized now she was only annoyed because she couldn't understand our conversation. I had taken the only earbud. "Do you have another translator for my left?"

He tilted his head quizzically. "Why would you need another?"

I stared at him a moment. Certainly, there was no evolutionary necessity for our species' divided brains. Heda thought aliens perhaps had only one consciousness per body, like animals do. But I had never considered what it would be like to be a creature like that. Wouldn't it be terribly lonely?

"Resa needs to hear too," I said at first, and then stopped in confusion. I'd never had to explain this concept before. "You see, we are two beings. Tria hears out of this ear, and Resa hears out of the other. Do you understand?"

The vertical pupils in his yellow eyes dilated and his crest twitched. Surprise? Curiosity? "I am not sure I do," he said, turning back to the table and getting another earbud, which he fiddled with till it would fit my ear. "Do you mean two halves of the same individual? Or two separate persons?"

Resa took the other earbud and put it on. I answered, "Two separate persons. That part of us is her, and this part is me." I gestured to her half of our body and mine.

"And who is talking to me now?"

"Tria."

"Does Resa talk?"

"Not usually."

"And can you do tasks separately? Like, at the same time?"

"Yes, of course."

Karnath flapped his hands excitedly, pacing around in a small circle beside the table. "This is excellent! This is unprecedented! And to think I thought I would have little to do on this expedition."

I smiled. "What is your field?"

"Exobiology. It is why I was assigned to you. We came mainly for radio data, but I was supposed to study any life forms we happened to find. I didn't expect an entire sentient being to study!" He paused, assessing me. "Why are you doing this? Is your planet so terrible, that you had to escape?"

"No!" Resa made an emphatic gesture also. "I was curious. This would be my only chance to study alien life, perhaps in my whole career."

"Brave of you. You couldn't know what we were like, how we'd treat you."

"I'm sure you'd do the same. Scientists have to take risks."

"I'm not so sure," he said, lowering his eyelids. "My career has involved few risks. Mostly squinting at single cells."

Something about Karnath—his open excitement, his humility—made me feel at ease, in this strange alien spaceship with the slick gray floor and the air just a bit too warm for comfort. Where Pav had been cold and abrupt, Karnath was eager to please. Even in the computerized translation, he sounded earnest and friendly.

"Ah—I should be showing you to your quarters. From what we've learned so far, your species sleeps at night, yes?"

Karnath led me down the hall and up some stairs. The steps were steep; I noticed Karnath's legs were long enough to have no trouble with them. He was roughly of my height, but more of his height was in his legs than mine. His joints also seemed to move a little differently than a Kinaru's—his knees seemed to have a ball and socket joint rather than a hinge. I hoped I would get a chance to see a skeleton, or at least a diagram of one.

"Before I bring you to your room, I suppose you'll want to see your planet from space."

"There are windows?"

"There is one in this room. Come." He lightly touched a door, which slid open soundlessly. Inside was a kind of conference room, with a low table and a number of seats on the floor which looked like half eggs—so a person could sit on the floor while still having something to lean back on. And beyond the table was a large window.

I went over to the glass and looked out. Far below, I could see the arc of Kinaru, mostly brown, with blue oceans here and there and some swirls of cloud. The southwestern mountains, where my father lived, seemed to be getting a little rain for once. Much of what was in view was shrouded in darkness, where night had fallen, but lights twinkled along the coastlines. I could pick out several cities and the darkness of the vast southern desert.

Beyond Kinaru were the stars—stars as I had never seen them, even in the northern tundra nights, when there wasn't a wisp of fog in the sky or a light for miles. Here there were millions more—billions. I knew the astronomers had found many too small to see from the surface with the naked eye, but that number had never meant anything to me before that moment.

My heart pounded, whether from my own feelings or from Resa's, I wasn't sure. She was crying again, delicately wiping the tears away with her palm. *It's so beautiful.*

"Are you experiencing a medical emergency?" Karnath's voice broke in on my reverie. "You have liquid coming out of one of your eyes."

I turned to him, smiling. "No, it's a normal response. The view is making Resa emotional."

He smiled back, baring a row of tiny, sharp, bluish-white teeth. It didn't suit his face at all; he must have been trying to put me at ease by imitating my expressions.

"You don't have to do that," I said. "I can learn to read your species' expressions."

He put a hand to his mouth, as if testing to see if he had done the smiling thing right, before closing his mouth and lowering his eyelids at me instead. "I often feel the same way about the stars."

That was an interesting revelation. I had wondered if his undivided brain meant that he had no left, but instead he seemed to have the kind of emotions Resa had, only incorporated into a single personality. How could that even work? For a moment I felt strangely alone. I was the only one here who could look out at the planet below and feel nothing.

"I made arrangements to be gone for some time," I said, after a moment. "Do you know—that is, will I be allowed to return? After this voyage?"

He flicked his fingers downward. "No. At least, not until your people qualify as developed. Manned spaceflight to your nearest planetoid is generally considered sufficient, if you meet the other requirements."

I stared out at my home. Now I did feel a little dismay. I wanted to return to my people with all the knowledge I'd gained. How many years before they were ready? Would Heda il Trambo live to see it?

The planet slowly fell out of sight, as the ship continued its orbit. I turned away from the window. "I suppose I ought to let you show me my room." I didn't want to admit it, but I was starting to feel exhausted. No wonder Resa was teary. It must be nearly midnight.

On the way down the corridor, I suddenly felt an uncomfortable wrench in my stomach, and my vision flickered. Resa let out a little yelp. Was I really so tired that I was near fainting?

Karnath reached out as if to steady my elbow, checking the gesture just short of my sleeve. "Oh! I am so sorry. I forgot to warn you. The ship just folded."

"Folded?" I asked, puzzled.

"We fold the ship through space, in order to travel faster than lightspeed," he said, making a folding gesture with his hands that completely failed to clarify anything. "When we pass through the fold, organic beings often experience some disorientation."

A little intimidated, I nodded. "Does this happen often?"

"Yes, periodically throughout our voyage. Our fold array is only powerful enough to take us a few light-days at a time, so each time we fold we must travel through normal space until the next fold point."

"So how long till we reach your planet?" I realized I had never asked. Would I be on this ship for years?

"Something between 26 and 41 days," he answered. "Pav will have a more precise answer, since it depends on the orbital position of each planet, relative to the mapped fold points. We also will be stopping briefly at a space station in a few days, so you won't be stuck on the ship the entire time."

My room was a tiny cell, with a bunk along one wall and a tiny chair and table built into the other. "The computer console is here in the table," Karnath explained. "There is a small lavatory through this door. Do you need anything else right now?"

"Not till morning, I think," I said, stifling a yawn. "Do you know how long our night is?"

He gave a nod, another awkward mimicry of my gestures. "I will call on you here in that amount of time."

CHAPTER THREE

Resa

I floated upward slowly through layers of dreams. The wind was blowing off the desert, blowing violet petals down into the river, but as I tried to catch them they turned to fish and slipped out of my hands. I felt achingly sad, and wondered why. Of all the things that made me sad, the wind was never one of them. It had never failed to comfort me, not in the worst of grief.

I tasted a metallic tang in the air. Hot and stuffy, a purple heat like a greenhouse. Old air, but with a faint touch of dampness and growing things.

Yes. I remembered now. The wind, the desert, the petals, the river, the fish...all were gone. Maybe forever.

Homesickness burrowed into my belly like a knife, and I fought the urge to curl my body around the ache. I didn't want to disturb Tria. So I curled my fingers instead, nails digging into the palm.

I had done the right thing. I knew I had. I loved Kinaru, but...

Tria stirred beside me. I opened my eye. *You're awake?*

Sorry, did I wake you? she asked.

No. I opened my fingers and let the pain slip out. *I've been awake awhile. I'm too excited to sleep.*

On the wall, where a window might be, was a painting in vivid blue and pale yellow—a yellow forest beneath a brilliant sky. The brush strokes somehow gave the illusion of depth, of space, and made the room feel less claustrophobic. My heart lifted a little. Art. These people had art; they valued it. I *had* made the right decision; I had.

I wanted to linger and look at the picture, but Tria stretched and went to check out the lavatory. The toilet was unfamiliar in design, but we were able to figure it out. The sink, at least, worked as expected and we were able to wash our face and drink some water.

I unbraided our light brown hair and ran my fingers through the snaggly waves. Personal care was my job. There was a small oval mirror, and I did what I could to fix us up.

In the mirror, Tria's side of our face was smooth and unruffled, and her hazel eye sparkled. I couldn't say the same of myself. My eyebrow wrinkled upward and a hot flush was visible even through the brown of our skin. For a moment I worried it was bad enough for even Tria to notice, but she wasn't even looking in the mirror. She stared into space, half-smiling. Excited for the day ahead.

I want my toothbrush, I said, turning away. *And my hairbrush. And my anti-odor spray. You should have told Karnath you needed our backpack from the room downstairs.*

I didn't want to put him out.

Sometimes, I said patiently, *putting people out is the more gracious thing. They want us to be comfortable.* It was typical of her not to ask. Rights are all about self-sacrifice. That, and they plain don't care very much about little things like body odor and slimy teeth.

We'll get it now, she decided. *You remember the way we came in?*

Tria

I paused outside the conference room with the window. I wonder what I would see if I looked out this morning. Just stars? How far had we traveled? How fast could this ship go?

I raised my hand to open the door with a touch, but before I reached it, I heard voices. Instinctively I lowered it. No one had said I couldn't go around the ship, but I still felt a little nervous about facing a whole group of Shatakazan at once.

My earbud picked up the voices better than my unaided ear could, and whispered their translation. Someone was saying, "That's ridiculous. Our charter is to conduct a passive study of Kinaru. Going to a completely different planet would be a waste of our sponsor's time and money."

"It's Curiosity's money to spend! And I think they would be delighted to hear we had found such a lead."

"If your sect want to do it, they can fund another expedition! Already you've saddled me with a stowaway, and intend to divert ship's resources to studying it. I expect it'll be underfoot the entire voyage."

"It's the least we could do, considering the mission was a failure."

"We collected terabytes of data, how can you call it a failure?"

"We barely had a month to study the Kinaru before we were discovered—and it wasn't any of *my* sect who was responsible for taking readings and making sure we weren't discovered!"

The other voice was silent a moment. Then she said, "Fine. Fine! Take it to a vote and see how that works out for you!" Soft footsteps approached the door and I darted away. If that was Pav, as I suspected, and she hadn't wanted me aboard, she'd be beyond annoyed to see me standing in the hallway. I was down the narrow, steep stairwell before the door opened.

My backpack was in the storeroom, exactly as I had left it. In the corridor outside my room, I met Karnath. "Ah, Tria il Resa," he said, flattening his crest. "You are awake earlier than I expected."

"Sorry," I said. "I should get on your ship schedule as soon as I can."

He helped me unpack the food I had brought in a large room he called the dayroom. There was no ship's cook, but there was a small alcove with heating elements and dishes, where Karnath helped me prepare breakfast for myself.

It turned out there was no chance of my getting onto the Shatakazan's sleep schedule. Their day was about the same length as ours, but they weren't diurnal like us. They tended to stay awake for ten hours or so, then nap two or three hours, then repeat. We compared time systems over breakfast—over my breakfast, I should say, since Karnath didn't eat. He apologized, saying he had already eaten this cycle.

I toyed with the idea of mentioning what I'd overheard, and asking what the political situation was. Pav and Karnath had mentioned their different sects, but how important was this? If Pav felt that hostile to me, did that put me in any danger?

I decided against it. If knowledge was power, knowledge they didn't know I had might be doubly so. I liked Karnath, but I had known him for a day. I couldn't be sure he would protect me, if it came to it, and that meant I had to be thinking about how to protect myself.

While I was still eating, another alien came in, a shortish one with a muddy brown crest, and hurried over to our table. "Your specimen!" the alien said excitedly. "I've been so eager to study it!"

"She can understand you," Karnath said mildly, his crest twitching upward a little. A dominance display? I looked at the newcomer, whose crest flattened slightly. Yes. The newcomer was either an underling, or simply abashed to have made an error.

Karnath stood up, his joints unlocking smoothly from his low, crouched seat. "Tria il Resa, this is Tazag 834 of Unity sect. Ze is our expedition's anthropologist. I am sure ze is eager for zir turn to interview you. No one knows more about your people's culture than Tazag."

I nodded, rising from my knees much more awkwardly. "I look forward to it."

A glance passed between Karnath and Tazag that I couldn't read, then Tazag said, "At your earliest convenience, Karnath," nodded to me, and went out.

What was that all about? asked Resa. *I can't read their body language yet, but I didn't get the impression that one liked Karnath.*

Perhaps just eager for his turn with us, and annoyed Karnath was allowed priority.

"I have a question," I said, kneeling back down. "With everyone else I've met, the translator supplied a gendered pronoun. This time it used a gender-neutral one. Is Tazag male or female? I can't tell."

"Ah, you have only two sexes! Tazag had hypothesized as much. We have three. Tazag is neutral sex."

I leaned forward, fascinated. "I have never heard of such a thing! I wouldn't have thought such an arrangement could evolve—what would be the evolutionary purpose of a third sex?"

"Our evolutionary ancestors lived in large groups, and clutched the eggs together. More adults to sit on the clutch were always helpful."

"And how do you tell someone's sex?"

"The crest color, usually. Males have green, females have yellow, and neutrals have brown. Though if someone is in the middle of a sex change, the color will be muddled and you may need to ask."

I blinked, deciding to leave the question of sex change for a later conversation. "And what about your families? Do you have three parents then?" I considered the linguistic difficulties. What would one call a genderless parent?

He made a downward gesture with one hand. "No, I have five. Two females and three neutrals. My genetic material came from a male friend, but as he isn't part of the household, he isn't considered a parent."

I thought of that for a moment. Resa said, *Five parents! I don't know whether to be scandalized or titillated.*

Neither! We are a scientist. Value judgments distract from the work of observation.

Still, I wasn't sure what to ask that wouldn't be wildly inappropriate. Our own marriage contracts are strictly heterosexual, arranged, and monogamous. Infidelity is extremely rare. Most of all, we don't discuss sex in polite company. But, as I had reminded Resa, I was a scientist. So was Karnath. Perhaps the truly inappropriate thing would be to let my upbringing stymie my investigation. I put down my utensil. "So with five parents... all of a household... are they all in sexual relationships with one another? Or are households created on other lines?"

"Sexual relationships are part of it," Karnath answered, without any sign of embarrassment. "One of my parents is asexual and emotionally bonded to two of the others. The rest have various interlocking sexual relationships. But I think the commitment is the important part. The decision to form a household. Sexual behavior outside of a household isn't forbidden—well, at least not in my sect."

"This is so foreign to me," I said. "We each have one partner. And there are no sexual relationships outside of that."

"Do you have a partner yourself?"

"No. I was assigned one, but that had to be broken off because of this." I waved my hand to indicate the ship, and the entire situation.

"How would you describe your feelings about this? Both having a partner assigned, and having to break it off. Don't your wishes enter into it?"

"With four people's different temperaments to be considered, it is much more rational to have the partners centrally assigned. We submit psychometric data to ensure everyone is compatible."

"But what did you *feel* when the assignment was made?"

I had to think long and hard about that one. Resa always knows how she feels. It's too easy for me to lose myself in the facts, forget to even notice if I have feelings. Finally I said quietly, "What was there to feel? I was at the point of my career where it was appropriate to request a match. And the board assigned us to one another, so we should have been well-suited. But... I can't say I felt that compatibility. Or that I regretted having to call the whole thing off."

I dropped my eyes to my plate, embarrassed at so much self-revelation. There was only one piece of preserved fruit left on my plate, which I ate.

"And Resa? What were her feelings?"

I looked up at him, startled. On Kinaru, rights do not often speak to lefts, since lefts so rarely speak. Instead the lefts communicate with each other through a nonverbal system of gestures and facial expressions which I can't follow. Then again, Karnath wasn't a right. I only thought of him as one because he spoke to me.

Resa chose to speak on her own, a rare occurrence. Her voice is different, throatier than mine, and she speaks slowly as she thinks of the words. "Trapped," she said. "Not ready. Guilty that I agreed. Love expected, not found. Walls closing in. Too late to take back my word. Didn't want to be like—" She cut herself off suddenly. "Like other wives and mothers. That life. Not how I saw myself. Not what I wanted."

You never told me any of this, I said, a little shocked.

*Why complain when the decision was made? It was a little late to pull out of it. It would have broken Rez il Tapa's heart. And it's not like you told **me** any of what you just said either.*

I always got the feeling you understood how I felt.

*I did. I always do. And it bothers me that you're so much in the dark about what **I'm** feeling.*

*If you want me to know things, you have to **tell** me! I don't read feelings like you do!*

Karnath was watching me quietly. "Have I upset you?"

I shook my head. "Resa... felt all this very forcefully. Please forgive her for her outburst." Resa reached for the little square paper napkin beside our plate and dabbed her tears. I flushed with embarrassment.

He looked at Resa's eye, then mine. "There is nothing to forgive, Tria il Resa. The process of inquiry can introduce questions that bring up great emotion. If there is any fault, it is mine for raising uncomfortable topics."

I shook my head. "You are right, of course. Science does require this sort of discussion. It would be wrong to avoid them simply because they are emotional." I rose from the table.

I got a tour of the ship—some of it. The lower levels, beneath the level where I'd come in, were command and engineering areas and I was politely requested to avoid these. But Karnath showed me an impressively high-tech medical lab, a biochemistry lab, and a room filled with computing equipment.

Most fascinating to me, though, was the corridor itself. When I had come aboard last night, I had thought the walls were a mottled green and yellow, but on closer inspection I saw it was a fine, transparent mesh, and the green and yellow substance was within. Tiny insects swarmed around in a gap of an inch or so between the mesh and the wall itself. "What is this?" I asked, touching the mesh with a hesitant finger.

"That is the biolayer," he answered. "You see, we have to light this corridor anyway, so it makes sense to use the light to grow algae. It produces a little supplemental oxygen, in addition to what the scrubber makes."

"What about the insects?"

"The insects are our food," said Karnath, and I stifled a surprised expression. Resa failed to do the same, her side of our face drawing down into a grimace.

Plenty of animals eat insects and you don't find them disgusting, I chided her. *You even breed them for your batsnake.*

That's different, she countered. *Thinking of him eating them makes me* *think of **me** eating them.* She gave an imperceptible shudder.

At least keep your prejudice to yourself. We are here as a scientist.

She subsided, and I answered Karnath's questions about our own diet. He was surprised to find we lived on only plants—apparently most sentient races they had yet encountered ate at least some animals. "Including the earthlings, we think," he added. "Which lends support to the hypothesis that you are only superficially similar."

"What do you mean, you think?" I asked. "How much do you know about these earthlings?"

"Barely more than what we know about you," he answered, spreading his hands apologetically. "Like you, they aren't yet prepared for us to make contact. Yet we can't even land on the surface, because their planet is much more populous than yours, and monitored by their satellite network."

"If they have a satellite network, doesn't that mean they're spacefaring?"

"Well, yes, more or less. They have at least visited their moon. But they fail on the other two counts—the place is a mess of war and poverty. It would be idiocy to attempt to deal with them. All they would do is take any technology we shared and convert it into weapons. And I can only imagine the harm it would do if they got a fold drive. It would unleash chaos on the galaxy."

I nodded, disappointed. "So we don't have so much as a genetic sample?"

"Well, not as such. But we have a great deal of data about them, because we can access their digital network. Much more than we have about your species. All we have of you are audio-only radio broadcasts. Not even any video."

At the end of the tour, we returned to the medical lab. "I've gotten permission from the captain to use the brain scanner. She was reluctant at first, as it takes so much processor space to run that we have to stop making folds while we're using it. But I have scheduled this time for it, and

I am extremely curious about this divided brain of yours. Would you be willing…?"

"Of course. I'm curious myself."

To my relief, the brain scanner was much less invasive than similar machines back home, which required a shaved head and wires sticking into the bald scalp. Instead it fit over my head like a helmet, making a mild humming noise. While it worked, Karnath asked me questions and showed me pictures. Delicately he tapped on my hands and feet with a long stylus. "Do you both feel this, or just one?"

"We both have some sensation in the opposite limb, and we can control it with the other's permission. Not in the face, though. Those are attached just to one side."

He looked at his readout. "I can see on the scan. The nerves for each side from the spinal cord pass through one brain hemisphere before terminating in the other. But the visual, auditory, and facial nerves don't cross over at all. Does that mean you can't see or hear at all out of that eye and ear?"

"Exactly."

"So you can't have any depth perception. No wonder your people don't eat animals. You'd have next to no chance of ever catching one." He gave a sibilant chuckle through his teeth.

"Why would we *need* to catch animals?" I countered.

"I suppose you wouldn't." He trailed off, staring at the screen. "Do you happen to know what happens if one half dies? Say, from a stroke or a blow to the head…"

"They both die," I replied in a flat voice.

"Even if the other side is undamaged?"

"They both die," I repeated. "Always." I felt sick. If he was asking these questions, he hadn't heard much of what tended to broadcast on Kinaru radio. The endless debates over cases like that. The question of what could be done.

"Hm. That's what I thought, looking at these scans. It doesn't even seem necessary, how thickly these nerves cross back and forth. And I would have thought the one justification for the brain division would be to give the body a spare, so to speak, but I see it doesn't work that way."

"No." I hoped he didn't ask any more questions. At least, not in front of Resa. Preferably not at all. Most of all, let him not ask if I knew anyone it happened to.

He glanced again at the readout. "Your heartrate is spiking. Does that happen when both of you are under stress, or does it happen with either?"

"With either. Though in this case we're both a little stressed. The thought of one of us surviving the other is... a little upsetting, as you can imagine. Or perhaps you can't. You're all alone, all the time."

He put his head to one side. "I suppose I am, if you put it like that. I never thought to be lonely, simply because I was the only person living in my own head. I can't miss what I never knew."

I was quiet. For the first time since I had come aboard, I was beginning to realize there were things I would have to hide from the Shatakazan. Things they could never understand.

CHAPTER FOUR

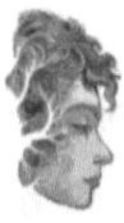

Tria

After the brain scan, Karnath left me to get his few hours of sleep, and I was left with Tazag. Ze was shorter than me by several inches, though still lanky like Karnath. Like the other Shatakazan, zir skin was gray and scaly; zir spiny crest was brown and half-erect.

We sat down at a small table in one of the ship's labs. "Really, to have any sense at all of your culture I would need a much larger sample size and several months to gather data," ze said, without prologue. "The radio surveillance yielded almost nothing—we had barely gotten enough to feed to the translator when you discovered us. But I have a truncated instrument which will help us to make a preliminary score for your species on several different axes." Ze pulled out a small computing device from a pocket on zir upper arm and started firing questions at me. "First: would you describe your planetary government as unitary, federated, diplomatic union, or no planetary government?"

I blinked. "Well, we have a First Minister—"

"The question is multiple choice. Do I need to explain any of the terms?"

terms?"

I sighed. With literally everything to learn about one another, a closed-ended interview was about the most unhelpful thing I could imagine. But I may as well play along. "Unitary."

"Is it democratic, aristocratic, oligarchic, representative—"

"Democratic," I interrupted.

"Does everyone vote?"

"Yes," I said, and then clarified, "Well, not *everyone*. Not children, for instance."

"Karnath told me about your species' divided brains. Is it one vote per consciousness, or one vote per body?"

"One per body."

"Do you discuss it among yourselves and make a joint decision?"

I hesitated. "Not really... voting is not a left kind of thing. It's written, after all... and it helps to be dispassionate..." I trailed off. I didn't know how to explain it without sounding dismissive of Resa's judgment.

"So one-half of the population is disenfranchised," ze said, writing it down.

I protested, "The laws we vote on are for the benefit of everyone!"

"That's what they all say," ze said in a tired tone, and moved on. I still fumed a little. Having only the rights vote wasn't at all like disenfranchisement. After all, we were in the same body! It isn't possible to ignore the needs of someone whose voice is always in your head.

The questions went on interminably, it seemed, but at last ze set the tablet down. "Well, this is very interesting. Your technological development score is 166, meaning your achievements are, on average, 166 of our years behind ours. However, your culture is highly advanced in neurology, moderately advanced in the other sciences, and deficient in communications and space travel. These go together, of course, because you would need a satellite network for the most advanced communications."

I nodded. "And what score would be required before you would officially contact us?"

"One twenty-four," ze said. "Though that's really an average. We focus on the few developments we can measure, like spaceflight and a satellite network. Some societies might be a great deal more advanced than this before we are aware, because we can't measure their development in other areas without landing, and if they have advanced global scanning and few unpopulated zones, we can't easily land."

Forty-two years, I said. *Forty-two years till they let us go back.*

Resa was shaken too, but she tried to stay optimistic. *That's of their years. We don't know how long their years are. And it's an estimate. Surely the Science Ministry will be focusing on space travel now.*

I took a deep breath. Better to put it aside for the present. Tazag was still talking, and I needed to stay focused. Later, I'd ask Karnath how long their years were.

"Your economic equality score is forty-five out of forty-nine," the anthropologist said. "I'm quite impressed. It's better than ours. Though, conversely, your personal liberty score is only five out of forty-nine. That means your species has less personal liberty than any species we have yet contacted. It's... well, there are any number of dictatorships that intrude far less on the citizens' private lives!"

"There really isn't any such thing as a private life, for us," I explained. "Or a private choice. Since each of us is affected by the choices of our other half, liberty would really mean oppression for half of the population. It's not that we like having our choices always decided by government, family council, or mediators, but it's a necessity. To leave the lefts unprotected... that would be disastrous."

Tazag made a note. "Interesting. I think the same might be extended to other species without your unique neurology. After all, isn't it central authority that always protects the weak? And it's inevitable that some will be in a position of weakness, compared to others."

Tazag went through the rest of the results—our peace score (high), our factionalization score (low to moderate), and our family structure (type 6). This was only of interest to me insofar as it got me thinking about what traits other species might have. What sort of government would a planet with a high liberty score have? None at all? But that seemed like utter chaos to me.

Tazag picked up zir tablet and started to rise. "Do you have any questions for me?"

Look how ze expects to leave after having gleaned what ze wants to know! Resa exclaimed, with some offense. *I thought this was supposed to be mutual!*

"Yes, actually, I have quite a few questions. My first is about sects. Every time one of you has introduced yourself to me, you name a sect. What are these?"

Tazag settled zirself back into the egg-shaped seat. "Hm. Well, our species has a very high score in personal liberty and individuality. However, so much individualism can come with a price of social atomization. So we form these groups. They might be considered akin to religions, though we haven't been literally religious for centuries. Instead, they describe our moral values. My sect's highest value is unity, the oneness of individuals with one another in mutual support. Politically, we tend to support a stronger government; socially, we engage in unifying events that strengthen our social bonds."

I nodded. "So are you born into them?"

"No. Or rather, we may be raised in one, but switch into another if we discover a greater affinity for that one. I was raised in the Curiosity sect." Zir mouth twisted in what I thought might be distaste.

Perhaps the reason he doesn't like Karnath, Resa said. *He doesn't like Curiosity.*

That's irrational. Karnath didn't seem to hold him any ill will.

People are irrational. You're always forgetting that.

"So there are members of different sects on this ship?"

Tazag flicked zir fingers upward, a gesture I was coming to recognize as equivalent to a nod. "This expedition was funded by Curiosity sect, but they accepted applications from all qualified candidates. Our expedition leader is a member of Liberty."

"So she makes all the decisions?"

"No, we vote on major decisions. She makes all minor decisions about ship's operations, and has an extra vote in the event of a tie. But since half the team is Liberty, she effectively makes the decisions. Her fellow sectarians tend to follow her lead."

"There are just those three sects aboard?"

"Yes. There are many others on Shatak, but this is a small crew."

I asked a few more questions about their system of government before letting Tazag go. To me, their radical individualism and liberty seemed like madness. Especially with several partners in every family. How did they ever work out those relationships without a panel of experts to ensure compatibility? And what about careers? People might waste years training for jobs they ended up not being good at.

Yet clearly they had managed enough community spirit to discover a lightspeed drive and explore dozens of other worlds. Perhaps there was some order to the chaos that I couldn't yet see.

Think about it, said Resa. *We'll have years on their world to study how it works. And I think I will like getting to make our own choices for a change.*

I suppose, I answered doubtfully. *If they will give us the freedom they have themselves.*

By now it was, by my chrono, about lunchtime. I might as well keep to my usual schedule, since time seemed to be meaningless to the Shatakazan. So I went to the dayroom by myself, hoping to find it empty as before.

But this time, it was almost crowded—about nine Shatakazan milling around in the relatively tiny dining area, crowding around the meal preparation area to claim foil packets of food and heat them up before decanting them into shallow bowls. I stood uncertainly at the threshold, scanning the faces. I was beginning to be able to notice differences in their features beyond crest color. Karnath didn't seem to be there, but I thought I saw Pav.

Nine pairs of yellow eyes turned to me and the hum of conversation quieted. I felt my face flushing and ducked my head. As if hiding my face could make me unobtrusive, when they all wore slick black bodysuits and I was in my loose, buff-colored tunic and pants. To say nothing of my brown skin and long, golden-brown hair.

I wove my way to the meal preparation alcove and selected something from the cabinet Karnath had helped me stock for myself. Vine grain, preserved butterfruit, and nuts. Again. For the foreseeable future. At least I had a variety of spice packets. Tapa's notion, I suspected.

The yellow-crested female I had mistaken for Pav moved over for me, and I saw it wasn't her at all. The expedition leader towered over me, while this one only came up to my chin. "Excuse me," I said by way of apology.

"It could never be an inconvenience to make way for you," she answered, lowering her eyelids and flattening her crest to her head. "I admire your courage. The first of your kind to make it to the stars!"

I smiled and inclined my head. "Thank you for the warm welcome." Perhaps this could be a friend, like Karnath. I emptied the packets into a dish, added water, and slid the dish onto the long heating shelf Karnath had shown me.

"I am Zin, the computer officer. Do please let me know if you encounter any difficulties on the *Galajak*. I know there are some who have been... less than welcoming." She gave me a sidelong glance before moving away with her food.

I stared after her, puzzled. *I suppose she's referring to Pav not wanting us aboard?*

Resa gave an inaudible sniff. *I don't trust her. Why should she mention that to us?*

It will take time for us to figure out the political realities here. She's probably looking for an ally, but why should she need one? Is there that much conflict on the ship? My food prepared, I went to the only one of the small tables that remained empty and nestled into the awkward egg-seat.

At a table an arm's length away, a female and a neutral sat, licking each other's faces with long green tongues. Their crests were both upright, but fanned outward in a gesture I had not seen before. I turned my head away automatically, feeling that I had witnessed something private.

Karnath came to join me before I had finished eating. He got his own food, which I tried not to look at. Luckily, if it really was insects, there was enough sauce in his bowl that I couldn't actually see them.

While he ate, he pointed out the people in the room. "Almost everyone is here at the moment. We tend to share a meal together at about this time. A few of the ship's personnel are still working."

"How many people are on the ship altogether?"

"Twelve. Six spacers and six scientists. It's a small expedition—after all, it was meant solely for radio surveillance. Most of the scientists are anthropologists or linguists, with one radio expert."

"And most of them are members of your own sect?"

"Ah, have you been learning from Tazag? Science is a popular career in Curiosity, but actually only two of us are Curiosity members, myself and Linguist Lex. Tazag is the only scientist aboard who is in Unity. But two of the ship's crew are Unity also, and the rest are Liberty, including Pav and our chief linguist." He pointed out the tiny insignia on his right shoulder. One symbol meant Curiosity sect, one showed his career of scholar, and a third showed his rank in that field, which was junior professional.

It was all rather complicated, but once I had absorbed the meanings of the symbols, it made it a lot easier to sort out the different people as Karnath pointed them out. The two beside us, so absorbed in their face-licking, were Talek, the second engineer, and Femat, the sociologist. Tazag was sitting a few feet to our other side talking to Resh, also of Unity sect, the second-in-command.

Karnath set down his utensil and pushed his bowl away. "I'm sure you can see from all this why I'm so eager to get as much done as possible while en route to Shatak."

I frowned. "No, I'm sorry, I don't at all."

"Right now, any work that gets done is credit to Curiosity. I'll have enough to publish a paper, and that will mean prestige for me and for my sect. Once we land—well, there will be no end of fighting about what university will get to work with you, but having already collected so much data myself, I may be able to put in a successful bid for my sect's main university. Meanwhile Liberty has no prestige to gain by prolonging the trip. Pav is eager to return so she can claim you for a Liberty university."

I nodded. There was something a little unsettling about being the prize in a political struggle between factions, but I didn't blame him for favoring his own. Who wouldn't want their name on the most important paper published in years?

It puzzled me, though. Tazag had acted, in front of Karnath, like ze was excited to study me, but once alone with me, ze had settled for checking off boxes. Where was zir scientific curiosity? For that matter, where was zir competitive spirit? If Tazag wanted credit for zir sect, why wouldn't ze push for more information, a more complete interview? Ze hadn't made any effort to be friendly, either. Was Unity uninterested in the sciences? But if so, why would Tazag have become an anthropologist?

The rest of the afternoon—afternoon by my chrono, at least—we spent studying each other's tissue samples. Shatakazan cell structure, seen through a microscope, was comfortingly familiar. I had a moment of pure wonder when Karnath fed the samples into a machine and the screen started printing our entire genetic code. "Genetic sequencing is that easy for you? We have been working for years on reading our own genome."

"It's only really difficult the first time," he said modestly. "Ah, you use deoxyribonucleic acid for your genetic material; that's not uncommon. We have the same. Here, I can compare your code with ours."

The computer overlapped the charts of his code and mine, then turned violet. "What does that mean?"

"It means there is no significant overlap in our genetic code. No relation, in other words."

"Did you think there would be?"

He flicked his fingers down. "But we always check." He bent once more over the keypad. "Let me just try something with the little data we have..." Another set of characters appeared on the screen, this one full of gaps. "This is what we have of human DNA. As you can see, it's not much. We hacked it back when they were first sequencing it. By now they have the whole thing, but we haven't accessed it yet. There's just too much data blasting from Earth—finding any one piece of information is like finding a single leaf in a forest."

He tapped the keys and the new set overlapped with mine. This time, some sections turned violet and some turned yellow, while most remained black. Karnath stared at it for some time. "I have never seen *this* before."

"What does it mean?"

"Whole sections are the same. Look." He pointed at the yellow. "But these sections are unique to you. Unfortunately, without more members of your species, it's hard to say how much is individual variation. Still, I think any human would have more correlation with the human paradigm than you have."

"So... a distant relation?"

"I think it would have to be. Huge portions of your genome are necessarily junk; there would be no reason at all for you to have the same junk genes as another species unless you were related." He put his hands over his face in frustration. "If *only* we had a full sample! Earth is so close right now, much closer than Shatak. If we could just go a *little* out of the way, and get within range to hack their network..."

"You can do that?"

"Only in theory. I already brought the idea up to Pav and she shot it down. And she has the votes to overrule me."

"Perhaps in another expedition?"

"These things are expensive. It will take some time to put together another, and get the money for it. Outfitting a ship isn't cheap. That's why it would be so convenient if we could stop off at Earth on the way." He took a deep breath. "Well. It is what it is. We will have to wait until we have more data. At any rate we have a very promising lead."

He went off after that to tell the other scientists about his discovery, while one of the ship's linguists, Jahac, of Liberty sect, helped me scan my books into the computer to teach it to read.

I had the idea of maybe asking him more about the ship's politics. Was there, perhaps, a way to lure some Liberty votes away from Pav, so that we could stop at Earth? I still knew almost nothing about the earthlings, but Karnath's excitement was contagious. Could I really be related to these mysterious aliens? Perhaps a stray comet, carrying organic material from Earth, had struck Kinaru and started all life on my planet. On the other hand, perhaps it was coincidence, just as our appearance was.

But Jahac did not want to talk about politics. He wanted to talk about the peculiarities in our language—words like right-mother or left-father, or our semiplural form that we use when talking about both persons in the same body. I finally gave up on probing his political opinions and asked him about his own language. I know nothing about languages—Kinaru has only one language globally. But he gave me a lengthy education on words specific to the Shatakazan's global dialect: specialized words for parents of each gender, a genetic father or mother, a partner of one's parent who isn't also one's parent, a mutual partner one shares with another partner, or a partner of a partner who isn't also one's own partner. He also gave me a brief tutorial on how to read the Shatakazan script, which was entirely phonetic and thus easy to master.

We were interrupted by a chime from his personal device. He stood up immediately, crest prickling. "We will have to continue this another time," he said quickly. "We are being called to a vote—I can't imagine why."

Karnath came back half an hour later, looking deflated. "I gave it another try. I told them the new information and requested another vote. Most of the team was simply annoyed with me for wasting their time. Everyone always votes as a sect, and the numbers haven't changed. Seven to five against."

"I don't suppose they'd let *me* vote."

He flicked his fingers down. "Only people who signed onto the original mission charter. Since we were all hired by the board on Shatak, we are their voice away from home. Or that's the thinking. Normally it works very well, so that we can alter our mission directive based on emerging circumstances. Now I think it was foolish for us to hire so many crew in Liberty sect. They're such a large sect, it's hard to avoid them. But despite their name, they can be... well, rather rigid. They reject anything that smacks of interference in a forbidden planet. That's why Pav voted against bringing you on board." He stopped abruptly. "I'm sorry, I probably shouldn't have revealed that."

"It's all right, I had that impression already." But he had piqued my curiosity. "I suppose some Liberty members voted to bring me on board though."

"Most of the scientific team did, plus the two Unity spacers. You were far too exciting a prospect to pass up, and technically it's not interference. Or no worse than we already had."

"The same could be said of a stop in Earth orbit," I said. "I just wish we could get them to see it."

Resa

That evening, Tria handed over control to me, so I could use both hands and feet. When we were younger, we used to fight for control. As a right, she's much stronger than I am, but I could wait till she was distracted and make a snatch for it. It took training for her to master guarding whatever mysterious gates lay between her and me.

Of course we didn't do that kind of thing now. We passed control between ourselves lightly, like a ball tossed from hand to hand. She had it more, of course, but she made sure I always had a chance. Which is more than some rights do.

I sat before the painting in our room, fiddling with the hat I was making. Fingerwork was much easier with both hands, that was for sure. The hat would be yellow, orange, and russet, the colors of leaves. Unsubtle colors, but I was glad I had chosen them. On this gray ship, I craved color like food.

The yarn tickled through my own fingers, but in Tria's hand, I felt only a faint echo of sensation. Was that how she felt things, or just the nature of the route the impulses had to take through her mind before passing on to me? Karnath's questions had left me wondering.

I liked Karnath. His face was like a snake's, or maybe a water reptile's, but I liked reptiles. It was only strange if you expected him to be something other than he was. And he felt genuine; he was like Tria, too excited by the prospect of a scientific discovery to have any ulterior motive.

About the others on the ship, I wasn't sure. They all had their own agendas, and Tria was so fixated on studying them I couldn't feel certain she was paying attention to their motives. And even if she did, what chance did she have of sorting them out? Even I didn't know why Tazag was so hostile, or what Zin meant by her friendliness. I didn't know anything about them, except that they were nothing like us.

The aliens that licked each other's faces, I envied. It seemed their version of kissing. Nobody had ever kissed me. So often I had read it in someone's eye, the way their touches lingered, the way they stood the slightest bit closer than necessary. Lefts don't miss that kind of signal.

But the rights would talk and talk and talk, as if they could turn the air blue with talk. They'd give their polite farewells and part. If we'd ever gotten married, then I supposed I would have been allowed my half hour or so, after Tria had gone to sleep, to spend that way. Tapa had wanted that, it was obvious. Perhaps I would have wanted it too, if the whole concept hadn't seemed like a cage. Nobody can love the bars of their own cage.

What would a planet be like where you could simply sit in front of the gods and everyone and lick faces? It had to be better than home. It had to.

But I shouldn't have *had* to leave home to get that.

Are you all right? asked Tria.

I flicked a stitch from one hand to the other. *Why wouldn't I be?*

You've cried a lot since we left.

I felt inside myself, the drained feeling, the stinging eye. She wasn't wrong. *Been a big day.*

Why did you agree to come? she asked abruptly. *Just to get away from Rez il Tapa?*

I lifted my shoulder and dropped it. *Not only.*

Leaving the planet wasn't the only way to get out of partnering with him.

Can you think of another way out? I couldn't. *If not him, it would have been somebody else. Or something else. My whole life... how much of it was I ever going to be able to control?*

She was silent a moment. *I've never wanted control. The councils that make all those decisions know what they're doing. They have our test results and everything.*

I worked another row without answering. If those people thought they could predict love with tests, they were wrong. I had seen exactly how wrong.

Tria went on, *My life has been shaped in satisfying directions. I don't need to be the one to shape it.*

My fingers fumbled as I tried to grasp what she had said. Did she think she was superior because she didn't want agency of her own? I guess she thought it was just another silly notion of mine.

I dropped several stitches, grinding my teeth. The more I thought about it, forming and discarding things to say to her, the madder I got. I tore the stitches off my fingers and threw the hat back into its bag. She was what she was and it wasn't her fault. But gods, I was angry anyway. Angry enough to slap her. And I couldn't say a single word because she would *never* understand.

I flung myself into bed and slapped my sleep stimulator onto my forehead. Not that I wanted to sleep, but if I was asleep she would stop talking. The cool metal gadget gave its faint hum.

In the last minute before I fell asleep, I saw my mother's face. Was *her* life shaped in satisfying directions?

CHAPTER FIVE

Tria

We reached the space station the following morning. Most of the crew gathered in the cargo room on the middle level, putting on sterilization bracelets and checking earbuds.

"This station is not run by the Shatakazan," Karnath warned me. "It's run by the Vray'la, which doesn't mean it's not *safe*, but—well, it's best if you stay by me. If we get into trouble here, the whole ship will be delayed."

"Are you sure it's all right for me to be on the station? I don't want to risk causing trouble."

He lowered his eyelids. "It would be criminal to let you miss it. Your chance to see your first aliens! Well, besides us."

There was a faint thump and the vibration of the engines cut out. Pav, Daz the navigator, and Gaj the chief engineer came up the stairs from the lower level. "We're cleared to enter," said Pav. "Keep your devices on your persons and return here by 9.75." We trooped down the curving ramp and through a short, flexible tunnel before setting foot on the station.

The first thing I noticed was the light. While the *Galajak* was always a little dim, except in the hallways where the biolayer grew, the station was almost blindingly bright. The light shone a little blue, giving an odd cast to everyone's faces. The air was cool after the warmth of the *Galajak*.

The station was large and busy, decorated in a garish style with bright colors everywhere and art made from patterns of glowing lights. Beside the airlock, a squat being, as tall as my shoulder, held up some kind of scanner. His skin was brown and craggy—he could have passed for a rock if he had closed his tiny red eyes. Apparently satisfied, he growled a few syllables, which my earbud rendered as, "You are cleared for entry to Far Expanse Station."

Here the group broke up. Pav went off at a purposeful pace, followed by most of the spacers and Jahac the linguist. Lex, the linguist; Prazad, the alien tech expert; and Talek, one of the two engineers, stayed with Karnath. The rest scattered on their own, apparently in a hurry to get away from the others. After months together, I could hardly blame them for wanting some space. "What should we show Tria first?" asked Lex. "Restaurants?" She crinkled her eyes roguishly. "Sex shop?"

I felt my face reddening. "Restaurants sound nice," I managed.

Karnath graciously stepped in to redirect the conversation. "We did test Tria's food earlier. She can eat anything we can. Just don't eat any Vray'la foods," he added, aside. "They make us sick and I can't predict what they might do to you."

We dodged through the crowds of aliens—mostly the rocklike Vray'la, but also plenty of Shatakazan and many I didn't know. I spotted creatures with rainbow scales, riding in hoverchairs with bubbling spheres along each side of their heads, presumably to provide water to their gills. There were four-armed bipeds, features invisible within silvery atmospheric suits. Of course this particular atmosphere would only be breathable for a certain percentage of species. But it was a shame I couldn't see inside the suits.

Talek claimed us a table in a small restaurant overlooking the concourse, sending Prazad to order something. From here I could see the floods of people below, hurrying from one airlock to another or stopping to buy something to eat at a food stall. "I feel strangely tired," I said, sinking down on a plain stool by the table. "Is there less oxygen here than I'm used to?"

"A little," said Karnath, "but what you mainly feel is the gravity. The Vray'la standard is about 115% of yours."

Lex peered over the railing. "Looks like Tazag and Resh found each other. I always thought there was something going on with those two."

Talek wrinkled zir nose. "Them? No, I don't think so. I feel like I'd have noticed."

I studied Talek curiously. Ze had the brown crest of a neutral, with gold specks sprinkled on zir brow ridge and the sides of zir face. I decided it was a cosmetic. Lex had some too, in blue. "Are shipboard relationships common?"

They all laughed at me. "What's uncommon is not having at least one," said Lex. "Hence why everyone's laying bets on Tazag and Resh. And one or two others..." Her eyes went to Karnath, who seemed not to notice.

He's one of the single ones, said Resa. *And Lex wants him.*

I can't say I'm that interested in their interpersonal drama.

You should take an interest in everything, she chided. *Or what kind of scientist are you?*

Talek put in, "Femat is another. I just told her this morning I won't be keeping company with her anymore. She's great at sex, but just so quiet. I need conversation, too. I feel bad, though, she seemed more disappointed than I thought she'd be."

"Hm, maybe I'll talk to her when we get back to the ship," Lex mused. "Daz is a fine lover but ze doesn't take up *all* my time."

Just then Prazad returned with our food: four violet-colored drinks and a bag of fried... I averted my gaze. Definitely some kind of beetle. Well, I would try the drink, at least. I took a tentative sip. It was warm as bathwater and tasted of salt, umami, and a faint funk, like a moldy basement. I lifted my hand to cover Resa's obvious grimace. Well, it would be too much to expect the food of other planets to be palatable to a tongue that wasn't evolved for them.

Talek leaned forward to peer around Lex at the people down below. Tazag and Resh were talking to a third Shatakazan, a female I didn't know. "Is that Banat?" ze asked Lex. "I didn't know the *Vatarax* was here."

"Yes, I saw it on one of the displays we passed. It's supposed to be docked at the far end."

"Well, excuse me, then. My old lover Saban is aboard, I have simply got to meet up with her. What are the odds?" Talek gently squeezed Prazad's arm before getting up and hurried off.

The rest of us decided to go to a theater down on the lower level, to enjoy a sensodrama. "You'll like it," Lex assured me. "On your planet you don't even have 2D dramas, do you?"

Prazad cleared his throat. "Only radio," he said, the first he'd spoken all morning. "They have all the technology necessary for color broadcasts, but they haven't happened to develop it."

We took a grav-tube down—a disturbing hole in the balcony that people simply jumped down, a gravity field slowing their fall. Beside it, a similar tube gently wafted people upward. I stepped into the field nervously, but it deposited me lightly on the ground.

Beside the tube was another restaurant, I thought at first. Unlike the other restaurants, where tables spilled out into the open spaces around, this one was surrounded with walls of etched glass. Inside, through a pattern of clear spaces, I could see beings slumped at tables or staring glassy-eyed in front of them. No one seemed to be eating anything.

"What is this place?" I asked Karnath.

"A dispensary," he said. "You know—for relaxants, hallucinogens, things like that."

"Mood-altering drugs?" I asked, wrinkling my nose.

"Yes, the Vray'la take a positive view of them."

"Not just the Vray'la," I said, scanning the clientele. "Look, there's Femat." Sure enough, she leaned back in one of the booths, yellow crest flat, staring into the middle distance. On the table before her were a glass of water and a few tablets.

"It's not our business," said Karnath, turning away. "As long as she's sober on duty, it doesn't matter what she does on her own time."

"I feel bad, though," said Lex. "After what Talek said. I'm going to talk to her."

Karnath tried to talk her out of it, but she slipped inside. We could see her bend down to talk to Femat. The other female flicked her fingers downward and waved her away.

"She would have asked for company if she wanted it," chided Karnath as we walked away toward the theater. "You shouldn't interfere."

"Well, I felt like I should try. Sometimes the best thing for rejection is a new lover."

He sighed. "And sometimes, people just need time."

The sensodrama was an interesting experience. We donned large helmets, designed to fit a variety of alien heads, and settled into a squashy gel which served for seating. Once the helmet was on, I could see and hear as if I were really there—in this case, at a Vray'la temple which had recently been excavated.

This is more like a documentary than a drama, Resa commented in disappointment.

Or an advertisement for travel to their homeworld, I agreed. *But it doesn't matter. It's still a fascinating technology. Look, when we move our head, we can look around!* The gel also transmitted tactile sensations, so that we could feel the stones of the temple.

After about an hour, the sensodrama ended and I took off my helmet. Karnath and Lex were still on either side of me, but Prazad was gone. We found him waiting outside the theater, crouching with his back against the wall. "Sorry about that," he said. "Those things make me sick."

"No need to apologize," said Lex. "We should be starting to make our way back, don't you think? I wonder if Talek found zir ex-lover."

We came upon zem on our way back. Ze hadn't had any luck. "It was the strangest thing, they had the airlock shut and wouldn't let me on! They told me she was still on the *Vatarax*, but couldn't come out and see me."

Karnath rubbed the back of his hand against his chin. "That *is* odd. And they wouldn't say why?"

"No. Said I had to speak to Banat, but I couldn't find her anywhere, and it's already time to go back. It's such a shame. I haven't talked to her in years."

We paused outside the dispensary. Femat was still inside, her chin resting on her chest and her eyes closed. The tablets on the table were gone. "We really should wake her up," Lex said. "I don't want her to get in trouble with Pav if she's back late."

She went in and shook Femat by the shoulder, leaning down to speak in her ear. Femat didn't move. Shooting us a look, Lex tried again, with no effect.

"Wait here," said Karnath. "I'm going to go help." He reached the table and dipped his fingers in Femat's glass, flicking the water into her face. This too had no effect. Karnath leaned down, bringing his ears near Femat's nose and mouth. Then he suddenly rushed into action, ripping off his sterilization bracelet and Femat's in order to feel for a pulse on the front of Femat's neck.

Lex turned brilliant yellow all over her face and dashed out of the dispensary. "She doesn't have a pulse," she gasped. "Karnath's doing first aid. Prazad, you call Pav. I'm going to flag down one of the stationers."

By the time Pav arrived, the Vray'la medical responders had brought Femat to a small medlab, where a Shatakazan doctor was examining her. "There was nothing you could have done," ze assured Karnath. "Time of death was at least twenty minutes ago."

"Do you have a cause of death?" Pav asked.

"Our blood scan shows a large dose of synemethin, and that would have been enough to kill her."

"The Vray'la relaxant?"

"Yes. It's toxic to us—much stronger than we need, and it interacts negatively with our lungs. She would have gone into a deep sleep and stopped breathing within a few minutes of taking it."

Pav bowed her head, considering. "I can't think why she would have taken synemethin. Everyone knows to avoid Vray'la drugs. Could the dispensary owner have mixed them up?"

"It's not impossible…" the doctor mused. "But—well—getting the drugs right for each order is his entire job! He'd never have a license to operate here if he wasn't conscientious. And he'll lose it for sure, if this is his fault."

Talek cleared zir throat. "Is it—is it possible she ordered it on purpose? Would the owner have given it to her if she did?"

"He's not supposed to," said the doctor. "But if your friend wanted to harm herself, she could have easily taken someone else's tablets. Everyone in there is under the influence of something, it wouldn't be hard to do."

Talek's crest flattened and ze looked at the ground, wrapping zir arms around zirself. I felt sorry for zem. Ze hadn't known she'd be that disappointed by zir ending their relationship. Could she really have wanted to take her own life over it? She was quiet, perhaps she'd had other worries. Talek couldn't blame zirself.

"Who saw her last?" asked Pav.

"I did," said Lex. "Well, we all did, but I went inside and talked to her. I suggested she come with us to the theater, but she wanted to be left alone."

"Did you notice if she had any pills, or what kind?"

She wobbled her hand in the air vaguely. "There were some, for sure."

"Synemethin comes in a pink tablet," the doctor added helpfully.

Lex chewed her lip a moment, then shook her head. "I really can't remember."

I can, said Resa, startling me. She had been quiet since we had found Femat. *Four white tablets. No pink ones.*

Are you sure? We didn't even go inside.

I'm sure. A moment passed. *Aren't you going to tell Pav?*

I hesitated. *She didn't ask us. And I feel... I feel like I shouldn't interrupt this investigation.*

It's not interrupting. It's contributing.

I didn't answer. I felt bad, but I also knew Resa could be unreliable, especially when she was emotional. Femat's death must have shaken her, and she was grasping for something to do to help. But, reluctant as I was to tell her this, I didn't feel entirely confident she really remembered seeing the pills.

Resa

On the way back to the ship, my hand started to shake. Seeing Femat lying there on the ground, while Karnath worked to revive her, had turned me as cold as ice and sent the world far away, as if through a tunnel.

By the time we stepped into the cargo bay, I was flashing back hard. My instinct was to curl up in a ball, rock back and forth, pull at my hair. But while Tria controlled our body, all I could do was shrink inside myself, till I felt like a tiny little point within the center of my heart. Let Tria calmly handle the practicalities. I was living in the past.

You're doing good, though, I reminded myself. You spoke up when you knew something. That shows you're handling yourself better than you did then.

Then.

We had been twelve years old. Old enough to be interviewed by the police. There hadn't been any doubt about who had killed them—the sleep stimulator was still on my right-mother's forehead, and the knife in my left-mother's hand. No one else had been around.

But they had wanted to know *why*.

They put us to sleep in turns, to do the interview. Just in case we would be more comfortable that way. But I was never comfortable without Tria; I kept reaching for her presence, like a tongue going looking for a missing tooth, over and over.

The nice woman from the police department smiled at me. "Are you verbal?" she asked kindly, meaning, could I talk. Not all lefts can, especially not so young.

I could speak fine, on a normal day, but not on that day. Not when I had just lost everything that mattered to me. And I wasn't sure what I could have said anyway. Had she been happy? Of course not, but you idiots have figured that out by now, haven't you?

So I shook my head, vision rippling with tears, and she left me with some paper and paints. As if I could somehow draw suicide. As if I could paint the reason.

Ignoring the brush, I dipped my fingers in the blue. Blue is a sad color. But blue wasn't sad enough, so I added black, mixing them together till the black sucked the blue down with it into darkness. I filled the paper and reached for another.

And that was when I saw the officer had left her folder behind. Open. Because if I couldn't speak, I couldn't read, could I?

Only I could. I read the whole file, carefully turning the pages with my clean third and fourth fingers. And then I put it back.

They knew. Not only did they know, they could have seen it coming. They could have stopped it. But they didn't.

I never told Tria what I had read in that file. I told myself she wouldn't want to know. But I was the one who clung to my ignorance. I didn't want to know what she would say or think. Because if, for one second, she had dared to blame my left-mother for what she had done, I wasn't sure I would ever be able to forgive her.

A scent brought me back to myself—a scent bearing nothing of the past. It was Karnath, leaning close, smelling faintly spicy, like dry copperbrush almost. "Are you all right?" he was asking.

I looked up at him, meeting his golden eyes. He was looking straight at me, but I couldn't speak. Instead Tria answered. "Yes, of course. What about yourself? You look greener than usual."

He wobbled a hand in the air. "That was... upsetting. I need to take some time to process it."

"Of course," said Tria, turning to go.

"I didn't mean alone," he said hastily. "Would you like to join me? Processing trauma verbally can be very helpful."

I don't find it so. I wanted to process it by squeezing someone's hand, or with teary embraces. Pressing oneself against the living to remember that life still beats in so many veins. But the sterilization bracelet I wore made touch impossible; it would burn any living cells I touched that weren't my own. If Karnath had even wanted such a thing.

I managed to say to Tria, *Yes. Go with him. He doesn't want to be alone.*

Tria

Karnath tucked himself into the egg-shaped seat behind his desk, drawing his feet up and hugging his legs against him. "I just can't wrap my mind around it," he said. "Why would Femat want to die?"

"Talek seemed to think it was zir fault."

"It makes no sense," he said, hugging his knees against his chest. "Femat had two long-term partners back on Shatak. Her relationship with Talek was only a month old. I just don't think anyone would end their life over the end of such a casual relationship."

"Maybe she had other worries. Maybe she had been waiting a long time for a chance like this." I took a deep breath to dispel my feelings of discomfort. This topic troubled me. I had wondered most of my life what could ever make a person choose to die.

Karnath sighed. "I suppose we'll never know. That's the most upsetting part of the whole thing. That we can't go back and ask a person why. I just keep thinking, maybe if we'd pushed her harder to join us... maybe if she had confided in Lex... "

"It isn't your fault," I said automatically.

He raised his head, giving himself a little shake. "What do they do on your planet when someone dies?"

"There are religious rituals..." I began. I remembered them vaguely. Resa was a believer, so we had attended the temple ceremony. There had been torrential sobbing, embracing, tearing of hair and clothing. She had seemed to get some closure from it, but it had done nothing for me. "People believe the spirits of their loved ones go to another dimension to dwell with their ancestors," I said at last. "I have never been religious, so I don't have that comfort."

"Has anyone close to you ever died?"

"My mother. Mothers." I cleared my throat. "I never discuss it."

His crest flattened and he looked at the floor. "I apologize. I meant to ask you, is Resa all right? I can't yet read her expressions very well, and I was worried this business might have upset her."

"I am not sure. Neither of us knew Femat. But she is being..." Paranoid, I wanted to say. But she wouldn't like that. "She's worried about it. She hinted to me that if Femat could easily have taken a tablet from another table, so could anyone else."

Karnath's crest flicked up and his eyes widened. "You mean—another person could have poisoned Femat on purpose?"

I nodded. "I feel it's a lot less likely than accident, or suicide."

"It's possible, though. It was a public place. Anyone could have walked by the table, and no one would have thought anything of it."

"Is there any tension between you and the Vray'la? Would one of them have targeted a Shatakazan purely on that basis?"

He flicked his fingers downward. "No, they're usually happy to have our business. They aren't interested in scientific exploration, so they don't mind us passing through their space on the way to other planets. Though any individual Vray'la—or, in fact, anyone—might have a personal grudge."

"Not for Femat in particular, though. Most of the people there wouldn't know her, and anyone who did know her wouldn't expect to find her there. Our visit wasn't scheduled far in advance—your team meant to stay on Kinaru much longer." I was leaning forward now, on the edge of the bed. If Resa's thinking was paranoia, it was catching.

Karnath held up a finger. "It could have been the idea of a moment. In fact it would have had to be. No one would have known we would be at the station, or that she would choose to go to the dispensary. But a person who disliked her could have been walking by, seen her through the window, and performed the switch on impulse."

I shook my head in disbelief. "Who could hate Femat that much, that they would choose to kill her without even an hour to think it over?"

"I don't know. This was her first time off-world, so far as I know. She's younger than I am. That doesn't leave a lot of time to make enemies in." He spread his hands. "Maybe Talek would know."

I frowned. "I'm not sure we should talk to anybody on the crew about this yet."

He stared at me a moment. "You think it could be someone on the *crew?*"

"No, I just meant I didn't want to spread worry and suspicion based on pure speculation," I said hastily. "But now that you mention it..."

"Well, Talek, at least, was in our group while we were on the station."

I shook my head. "No, remember? Ze went off looking for zir friend, before we ever passed the dispensary."

"So the only ones we can be sure of are Lex, Prazad, and ourselves?"

"Prazad stepped out of the theater. He said it made him sick."

Karnath pursed his lips. "For that matter, we all had helmets on in the theater. Any one of us could have stepped out, switched the tablets, and come back before the sensodrama was over, no one the wiser."

I rested my elbow on my knee and my chin on my fist. "This is bad. Because now that I think of it, it's much more likely for someone on this ship to have done it than anyone else. The chance of running into someone who knew her enough to dislike her is vanishingly small. Whereas on a ship like this, everyone knew each other, and any of them might harbor hard feelings."

"But for Femat? She was quiet. Generally friendly. Did her work well. As a sociologist, she worked mainly with Tazag, but I never heard them argue. I just can't imagine anyone having hard feelings." At last he shook his head. "No. No, I think we're being too paranoid. None of these possibilities are remotely likely. Whereas either an accident or suicide seems fairly plausible."

I checked my chrono. It was getting late, by my body's time, and I made my apologies. It wasn't until we were out in the hall that Resa said, *But all of the pills were white.*

It took me a long time to fall asleep that night. More and more, I thought Resa was right. But if it was someone on the ship, I didn't know who I could trust with Resa's recollection. Maybe not even Karnath.

CHAPTER SIX

Tria

I spent the next "morning" with Tazag, Lex, and Jahac. This time we had an open-ended discussion: about our system of government, about our mediation system for when there are disputes between partners, and about our history. They had spent most of the time since we had left Kinaru listening to the radio broadcasts they had collected, so they had enough information to ask interesting questions.

"So how far back would you say your written history goes?" asked Tazag.

"Eight thousand years," I said proudly. Our ancient epics from early history were beautiful and poetic—every schoolchild has to read them. I wished I had had a copy to bring.

"And in all that time," Lex asked, puzzled, "you have always spoken the same language? Planetwide?"

I nodded. "Of course it has developed some in that time. Those old stories are very archaic; it's difficult to read them."

"Our own study has suggested that a language will mutate to the point of unintelligibility within a millennium, unless it's artificially held steady by written texts."

"Which ours is. We learn proper global dialect in school, in part from our historical epics."

"And there are no regional dialects?"

"Of course there are some differences. But it's mutually intelligible throughout the planet. Of course, as I'm sure you know, a great deal of the planet is inhospitable to life because of the aridity. We mostly live within a few hundred miles of the coastlines. And early in our history, people were confined to the coastline of a single ocean. So no group was so isolated that they wouldn't need to talk to people from other regions."

"I suppose not," said Lex, making a note on her device.

"And what about the population?" asked Tazag. "Our measure of visible cities suggests perhaps 800 million, but surely we've made an error. Is there a large rural population?"

"No, 800 million sounds about right."

Tazag's crest fluffed slightly in surprise. "That seems tiny for a race that's old enough to have reached this stage of advancement. Do you have a very low birthrate?"

"Most families have two or three children. In the past people chose larger families to help with farmwork, but at this point people prefer to have only a few because of the effort it takes to give each child a proper education."

Ze rubbed zir chin with the back of zir hand, still puzzled. "And your lifespan? Is it very short? Are you much prone to pandemics?"

"I don't know what would be considered short. We live one hundred to one hundred twenty years, on average."

Tazag made a conversion on his tablet. "So perhaps one hundred fifty of ours. That's actually fairly long, compared to other races we've studied." Ze tapped away on the tablet for awhile.

"What are you thinking?" asked Lex, tilting her head to one side.

"The only way I can make these numbers work is for the Kinaru to be a very young race," ze murmured. "How old are your prehistoric archeological sites?"

I frowned. "There aren't any. Our history goes back much further than our archeology. People were living mainly in skin tents at that stage, so they wouldn't have left much."

Tazag stared at me a moment fixedly. Then ze stood up quickly and turned to go. "I need to work with these numbers for a while. Please excuse me."

I looked after zem. Ze'd gotten me thinking as well. I had no idea most planets had a longer archeological history than ours. It made me wonder, was there some kind of cataclysm at some point? There was no historical record of one, but it would explain why we had no fossil record of our own evolution.

In the corridor outside, I spotted Pav. Before I could second-guess myself, I hurried up to her. "Excuse me, may I speak with you? Privately?"

Tilting her head in surprise, she ducked into the conference room with me. Outside, the stars were thick as ever, spotted with nebulas. I pulled my gaze away from them and back to Pav's face. "I wanted to talk about Femat's death, back on the station. I... Resa thinks that it might have been murder."

She turned to the table and sat down, waving me to sit as well. I hunched into the egg-seat. "Of course we considered that possibility," she said. "The station police and the consul both agreed we couldn't rule it out. But we couldn't confirm it either. The only surveillance camera was directed behind the counter, to monitor for theft."

"Could you tell if the order was filled correctly, at least?"

"It seemed to be. The dispensary owner was emphatic that he never mistakes an order. The only Shatakazan customer he had had during the period ordered six tablets of prodexin, and that's what he put on the table. He was sure about that. He always doublechecks when serving non-Vray'la."

"That was what Resa said. She says she saw the tablets in front of Femat, when we looked in, and they were all white."

Pav bowed her head, pulling absently at her lower lip. "That does narrow the window in which it could have happened."

"Did you ask the owner if anyone came in without ordering anything?"

"Yes, he said two Shatakazan came in, at different times, to talk to Femat. Or the same one twice. He said," she reported acidly, "that we all look alike."

"He didn't even know the crest color?"

She flicked her fingers downward. "Vray'la don't see in the same spectrum as we do."

"So it could have been any Shatakazan."

"Or any of the Vray'la patrons, or other alien patrons, of whom there were a few."

"Why would any of them go after Femat?"

"A racist, most likely. They exist everywhere. Some people develop a prejudice against a certain species and can't be talked out of it. Of course the station police did not care for that suggestion. They insisted it had to have been suicide. I have trouble with this theory, because I feel we would have noticed if she were depressed. And if she had been, she could easily have gone to Resh or Karnath for a prescription and felt better in a day or two." She spread her hands in frustration. "The sad fact is that we may never know what happened to her. I wish we had more to tell her family."

I nodded. It had given me considerable relief to talk to her. At least I didn't have the guilt of withholding Resa's report. And her openness to discussing it with me reassured me that she wasn't hiding anything. Probably.

I found Karnath in the dayroom, finishing a meal. "I asked around a little," he said quietly, when I joined him with my tray. "In a casual way. I didn't want to spread paranoia, but I was curious whether the others stayed together while off the station."

"And?"

"It seems they did. I talked to Gaj, and she said she was with Pav, Jahac, Daz, and Zin the entire time—well, until we called Pav away. After ordering the material they needed from the supply shop, they went to a low-grav gym to play float-ball. No one could have left without the others noticing, or they would have left their position open and dropped the ball."

"Well, that leaves someone accounted for, at least," I said, sighing. "I spoke to Pav just now. She suspects it was a racist attack by a stranger on the station. I don't know how common that is."

He screwed up his mouth. "Not very. But, *shells*, none of the possibilities is very likely!" His voice rose loud enough to draw glances. He sighed, lowering his voice. "I just—I don't like it. I don't like the thought that it could be one of the crew. We've been together over seventy days on this ship. I thought I knew everyone better than that."

"You probably do," I reassured him. "The idea that one of us did it is highly unlikely. Try to put it out of your mind."

He nodded. "I will try." For a moment he toyed with his empty plate. "I need something else to occupy my mind. I'm going to watch some videos. Would you like to come?"

"Oh, certainly," I said. "I have never seen a video."

"Come on then," he said, piling my tray on top of his. "Let's go see what you might like."

He brought me to the lab with the largest vidscreen, using his personal device to scroll through the options. "What are you interested in?" he asked. "Fiction, non-fiction, historical?"

Too many choices. "What do *you* like? What do you watch for fun?"

His crest flattened in embarrassment. "Oh, I don't know if you'd like any of that. Everyone laughs at me for it. They say I'm obsessed."

I smiled. "Now I have to know."

He glanced down at his device. "Oh, all right," he said, flicking the screen to make his selection. "It's... Earth comedy broadcasts. I've always been obsessed with Earth. It's one of the most fascinating planets we've ever discovered. Most we find don't have intelligent life, and most that do have it are very primitive, so we don't interact with them and have no way of finding out much. Earth is right on the edge—advanced enough that we can keep track of what they do, but still wildly primitive in so many ways."

"Primitive how? It seems they have more technology than we do."

"Yes, but also a great deal more unrest. Some areas are fairly developed, others are in dire poverty and warring with one another for resources and dominance. Pandemics sweep the planet from time to time; their medical infrastructure is insufficient to combat even those diseases they know how to cure. Even the civilized countries are rife with corruption and crime."

"The mirror image of Kinaru," I said. "We failed to qualify for contact because of our lack of technological development, but socially even Tazag agreed we are advanced."

"There are many on Shatak who think we should make an exception for Earth. Visit one of the more developed countries, perhaps help them along."

"I still don't understand why you don't. After all, my own planet will almost certainly develop space travel faster now that they know you're out here."

"The worry is giving a planet technology before it's ready socially. Already Earth is a great deal too technologically advanced for its own good. When they first split the atom, instead of using it for power, they made bombs out of it. And that was one of the nations we had categorized as more civilized."

"Maybe that's just... their nature. Is it possible they're just too unstable to ever be ready?"

He waggled a hand uncertainly. "I don't think so. I've watched a great deal of their video broadcasts and they seem... well, like anyone. Perfectly capable of kindness and generosity. It's very normal for a planet at an early stage of development to be divided into competing nations, to be prone to warfare, to have steep class differences in standard of living. Their trouble is that they're racing ahead technologically at light speed. I don't know how they do it. But it would be disastrous if they developed a fold drive and brought all that chaos out into the galaxy. They need time."

"So they're dangerous, but you like them?"

"I'm intrigued by them. Not sure I would like to actually face a human in person, but in their entertainment broadcasts, they're very relatable. They seem almost Shatakazan." He selected a program and cast it onto the screen.

I settled in to watch it, curling up diagonally in the egg-shaped seat and bracing my knees against the opposite side. The picture was a little grainy, but my earbud translated the earthling language as seamlessly as it did with Shatakaz. The program was about several young adults living together in a city dwelling. "Is this a family?" I asked. "Like the Shatakazan have?"

"Oh no, their family structure is a good deal more like yours. But in this region, it's common for young adults to spend time living alone or with friends before establishing a household. All of them are looking for mates, which is what provides much of the program's drama."

Sure enough, it was mainly about romance—very unstructured, awkward romance with disappointing results I could have predicted. Always one character would want a romantic pairing with someone who wasn't interested, or the romance would seem to be going well and it would all fall apart over a quarrel. "This is terrible!" I exclaimed at the end of the program. "We have nothing like this on Kinaru. Our relationships are *rational.*"

You should have read my graphic novels, Resa said. Where there is no drama, people will create drama. It's exciting.

Perhaps in fiction. But imagine if real life were like that!

Karnath inclined his head. "On Shatak, as well, we have fewer complications."

"Really? I would have thought, with so many people involved, your relationships would be difficult."

"They are very … informal. It helps that we can usually tell through body language when someone is interested. After a few sexual experiences together, it is easier to tell if you are compatible with them."

I furrowed my brow. "Sex first, then commitment? That's… different."

"Of course," he said. "How can anyone expect to make a rational decision about compatibility when under the influence of frustrated sexual desire?"

"That's why the social arrangements board makes these decisions for us," I said. "Obviously the people involved will be the least able to be objective."

Karnath regarded me. "But think of your own arranged partnership. That was hardly any better. A happy ending is never guaranteed in romance, and the emotions involved guarantee that mistakes are deeply painful."

I thought of Femat, and how she had been disappointed when Talek had ended their relationship—perhaps even to the point of suicide. That seemed worse than if I had ended up with Rez il Tapa. "Do you have anyone?" I asked. "Back home, maybe?"

He flicked his fingers downward. "I have not been lucky in that respect. I've had relationships, of course. The casual ones, I find unsatisfying. Sex without emotional intimacy doesn't appeal to me. But the more serious relationships I've had have ended for one reason or another."

"Do you think our system would work better for you?"

He rubbed the back of his hand against the bottom of his chin thoughtfully. His scales made a faint zipping sound. "It seems something would be missing with that approach. Where is the... the spark? The chemistry?"

I looked back blankly. *I am not really sure what he's talking about.*

That's just the sort of thing you rights always fail to understand, Resa responded, sounding annoyed. But she wouldn't say anything else.

I looked at my lap, feeling embarrassed. When Resa referred to some special left thing that I wouldn't understand, I always felt a little foolish. But with Karnath agreeing with her, it was so much worse. What if every sentient species in the galaxy knew about this mysterious spark, except me and maybe other rights?

Karnath tactfully switched to another program, and I tried to put my thoughts to one side. The Kinaru way worked. It didn't matter if no one else in the galaxy understood.

CHAPTER SEVEN

Resa

We parted with Karnath after a few hours. Tazag apparently wanted to discuss something with him. "Probably the interview I had with zem this morning," Tria told him. "Ze was very interested in our history and population growth. Perhaps you will have some insights."

While he was seeking out Tazag, we went to the dayroom for dinner. This time of day, there were no crew around; they didn't need to eat as often as we did. I ate in silence, thinking of the Earth drama we'd watched, and Karnath, and my mother. I was learning too much, too quickly. I needed time to process, but things wouldn't stop happening.

If we had been on Kinaru, I could have gone for a walk, breathed fresh air, felt the strength in my body and the sun on my hair. It had always helped. But here there was no air that wasn't stuffy and hot.

On our way out, though, we passed Karnath in the corridor. He and Pav were nose to nose, crests both fully erect, having a heated conversation. Neither looked at us, so we turned sideways to edge past them.

"...If you aren't on this mission to increase our knowledge, what are you even here for?" Karnath was saying.

"I am here to carry out the charter! And the charter is to study Kinaru. Not Earth."

"It seems the two may be the same topic!"

"How? It makes no sense. Neither species has interstellar travel, and neither has any sign or any history of having had it in the past. The comet theory is the only logical one. And that's interesting but hardly groundbreaking. There is nothing new we could find out on Earth."

"But after what Tazag said, perhaps the settlement of Kinaru was not as far in the past as we think! Isn't it just barely plausible…"

Tria slowed her steps, turning her ear toward them to hear better.

What are you doing? I demanded. *I'm pretty sure eavesdropping is rude in every culture.*

I want to know what Tazag's theory is! But she faced forward again and moved along to our room.

I started yawning before I was even finished changing into my nightshirt. I passed control back to her. *These days are exhausting,* I explained. *Do what you want, I'm going to sleep.*

I'll just stay up a little longer. I have to read more text into the computer to help the reading program along.

I fetched my sleep stimulator and held it in my hand as Tria took her seat at the computer. It was a small metal circle, with reusable adhesive on one side. Somehow it made the kind of electrical waves the brain needed to fall asleep. It wasn't my favorite way to go to sleep, but it isn't easy to sleep while sitting up, while Tria is still working on something. With a reluctant sigh I adhered it to my forehead.

My dreams were jumbled and confusing. Femat, sitting at a table, preparing to eat four white beetles. The entire crew of the ship, engaged in what I thought was an orgy but which turned out to be a medical examination. My mother, smiling as she used to. Partway through the dream, a strange wailing noise started breaking through. Pav opened her mouth to speak, but the wail came out of her mouth. Then it was coming from my octomonkey, which was perched on the DNA scanner, howling.

Finally I awoke to Tria slapping my arm. *Resa. Wake up. Something is happening.*

My eyes snapped open and I pulled the sleep stimulator off. *What— where—what is going on?* Shaking myself, I remembered where I was: in space, aboard the Shatakazan ship, in my bunk. The high-pitched wail was still sounding, and the lights were flashing on and off.

Some kind of alarm, said Tria. *I'm not sure what it means.*

My chest clenched, thinking of terrible things it could mean. Venting oxygen. Engine meltdown. Imminent death.

Don't panic. Stay calm. She forced our breathing to stay slow and deep. Reaching out, she touched the door to slide it open. It still worked, and we stepped out into the hallway.

At first I saw nothing but the flashing lights, which luckily didn't go all the way dark in between flashes, so I could still see. Then several people ran by. "What's the emergency?" Tria called out. "What am I supposed to do?"

One of them stopped and turned around. It was Jahac, the linguist. "Medical emergency," he said. "Go back into your room and stay there."

I resisted. *We have to go see what it is! Who could be hurt?* She compromised by staying where we were, in the doorway.

A moment later a crowd of people came hurrying up the narrow stairwell, supporting a stretcher. They leveled out when they reached the top and tore past us toward the medlab. At the head I saw Resh, the second-in-command, trying to wake the unconscious person on the stretcher. We leaned forward to catch a glimpse. It was Pav, the yellow of her crest tinged with gray.

They turned into the medlab and I didn't see them anymore. A moment later Karnath came running. He saw us but didn't stop. A small crowd was gathering outside the medlab, because there was no room for everyone inside, but Karnath passed them and went in.

I stayed in the doorway, clenching and unclenching my hand anxiously. True, she had seemed to dislike us at first, but since then she had made an effort to be kind. And what could have harmed her on this ship?

At last the crew started trickling back out of the medlab. Tria called to Jahac as he passed by. "Is she all right?"

He gave us a steely look, crest flat to his head. "No. She is dead."

I gasped and covered our mouth with my hand. *Dead? But how? She was fine, just last night!*

Tria checked her chrono. *We saw her only two hours ago. You haven't been sleeping long.*

I stopped myself from answering. What I needed wasn't a fact check. What I needed was someone to listen and comfort me. May as well ask for one of the moons.

Karnath came out after most of the crew had already passed by, his crest flat and his step drained of its usual energy. "I don't understand it," he said, rubbing his forehead. "That voltage shouldn't have been enough to stop her heart."

"What do you mean?" Tria asked. "What happened?"

"She seems to have been electrocuted by a faulty circuit in the command room. The engineers are going down to investigate it now, to figure out how the fault occurred." He took a slow breath in and out. "Resh and I tried to restart her heart by shocking it, but it had no effect."

"What happens now? What are people going to do?"

"Aside from the engineers, there isn't much anyone can do. Resh will have the responsibility of making an inquiry to understand where the fault was and how to prevent future accidents. But for the rest of us... we will probably take some time to process, if our duties aren't immediate. Liberty sect will hold another rite." He stared at the ground. "I just—I can't understand it. Two in one mission."

Resh was last to come out of the medlab. He stopped in the corridor beside us. "Karnath, I think we need a change of policy for your test subject. She should stay in her room unless accompanied by someone."

"Do you really think that's necessary?"

Resh flicked his fingers up. "At least until we understand what went wrong. If something happens to her, our entire mission is wasted." He looked at me a moment. "My apologies for the inconvenience." Then he touched the panel beside the door to shut it. I reached out to open it again, but it was locked.

So that's how it's going to be. I could detect a note of annoyance in her thoughts. *I'm one of them until something bad happens, and then I'm a test subject.*

I stared at the closed door. I wished we could have talked to Karnath longer. He looked how I felt: shocked. Sad. A little frightened.

Are you sure it was an accident? I asked.

Didn't Karnath say it was?

He didn't seem so sure. I thought of his frightened face, green leaching over his cheekbones. Accidents don't make you afraid, not if you already know what caused it.

Let's go back to bed. I'm sure we'll know more in the morning.

But I lay awake a long time, thinking it over. Two deaths now since we had left Kinaru. I didn't truly believe either was an accident.

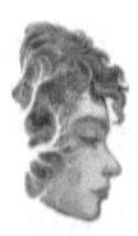

Tria

I was awakened the next morning by the door sliding open. "My apologies, Tria il Resa," said Karnath. "I did not mean to wake you."

I sat up, pushing my hair out of my face and looking at my chrono. "It's all right. I'm usually awake by now."

"You lost some sleep." That was one way of putting it. "We've been talking about Pav's death as a crew, and we... hm... people feel that you ought to be questioned."

"Me?" I got to my feet. "Why me?"

"I should have clarified. We are all engaged in a questioning session. A consensus was reached that you ought to be a part of it."

"I see." I looked down at my rumpled sleep shirt. "Is it all right if I get dressed first?"

"Of course." He withdrew from the room and we got ourself ready. I wondered if he had locked the door behind him, but no—when I was ready, it opened at a touch.

The whole rest of the crew was gathered in the conference room with the window. Every seat was full but two. Karnath directed me to sit beside him at the foot of the table. I could feel every eye on me as I awkwardly folded myself into the seat.

Resh addressed the whole room in a measured tone. "To summarize what we have discussed so far. Pav was electrocuted by touching a control panel in the command room, which should not have been electrified. She was found by Talek and Daz, who entered the room looking for her after being unable to raise her on her device. Talek activated a medical emergency alarm and I arrived on the scene a moment later. Talek, Daz and I transported her to the medlab. First aid was provided by myself and Karnath, both of whom are certified in basic emergency care. Standard procedures were followed. Death was pronounced at time 14.27 by Karnath. While it was not possible to ascertain the time Pav received the shock, she was seen entering the command room at 14.08, so the shock must have resulted at some time between those two points.

"The panel was inspected and found to be electrified. Technician Gaj has assured us that very panel was checked and found in sound condition just three days ago. Likewise Talek touched the same panel at 13.38 the day of the incident, and noticed nothing out of the ordinary. On disassembly of the panel, Gaj, Talek, and myself observed that a wire was bare and touching the surface of the panel, which caused the shock. The power running through the wire was measured at 45 units, which would be expected to be enough to stun but not kill Pav. Karnath has theorized Pav may have had a small weakness in her heart which made it respond to the shock more strongly than expected. This cannot be verified at this point without a prior medical scan, which we do not have in our data banks. We will have to request the data from Shatak upon our return." He scrolled further on his tablet. "I will take a vote to approve this account of the incident."

Everyone stretched out one hand, palm up, and Resh bent over his tablet to record the vote—apparently, a unanimous approval. No one looked at me expecting a vote, so I waited quietly.

"I will now open the questioning session to discussion."

Jahac immediately said, "It has to have been deliberate. If the panel was fine three days ago, someone tampered with it."

Several people flicked their fingers upward. Gaj corrected, "Not necessarily. If it became overheated perhaps the casing melted."

"But why would it have done that?" Jahac argued.

Resh spoke up. "I will place in the record that there is some question whether this death was accidental."

Daz glanced at me. "When we came downstairs looking for Pav, we found the door at the top of the stairs was not locked. I thought we had agreed that while we had the alien onboard, we would keep that door locked."

"Probably Pav was the one who forgot," said Talek. "She had just come down from the upper level a short time before."

Are they suggesting we did it? Resa fumed.

I was staggered too, but I tried to remain rational. *They don't know us. They have to consider it.*

They're not considering it! They're assuming it!

Karnath spoke up. "I believe Tria il Resa has avoided that area as I requested."

"But you've admitted you haven't been with her at all times," countered Daz.

"No one has actually seen her go down there, have they?"

I'm going in, I said. "Can I talk?" Resh flicked his fingers upward, and I went on, "I haven't been down there. Karnath said not to so I avoided it entirely. I know that I haven't the slightest idea how your systems work, and I wouldn't want to break anything. Can't you swab the door for genetic material or something?"

There was a silence, then Karnath said, "That's the problem, you see. You have a sterilization bracelet. It prevents pathogens from reaching you, but it also prevents you from depositing anything. You couldn't have left cells even if you did touch the door."

I rested my head on my hand. This was very unfortunate. But of course no one had thought of a crime happening when it had been decided.

Resh continued, "In the event of a death that has not been ruled accidental, procedure dictates we all describe our whereabouts at the time of the crime."

This part took some time. The two technicians who had discovered Pav, Talek and Daz, had been working on the sensor array on the middle level since about 13.00. They had called Pav to reactivate it, as they had finished their diagnostic, but had received no answer and had gone looking for her. The two linguists, Jahac and Lex, had been working together on the radio data they had gathered on Kinaru, with the help of Prazad. Gaj had been sleeping, and her roommate, Zin, the ship's computer expert, had been working on the terminal in the same room.

Resh was next, and said without a trace of embarrassment, "Tazag and I were engaged in sexual intercourse at the time. We were together from about 13.25 till the medical alert sounded."

Tazag flicked zir fingers upward, the brown color spreading across zir brow and the sides of zir face. Well, at least someone was embarrassed. I certainly was.

Resh entered his testimony into his tablet and then glanced at Karnath. "Where were you?"

"Until about 13.00 I was talking to Tazag. After that I encountered

Pav in the corridor outside, where we had a discussion about our mission parameters."

"I think it would be appropriate to call it a heated argument," interposed Jahac, giving Karnath a look that could only be described as venomous. Even I could tell that.

Why does he hate Karnath so much? I asked Resa.

That's not a look of hate, said Resa meditatively. *Anger, maybe, or hurt. He looks like he's been slapped.*

"I will record that it was described as heated," Resh said dispassionately, making another note. "Continue."

"After that I went to my room."

"Does anyone share with you?"

"Lex does, but she was out. Studying the transmissions with the other linguists, apparently."

"What were you doing?"

His crest flattened a little in embarrassment. "Watching Earth comedy videos."

There was a hissing chuckle around the table. "Why?" asked Resh.

"I enjoy them. It's an old hobby of mine."

"It seems you have accounted for your time," said Resh. "However, I must make a note that during some of that time no one was able to confirm it."

Karnath flattened his crest and said nothing.

"Last I must ask our visitor, Tria il Resa. Where did you go after leaving the dining room?"

"I went to my room. I worked on the computer a little and then I went to bed. I didn't wake up until I heard the alarm."

"Can anyone confirm that?"

I shook my head, and then added, "No."

Resh made a note. "I suppose I must close this questioning session ambiguously. Since it is the opinion of Gaj and Talek that the wire would not have malfunctioned on its own, and since not everyone is able to account for their actions during the time in question, we cannot rule out the possibility that the incident was intentional. Still, since the voltage was so low, it seems unlikely that anyone meant to kill Pav. Are we agreed to enter this discussion into the ship's record?"

Most voted yes. Jahac stared down at the table and did not vote. Suddenly Karnath burst out, "Doesn't this strike anyone as suspicious?"

"Of course it does," said Resh. "That is why this session is taking place, so that a full investigation can happen when we reach Shatak. These statements will be important in any trial."

"I mean, for two suspicious deaths to happen so close together," he clarified. "What are the odds that even *one* crew member would die on a mission as uneventful as this one? Let alone two, and both in circumstances that make it impossible to rule out murder."

Jahac gave an angry hiss. "Really, you?" he demanded sarcastically.

Karnath lowered his head and flattened his crest. I gave him a sideways glance. I would have expected him to defend himself, but instead he seemed hesitant to cross Jahac. Why?

Resh was the one to answer. "If anyone has any ideas how we might resolve this to everyone's satisfaction, I'm eager to hear them." No one had anything to say, so the record was approved. Resh went on, "From now on, I will command the *Galajak,* and all concerns may be brought to me. I request the technical staff to make a thorough check of systems before we continue."

People left singly or in groups, talking quietly, until no one was left but Karnath and me. I stared at my lap, avoiding his eyes. *This doesn't look good for him,* I said to Resa. *Everyone saw him fighting with Pav. And he has no real alibi.*

He didn't do it, she answered confidently.

How do you know that?

He just doesn't seem like he would ever do anything like that.

I frowned in disappointment. *I was hoping you had something better than a hunch.*

Finally looking up, I saw Karnath gazing at me. "They should have let you and Resa be witnesses for each other," he said. "I didn't think of it until now."

"I don't think anyone would have allowed that," I said. "They don't know or trust either of us, and of course it's pretty plausible that we'd cover for each other if we had done it."

"For everyone else they accepted one witness. Didn't matter who. Even a lover."

"I suppose so." I turned it over in my mind. "So you don't think I did it?"

"Of course not. If you had done it, I don't think you would have suggested they swab for your genetic material. And I doubt you would know enough about our systems to know what to do." He paused, looking at me. "You think I did it."

Resa flicked her fingers downward. But I lifted my shoulder and dropped it again. "I don't know what to think. I know how badly you wanted to get to Earth. And without Pav, you'd have the votes to do it."

His eyes widened. "I hadn't even thought of that. But I couldn't ask for another vote, not now. Everyone would think I had done it."

I nodded slowly. "Wiser not to. I want to go as much as you do. This lead demands to be followed. But we do have time. Who knows how many years I'll be on Shatak before I can go home. And maybe in that time there will be another chance."

"I am sure there will. It would be a disappointment for me, because surely when we return a more senior scholar will take over this project. But the important thing is that the puzzle is solved, that science advances. And it will."

You're right, I said to Resa. *He didn't do it. If he did it to change course, he wouldn't agree so quickly to abandon that plan.* To Karnath I said, "So how are we to clear ourselves? I don't want everyone to wonder forever if one of us did it."

"I'm going to talk to Zin," he said. "She is the ship's main computer specialist. Both of us were on computers at the time. If the computer logs any kind of record of what we did, she'd be able to find it."

He stood up to leave, but I interrupted. "One more question. Why doesn't Jahac like you?"

His crest flattened and he sat back down heavily. "It's … it's not really important."

"He clearly thinks you did it. He was trying to suggest as much. I want to know why."

"We... we were lovers, once." I looked down at the table to hide my surprise. I kept forgetting that gender was irrelevant to them. "On a previous mission, we got close. I meant to keep the relationship going when we got back, but... I couldn't stand his other partner. And she disliked me. He was willing to keep seeing me on the side, but I broke it off. I didn't want to be someone's bad decision, the one his partner would resent. But he was hurt. In his mind, I had forced him to choose between me and her, and had punished him by leaving when he wouldn't choose." He rubbed his hand over his eyes. "On this mission, he and Pav were growing intimate. He's deeply upset at her death and all that anger is going toward me because I hurt him before. I don't know how to fix it."

"I'm sorry." Such useless words. Resa carefully patted his shoulder, on his uniform where it wouldn't singe his skin. "I shouldn't have pried."

He stood up again and went to the window. The stars outside were still; the ship wouldn't move until it had been fully checked over. "Come," he said at last. "There is still so much to learn. We can't let this tragedy stop us from studying all we can."

CHAPTER EIGHT

Tria

We spent the rest of the morning in the medlab studying each other's pharmacology. The idea of medications to rapidly cure depression had fascinated me. Shatakazan medicine far surpassed ours, and Karnath cheered up considerably as he showed off the different medical equipment they had. It was a relief to find out that most of the medicines they used were compounds I recognized as non-toxic to Kinaru—though most of them wouldn't be effective, either.

"It's a shame," I said. "I had been hoping that you would have treatments for some of our ailments, which we would be able to share when I finally return."

"We will certainly be able to help you develop new medications for your unique needs," he said. "And once they have been discovered, anything can be easily synthesized with this." He gave a proprietary slap to a boxy machine in the corner.

I peered at the screen on the front. "Something that mixes medications?"

"Better. It synthesizes them directly on the molecular level." He showed me how to select a compound or even draw in a molecular model. "What's one Kinaru medicine you might need?"

"Ibuprofen, I guess." Tentatively I drew the diagram on the screen.

Karnath punched in a dose and the machine gurgled a moment. When he opened the hatch on the front, there was a small, colorless crystal. "Is that it?"

I took it out and sniffed it. "Yes, that's it all right. Though a normal dose would be a quarter of this. How big are your units?"

After more messing around with the synthesizer, I admitted myself impressed. "So much work, of so many chemists, making medications all over Kinaru, and a device like this can do it in minutes! It's such a shame my planet has to wait."

He hiked himself up onto the metal counter and sat there, kicking his feet. "It's not as simple as that. If we gave this synthesizer to your people, it would disrupt your pharmaceutical industry and put all those chemists out of work."

"Won't that have to happen eventually anyway? New inventions happen."

"Yes, but not all at once. That's the worry, dealing with developing planets. It could leap you a century ahead in technology all at once, meaning endless disrupted industries and unintended consequences. Every new technology has social and legal ramifications which aren't immediately clear."

"Well, you'd be there to explain it all."

He looked down at his lap. "Isn't it—no. We're not—hm." At last he said, "The people of Shatak, on the whole, are not eager for that level of oversight over anyone else. Normally when a planet is declared sufficiently developed, we might send a first contact team to make the introductions, offer a treaty, and explain anything truly necessary. After that, the Shatakazan government has no further involvement. Sects and private corporations can then send ships, if they want to, and trade with that planet as an equal partner. We're not in the habit of shepherding planets through the process more carefully."

I blinked. "It seems like it would be much better if you did. All those pitfalls you mentioned are still going to be there, after all."

His crest flattened in embarrassment. "I suppose it is a little selfish of us. Our law was intended to keep private corporations from exploiting planets too ignorant to realize they were being taken advantage of. But that's as far as anyone has been interested in protecting aliens. The actual task of assisting foreign cultures in adapting to new technology—well, it would take a great deal of manpower. I'm not sure anyone wants to do it."

"Oh—of course," I said, feeling embarrassed myself. The Shatakazan had been so gracious that I had failed to consider that there might be limits to their generosity. "Of course you have no obligation..."

"And besides," Karnath added quickly, "not every planet would appreciate that sort of relationship. One where we made ourselves the judge of what technologies you could have, and when. Resentment would build, and you would end up blaming us for everything that went wrong."

That's a tidy excuse, said Resa. *If the Shatakazan are holding out on a cure for cancer or something, none of those reasons can really justify it.*

They don't owe us anything, I argued. *They have their own needs to think of. We can't take on responsibility for every suffering person in the galaxy.*

You wouldn't *stand for it. Not if you were making the choice. If the Shatakazan were in need of something you could provide, you would do it.*

I didn't answer. She was right, of course; if the situation were reversed, I would expend quite a lot of extra resources and accept the risk of some resentment, just to feel I had done what I could to bring the blessings of my greater technology to people in need of it. But did that make me generous, or simply a busybody? The Shatakazan way—the Liberty sect way, I supposed—might be hands-off, but it was meant respectfully.

Karnath slept through the middle of the day, while I read more about Shatak on the computer. He reappeared in the dayroom as I was sitting down to lunch. "Did you get a chance to speak to Zin?" I asked.

He flicked his fingers up. "She said she will try to access the use records on my terminal when she is off shift. Right now she is busy checking the computer systems. If there is any fault in the navigational computer when we take our next jump, we could land in the middle of a black hole."

Resa shuddered. I said, "Is that something we need to worry about?"

"Oh, no. The computer has many failsafes and Zin is excellent at her work. I am not concerned." He took a bite of his food. "Now that we know you can eat our food, do you want to try anything of our ship's rations? The vegetable portions, of course."

I shook my head. "I don't think very much you eat is palatable to me. My tastes seem to have evolved to match Kinaru food." Suddenly I started and slapped the table. "Can we analyze the DNA in that?"

He tilted his head, puzzled. "Certainly we could, if any of it is sufficiently unprocessed... like those grains for instance, in their raw state, might have some genetic material. But why—oh." His crest flicked upright and he flapped his hands. "To see if it shares the Earth DNA as well! Excellent thinking!"

We rushed through our meal and collected samples from my food cabinet. In the lab, Karnath carefully prepared the samples and inserted them into the analyzer. It hummed softly. My heart was pounding. This could confirm the comet theory—that all life on our planet was seeded from an Earth organism. Or it could only lead to more questions.

The unreadable characters printed themselves on the screen. Karnath set it to compare with the Earth DNA, and the two sets overlapped. The screen turned purple. No match.

He looked over at me with big eyes. "So you are related to the earthlings ... and the grain you eat is not. There must be two separate evolutionary lines on your planet! Let me see..." He pulled up my own code and overlapped it with the grain. Purple again. No common genes at all.

"Would you really expect there to be common genes between a

sentient creature and a plant?"

"Of course. The smallest bacterium on Shatak shares some genes with us. Now most of those genes aren't used in our own genome—they're junk, leftovers. A few might still be used in metabolic processes. But they show we are related. That's how we were able to prove evolutionary theory."

"Did we just... *disprove* evolutionary theory? For the Kinaru, at least?"

He flicked his fingers down. "No, but we have shown your evolution was independent. It includes some of the Earth genes... and something else, something that I assumed must have arisen on Kinaru, but if so, it's completely separate from the genes in these grains."

We analyzed all the samples we could, but in the few that had any DNA remaining, none were a match with mine.

"Well," I said, staring at the screen, where Karnath had displayed a tiny version of each of our comparisons, "this does explain a great deal. We had begun to sort animals and plants into evolutionary trees, but there was a great deal of debate on where to place ourselves. Most of the animals on our planet have six or eight legs, for one thing. It was taken by religious people as proof that we were directly created by the gods."

He gazed at the display. "Not by gods, I think ... but that leaves us no closer to understanding by whom."

Just then his tablet chimed. He took it out to read the message. "We're being called for a vote. Again."

"Should I wait for you in my room?"

"No, come along. You're part of the crew, if not officially."

Resh frowned at me when I came in. "I did not ask you to bring her," he said to Karnath.

"I couldn't leave her in the medlab by herself," he argued.

Resh chose to let it go. "Everything has been fully checked and we are ready for our next jump," he began. "This is the last opportunity for another vote about whether to divert to Earth."

"So?" Jahac argued. "We have already voted. There is nothing new to change the votes. Except Pav's death, and it's sickening to think anyone would take advantage of her passing to push their way against what she wanted. We need to return to Shatak as quickly as possible to return her body to her family."

There were mutters of agreement from around the table—mainly from the Liberty crew members.

"That is one argument," said Resh. "Shall we vote on it? Or are there other considerations?"

I shot Karnath a glance. He looked back at me, torn. "I couldn't," he murmured.

"I'm sorry, Karnath, do you have something to offer?"

Karnath took a deep breath. "I do have new information. However, I hesitate to argue in favor of a course change in light of Jahac's argument. I do not want to disrespect Pav."

Tazag turned to him eagerly. "At least give us the information so we can make a fair choice."

Reluctantly, Karnath described what we had discovered. "This may disprove the comet theory. If a comet landed before life had developed on Kinaru, all life on the planet would be descended from this strain. Or if it landed after, it seems unlikely that it could simultaneously develop on the planet without any genetic transfer."

"Perhaps in separate regions?" Tazag suggested. "It's an interesting theory, but I will have to leave it to you, as the biologist, to weigh its plausibility."

"That's the thing, I can't. Not without more samples either from Kinaru or Earth. I need a full earthling genome in order to tell how closely the Kinaru are related. Is this a few random strands, or most of the genome? If only they had harvested more data on the last Earth expedition. I understand that no biologists were included, which may be why no one realized how necessary it was to obtain it."

Prazad, the alien tech specialist, spoke up. "Perhaps you don't understand just how difficult it is to harvest the data in the first place. In order to leave no trace of our presence, we have to record passively only. So unless they are constantly emailing the entire genome to each other, we're not going to have it. We have a great quantity of news programs and entertainment broadcasts and millions of pictures of animals with humorous captions. That's simply the nature of the process."

"In that case there is no point in going to Earth," Jahac said. "We're never going to get the genome even if we do."

Zin, the computer expert, spoke up. She was small of stature and even slighter of build than the others, but her crest was fiery yellow and she moved her hands energetically as she spoke. "I think I can make an active search for the data without leaving a trace. That's really the goal, right? And I'm good at what I do. I feel confident I can pull it off."

The debate went on for some time longer, but in the end the vote went exactly along sect lines. The five Liberty crewmembers voted to continue to Shatak, while the two Curiosity and three Unity members all wanted to continue to Earth. As acting leader, Resh was allowed a second vote to break the tie. He ordered calculations to be made for a jump toward Earth.

Resa

Earth.

Exactly where Tria wanted to go, following a lead on the biggest mystery of her career. They hadn't let her vote, but the answer just happened to be what she wanted. Funny how it always goes that way.

For my part, I was suspicious. Two deaths, and then suddenly Tria and Karnath got what they wanted. With a prize like that, they wouldn't keep pushing for answers. They were too excited to go to Earth at last, to solve their own mystery. I thought, privately, that the mystery of where our genes came from was academic, while who killed Pav and Femat was vital. But since that last vote, Tria hadn't said a word about the murders.

Karnath had been even easier to neutralize. The second Jahac had cast suspicion on him, his focus had switched to clearing his own name. It didn't matter that no one was taking Jahac's outburst seriously. It mattered to Karnath. He wasn't over Jahac, any more than Jahac was over him. He wanted his ex-lover to think better of him. Nothing wrong with that, but it left no one still turning over stones to find the real murderer.

Not that I could do better myself: I couldn't. There was something in Resh's impassiveness that worried me; something in Zin's friendliness that rubbed me the wrong way. Something in Pav's hostility, too, had seemed inexplicable, though Karnath hadn't thought anything of it.

Was it just that I didn't understand Shatakazan? Probably. I was learning to read their eyes, crests, and color changes as clues to their mood; but there was so much more to understanding a person than that. What were their relationships, their cultural expectations? Talek was protective of the little radiologist, Prazad, but why? Gaj wouldn't make eye contact with Zin, but why?

When I had first arrived, the Shatakazan's openness had startled and thrilled me. They easily reached out and touched one another, cupped cheeks, licked faces. Half the crew was sleeping with the other half and completely unembarrassed about it. So I thought they would be easy to understand, but it wasn't that simple. It was like beginning one of Karnath's dramas halfway through. You had to know the history to be able to follow along.

Why didn't I ask Tria to dig more, find that history for me?

I suppose because I felt I had already asked too much.

Tria

In the morning, I was awakened by Zin poking in her yellow head. "Sorry, didn't realize you'd be sleeping. You Kinaru do sleep a lot." She gave a sibilant chuckle.

"It's all right," I said, checking my chrono. "I should be getting on with the day. Did you need something?"

"Yes, I just went through Karnath's workstation like he asked me to, to find the activity logs. Can I go through yours as well?"

"Of course. Were you able to verify his story?"

She half-lidded her eyes cheerily. "Oh, I think I'd better save the report for the crew meeting, after I've checked yours."

Strange, I said. *Why couldn't she just answer?*

It must be yes, though, or would she be smiling like that at you?

I slipped into the lavatory to get ready, feeling uneasy. If they weren't able to back up both of our alibis, we'd have that cloud hanging over our heads the whole expedition. Surely Pav's death was really just an accident, since everyone else had an alibi and I felt confident Karnath hadn't been involved. But who would believe it? Jahac certainly didn't. I wasn't sure about anyone else.

The meeting was called shortly after I'd finished breakfast. Karnath and I were the last to enter the conference room. Resh followed us with his eyes the entire way to our seats. "We have a report from Zin about your alibis at the time of Pav's death. Please sit down."

Zin put two thin sheets on the table. "Here are the printouts I obtained for Karnath's and the alien visitor's workstations. As you can see, I was able to access the usage logs of both workstations. Both showed no one was logged in at all at either workstation during the time window in question."

There was an excited murmur around the table, as the printouts were passed around. I turned to Karnath. "How is that even possible?" I whispered. "I *know* I used the computer. Can there be a mistake?"

Karnath looked worried. "Not with Zin. She's good. We were lucky to even get her on such a minor mission."

"If it's not a mistake…"

"She's lying," he said, dropping his voice even lower. "She erased the evidence I asked her to look for, and printed out the 'proof.' And I have no idea why she would do that."

The printouts finished their circuit of the table. Karnath gave them no more than a glance before passing them on.

"What do you have to say, Karnath?" asked Resh neutrally.

"I have no explanation," he answered. "I know I told the truth about what I was doing. But I don't know why the computer failed to record it. It must be an error of some kind."

"Is that possible, Zin?"

She flicked her fingers downward. "Every computer makes a record. Not many people are aware of that." Her eyes slid over toward Karnath.

"I was aware of it, which is why I asked you to look for it!"

"You didn't ask me to look for it," said Zin, her face clear and unruffled. "It occurred to me on my own, and I obtained permission to look from Resh."

Karnath's crest was standing completely on end. For a moment I was concerned he would say something rash, or start a fight, and cause more trouble. But instead he took a deep breath and the green quills relaxed. "I see that my word is being cast into doubt by this testimony of Zin's."

Jahac spat, "If by that you mean, you are now exposed as the liar you are!"

"Please refrain from heated remarks, Jahac," Resh said mildly. "In light of this evidence, it seems that we must assume his denial of having tampered with the panel is also suspect. Perhaps he did not do so, but we cannot rule it out."

Gaj volunteered, "I suggest Karnath be confined to quarters until the conclusion of our mission. He can still contribute as needed through the ship's network. Any trial will have to wait until we arrive home."

Lex objected, "What does that mean for me? I share a room with him."

"You will have to transfer out," said Resh. "You can sleep in Pav's room."

They're all making plans as if it was decided! Resa complained. *Surely this won't pass a vote?*

But it did. Everyone was well aware of Zin's computer skill; if she said it wasn't possible that the printout could be in error, they believed her. After all, why would she lie?

As I left the room, escorted this time by Tazag, my mind was absorbed by the same question. Why *would* she lie?

After several hours in my room, I was no closer to an answer than before. Zin was a member of Unity, not Karnath's sect, but she had never seemed to dislike him. And she had been completely friendly with me. I tried to remember her own alibi for Pav's death. She had said she had been working on the terminal in her room, while Gaj slept. Could she have stepped out without waking the engineer? It was certainly possible. And I imagined she'd have the expertise to strip a wire and electrify the panel. I wished anyone had thought to question her alibi earlier. Though I suppose she would have simply done the opposite of what she had for Karnath and me, and produced a record of having been logged into her workstation at the time.

But if I tried to connect this with Femat's death, Zin was out of consideration. She had been with Pav the entire time. Who else could I consider? Jahac's animosity toward Karnath seemed suspicious, even for an ex-lover, but he had a solid alibi for both deaths. Resh, I was tempted to suspect because of his lack of interest in solving the murder, but he had been with Tazag both times.

Could they really be unrelated? It hardly seemed possible. Both deaths fit the same pattern: plausibly accidents, not violent or showy. Whoever had done it hadn't been angry, and had had no interest in confronting the victims. And they hadn't wanted to make enough fuss to delay the ship at the station. They had wanted to quietly get rid of two people while leaving everyone in doubt whether a murder had occurred.

The victims, however, seemed to have nothing in common. One was a spacer, the other a scientist. One was the leader of the whole expedition, the other almost the youngest. Both victims were in Liberty sect, but the same could be said of half the crew. Would any Liberty crew member have done as well?

I switched on the computer terminal to read up on sects. There was plenty of information in the ship's data banks. I learned that Liberty sect had controlled the central government for a century and a half, and over a third of the planet belonged to it. There were dozens of other sects, of which Unity was a fairly minor one. Curiosity was small too—only popular among scientists.

In many ways, they served much the same function as our government, when it came to providing for those unable to work, paying for young people's education, and funding scientific endeavors. That meant the government itself was, by my standards, fairly minimalist, focusing on policing crime and coordinating the sects when they wanted to work together. In part this was because it was mainly controlled by Liberty, which, true to its name, was strongly opposed to excessive government intervention.

A little bubble popped up on the side of the screen—a video call from Karnath. I answered it. "I didn't realize we could still be in touch," I said. "Are you all right?"

He blew out his cheeks with a slow outward breath. "I suppose. I am still upset that we are suspected of this crime. I thought people knew me. I thought they respected me as a scientist and a person."

"People are scared," I said. "And I'm scared too. If Zin was willing to lie about us, it makes me think it wasn't an accident. Either she did it, or she is covering for someone who did."

He inclined his head. "I've come to the same conclusion." He rubbed his hands over his face. When I had met him, he had usually been cheerful and excited to learn more, but all of that positivity was gone. Now he looked strained and frightened. "What I don't understand is why. Why would anyone on the crew want anyone else dead?"

"Were there any personality conflicts?"

He shook his head slowly from side to side. "Nothing major. Our time on Kinaru was relatively free from drama. I can see how anyone might hold some resentment against Pav for letting you discover us, but that hardly seems something to murder anybody about. Zin no more than anyone else. She seemed to like Pav, I thought. Femat too. She is friendly with everyone."

"She was friendly with you and me before lying about us," I argued. "So we can't rule out some secret grudge that she covered very well."

He allowed that with a gesture. "But perhaps it was something more pragmatic. What was the main effect of both deaths?"

"Changing course," I said. "Going to Earth."

"Yes. But so far as I know, we're the only ones who were really pushing for that. Others voted with me, but I didn't notice anyone else being insistent about it."

"Maybe they kept their enthusiasm to themselves because they knew they didn't have the votes."

He rubbed the back of his hand against the bottom of his chin. "But on the last vote, when the motion finally carried. Who proposed the new vote?"

I thought a moment. "No one really did," I answered. "Resh seemed to be trying to push you into suggesting it, but you were hesitant."

"Tazag seemed enthusiastic. And Zin was the one who said she was sure she could get the genome if we did."

"A lot of people seemed interested after you spoke. And, well, five did vote to change course."

He was quiet a moment. "I guess I don't understand why anyone would want to go to Earth badly enough to kill for it. There will be another mission there eventually."

"Perhaps more will become clear once we reach Earth."

"We'll reach orbit the day after tomorrow. But I don't know how much we'll be able to find out, without having freedom to move around."

"I'm not going to be confined, so far as I can tell," I said hopefully. "Or if I am, people will still be coming to see me and ask questions. Perhaps I can find out what is going on, and let you know."

"You do that," he said. "I'll try to keep track of anything I can on the ship's network. If we can find out what's happening, perhaps we can convince the others we aren't to blame."

I nodded, feeling a grim resolve. This wasn't how I had thought this journey would go—I had expected anything from discovery to danger, but I certainly hadn't imagined we'd be investigating a murder. But I had to, now. Both to save myself from being treated with suspicion, as a sub-sentient and violent specimen, and to prevent Karnath from possibly being convicted of murder when we arrived to Shatak.

"I will do everything I can to clear our names. And, if possible, find the real murderer."

CHAPTER NINE

Resa

Tria took our confinement to quarters in good grace. I did not. I jiggled my knee incessantly while she did research on the computer, and every time she took a break I paced. It took four steps to cross the room. Six if I took it on the diagonal.

What made it worse was that Tazag, who was supposed to bring us to the dayroom to eat, was consistently hours late. Nothing to do meant nothing to distract myself from how hungry I was.

Ze'll come for us eventually, Tria said. *Try to think of something else.*

Like what?

Like Earth. On her workstation, she brought up a picture of it. *Is it pretty to you?*

I studied the little marble of blue and white. So much water. I wondered if the earthlings lived on boats, sailing those endless oceans. I wondered what the wind smelled like, coming off the sea, laden with moisture. We had never been to the sea before.

The people, now: that might be even more interesting. Karnath's dramas had made me curious. There were people who looked like me, but living their lives in such freedom, such emotion. Tria had scoffed, but why *shouldn't* it work?

Everything we had been taught said it wouldn't.

On Kinaru we tell children stories of the desert cat and the burrowing owl. The owl is sensible and curious, while the cat is a bit of a trickster, always landing herself in trouble. Picking fights with spined lizards, trying to kiss her reflection in water, following mirages. In some of the versions, the gods put the cat and the owl into the same body, making the first Kinaru. This keeps the cat out of trouble. The owl gets—I can't remember what the owl was supposed to get out of the deal.

In any event, since the owl is wiser, the gods make her stronger, so that she could keep the cat out of trouble.

By the look of it, humans weren't like us. They were impulsive, emotional, willful. Did the desert cat rule inside them, instead of the owl?

No. They'd never have survived if it did.

Tria

Tazag finally arrived at my room, over two hours past lunchtime. "Finally," Resa burst out. "I'd thought the desert cat had eaten you."

Tazag gave me a puzzled look, while I reddened. I wanted to chastise Resa, but what would be the point? It was my own fault for not guarding my control better. I left it alone, usually, both because I trusted her and because sometimes she came out with something surprisingly helpful. But she was still a left. Thinking before she spoke was probably beyond her.

I hurried to cover over her rudeness. "What I mean to say is, you are later than expected."

Tazag made a dismissive gesture. "I was delayed."

In the dayroom, I prepared grain, legumes, nuts, and vegetable sauce. Resa slipped several foil packets of fruit into her pocket. I didn't interfere—better she have something to eat than be hungry and irritable the next time

Tazag was late.

"When do we reach Earth?" I asked Tazag, sitting down across from zem.

Ze sighed. "Since I have to be here anyway, I planned to put this time to some use with another interview. I thought we could discuss crime and social problems."

"How about we get the news out of the way *first*, and then I'll answer your questions?"

That's the way, said Resa. *He needs you. Don't let him get what he wants for free.*

Ze grudgingly flicked zir fingers upward. "We arrive in Earth orbit in three-quarters of a cycle."

I did some mental math. Early tomorrow afternoon, then. "And then what happens? How do we monitor the earthlings' transmissions without being seen?"

"We can mask our presence with our holographic projector," ze answered. "We can also make ourselves invisible to radar."

"Radar—is that a technology the earthlings have?"

"Yes, it allows them to detect even ships they can't see. We have to be very careful to stay ahead of their current technology."

I nodded. "And then Zin can interact with the network without being detected?"

"Yes. Of course. You know all this." Ze seemed annoyed. "Now I would really like to know if you have any estimate of the crime rate on your planet!"

I sighed. That was probably all I was going to get. "Very low," I said. "Crime is irrational; we are all taught at an early age how to be rational."

"Can you even *be* irrational?" ze asked. "I mean, the rights. Aren't you naturally unemotional?"

Raising a finger, like I remembered my primary teacher doing when she said the same thing, I recited, "Absence of emotion is not rationality.

Even a calm mind is prone to bias and error."

Ze made a note. "So you learn all of this in school? Just the rights? Do the lefts go to school?"

I smiled. "Well, they are *at* school. But no one really expects them to learn anything. They cause a great deal of trouble. We have to schedule plenty of breaks so that they can do the things they prefer."

Remember when you and all the other lefts made quiet tapping noises whenever the teacher's back was turned? I asked Resa. *And she couldn't guess who was making it, because everyone was making it?*

She smiled. *Those were good times.*

At the time, I had been annoyed with her. I was there to learn and she wouldn't stop being disruptive. And the teacher never wanted to discipline lefts; she said they couldn't help it and it was our job to find a way to control them. But Resa and I have always been close; there was no way I could punish her, even though I was angry.

But now I only had fond memories. I certainly had managed to learn in school despite her irrepressible behavior, and as we got older she learned to bring something of her own to play with without distracting me, because she wanted me to succeed and qualify for an academic posting. I squeezed her hand affectionately, and she returned the gesture.

Tazag was writing and noticed none of this. When ze looked up, ze asked, "But the crime rate. What crimes are most common?"

I thought it over. "Theft. Smuggling goods to avoid paying taxes. Graft. That sort of thing."

"No crimes of passion? If the rights wouldn't, what about the lefts?"

Here I hesitated. "We take care of the lefts. We do not put them in a situation to be carried away by emotion. And we are stronger than they are. It is not possible for them to take over if we resist them."

It was the closest I had come so far to lying. I wondered if Resa would call me on it, but she was silent.

I watched Tazag narrowly as ze wrote. As a Unity member, ze had voted for the course change. Did that mean ze stood to gain by the killings? Yet ze had had an alibi for both.

Tazag dropped me back at my room as soon as I had finished eating, sending Lex in zir place when it was time to take me to dinner. I had no objection. Better to send someone else than to forget about me.

In the corridor, I asked her, "Have you seen anything of Karnath?"

"Yes, I bring him his meals. He is well. Though I am sure he must be anxious. He must stand trial when we return home, and the penalty is lifetime imprisonment."

"Do you think he did it?"

She was silent a moment. "I don't know. I trusted him, but I trusted Zin as well. One of them must be lying, but I can't imagine that either would."

"Does my testimony count for anything?"

"Not really," she said coolly. "I know nothing about you. No, I'm afraid it must all wait for the trial. They can be tested for truthfulness, and then we will know."

That was new information. If the trial process involved a reliable test for truthfulness, then the culprit must know they couldn't evade justice. Did that mean they had done it for some altruistic end, accepting a lifetime imprisonment in order to do something important, something that involved changing course to Earth? Or did they have no intention of returning to Shatak at all?

No wonder Karnath was worried.

After dinner, Lex escorted me to the medlab, to meet Karnath, who had been escorted by Tazag. "I will wait outside," said Tazag neutrally before they both left.

Karnath lowered his eyelids at me. "Are you well? I requested time with you mainly so we could talk, but I also want to have a look at your blood if you don't mind."

"Whatever you like," I said, hopping onto the exam table and extending my arm. "I've been all right."

"Good. Have you heard any news?"

"Only that we will arrive at Earth tomorrow afternoon. I can't remember what that is in your time."

"12.5 or so," he said absently, as he delicately inserted a needle into my arm without touching my skin. He was good—it barely hurt. "I talked to Lex awhile, but she had nothing but gossip. She said Zin is sleeping with Gaj now, and Talek had an upset stomach and missed zir shift." He withdrew the needle and handed me a piece of gauze.

I frowned as I pressed the gauze into my elbow and bent my arm. "Gaj is head engineer, right?"

"Yes. And Talek is the assistant engineer. Do you think—"

"That Zin could be trying to neutralize people one by one? I certainly do."

"But to what end? Controlling the engines is nothing without controlling navigation, and Daz does that. And ze would normally take orders from Resh." He set the vial of my blood in the slot of a machine. "Resh should also be checking up on Talek's stomach. We are on a controlled diet in an aseptic environment. Ze shouldn't be ill."

"Wouldn't you normally be the one?"

"Well, yes, but Resh has medical training as well. He is trained in a variety of specialties—that is expected of command staff."

I rested my chin on my fist. "If Resh did check on Talek's illness, and found something amiss, he'd hardly tell either of us."

"That is true. If I were investigating something suspicious on board, I would keep it to myself till I could make an accusation." Karnath was silent awhile, peering into the microscope. "These cells—I assume they are immune cells—are impressively vigorous! Do you get sick often?"

"I have had colds a few times. A fever once. Once there was a bad stomach virus that went through my school, when I was a child."

"Are there major diseases on your planet? Pandemics?"

"No, nothing like that."

"Perhaps these cells are responsible. I wish I could get some pathogens to test them on. I think they'd hold their own. Then again, if your species isn't related to any of the animals, and the population is low and spread out, that too would tend to discourage major illnesses." He motioned me over to look. I gazed at the cells for a while, and then gave Resa a turn. The cells themselves were nothing new to me, but the microscope was far beyond ours. With a turn of a dial, I could see inside the tiny organelles.

For the sake of fairness, Karnath took a sample of his own blood for me to look at. It was green, and the cells looked very different from mine. I tried to focus on them, but my mind was elsewhere, turning over the list of suspects in my mind. Zin headed the list, but she could not possibly have killed Femat. Pav herself had attested to that.

Suddenly I straightened up from the microscope. "Maybe we're looking at this all wrong," I said. "It's clear that no one person could have killed both Femat and Pav. Everyone who could have killed Femat has an alibi for Pav's death, and vice versa."

"But the *coincidence*," he insisted. "It *can't* be unrelated."

"I didn't say unrelated. What if it's a conspiracy of several people? They could provide each other with alibis."

Comprehension dawned. "Like Resh and Tazag. They were together on both occasions."

"And Zin could be covering for them. Perhaps she feels loyal to them because they're in the same sect?"

He shook his head. "I can't imagine covering up a murder for someone because they were in my sect. It's a bond, yes, but not that tight."

I leaned back against the worktable and folded my arms. "Here's one thing that's odd. Why are there three Unity members on a crew this size?

That's 25% of the crew, for a sect that's less than 1% of the population. And they're not mostly spacers or scientists. So why are they all on the *Galajak* together?"

Karnath rubbed his chin. "That's a very good question. Zin, especially— she's very prestigious in her field. I have often wondered why she took this posting, when there are better ones available."

"What is Unity all about? What do they want?"

"Mostly they just hate Liberty. They think such social atomization is bad for us, and that sects have too much power to legislate for their members. They want a strong centralized government."

I frowned. "That doesn't shed any light, I'm afraid."

He pulled out his device. "This is just a hunch, let me look something up..." He swiped at it for a moment before raising his head. "That person Resh and Tazag were talking to on the station... that was Banat, right? Talek recognized her?"

"Yes... from some other ship, I don't remember the name."

"The *Vatarax*," he said. "Banat is in Unity too. And it was just after they spoke to her that the murders began. Is it possible that it's a wider conspiracy?"

"You would know better than I how plausible that is."

"Such a thing hasn't happened in centuries," he said slowly, leaning against the genetic analyzer. "When a sufficient number of people are discontented, the sectarian coalitions in the legislature rebalance themselves, such that the most common viewpoints are represented. But Unity isn't that popular. They'd never win democratically. Perhaps they despaired of change by the usual route, and decided to abandon the democratic process."

"But how?" I asked. "Redirecting a small ship to Earth doesn't seem likely to have much impact, one way or another."

He shook his head slowly. "I can't see it either. There must be some larger plan involving a lot more than just the *Galajak*. But I can't fathom what it might be. I do know one thing, though." He pushed away from the analyzer and stood up straight. "No matter who is behind this, or what their goal is, going to Earth must be part of the plan. I hate giving it up when it was my idea, but we can't go now. I'm changing my vote." He lifted his device.

"Wait!" I cried, lifting my hand. "Think for one second. If someone killed two people to go to Earth, are they really going to let you live to change your vote? If you call everyone to a vote, the murderer will target you."

He flushed green and put the device back in his pocket. "I hadn't even thought of that."

"We have to find some way to let the others know without a meeting. I just don't know who to talk to that we could trust."

"Lex, maybe? She is in my sect and voted with us. If both of us agreed to change our votes, they could never catch up without killing almost all the crew."

"So long as she's not in on it," I said darkly. I thought of the cheery, talkative female. Who could be less likely to be part of a murderous conspiracy? But reason demanded I not discount anyone just because of subjective impressions.

"The other possibility is one of the spacers. We can't get to Earth without them."

I nibbled my lip. "Discounting Zin and Resh, that only leaves Gaj, Talek, and Daz."

"But Talek is ill. And Gaj... if we come to her accusing her lover, she won't want to listen. Daz is the only one we can really have a chance with. And losing our only navigator would be a big hindrance to them."

I bowed my head. "No matter who we talk to, there's a risk. I think we should at least try with Lex and Daz. Next time Lex brings you food, maybe you can talk to her?"

He nodded. "And I will ask her to bring Daz as well."

The next morning I woke to see someone standing over my bunk. I had a moment of panic, thinking it was the murderer, come to stop me from asking any questions. But as my vision adjusted, I saw it was only Lex.

"Sorry," she said. "I didn't know how to wake you without startling you."

I rubbed my face. "Have you been there long?"

"No, I just came in. Karnath wants to talk, and he said you would want to be awakened."

Checking my chrono, I saw it was only about an hour before I would have woken up anyway. Resa was dozing still, and I let her be. I pulled on my clothes and shoved my feet into my boots. It would do for now. I don't have the dexterity to tie the laces; I would have to wait for Resa's help to do them.

She led me to Karnath's room and unlocked the door. Karnath leaped to his feet. "Good, you came. But where is Daz?"

Lex flicked her fingers down. "The last fold is soon; ze couldn't leave zir station."

Karnath sucked in his breath and let it out, puffing out his cheeks. "Well. It will have to do." He sat down in his chair, inviting Lex to take the other. I sat on the bed, pulling my legs up under me.

Resa stirred, waking up at last. *What's going on?*

We're trying to stop the conspiracy. Try to keep up.

Karnath filled Lex in on what we had speculated. She rubbed her chin, looking doubtful. "You don't have any proof of any of this. These deaths could still both be accidents. And I only have your word that Zin lied about your computer records."

He flattened his crest in acknowledgement. "This is true. But if I wanted to go back home to Shatak, there would be no reason for me to vote for a course change. If I killed Pav and Femat, the only reason I can think of would be to go to Earth. And I'm telling you I don't want to go to Earth anymore."

"You're asking me to change my vote? You were the one who convinced me to vote to go to Earth in the first place!"

"I know," he admitted. "But do you see how suspicious it is? What if I played into their hands by suggesting the course change?"

She sighed. "Fine. I'll change my vote."

"Can you quietly go around the crew and tell them to gather? Save the Unity members for last. Maybe start with Daz, they can't make the last fold without zem."

Rising to her feet, she said reflectively, "Daz will agree, at any rate. Ze never wanted to go to Earth." She tapped the door to open it.

Nothing happened. She moved to the door panel and tried to unlock it, but turned around, cheeks flushing yellow. "Someone's come along while we were in here and locked it from the outside."

Karnath joined her at the door, but had no better luck. "Can you just call zem instead?"

She took out her device. "Frass, I'm off the network. Check yours."

He looked at his and flicked his fingers down. "No good. Zin must have shut us out." He switched on his computer console. "This, at least, seems to still be working." His fingers rattled over the keys.

At last Prazad's face appeared. "Karnath? Do you know what's going on?"

"Why, what's happening there?"

"Our door is jammed. Like it's locked from the outside. Jahac is here with me, we were both working at our stations, but when I got up to go the the media lab I couldn't get the door open. I tried all the spacers but I guess they are all busy, being so close to Earth and all."

Karnath's mouth tightened. "Prazad, I think we may be in the middle of a mutiny. I believe we have been intentionally locked in."

Green color flooded into Prazad's face. "Do you think Talek's all right? Ze was the first one I called … I have been so worried since I heard ze was sick ..."

"There's no reason to think ze isn't all right. I think Zin has been cutting communications—" As if to demonstrate the truth of his words, the screen suddenly went dark. He took a deep breath and slowly turned his chair around. "Too slow," he said. "I should have gotten on this faster—shouldn't have taken so long to figure it out—should have spoken to Daz last night..."

"Nothing to be done now," said Lex. "Though for my part, I think I believe you now. If you were behind any of this, you wouldn't be the one locked in here." She went back to working on the door panel. "If I had any technical skills at all ..."

A few minutes later, we folded. As the dizziness faded, I felt the normal-space engines begin their faint vibration.

Karnath gnawed on a thumb. "I just can't see the importance of Earth. Its interest is purely scientific. I know why *I* would want to go there, but why would anyone in Unity?"

I closed my eye a moment. What was special about Earth, besides its possible connection to my planet? Its savagery, perhaps? "It's forbidden," I said at last. "So it would be a good place for a secret meeting."

Karnath beamed at me. "Of course! They might have planned some meeting with someone from the *Vatarax*. Remember Tazag and Resh were talking to Banat, at the station."

Lex turned from the mess of wires she had made of the locking panel. "Maybe that's why Talek wasn't allowed to go aboard to talk to zir old lover. The *Vatarax* might have already been taken over."

"Talek's lover might be dead by now," he said soberly. "A cargo ship like the *Vatarax* would have a crew as large as ours. If they wanted to take control over the ship, they might have had to kill even more people."

"But what's worth killing for?" I asked. "Lex, you told me that once we get back, everyone will have to be tested for honesty. If that's effective, the murderers won't be able to get away with it. So they must have some kind of plan that doesn't involve returning to Shatak."

"Unless they plan to kill all the witnesses," Karnath said hollowly.

Lex had no response to this. Instead she turned back to the locking panel and started randomly yanking at wires. They broke with little sparks, but the door stayed shut.

Suddenly it slid smoothly open and I started to jump to my feet. If we got out of this room, there might be some way to retake control of the ship. But in the doorway stood Tazag, holding a weapon of some kind. Lex hadn't gotten the door open. Tazag had opened it. I sank back onto the bed.

Lex wasn't cowed by the weapon. Her arm flicked out toward Tazag, almost too fast to see, but zir weapon gave a soft buzz and Lex folded to the floor. Karnath had also leapt to his feet and started toward her, but the weapon took him out next.

I froze, horrified. Had I made the wrong choice? Perhaps if we all had rushed zem, we might have gotten the weapon. Now the others were down, perhaps dead, and Tazag had zir weapon trained steadily on me.

"Don't be alarmed," said Tazag. "They're only stunned." Ze lowered the weapon, but kept it ready in zir hand as ze stepped into the room.

"What do you want?" I asked tightly.

"You. It's really unfortunate that I can't study you any more myself at present, but I have arranged for someone else to do so. I'm onto you, you see. I know your race isn't as unique as you claim to be. Karnath was right the first time. You're human."

I shook my head in disbelief. "That's not what we found."

"Of course you wouldn't admit it. But I will soon have proof, once you've been compared with the humans directly."

"So you have the genome already?" I furrowed my brow. Somehow, of all the things I had speculated, actually carrying out their mission had not crossed my mind. What was the point of confining us all in Karnath's room if they had nothing to hide?

"Oh, no," Tazag said. "That would take ages. We'll be landing shortly."

"Against your planet's policy?"

"Planets don't have policies," ze said harshly. "People do, and we have made a new one."

"What gives you that right?" I asked, mainly to keep zem talking.

Zir crest stood on end and ze looked down at me in disdain. "What gives *you* the right to legislate for half your population? I had hope for you at first, but you're no different from Liberty. You think because your methods are democratic, you can't be oppressing others."

"And you think, because your cause is right, it's acceptable to kill two of your crewmates?"

"I never killed Pav," ze retorted. "Zin stripped the wire, and Resh finished her off while giving first aid. I had nothing to do with it."

"So you killed Femat."

Ze gave a grimace, probably realizing I was only stalling. "I need you to come with me. Are you going to cooperate?"

I looked from Karnath to Lex. No point in resisting; ze would only stun me too. I flicked my fingers up.

I followed zem down the corridor. No one was around. Not till we came down the steep staircase and into the storage room. There I saw most of the crew gathered. Daz was there, hands on zir head. Zin stood over zem, pointing a weapon, different from Tazag's stunner. Gaj sat nearby, yellow with distress, with her crest flat to her head. And Resh stood in the middle of the room, directing it all.

I took it in. Just as we had guessed, the three Unity members had been at the center of the plot. Daz had had to be threatened so that ze would navigate the ship down safely. Gaj had been manipulated; she looked ashamed of herself.

"You," I said to Resh. "You seemed so impartial. Why spend all that effort trying to look innocent when, in the end, you were simply going to use force?"

"It was important that no one suspect too far in advance," he said.

"With only three of us in a crew of twelve, we had to neutralize people one at a time. Now, of course, there is no need to keep any secrets. We have the entire ship in our power, and we won't be returning to Shatak until things are... much different."

Just as we feared, Resa said. *I think it's time to panic.*

There has never been a situation that was improved by panicking. I took her hand and held it tightly. I didn't want to admit that I, too, was afraid.

"So was Tazag telling the truth? You're landing the ship?"

"Oh, we already have," said Resh coolly. "Congratulations on a very smooth landing, Daz."

Daz looked daggers at him, brown crest flicking upright. "Eat frass, larva fucker."

Resh paid the curse no mind. "Zin, are our contacts satisfied with our landing? Are we adequately concealed?"

She checked her tablet. "Yes, they will be here soon to pick up your specimen. Should we send the biologist too?"

My breath caught in my throat. Part of me hoped he would say no. Better for Karnath to stay safe on the ship—or relatively safe, at least. But on the other hand... Karnath was the one person I could trust on the ship— on the whole planet. I didn't want to go out there alone.

"Yes, bring him," said Resh. "The earthlings don't have the ability to even know what they're looking at. And bring rations for both of them."

Zin left and came back a moment later with Karnath, who carried a bin of food. He looked ill, his face a uniform green. But his face was resolute. He flattened his crest at me by way of greeting, and stood where she directed him.

Zin clasped a sterilization bracelet on him before turning to Daz and Gaj, aiming her weapon once more. "Go back up, you two. I don't need you down here anymore." She followed them up. A moment later we were being led down the disorienting curved ramp, to stand under the power of real gravity again. Resh walked in front, followed by me, then Karnath, with

Tazag in the rear.

At the end of the ramp was a circular airlock, which Resh opened. The air that rushed in hit my face like a damp blanket—humid, but cooler than the ship's overly warm air. We filed out into the darkness.

CHAPTER TEN

Resa

Fresh air at last. But it wasn't dry and bracing like the air at home. It was damp like a jungle, complete with the chatter of animals. More foreign even than the stale ship air.

I clenched and unclenched my fist over and over, as we were made to walk through damp groundcover, past shadowy humps of trees. Funny how I had longed for real ground under my feet, a living planet, and suddenly I had it and didn't want it. I wanted the faint blue light of phosphorescent flowers, and the flutelike song of night birds.

I glanced up to see the stars. At least they should look the same. But instead a heavy sheet of cloud was over the sky. It glowed with an orange light.

We continued walking through the damp plant life until we reached a road that wound through the park. Resh shone a small hand light around, illuminating yellow stripes in the middle of the road. A moment later, a pair of bright lights appeared in the distance along the road, rapidly coming nearer. A ground vehicle pulled to a stop beside us and the hatch opened. A handlight played along us, so that I couldn't make out the figure holding it. An earthling? Or a Shatakaz that had been hiding here already?

We were bundled into the rear compartment, with Karnath beside us. Tazag got in front, while Resh turned around to head back to the ship. The vehicle peeled away, bumping me around the compartment.

I could feel a panic attack starting. Tria was trying to keep our breath slow and steady to calm me, but every time she got distracted with something I started hyperventilating again. *It's okay, it's okay, we're going to be okay,* she repeated. *Take your fear, put it in a box, put the box on the shelf. It's what I do.*

I held her hand in a vise grip. Sometimes her attempts at rationalizing me out of my feelings only made me angry, but this time it was what I needed. If she could remain calm, perhaps we would be all right.

Karnath reached across us to fumble in the darkness. "They have safety belts. Here." He pulled the webbing around us and fastened it. "Try not to worry." His voice wobbled nervously, belying his words.

I peered at the dark shape of the driver's head. I couldn't see anything like a crest. Tazag was talking to the driver in a low voice. I couldn't make it out, but my earbud helpfully picked it out and translated. Ze was saying, "Will we be getting an extra bonus for this specimen? I am not yet sure how it could be useful to you, but our contact did say you wanted it and it was an extra effort for us to deliver it."

"I was told so," the driver said gruffly. His voice was deep, like a Kinaru male. An earthling, then, a male earthling.

"They're speaking English," Karnath murmured. "We must be... hm... if I had to guess, the United States."

"Is that one of the more developed countries?" asked Tria.

"Yes. Though not necessarily one of the most peaceful."

That doesn't make me feel better, I said. But trying to listen to Tria and Karnath was at least some distraction.

The road wound on and on. For a long time I watched the yellow stripes curve left and right without any sign of another vehicle. After about an hour I started to see others. Their lights, coming from the opposite direction, shone in my eye and almost blinded me. But I kept looking around, both inside and outside the vehicle, hoping for some kind of clue to what was happening.

The vehicle was like a Kinaru groundcar, though the engine was quieter and the design sleeker. Also we never drive at such a breakneck speed. I had never driven a groundcar myself; like most people, we usually took the train. But this was clearly a secretive operation; they wouldn't have wanted to bring us on a train.

The man in the front was heavyset, with hair cropped short. His hands, which gripped a wheel that controlled the vehicle, were like big mitts. Not much chance of beating him in a fight, if it came to that. But if it came to that, I didn't know if Tazag still had his weapon.

I leaned my head on the cool glass of the window, feeling like I ought to be tired since it was dark outside, but by my body's time it was still only afternoon. I could see lumpy dark shapes beside the road—trees? Buildings? It was impossible to tell.

The fear in my belly formed a cold knot. I felt we were sailing, without wind or sound, on a river of darkness. From nowhere to nowhere.

Tria

At last the car pulled down a winding drive and into an open area beside a building. It pulled to a stop, and the driver opened the door.

I was tempted to be stubborn, to make demands and threats, but I could see the big man could drag me out bodily if he wanted to. And I had given Zin my word to cooperate. I fumbled for the release on the safety belt and crawled out of the car.

Here in the paved lot beside the building, there was plenty of light from big lamps set on tall poles. On the steps in front of the building were a number of people waiting for us: several men in dark suits and a woman in a light-colored jacket.

One of the men stepped forward and greeted Tazag. "Right on time, Mister Tazag—it is you, right? The email said it would be just you and the other alien, but I see you brought somebody else."

"This is Karnath. He is an expert on this life form. He isn't part of our group, so watch your back around him."

The man laughed. "I certainly will do that, buddy. But I watch it around you guys too."

Tazag flatted zir crest uncomfortably. "Naturally."

The driver unloaded our supplies from the back of the vehicle, then he and Tazag got back into the front and were gone. I watched them go, feeling desolate. Not that I missed Tazag, but with zem gone, I had no means to get back to the ship. In the darkness, I had no idea how far we had come or in what direction. And while the ship may have been full of strangers, and some enemies, it was the only way I could ever get home. The earthlings didn't have the capacity, even if they wanted to. Considering they had apparently agreed to study us for Tazag, I doubted they had any intention of letting me go.

The woman came up to me. She was light-skinned and a little taller than me, with gray hair. "Pleased to meet you," she said, sticking out her hand and smiling broadly. "I'm Dr. Karen Townsend, head researcher at this facility."

I stared at her hand awkwardly. I had noticed this from the video broadcasts: humans were incessantly touching one another and seemed to have no regard for personal space. In any event, with the sterilization bracelet on, I couldn't return the gesture without burning her skin.

"Apology for not returning gesture," said Karnath. I looked at him in surprise. Then I realized he was speaking in broken English, and my translator was passing along his poor grammar. "We are pleasured to meet you also. I am Karnath and this person is Tria il Resa."

Dr. Townsend laughed. "You don't have to try to speak English, I have a translator." She lifted her gray hair, which was in a fluffy bob around her face, to show the bud in her ear. "Mister Karnath, Miss il Resa, please come this way and I'll show you your accommodations."

The facility was not large, and it seemed to be empty except for us. All of the windows were fogged to obscurity; I could see the glow of streetlights but no objects beyond. "What is this place used for?" I asked.

"Oh, all sorts of projects related to our contacts with the Shatakazan. Research and development. Haven't done any biological research yet, because the Shatakazan don't want to volunteer to be studied. I understand you have agreed to cooperate with our research?"

"I'm... not sure what, exactly, your research is. I left my planet to study other life forms, and of course I mean this study to be mutual." Resa added, *So long as they're not planning to cut us up.*

"Well, honestly I'm not sure myself. Tomorrow you'll meet the biologist who will work with you, and she can decide on the scope of the study. Mainly we're curious about how closely you are related to us. That's why we agreed to Mister Tazag's suggestion."

I exchanged a glance with Karnath. I disliked this diplomatic tone, where she chose to ignore our real situation. Or had it been concealed from her? We would soon know.

We walked through a long lab with various equipment, nothing as advanced as the Shatakazan had, but still impressive. There was a room of blinking computer servers, a number of small offices, and a room with five or six locks, which she didn't open, with red labels in English writing on it. Finally she landed at a tiny, windowless room with a narrow bed, a chair, and a storage compartment full of drawers. "I really must apologize for the accommodations. This place wasn't made to keep people overnight, and the message only said one person was coming. I'll have another bed in here sometime in the morning. And there's a bathroom through that little door there."

What caught my eye, though, was a heavy lock on the door, with a glowing red light where Dr. Townsend had had to scan her badge to open it. For all her kind words, we were going to be prisoners.

"Well, I'll let you freshen up and rest. We won't start any serious study until tomorrow, whenever you're ready." With another brilliant smile, she left us in the cell.

I turned to Karnath. "Well, it could be a lot worse."

But he had sat down on the bed and was wrapping the blanket around himself morosely. His crest was flat and his face a dark green. Huddling with the blanket around his shoulders, he said nervously, "I fail to see how this could be any worse."

"They're... being friendly, at least?" I offered. "I don't think they'd waste time bringing us a bed if—"

"If they're just going to cut us up to see what's inside?" His voice was getting high and panicky.

I came to stand in front of him and bent down to look him in the eyes. In a firm, steady voice I said, "They are *not* going to do that because we are not going to let them. Okay? We aren't powerless in this. We will find out what resources we have, and use them to keep ourselves safe."

He blinked back at me. His yellow eyes were dilated almost to full blackness. I'd never seen him like this. He took a long, shaky breath. In a small voice he said, "I suppose this isn't frightening for you. You've done all this once before."

I came over and sat beside him on the bed. "It's very different to choose to go than to be kidnapped," I said. "And, if I'm honest, it was frightening then too." Resa reached out and squeezed his shoulder through the blanket.

"You handled everything so gracefully, and I—it's like I said before. I'm not comfortable being on the other side of things. I like doing research, not *being* research." He combed his seven fingers through the multicolored fringe of the blanket.

"We will get our chance to research them too, it sounds like. And knowledge is power. The more we can learn, the better our chance is of getting out of here."

He brightened at that, the green receding a little from his cheeks. "Do you think it's even possible?"

"I don't know," I confessed. "But we won't know unless we try. And the first step is to gather as much information as we can."

He sat up straighter and took another deep breath. "All right. Let's consider what we've learned so far. Resh, Zin, and Tazag are involved in a conspiracy which hijacked the ship and brought it to Earth. What do we know about their motivations?"

I thought it over. "They didn't say. Tazag said I would be studied and it would finally prove that I was really human. But I don't know if that is the reason they landed."

It's not, said Resa. She was calming down at last, too, distracted by the puzzle. *It's Tazag's pet project. Zin sounded like she thought it was a waste of time.*

I conveyed her words. Karnath nodded. "That makes sense. Tazag has always been convinced you were transplanted earthlings, but the first murder was after we arrived at the station. I think the three were awaiting a signal from the Vatarax."

"So it's a Unity plot, like we thought. But what would Unity want with Earth?"

"I'm not sure. I wouldn't think Earth would have anything to offer, compared to other planets. But it's certainly an exchange of some kind, they spoke of a bonus."

"They must be planning another meeting elsewhere, to deliver whatever it is they're trading. Somewhere closer to the ship. This facility is just for research, after all."

Karnath nodded. "We need to decide how much we should cooperate with their research. Obviously Shatak's law is 'not at all,' but that hardly can be followed at this point."

"As far as biological research is concerned, I think we can safely share all our work with them. Unless you can think of a way that *that* can be used as a weapon."

He considered it. "I think any research avenues that might have military potential could be headed off in advance."

I smiled. "I'm glad, because—as unfortunate as everything else has been—we will finally get our chance to solve the mystery we've been working on since we met. The question of just how closely related to the earthlings my people are."

"Having seen them in person, I have to say perhaps Tazag was right. The likeness is almost exact. I expect we will find the genetic correspondence is very close. But I can't imagine what that would mean. Perhaps the earthlings can tell us if there is any legend of space travel in their past. I certainly heard nothing about it in all my study." He blinked slowly. The green color had completely receded from his face; he looked more tired than frightened now. "Did Tazag say anything else to you while I was stunned?"

I cast my mind back. "Ze had a little rant about democracy. Ze thinks it's meaningless if the strong oppress the weak. That's not the first time I've heard that from zem."

"It's basically Unity's entire idea. They object to some of the sects on Shatak. Some of them have strict rules and arguably aren't good for their members. For instance, some are against technology and others forbid sex. Liberty's position has always been that, as long as no one is forced to join or remain, it can't be oppressive. But Unity points out that people are raised in these sects, and children can't really consent to that sort of indoctrination."

"Couldn't the sects just accept adult members?"

"How would that even work? Parents are going to teach their values to their children." His eyelids lowered at a happy memory. "I loved going to a Curiosity school as a child. There was no limit to what you could learn.

We had school morning *and* afternoon, and we competed in academic games instead of sports. I was able to enter university three years early and was the top of my class. I wouldn't want to give that up for a generalized global education, where everyone learns the same..." He trailed off, giving another slow blink. "I apologize, Tria il Resa. I have been awake for over half a cycle, not counting being stunned, and I am exhausted. I can barely put my thoughts together at this point."

I nodded and moved off the bed to the desk chair. Karnath curled up into a ball, still wrapped in the blanket. Earth must be cold to him, after the heat of the ship, which surely mimicked a hot planet. I personally found it refreshing, though it was still warm for night. The humidity must trap the heat. Kinaru was never this humid. Resa kept fidgeting with our hair, which had transformed from wavy to frizzy from the moisture in the air. But we, too, had had a long day, and I eventually fell asleep with our head pillowed on our arms.

CHAPTER ELEVEN

Tria

The next day was a whirlwind of confusion. The new bed arrived while I was still asleep and drooling on Resa's arm. Karnath was wide awake and alert, having had all the sleep he'd need for half a day, but I drowsed through the morning. *It's just as well,* I said to Resa as she complained about it for the tenth time. *We'll be adjusted to Earth time by tomorrow.* At least the small bathroom had a shower. I fiddled with the dial until I managed to make it cold enough to wake me up.

Earth's day was close to the length of ours, and the earthlings preferred to sleep at night like I did instead of catching naps at noon and midnight like the Shatakazan. So as the day progressed, more and more people arrived at the facility. We were introduced to a new biologist, who had apparently just been hired to study us. She was younger than Dr. Townsend, with long brown hair tied back at the nape of her neck and thick glasses. Her name was Dr. Eleanor Carroll, and she nodded at us awkwardly. Apparently she had been told we wouldn't shake hands.

Assisting her was a young man who had been reassigned from another department in the same building. His skin was even paler than the others, sprinkled with ginger dots, and his hair was a brilliant orange, like broadleaf trees. His name was Mike Herriot.

"Greetings, Dr. Eleanor Carroll," said Karnath, extending his hand with the fingers upward.

She ducked her head. "Eleanor. Please."

I smiled at her, in what I thought was a friendly way. But Eleanor looked alarmed. "Can you please lift up both your arms straight in front of you?" She pulled a tiny light out of her pocket and started shining it in our eyes, a concerned expression on her face.

Karnath raised a hand. "That isn't necessary, Eleanor. She isn't having a stroke. Her species' expressions are asymmetrical." He explained about our divided brains, to the fascination of the earthlings.

"I suppose that answers that question," said the biologist. "Tazag said they had speculated you were related to us, and you certainly look superficially the same, but we have nothing like that. I mean, our brains are structurally divided into hemispheres, but they aren't separate people. We have no awareness of when we're using one or the other."

"It's not that simple to dismiss," I said. "We had a fragment of genetic information of yours, which we compared against mine and found some areas of overlap. We were hoping we could get a full sample to analyze."

"Of course," said Eleanor, rubbing her hands together in excitement. "It certainly is worth a look! But I have to warn you, it will take weeks to analyze a new strand of DNA, with the equipment we have. I don't suppose you brought any of your own?" She looked hopeful.

"No, but I have the full analysis that we did." He took his personal device out of his pocket and opened the file. "All I have to do is translate this into your terminology, and compare it with previous analyses you've done of human DNA. And also, perhaps, DNA of other Earth life forms. What we want to find out is whether the Kinaru share some very early ancestors with a life form on Earth, or whether the branching happened later."

Karnath spent most of the day with Eleanor, trying to understand the terms used in Earth genetic analysis and translate my genomic information into a form comparable with the format they used. At a nearby table, I attempted to do the same thing with the protein, carbohydrate, and fat molecules in food. Without an analyzer, I would have to painstakingly examine the molecular structure of each molecule and compare it to the structure of the molecules I already knew Kinaru could digest. Mike Herriot helped, by leafing through a fat biochemistry textbook until he found the molecular diagrams and reading aloud any relevant text.

I found myself longing for the technology on the ship. It could have absorbed and translated English writing in a few hours. For that matter, all of this would have been unnecessary because we could have simply plugged in the leftovers from Eleanor's breakfast and it would have immediately displayed any matches. But from what I could tell, most of the molecules did match. The ones that didn't were simply indigestible to me, not poisonous. I recognized the alcohol molecule. "I know that one! It's a byproduct of fermentation. It's a mild poison to us; trace amounts are all right, but you wouldn't want to drink a cupful. Can earthlings metabolize it?"

Mike grinned. "Well, sort of. What sort of symptoms do you get from alcohol poisoning?"

"Oh, a whole variety of neurological effects. Drowsiness, poor coordination, hampered judgment. Then later on, headaches and vomiting."

"Yeah, we get that too. But people still drink it."

"On *purpose?*"

"Well, yeah. Sometimes you kind of want to... I dunno, depress the higher functions so you can relax and let go."

I frowned. "I have no desire to do that. And Resa doesn't need to. She's basically always like that."

I resent that! I have higher functions!

Oh, you know what I mean. I never knew you to need a chemical to relax with.

Mike flipped to another molecule. "Here's another drug we like to use.

Caffeine. Helps us wake up in the morning."

I studied it. *I need that*, groaned Resa. *I am so tired.*

"No, I don't think we have that on Kinaru." *And we're not experimenting on ourself either. What would they do if we had a terrible reaction? They don't know enough about our biology to doctor us.*

A lot of the molecules were from animal foods. The amino acids looked all right, but the sheer amount of protein and fat seemed excessive. Besides, I couldn't imagine shoveling animal corpses into my mouth, however carefully prepared and disguised. And Resa would never stand for it in any event.

Over lunch—out of the bin we had brought; neither of us was quite ready to try Earth food—I asked Karnath and Eleanor what they had learned.

"Well, we've successfully transformed all the data I brought into their format," Karnath said. "My device doesn't have much processing power when it isn't hooked up to the ship's network, but I could manage that much. Right now I'm trying to connect to this facility's network so I can send the information to Eleanor's computer. If I can't do that, we'll have to compare the data by hand, which would be... well, it would take the better part of a year, unless we had more people to work on it."

I looked at Dr. Townsend, who was eating some brown substance between slices of bread. "I don't suppose there's any chance of that?"

She shook her head. "My experience with the government is that they're always willing to spare budget and people to investigate the tech, but I'm afraid they consider the biology a side project of merely scientific interest."

"So Tazag's people are selling you tech?" I exchanged glances with Karnath. Exactly what the ban on landing here was meant to avoid!

Dr. Townsend fixed her eyes downward. "I've said too much."

"At some point we do have to talk about our position with you," Karnath said. "You're working for the government—the American government, I assume."

Townsend's face was guarded, impassive. "Yes."

"And you've been asked to study us. Our consent isn't really needed. We're prisoners."

"I thought you planned to join us in our study."

"Yes, we've been helping you, mainly in the interest of science. But I'm curious whether our cooperation earns us any trust from you. It would take you immense time and resources to analyze Kinaru DNA, while with our help, I hope to have the information in your computer within a few days. And at any point, if we're not content with the situation, we can stop helping."

I glanced at him with respect. I had already gotten lost in the science, which I knew was a temptation for him as well. But he had not forgotten we were prisoners, and he was going to leverage what he could.

Dr. Townsend eyed him doubtfully. "What exactly do you want?"

"I'm not sure yet. Can we go outside? I feel I've seen nothing of Earth, and I've always wanted to come here."

"No. I'm sorry. This project is secret. You can imagine the hysteria if people found out there were aliens around. Doubly so if they found the government was keeping it from them."

Karnath rubbed his chin. "Can we have a television?"

Dr. Townsend smiled at that one. "Any little comforts that can have a positive effect on your mental health—if it's reasonable to get."

He nodded. "We'll let you know if we think of anything else. If we are to be colleagues on this project, we want to be treated like colleagues. Being kept in the dark like this is very disconcerting."

Resa

Karnath slept after lunch for a few hours, while Eleanor and Tria played with blood samples. Eleanor wanted to see if Earth pathogens could infect us, but our blood seemed resistant to anything she could fling at it. Karnath's cells, meanwhile, were too different to be susceptible. "I guess those bracelets you have are unnecessary," she said.

Tria took hers off and slipped it into her pocket. "If you're wrong, you get to be the first person to ever treat a sick alien."

Eleanor chuckled, taking all the sample dishes and carefully shutting them in the autoclave. She stripped off her gloves and dropped them in the incinerator. "While we're at it, why not expose yourself to even more Earth stuff. Perhaps a try at some human food."

She hesitated. *Might be weird.*

Let's, I urged. *I'm so tired of the same things all the time.*

"All right," she said at last. "But just plant foods."

Eleanor took us to the facility's kitchen and sat us down at the oval table. Earth chairs weren't quite like ours, but at least they accounted for legs that weren't double-jointed. I relaxed against the padded backrest and watched her rummage in the cupboards.

I liked her, I decided. She seemed like a real scientist, like Heda or Beva back home, not a political type like Dr. Townsend. Where Townsend's hair stayed perfectly in place like it was lacquered, Eleanor's was fluffing out of its ponytail into a fuzzy halo. Her thick glasses made her eyes look enormous, like a burrowing owl's.

She looked nothing at all like my mother. But something about the way she puttered around the kitchen made me think of her.

"I think your first Earth food should be ... ah, of course. Cocoa. It's usually made with animal milk but I can make it with this, it's made from nuts." She retrieved a carton from the refrigerator and turned on the stove. "My daughter can't have real milk so it's how I usually make it anyway."

"You have children?" asked Tria.

"Just her. And some cats." She grinned. "Mia loves cats and I can't seem to say no. We have five now."

"Resa would love that, she is obsessed with animals of any kind." We watched her stir some brown powder into the pot. "Do you have a partner?"

"No," she said forcefully. "Don't have one, don't want one. I've had enough of marriage for a lifetime, I think."

I warmed to her a few more degrees. Divorce isn't common on Kinaru, but I've always approved of it. She didn't need a spouse, not when she had a microscope to play with.

"What about you?" she asked, pouring the drink into a mug and putting it in front of us. "Got anyone back home?"

"Thankfully, no." Eleanor tilted her head in confusion. Tria clarified, "Well, it would be unfortunate if I did have someone, since I don't foresee being able to get back."

"Ah. That is true." She poured another cup and sat down across from me. "Well, at least you have Resa."

"Yes. I am never lonely."

"Karnath filled me in on all the brain scans he did, but I'd love to run you through some practical tests. Separate personality and skills tests, that sort of thing."

"Whatever you want."

I took a careful sip of the cocoa, remembering that nasty Shatakazan drink we had tried on the station. But this was delicious; hot and sweet and just the faintest bit bitter. Nothing quite like home, but it sank into my tastebuds like it was meant for them.

Just then Karnath came in. "I have set up a script to connect my device to your network," he said to Eleanor. "It will take at least a day to complete, and if it fails I will have to try another."

"Cocoa? Tria tells me your planets have similar starches and amino acids so it should be all right for you."

He took a tentative sniff at the pot and drew back, crest prickling. "No. Not for me, I think."

I smiled at his reaction. I was so glad he was here with us. His little gestures, his science talk, his nimble many-fingered hands, all gave me a warm feeling at the heart. Eleanor was starting to make me feel that way too, like I had felt with Tria's old science team. We weren't a team really, we were a scientist working for the enemy and two prisoners. But tell my heart that. It looked at Eleanor and Karnath and declared: Team. Tribe. Family.

Tria

We were locked into our room in the early evening, when Eleanor left for the day. The television Dr. Townsend had promised had not yet arrived, so there was nothing to do but sit on our beds and wait to get tired. "I suppose I could recite you a poem," I offered. "We all have to learn our historical epics in school. I have a few of them memorized."

"I'd like that," he said. "It's a shame you never recited one for…" He trailed off, probably remembering Tazag's treachery. In a quiet voice he finished, "Well, Jahac would have liked it. He loves poetry."

I closed my eye a moment, considering which to choose. *I feel strange, reciting any of them to him. What if he doesn't like it? I've never heard anyone criticize them.*

Then you never asked a left, Resa answered. *I've always found them a little bloodless.*

I raised my eyebrow, startled. What exactly did she want them to be?

"So are they religious legends?" Karnath asked. Perhaps he thought that accounted for my hesitation.

"No," I said. "The Kinaru didn't develop religion until much later."

He tilted his head curiously. "The Shatakazan were religious since prehistoric times. We have artifacts believed to be religious from over a hundred thousand years ago. It's only in modern times religion has fallen out of favor."

I blinked. A hundred thousand years was an unthinkably long time. I didn't think sentient life had even evolved on Kinaru that long ago. Without artifacts, it was impossible to tell. "Interesting," I said. "Our religion arose only at the beginning of the classical period, about two thousand years ago, when we first began living in cities. The most popular theory at the moment is that pastoral people had no use for religion, since they were already close to nature. In cities, lefts in particular would have begun to feel alienated from nature, and religion became a way of satisfying some kind of emotional need." I paused, feeling unsure. *I hope that explanation isn't dismissive of your faith.*

No, said Resa, *there's some truth to it. I feel in temple a lot of what I do in nature.*

I decided on the First Lay, which was my favorite. It told of how Fola il Gendo had invented fire. At first, the fire had devastated her tribe's gathering grounds, but eventually the tribe had learned how to confine and control it. The themes of curiosity and caution were explored and held in tension, without ever being fully resolved.

I could feel my cheek flushing as I recited it, knowing its perfect cadences must be completely butchered by the translator. It was universally considered the ideal against which all other poetry should be measured—it went on for three thousand lines without a single error in the meter. The other poems in the book were similar; in the pastoral period there clearly were very specific expectations of how a poem ought to be.

Though I could see why Resa didn't like it. The modern poems she enjoyed were meterless, short poems about flowers and things. Left poetry. Though no author had been attributed, the First Lay had obviously come off the pen of a right. All of them had.

Karnath bowed his head quietly while he listened. When I finished the recitation, he raised his head. "Why did Fola il Gendo stay beating at the flames till she suffocated on the smoke?" he asked. "She should have fallen back toward the camp. The other tribespeople could have put it out at that point."

I blinked. "But it was her responsibility. A person should accept any amount of suffering rather than cause it to another."

"I don't think I agree with that," he objected. "Her individual life mattered, too."

"Of course it's easy to pick apart her motivations after the fact," I said, frowning. "She didn't have time to calculate whether the tribe could control the fire without her. But she had formed the habit of considering others before herself. For us that is the definition of virtue."

He rubbed his chin thoughtfully. "I suppose that's what Tazag meant when he said your society was communitarian. We are more individualistic than that. That attitude sounds to me like a lack of legitimate self-interest."

"Well, it clearly works for us. We have been able to eliminate poverty and war, and in less time than it took the Shatakazan to do the same, from what I read on the *Galajak*. Don't you think that comes from our belief in altruism? Well, that and our divided brains, which keeps emotion..." I hesitated, choosing my words carefully. "As a source of enjoyment rather than a guide for major decisions."

He was quiet for a few minutes, expressions flitting across his face as if he were debating something with himself. An odd notion, given he was only one person. At last he seemed to make up his mind. "There's something I've been meaning to ask you about," he said slowly. "From your descriptions, Kinaru sounds like a paradise. Long lives. Hardly any disease. No violent crime. Or so you told Tazag. I read the transcript of your interview with zem, but I never had a chance to discuss it with you."

"Did it interest you?"

"Yes, but ... My apologies. I hate to sound suspicious, especially after all that has happened. But while I was confined to my room, I spent the time reading the transcripts of the radio broadcasts we recorded back in Kinaru, which the computer had finally finished translating. And there was something that kept appearing which puzzled me. It concerns me that you didn't mention it when Tazag asked."

I chewed my lip. I had a feeling I knew what he was talking about. "I didn't say anything to Tazag that was untrue."

"No, but—when he asked about violent crime, I would have thought you would mention murder-suicide. It's mentioned again and again in the broadcast data. This sounds a significant problem and I don't know why you didn't mention it."

"I . . . I was not trying to conceal anything, or make us sound better than we are," I said defensively. "I simply am not comfortable discussing it."

"Should I consider it a taboo? We don't have to discuss it at all, if your culture forbids it. But since it was broadcast openly on the radio . . ."

"It's not a taboo," I said shortly. "It's just me. *I* don't like to talk about it."

"May I ask why?"

I hesitated. "I don't want this in any report, whether to the earthlings or to your people if you get a chance later. But since you are my colleague, and you asked, I think you deserve an answer."

He nodded respectfully, flattening his crest.

"Our mother died by murder-suicide." My voice was flat. "Ava il Poti. Ava was asleep, under a sleep stimulator, which was normal for her. Poti must have secreted a knife at some time earlier, and slashed their throat. Death would have followed quickly. They tell me Ava never woke up. Poti . . . would have suffered."

"What motivates this sort of crime? I can't imagine . . ."

"Neither can anyone," I said. "We were twelve years old. We were interviewed, together and separately, to see if we knew anything. But neither of us had a clue. They were both good mothers. My fathers and I are—not close. Neither of them. So if they had a theory, they didn't share it with us."

"But it would have to have been a major grievance against Ava, to be willing to face death in order to kill her."

"Not necessarily," I said. "For all we know, she simply wanted to end her own life, and could not without ending Ava's. Lefts are . . . prone to strong emotion, as you know. Perhaps she was depressed."

He stared at the floor a moment. "I cannot imagine … to be so bound to another that you have no choice to leave, no choice even to die without affecting them. In a way, it's a marvel it doesn't happen more often."

"That's why our society is set up as it is. You surely read Tazag's report, that we have a vanishingly low liberty score. And this is why. Every decision has to be made through a council, or a test, or a mediator, to reduce occasions for conflict. We work very hard to keep the peace. It's a matter of life and death."

"I see." He reached over to the desk, where a box of tissue had been left for us, and pulled out a square of it to offer to me. I stared at it for a moment, puzzled, but Resa reached out and took it. She was crying, and needed to wipe her face. I felt a stab of guilt, first that I had talked about the topic at all, which never failed to make her cry; and second, because I had failed to even notice.

"I thank you for honoring me with the truth, Tria il Resa," said Karnath, flattening his crest at me respectfully. "I won't ask any more about it."

"Thank you." My voice was husky with Resa's tears. "Please don't share this with anyone."

"I understand." He gently laid a hand on Resa's knee in a comforting gesture. It was odd having Karnath interact with Resa on her terms, with eye contact and expressions and occasional touches. Since I had a relationship with him too, I thought of him as a right and expected him to focus on me; but he was just as much a left as a right. Both in one.

I wasn't jealous, of course. It was just a new experience for me.

CHAPTER TWELVE

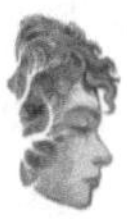

Tria

We were interrupted by a knock at the door, followed by the beep of the door unlocking. Dr. Townsend poked in her head, still well-coiffed at this time of night. "Karnath, I might need you," she said. "Do you know anything about first aid? The others said you did."

I sat bolt upright on the bed. *Others? The rest of the crew?*

It must be, said Resa excitedly, her tears forgotten. *They could easily get a human doctor.*

Karnath rose to his feet. "I do." He went after her, and I hurried after him before the door could swing shut. Townsend gave me a glance, but didn't say anything.

She brought us through the lab and down a hall toward the far end of the building, where we hadn't yet been allowed to go. "We really aren't equipped to be keeping all these people here," she said in some annoyance. "But they needed a place to store them that wasn't near—that is, a place to store them. They arrived tonight but the green one seems to be having some kind of medical emergency."

I exchanged a glance with Karnath. Jahac, maybe? It must be him or Prazad. But it was odd she hadn't said "green-crested."

When we entered the room, I saw what she had meant. There were three narrow cots, and Prazad lay on the middle one. He was curled in the fetal position, but from what I could see of his face, it was entirely green. He certainly did not look well. Strong stress always made their chromatophores activate; I knew that much about Shatakazan physiology.

Jahac knelt beside the bed, feeling Prazad's pulse in one limp hand. Lex paced, cheeks tinged yellow and crest prickling. "They took us out of the ship tonight," she said abruptly. "The van had no windows, I don't know where we are."

"This is a lab," Karnath said, putting a hand on her arm to soothe her. "It's just humans here, but they don't seem too hostile."

"Well, Prazad was frightened by the trip. He said they might be going to do experiments on us. And he's still worried about Talek, we never saw zem so we can't know if ze recovered. None of us could say anything that comforted him, and of course it's hard to calm someone down when you're frightened yourself. We didn't even know what had happened to you."

"I fully understand," said Karnath. "I was shaken when I was brought here, as well. Tria helped to keep me calm." He caught my eye, lowering his eyelids appreciatively.

I felt pleased. I had been afraid my own stoicism that night would be a cause for resentment or frustration, but it was true, he had seemed reassured.

Going over to the cot, he gave Prazad a quick examination. "He'll be fine. I could snap him out of it now if I had any medication to work with, but as it is, we'll simply have to wait it out." He turned to Dr. Townsend. "Do you have anything to warm him up? A heater, a heated blanket?" She nodded and went out, locking the door behind her. While she was gone, he gestured Lex and me in close by him and Jahac. "We've found out Tazag and the rest are trading tech to the earthlings. Not sure yet what they get out of the deal."

"Minerals, I guess?" suggested Lex. "Unity could use the financial help. If they didn't have any resources to trade, I suppose they might be desperate enough to trade tech."

I shook my head slowly. "That doesn't seem right. Making money on mineral trading isn't going to get them off the hook for the two murders. Didn't they say they weren't returning to Shatak until things were much different?"

Jahac eyed me respectfully. "I fear something larger is going on back on Shatak. Some kind of coup."

Lex's cheeks yellowed further. "I wish we were there."

"Our most important duty right now," Karnath said, "is to stay calm. When Prazad wakes up he will have to be kept as calm and safe as possible. To the best of my knowledge, we are in no immediate danger. I will try to come back again tomorrow and see how he is, if they'll let me."

Townsend returned at that moment, carrying a floppy red bottle full of hot water and a heavy blanket. Jahac carefully nestled the bottle against Prazad's abdomen and tucked him in.

"Is he going to be all right?" asked Townsend.

"Yes," said Karnath, crest bristling a little. "This response is normal to us in times of trauma."

Townsend couldn't read his gestures as I could, or she might have realized he was being pointed. "Come along then. In general I think it's best you stay separate."

Back in our room, I perched on the edge of my bed. "It's a relief to find they are all right."

"Only the science team," he answered, leaning against the wall, cheeks green with concern. "Where are Talek, Gaj, and Daz? The last two were well when we left, and they didn't seem to have joined with Tazag's group."

"They could be dead," I said bluntly, then regretted it when I saw his crest flatten. But the next idea I had wasn't much better. "Or they could have left. Unity would need them to operate the ship."

A wave of green rippled over Karnath's face as he considered that possibility. Then he took a deep breath. "We can't get ourselves panicked over it. We need to keep prying for details."

By now my exhaustion had caught up to me and I went to bed, but I lay awake for some time. I felt disconnected, disoriented. Had it only been such a short time since I had left Kinaru? The rest of the polar expedition might not even have gotten home yet. I imagined Heda il Trambo, returning to the university brimming with the news. And then . . . then going to my father, and telling him we were gone. Or perhaps it was Rez il Tapa who would go. I wondered if Tapa would cry.

I felt an ache, somewhere in my chest. *You knew this would happen,* I said to Resa. *You knew we'd be homesick.*

Yes, she said. *So you understand now?*

I turned onto one side and looked over at Karnath, sitting on the bed with his feet drawn up, reading something on his device. "Was this a huge mistake?" I asked.

"What? Failing to consider the possibility that multiple people had conspired to kill Pav? Not moving faster once we realized it was a murder? Trusting Zin?"

"Leaving home," I said in a small voice. "Coming away with you. I thought . . . I thought it would be madness to let an opportunity escape, if there was more out there than we knew. But maybe it was just as unreasonable to come. It never could have been safe. I knew that when I left."

"And yet," he said, "you're not the reason we came here to Earth. None of this is your fault. And perhaps it is fortunate, if it puts you and me into a position to do something about Unity sect's scheme."

"You really think we can?"

He tilted his head to one side, thinking. I shouldn't have asked the question. I knew Karnath never was one for the comforting lie, and the comforting lie was what I was looking for. At last he said, "I know that if we were not here, we would not have any chance. And since we are, we have some chance, however small. We at least may be able to find something out, and use that information, even if we can't yet see how. So—in that light, I don't think you have made a mistake."

With that, I turned back toward the wall and fell asleep.

The next morning Karnath asked after Prazad as soon as Townsend came to let us out. "He's awake," she said, "and seems to be fine. You're not needed."

"I would really like to see him for myself," he protested.

"The higher-ups wouldn't like it," she said. "Unless there's a real necessity, I'm not authorizing any more visitation."

Eleanor arrived about half an hour later, dropping her purse, phone, keys, and badge on the long table of the lab in a big heap. "What are you doing?" she asked without any greeting.

"Trying to get onto your network still," said Karnath. "It's more difficult than I thought it would be. I can detect the signal, but my device can't make sense of it."

"I don't know anything about that," she said apologetically. "You might ask Mike to help you."

"Did you hear about the three more Shatakazan that arrived last night?" I asked her in a conversational tone. Townsend could be cagey, but Eleanor might say more, if approached carefully.

"I heard they would be handing them over after dark," she answered. "So they got in all right?"

"More or less. One of them had a medical issue, but Townsend says he is all right now."

Her eyes gleamed behind her thick glasses. "I wish I could study them. Not that you aren't a delight, Tria, but the Shatakazan are so much more alien, we could learn so much. But they tell me it's not in the agreement."

"Do you know if more will be coming later?"

"I don't think so, they said there was nobody on the other ship but the

Unity guys."

Karnath said nothing in response to this, but his crest prickled and I knew he had heard. Another ship! Could it be the *Vatarax*, that had been at the space station with us?

"It's just that some of our friends are still missing," I said plaintively. "Spacers—they flew the ship."

"Oh, if it was the tech people they're probably teaching our people how to—" She cut herself off. "I keep forgetting, I'm not supposed to talk to you about any of that. Karnath." He looked up, as if he had not been listening up to then. "What do you think about the network? Is there something else you could try, or should we be trying to find a way to compare the data manually? It occurred to me you might have some kind of optical scanner that could grab the data off our screens."

He tilted his head to one side. "I am uncertain if my device has the processing power. I'm not ready to give up on connecting to your network. It theoretically should be possible, it's just that I'm not an expert in alien computer systems. The only one on our ship was Prazad, and Townsend won't let us see him."

Eleanor put her chin down. "I'll talk to her. I'm not resigned to spending weeks scanning through pages of data."

Townsend must have relented, because Eleanor was soon scanning her badge and letting us into the room where the other scientists were kept. As we had heard, Prazad was sitting up in bed. His crest looked a little wilted and his color dingy, but he brightened a little when he saw us. "Karnath! They said you were here, but a part of me worried they were only trying to reassure me."

"Are you going to be all right now?"

"I think so. Normally I have meds on hand, just in case, but I was not able to get them before we were taken from the ship."

Karnath's crest prickled at this. Then he sighed. "Well, we must make do. They don't have any medical synthesizers here. I brought you a bit of a problem, if you feel up to it." He held out his device.

Prazad seized it. "I need something to keep me busy. What's the problem?"

Karnath sat on the bed beside him, explaining what he had done so far. I sat on one of the other cots, beside Lex, who was idly picking at a dry scale on the back of her hand. "How are you managing?" I asked in a low voice.

"Better than he is," she said, jerking her chin over to Prazad. "I'm so worried about Daz. And the others, of course, but ze is my lover."

"I asked after the spacers," I said, moving over as Jahac came to join us. "It sounded, from what the scientist said, that they were alive. It seemed like she was going to say they were with the ship, but she cut herself off."

"Did she say anything about Talek?" Jahac asked, leaning in and pitching his voice even quieter than mine. "It would mean so much to him." He tilted his head to indicate Prazad.

"No, she just said tech people. Why is he especially concerned for zem? Are they lovers?"

He flicked his fingers downward. "Quarter-siblings. It's his first time in space, and ze got him the assignment. I think ze was worried about his anxiety, and thought he would be better off with zem. Now it's just that much worse for him because he doesn't know if ze's all right."

"I will find out anything I can," I said. But I didn't feel encouraged. Eleanor didn't seem to know very much about what was going on outside the lab.

Neither Lex nor Jahac had any further questions, so I turned my attention back to Prazad, who was saying, "Your problem is that here, where it asks what numeric system to use, you put in decimal."

"But the earthlings use decimal," Karnath protested. "I do know that much."

"You would think, because that's what they use for counting, but in computer systems they also use binary and hexadecimal. Just select all three and then run the program. It should work." He made as if to hand the device back, and then hesitated. "Do you know you have a virus on there? It's using a lot of power."

Karnath took it and peered at the screen. "No, I didn't. You think I picked it up from the network here?"

"No, you haven't gotten close enough to a connection. It's just funny because I know Zin found a virus in the *Galajak*'s computers on the way here from Kinaru. She complained about it to me, but I didn't get a chance to look at before…" He trailed off. "Before all this. It didn't seem to be doing anything, but it was impossible to get rid of and had gotten into the core programs. She couldn't figure out where we had picked it up."

"Strange," said Karnath, sliding the device back into the pocket on his upper arm. "I'll look at it tonight. But before I go, I did want to talk a little about the situation. I don't know if Townsend will let us see you again. One of the scientists let slip that there is or was a second ship here on Earth. It sounded like she was about to say the techs were teaching the humans how to use it."

"The *Vatarax*," Lex suggested. "Do you think they might be selling one of the ships to the humans?"

"That was my thought too. I had the idea of looking out for an opportunity to escape, and trying to reach either ship."

Lex's crest prickled. "Are you crazy?" she hissed. "What hope do you have on a savage alien world of even surviving, much less finding the ships?"

"We can't stay here forever," I pointed out. "Perhaps if one or two of us escape and come back for the rest when we've found the ship. I could. I can pass for human, after all."

"I can't possibly," said Prazad. "I'd only slow you down."

"Karnath speaks human." Jahac still avoided looking directly at his ex-lover. At least he was no longer hostile.

"English," Karnath corrected. "Which luckily is the right language for this region. I could go."

"If it's all the same, I'd rather not," said Lex. "The two of you have the best chance of success. More people would only increase the risk."

"Don't take unnecessary risks," said Jahac, his eyes fixed on a point between Karnath and me. "Wait for a good opportunity. There's no emergency."

We were interrupted by Townsend opening the door. "I meant you to let them in and stay in there with them," she was saying over her shoulder. "Who knows what they're plotting in here."

"But the door doesn't have a scanner on the inside," Eleanor protested, passing Townsend to come inside. "I didn't want to get stuck in there all day." She stopped in front of Karnath. "Did you get it done?"

"I got what I needed," he said, rising. "It will take some time to work, but Prazad thinks it will be successful this time."

Prazad's corrected program completed as predicted, and Karnath transferred my genome to the facility's computers to compare it to a human sample. The analysis took days. If we had been comparing two earthling samples, Eleanor assured me, it would go a lot faster because we would restrict our search to certain genetic markers, but in this case, they had to go one nucleotide at a time.

I spent the time doing countless tests. Or sometimes I simply waited while Resa did tests. My eye would be covered and an earphone put over my ear so I couldn't accidentally help her.

Eleanor showed me the results, when it was all over. "Both of you are equally intelligent," she said, gesturing to the printout. "But in completely different areas. She was like lightning on the spatial reasoning tests, and her ability to make connections was highly impressive. You, on the other hand, are much more advanced than an average human on verbal skills and logic, but you basically failed the spatial tests."

"I could have told you that," I said. "Rights and lefts have different skills."

"I know, but I was curious to see just how different. And whether it left you with more, or less, ability than an average human. It seems that, combined, you're a great deal more intelligent. Or should be. It seems the lefts don't have access to an education?"

I drew back a little uncomfortably. "They go to school with us."

"But the education isn't intended for them. It doesn't focus on their skills or adapt to their abilities."

"I suppose not. But they have plenty of opportunities to do the things they like. Sports, for instance, or drawing, or crafts."

"That's good, and certainly Resa doesn't seem to have been held back too much from achieving her potential. But I wonder if your people expect too little of them. Everyone likes a challenge."

"You may be right." I frowned, wondering if Resa was listening to any of this. She didn't seem to be. She was paging through a picture book of animals on our lap. Earth animals were all four-limbed and most of them seemed to be furry.

Karnath was at the other side of the worktable, at the computer. "This is so slow," he complained. "I could have analyzed the DNA of every plant and animal on this planet in this amount of time, if only I had the ship's computer to work with."

"How does it look so far?"

"There's certainly a great deal of correlation," he hedged. "Closer than, say, humans have with apes. But there's a great deal that's different, too. Whole new sections, especially in areas Earth scientists have identified as having to do with the brain."

"That's expected, right?" I asked, circling the table to look over his shoulder. "We know already that our brains are different."

"Yes, but ... what's strange is that none of the additional DNA so far appears to be junk. And very little of the human DNA is omitted. There are just these—additions." He showed me areas on the computer that he'd color-coded. "And there are tiny corrections elsewhere. Apparently you can synthesize a number of vitamins the earthlings can't."

"Corrections? As if we were somehow more evolved?" I glanced at Eleanor, feeling a little embarrassed. I didn't mean to imply that we were superior.

He tilted his head. "Yes … except, look. Here's a gene from the human genome. It repeats several times with slight variations. Or this one, with extraneous material that has nothing to do with the enzyme it's supposed to be making. Evolution is a messy process. But look at this gene, it's so— tidy. There's nothing inessential in it; no randomness, no repeats."

I squinted at the page of symbols. Kinaru had only just started investigating the nature of DNA; matching which genes went with which traits was far beyond us. "So what are you suggesting?"

"I can't be sure, because the closest my people have come to gene editing is correcting small defects by grafting in healthy DNA from another cell. Not creating it from scratch. But that's what this looks like to me. It looks like this DNA was … *written* by someone. Not borrowed from another life-form, but actually created artificially."

I stared into his golden eyes in shock. Artificial? It was unnerving, thinking of my own genes being the deliberate work of someone else. Not part of nature at all.

Eleanor nodded. "That does make sense. Presumably whoever did the genetic engineering also planted your people on your planet."

"Are you *sure*?" I asked Karnath.

"Of course I'm not sure," he said, without annoyance. "I think I just said that. I need to do more analysis. But that's where the data seem to be leading. I'm open to an alternate hypothesis."

Every evening, the scientists at the facility would go home, leaving a guard to keep an eye on the building. Karnath and I were escorted to our room—very politely, but firmly nonetheless. We would not be allowed to wander the premises undetected.

We spent our evenings watching television. Karnath had mainly requested it so that we could find out the situation on Earth by watching the news. There seemed to be considerable unrest globally, but Karnath assured me it was always like that. "There are hundreds of nations," he explained, as we sat on his bed, watching the screen on the opposite wall, eating an interesting Earth product called popcorn. Karnath liked it with salt. He had no interest in sweet flavors at all, but loved salty and savory things. "Naturally with so many conflicting interests, there is always unrest in one place or another."

"But is it always this violent?" The screen showed fires, riots, rockets.

"More or less. I told you there was a reason we didn't go here. I'm a little concerned about the rising tensions with Russia. We had thought the competition between them and the Americans was basically over, but now they report on it daily. It's concerning in a way these smaller conflicts aren't, because they could actually pose an existential threat to the earthlings. They have weapons that are capable of poisoning the entire planet."

"Do you think it's an immediate worry?" I imagined one of those rockets landing on the building, with us locked inside and unable to escape.

"Oh, no. Open war between those two nations has been a worry for earthlings for decades, but they have never quite done it. They all know they could destroy themselves that way."

Resa grabbed the control and switched the channel to an animal show. "I think this is making her nervous," I said to Karnath, by way of apology.

Not that, said Resa shortly. *Thinking.*

I raised my eyebrow, but said nothing. It seemed strange to me that she could think best while also watching a program that interested her, but

I didn't question her process. I already knew she thought nothing like I did.

At last, as a spotted savannah predator took down a ruminant, Resa spoke. "The one thing only Earth has."

He tipped his head, recognizing her throaty voice and different way of speaking. "What is, Resa?"

"Dirty weapons. You know."

I interjected, "She means nuclear weapons. We are aware of the damage nuclear radiation can do."

Karnath still wasn't following her. "Yes, I said Shatak and other civilized planets don't have them."

"So why go to Earth?" Resa insisted, her tone growing frustrated. "Diamonds from the Violet Mountains."

I frowned, puzzling through her metaphor. "The only place on Kinaru to get diamonds is the Violet Mountains," I explained.

Karnath sat bolt upright, crest prickling. "She is saying nuclear weapons are the only resource Earth has to tempt Unity to come here!"

Relieved, Resa flicked her fingers up. Explaining it had been a challenge, especially when she hadn't yet thought her idea through.

I felt the blood drain from my face. "You think Unity came here to trade for nuclear weapons?"

Am I wrong?

"They must have," said Karnath. "And I should have thought of that sooner. They are a small sect, not able to seize control politically. Yet any attempt to grow in status through trade would be far too slow to justify their confidence that things would be different when they returned." He shook his head slowly from side to side. "An earthling would have realized this much more quickly. But you and I both come from planets without war. It is hard to grasp why anyone would choose that route."

"Tazag is convinced zir cause is righteous," I said. "I can easily imagine zem justifying any amount of violence in the name of ending oppression."

"It's just..." He rubbed his forehead, crest smoothing itself back down as he absorbed the implications. "For a small sect to win against such overwhelming numerical odds, they'd have to strike by surprise, and as many major targets at once. The loss of life would be catastrophic. Liberty City, the center of government, would naturally be a target. My family lives near there." His cheeks flushed green.

I felt suddenly aware of the difference between us. I was trying to solve a puzzle, but for him it had just gotten deeply personal. Yet I wanted to show him I did not intend there to be any difference, so I said, "Jahac said to be cautious about planning to escape, that there is no emergency. But I think the situation has just changed. We should attempt to escape as soon as possible."

He nodded, face clearing as he replaced fear with determination. "Yes. I only hope it isn't already too late."

CHAPTER THIRTEEN

Tria

Escaping would be easier said than done. There was the lock on our door, the lock on the outer door, the guard that roamed at night or Dr. Townsend at her desk by the front door in the daytime. And if we surmounted all these obstacles, there was the question of surviving on Earth. I had only the faintest notion of how dangerous it might be out there; Karnath's comedies showed a harmless place with no bigger problems than embarrassment and romantic rejection, while the news broadcasts seemed eager to convince the viewer there was danger all over the country. Either way, it would be dangerous for us unless we could conceal our identities. I couldn't imagine earthlings accepting aliens without hesitation.

If we could convince Eleanor to assist us, all of this would be made a great deal easier. But I was doubtful. She was always friendly, in an absent-minded sort of way, but that didn't necessarily extend to betraying her colleagues. I struggled to decide how much I could trust her with. If she already knew Unity was here for nuclear weapons, mentioning it wouldn't change her mind. More likely she would tell Townsend everything I told her.

I found her the next morning at the computer, anxiously typing with a furrowed brow.

"What's all this for?" I said, gesturing at the screen. "I thought we would be looking at the DNA more today."

She flicked her eyes at my face and then back to the screen. "Dr. Townsend says I need to be more careful what I say to you."

"It makes no sense to keep secrets from us. Who would we tell?"

Sighing, she lifted her hands from the keys and looked up. "Well, suffice it to say that our discovery of yesterday has interested the higher-ups, and Dr. Townsend is going to a meeting today to present our findings. By rights you two should be there, but of course you won't be. Even I am not going to be in on the meeting. I'm supposed to type up everything we've learned so far and Townsend will be presenting the data. Which seems a waste of her time when we may as well email it, if they don't even want to discuss it with *any* of the scientists who have actually been working on the project." She shook her head in frustration. "I mean, I understand that technically you two are prisoners, but I'm not. Why would they hire me if they didn't think they could trust me? Why not lock me up too? It's ridiculous."

Ah, academic politics. Some things are the same on every planet. "Maybe they trust you, but Townsend wants to make it look like she made these discoveries."

Eleanor nodded. "Yeah, probably. But it burns me up. It's bad enough that even if I did get credit for my work, it would all be too top-secret to publish and I'd still have nothing to put on my CV. I knew it was going to be like this when I interviewed; they were too cagey about what the work actually was. Never would have taken it if I weren't desperate."

"How can you be desperate? You're obviously very good." I meant it; I wasn't *only* trying to soften her for an appeal later.

She sighed. "It can be hard to get a good job in academia. I took some years off to have Mia, and after my divorce I found myself needing a job in a hurry. Spent the past two months answering *phones*. I was hoping this position would help restart my career, but no luck. At least it will pay the bills until I find something better."

"I'm sure you will eventually," I said politely. So far I had been nice enough, but I wasn't sure how to lead the conversation where I wanted. *A little help?*

*Can't you read her body language at **all**?* Resa answered in some exasperation. *She keeps going back to her work, trying to get it done. You'll do better to talk to her later.*

I moved off, finding Karnath talking to Mike in the kitchen area. "I'm going out anyway," Mike was saying. "And Dr. Townsend told me to supply you with anything reasonable you wanted."

"In that case, I would really like a warmer garment." answered Karnath. "Perhaps a sweater, with a hood. Or those things you keep your neck warm with—scarves. I understand this temperature is comfortable for you, but my own planet is much warmer. My crest in particular is prone to chill."

I interjected casually, "Oh, if you're going out, can you get a change of clothes for me as well? The ones I came in are beginning to take on an odor."

"Will do," said Mike, making a note in his phone.

He returned some time later with the things we had requested: a gray hooded sweatshirt and a blue scarf for Karnath, and a set of knit athletic wear for me. It clung in ways I wasn't used to—Kinaru clothing is always cut loose—but it fit tolerably well. Better still, it was black, which I hoped would help me remain inconspicuous.

Dr. Townsend returned that afternoon and shut herself up with several of the others in a back office for close to an hour. For a moment I hoped this was our opportunity, but one of the interns sat at the front desk the entire time, eyes fixed on the door. They had no intention of being careless with their captives.

Eleanor returned to the lab in some kind of mood. Even I couldn't help noticing she was stomping a little, lips pursed. She started opening drawers and slamming them again, muttering, "This stuff should have been *organized*, it's like they got a list of what a bio lab should have and just dumped all of it in random drawers."

I came over and sat down on a wheeled stool near her. "Is everything all right?"

"I guess," she said. "But I was hoping to be able to do some *actual science*. After all it's an *enormous privilege* to be working with the first alien ever studied on Earth. The *least* they could do would be to follow the most fascinating lead we have." She slammed another drawer shut and pulled open the next.

"How do you mean?"

"I mean, we made an amazing discovery yesterday! Or at least, a lead on one. If you are really genetically engineered, we could get a look at the first artificial genes that have ever been studied. Even Karnath said they haven't done so much on his planet. If we could see how it was done, it could help us understand more fully how genes work! To say nothing of the application toward creating our own genes, for instance in agriculture. It could be huge! It could be the biggest thing to hit the biology community in a decade."

"I don't understand. They don't want you studying my DNA?"

She shook her head, shaking more hair loose from her ponytail. "They feel that we have an answer now, and that's all we needed. The aliens, apparently, were intrigued but didn't have further questions. And our guys only care about things that have monetary or military applications. Ha! I thought only the private sector was that obsessed with applications. A government funding project should be able to dedicate resources to long-term projects, stuff that might not pay off for years." She finally found what she was looking for, a drawer full of glass vials which she began piling on a tray.

I stared at her in alarm. "You don't mean they're shutting down the whole project?" Not that I wanted to be studied, but if I wasn't a valuable specimen, I supposed I'd be shoved into the back room with the other scientists and have an even harder time escaping.

"Oh, no, they're letting me keep going with your immune cells. Dr. Townsend must have pitched them as more immediately promising than they are, in the hopes of keeping funding going. You know how they do. So now she wants me to pull a cure for ebola or HIV out of a hat, in a span of months not years. I told her that didn't sound likely, but she said that without having to go through an ethics board, like you do with human subjects, it should go much faster."

I didn't like the sound of that at all. "So because I'm not human you don't have to be ethical?"

She looked up at me sharply. "Oh, don't take it that way. Of course I will make every attempt to keep you safe. Legally, she tells me, I'm not required to, but I feel you're very close to being human anyway." From another drawer, she took out a syringe. "I feel confident I can keep any risk to you to an absolute minimum."

This didn't sound promising, but I pushed further. "Even if it cost you this job?"

Her face fell. "Oh. I . . . I see what you mean. You don't trust Townsend and the others. And so you think maybe you can't trust me either." I nodded. "Tria, I like you. You're a nice person and a good scientist. But I do have a daughter to think of, and I'm living month to month on bills. You can't put me in a position to choose. And I'm hoping Townsend won't either. After all, your well-being is necessary to this project."

I fell silent. Resa asked, *Why don't you tell her what you have in mind?*

She's not going to be open to it. Even I can tell that.

But if you told her about the weapons!

She says she respects me because I'm almost human. These weapons are going to be used on Shatakazan. They're nothing close to human. She won't care. Certainly not more than she does about her daughter.

Eleanor had her vials ready. I hadn't been listening when she had asked for my arm, so she gently reached out and took Resa's. "I'm sorry, you have to use this one," I said, offering mine. "Resa is more sensitive than I am; the needle will hurt her."

Eleanor smiled and accepted my proffered arm. "How selfless of you!"

*What would be even more selfless would be if you would **listen** to me,* Resa grumbled.

In the end, the decisions are my responsibility, I countered. *I can't risk her telling Townsend how much we know, or what we're planning.*

CHAPTER FOURTEEN

Tria

That night, Karnath had better news than I did. He had been able to scan Eleanor's badge when she had left it in the break room after lunch. "I am confident that the copy on my screen will be enough for the optical scanners; they're not that precise. And look," he added, showing me some greenish-gray slips of paper. "Money. You need it for everything here. It's very capitalist."

"Where did you find it?"

"Eleanor's purse." He saw my disapproving look. "I'm sorry, but I think we need it more than she does. Unless she was willing to help us?"

I shook my head. "She told me she can't afford to get fired and will do what Townsend says."

"We're going to have to break out at night," he said, pocketing the bills. "I watched the front desk, but they are very careful to have someone there all day."

"It's just as well. Late at night, when it's dark out, we'll have better luck avoiding notice."

"But what about the lock on this door? The only scanner is on the outside."

I chewed my lip. "Well, they're electric, right? Can't your device do anything?"

He flicked his fingers downward. "They're not connected to any network. I tried last night."

Maybe I can pick it, said Resa. To my shock, she pulled a small kitchen knife from her pocket. *I picked this up in the kitchen. Might be able to pry back the bolt with it.*

My stomach sank. *Resa, why didn't you tell me?*

You didn't notice? Well, I hope if you didn't, the earthlings didn't either.

I took a deep breath. *Resa, do you understand why I would be upset that you had a knife on you I didn't know about?*

She was silent a moment. *Seriously? You're afraid of me? We're not our mothers. I'm not Poti. And more importantly, you're not Ava.*

What's that supposed to mean?

Karnath was watching my face. "Is everything all right?"

I shook myself. "It's fine. Resa is going to try to pick the lock."

He glanced at his device. "Not yet. It won't be dark for hours."

We waited, trying to watch television but without much focus. Resa was nervous and fiddly.

At last he checked his device and said, "It's fully dark outside, and most of the humans will be sleeping. It's time."

I listened at the door until I heard the guard's quiet tread, passing our room and heading toward the back of the building. There was a soft beep as he passed through the door leading into that section. *We're clear. Go ahead.*

Resa went to work, prying the knife through the lock. She cut herself once and let slip a curse. Then finally I heard the lock slip back. "We got it! Should we go?"

"No, leave it shut and come away from the door. When the guard has moved on from the back room, we'll make our move."

I sat back down, trying to look relaxed when my heart was pounding. On the screen, a woman was chopping vegetables. "This is it," I murmured. "If we screw up, we can't go back. Only forward. Do you have everything you need?"

"This thing has no end of pockets," he said, digging his hands in deep. "I just wish I had more to put in it. Like a weapon, maybe."

"I really hope we can get through this without hurting humans," I said. "This isn't their fault."

"I will fight them if I have to," he answered. "If they try to stop us, we don't have a choice."

I took a deep breath. "I guess not."

"This isn't what either of us were trained for," he said. "But we seem to be the only people available."

At last the guard finished his circuit and passed by our door once again. We waited till his footsteps had passed into the back section before we stole out of our room. In the dark, the room looked full of ominous shadows; the only light was the pale gleam of streetlights through the frosted windows and the red glow from the exit signs.

Karnath scanned his device at the front door, and it let out a loud beep. But I did not hear the lock slide over as usual. He seized the handle, but it didn't budge. Bending down, he laboriously sounded out the text on the tiny screen. "Lock … out … mode … system … armed. There's some kind of security system switched on at night," he hissed.

I scanned around the area of the door. Sure enough, there was an illuminated panel on the wall beside the door. "Could that be it?"

He flicked his fingers up and turned to his device. "This one's got a wireless connection, I should be able to hack it. Just stay down." We moved a little way from the door to crouch by the front desk. Coming from the interior of the building, the security guard shouldn't see us here.

The device was still working on the security system when a creak in the floor alerted me to the guard's presence. I turned my head and caught Karnath's eye, and we both froze, scarcely breathing.

The footsteps came nearer, and a flashlight beam slashed in front of us. Just then, the security panel's lights changed from green to red. I held my breath, hoping the guard wouldn't notice. But instead I heard him grunt, and he moved closer, passing in front of us to inspect the panel. I looked desperately at Karnath. We were fully in the guard's view now. If he turned, he'd see us, but if we moved to get out of his sight, he'd surely hear us.

We held our position while he studied the alarm. "That's weird," he muttered. "I know it was set before." He lifted a hand to reset it, and then dropped his hand, reconsidering. To my horror, he turned around and shone his flashlight around the room..

For half a second we were blinded by the flashlight beam. Then suddenly the beam was off, and Karnath was no longer beside me. I hadn't seen him leap for the guard, but now the two of them were grappling together.

It had never occurred to me to ask how Shatakazan were at hand fighting; it wasn't a popular sport on Kinaru. But the answer would have been, *very good.* Karnath's reflexes were quick and his flexible limbs allowed him to pin the guard's arms from behind and sweep his legs out from under him. The man hit the floor hard, his head bumping the wall as he went down. His limbs relaxed suddenly.

Karnath scrambled off the guard, looking at me in horror. "Is he dead? I didn't mean to knock his head like that."

"Unless human heads are much softer than ours, he is likely to recover." I stood up and checked the man over. "He's just unconscious. Nice work."

Karnath scanned the badge image a second time, and this time the lock engaged. Outside, the parking lot was empty and quiet, like the first night we'd arrived. The bright lights illuminated every corner, and for a second I hesitated, afraid to leave the tentative shelter of the door. Then Karnath grabbed my arm and we bolted for the cover of some brush at the opposite side of the lot.

The bushes were dense and full of scratching twigs. We blundered through, making an obscene racket. Karnath pulled me along, though I could barely see which way to go. His eyes were much keener than mine in the dark. After a moment we broke through into a clear space.

I blinked and looked ahead. It was another parking lot of another empty building. Karnath scanned the writing, struggling to decipher it. "I think it's a medical office. This whole area is some kind of business park."

"We have to get as far from back there as we can, before the alarm goes up." We ran along the edge of the parking lot, staying close to the shrubbery and out of the light.

Sure enough, at the end of that lot was another dense patch of brush and then another lot. This one was full of cars, and the lights were on in the building. Music drifted from outside. "A restaurant," Karnath hissed. "We're getting closer to civilization, and I wanted to get further away."

We turned to the side and plunged into the thicket of bushes. After a moment, the dense hedge thinned and I found we were in a patch of trees. I bent over with our hands on our knees, breathing hard. Karnath took out his device. "If I can still access the global network from here, I can get a map." A moment later he sighed and put it away. "No. I only had access through the building's network, and we're out of range."

We struck out in the same direction we had been going, fighting through hedges and crossing parking lots to keep from getting off track. Once we had to cross a wide street, but there was no traffic. After that we followed the edge of the road, sometimes passed by cars. At first, we leapt for the cover of the trees when we saw their headlights approaching, but after a while we found they never stopped, and we started ignoring them. With Karnath's hood up, and me in my Earth clothes, there would be nothing remarkable about us.

We passed some brightly lit businesses, but most of the buildings that lined the road were shrouded in darkness. Smaller roads wound into darkness. "Residential neighborhoods," said Karnath. "No good for us."

Resa's complaining was growing insistent by the time we reached a large park. A big sign loomed in the darkness, illuminated by a floodlight below. There was a metal bar across the entrance to shut out cars, but it was easy enough to duck under.

Inside, it was disappointingly flat and treeless. There were fields marked out with lines and fences, for sporting events; clusters of ladders and ramps, for children to play; and a huge shelter full of wooden tables beside a large pond. Karnath looked around in frustration. "This area is so populated," he complained. "I thought there might be a *little* patch of wilderness."

I pointed toward the picnic shelter. "That should do for a place to rest overnight. If we're on our way before people start getting up."

We lay down under one of the metal tables. The floor of the shelter was concrete and the opposite of comfortable, but I was so tired I barely cared. *My foot hurts from walking,* Resa fussed.

A lot more of that in our future. I thought of how long we had spent in the car, on the way from the ship. My chrono had read an hour and a half, Kinaru time. But I didn't know how fast the car might have been going. Much faster than any groundcar on my planet went, for sure.

I fell asleep with the constant buzz of insects in my ears.

CHAPTER FIFTEEN

Resa

I woke to Karnath shaking me in the predawn grayness. The air was cold and damp on my face, and a few birds were starting to sing out. "I saw something," he hissed.

We crawled out from under the table and clambered to our feet. I peered around in the dimness. His eyes could handle it better than mine; I saw nothing but humps of vegetation black against the sky. "Not here," he whispered. "I was on the roof of the shelter. There are earthlings coming this way. They have animals with them."

That doesn't sound too worrisome, I said. *I bet this is a great place to take pets for exercise.*

At this hour?

Karnath scrambled quickly on top of the structure, his seven-fingered hands and long toes finding easy grips on the wooden posts supporting it. I stood on the ground uncertainly until he reached a hand to help me up.

From here I could see the winding path through the park that we had followed to get here. Sure enough, there was some movement near the entrance. But in this light, I couldn't clearly make out what.

"Five earthlings in uniform," said Karnath. "One animal . . . I think it's a dog."

Dogs are nice. I sent Tria a mental image of one.

She asked, "Aren't dogs the ones they walk on leashes all over?"

"They also use them to track people," he said tightly. "They have a powerful sense of smell."

We turned and slid down, Karnath following. "They track us by our *scent?*"

"They sniff it out on the ground. It'll follow our trail anywhere we walk!"

I turned to glance back toward the dogs, now out of sight again. On television they had been big friendly waggy creatures. But it was true their teeth were sharp, in strong jaws. My heart started pounding. I whimpered aloud, "They could *eat* us."

They're not going to eat us. We'll find a way around them and get to the road. She bent our head, thinking. "Quick," she said at last. "Take off your shoes. We'll wade through the pond. That should disperse the aromatics we're shedding." Already she was kneeling down so I could get at the laces of ours.

"Of course!" Karnath slipped his shoes off, and together we waded into the water. It was cool but not freezing, and the mud squelched through my toes on the bottom. As quickly as we could, we followed the edge of the pond until we reached the creek that fed it. Here, the water was colder and the bottom was rocky, painful on our half-numb feet.

The device in Karnath's pocket gave a faint chime, and he pulled it out. "Hm. That's strange," he said softly. "I had given up on ever connecting to the global network from here, since access to it seems to be restricted to paying subscribers. But the script I was running to attempt it has just completed."

"Does that matter right now?" Tria asked, glancing back over her shoulder. The creek had run into a patch of trees, so at last the pond was out of sight. None too soon—last we had looked, the dog and its handler were almost at the shelter.

"It does if I can find a map." He passed the device to me. "There."

Sure enough, there was the park, with the creek running through. I passed it back. "Where should we head from here?"

"We will be reaching another road soon. We can get out of the water there; it's busy and that will hopefully help mask our scent. And from there, probably west. East and south of here are both densely populated areas. We know most of our trip was in darkness, without passing many lights. West seems the best chance at bringing us closer to the ship."

Just as we reached the road and put our shoes back on, the sun finally rose, bathing the trees in light. I blinked, startled. In the predawn light, everything had looked gray and pale. All at once all the vegetation had turned a brilliant, emerald green. Green groundcover. Green trees like round puffs. Green shrubs. Only the road was black, striped with yellow and white. Cars sped by, sending gusts of unpleasant-smelling exhaust into our faces.

At home, the leaves were all shades of red and gold. Copper-colored brush; gold fringe trees, ocher berry vines. The only green was the little flashes of wings from flying reptiles. Here, there was so much green it exhausted the eyes. Green as bile or arsenic.

I can't say what I had hoped for when I first thought of coming here. But I certainly had not imagined this planet would be so much like a poison. Its color was like a warning signal: stay away, we are going to kill you.

Tria

We hurried along the road as fast as we could, our shadows stretching out before us, hoping to put as much distance between us and the uniformed earthlings as possible. The road twisted and turned, still heading roughly west. "I think this may be the road we took to get to the lab," Karnath said, examining his device as he walked. "It passes through a few small towns, but it's much more rural than the other major routes in the area."

I grabbed his arm as his feet strayed over the white line bordering the road. "You'll have to look at that thing later. A car is going to hit you, the way you're not looking where you're going."

He chuckled and stuffed into his pocket. Instead he pulled out a can of nuts and handed it to me. "Hungry?"

I snatched them eagerly. "You should put your scarf on, now that it's light."

He pulled it out and tied it around the lower half of his face. "How is this?"

I took a sideways look at him. "Not too bad, if you keep your chin down. The hood of your sweatshirt shades your eyes." With his hood up, all I could see of his face were his golden eyes with their vertical pupils and the green of his brow ridge. His crest made the hood of the sweatshirt stick up a little, but that couldn't be helped.

We walked steadily all morning, as the sun got higher overhead. That was when I learned that a damp heat is infinitely more uncomfortable than a dry heat. The orchard country where I live is hot and dry, and where the irrigation ends, the wind comes off the steppes like a blast furnace. But it never sapped my strength like Earth's humid air.

Karnath didn't mind the heat or the humidity. "I live in the jungle, myself. It's hotter than this and the moisture in the air condenses on your face and drips off the end of your nose." He gave a sigh, thinking of it. It was a strange thought, the two of us, both so far from home, missing such opposite things. "But the walking is wearing. My people are not great walkers. Did you know that the early humans hunted things simply by following them, at walking pace, until they died?"

I shuddered. "Humans frighten me. How does one go from that to a civilized people?"

"Not all at once, of course. They have a brutal history. But they don't seem like that now. What about Eleanor?"

I allowed that, with a gesture. "But they aren't all like her. The government is selling weapons to Unity. What kind of people sell weapons without knowing what they might be used for?"

He sighed. "I won't deny there are some terrible humans. Just—try not to generalize. They're an entire species, as heterogeneous as—well, as my people. I was going to say, as yours, but your people aren't that different, are they? One language, one government, one culture."

"I suppose it's because we were planted there. There wouldn't have been time enough to differentiate." With all that had happened, I hadn't had much time to think about that discovery. It was uncomfortable to think of having been artificially created. But it explained why we weren't related to any animals.

"Why do you suppose anyone would do such a thing?" Karnath asked. "I can't see the purpose of taking humans, altering them, and putting them elsewhere. Some kind of perverse science experiment?"

"To improve them, I suppose," I said. "I mean, you were the first to tell me this planet is a mess. Someone must have tried to fix their most obvious defects, probably from an altruistic motive."

Karnath's hood jumped a little; his crest must be bristling. "That sounds a little arrogant."

"I'm sorry, I didn't mean to offend."

"It's not that it's offensive. It's that it sounds less like an educated guess than like an assumption founded on ego. You feel your planet is best, so you assume it must be. That's the sort of thinking they always warned us about, when I first started studying aliens. You have to be alert for errors based on your limited perspective."

I raised my hand, fingers spread. "I really don't think this is subjectivity. Even Eleanor said the genetic alterations were an improvement. And think of all the anthropological data Tazag gathered. No war, little crime, no poverty. Compare that with Earth." A noisy truck passed, leaving us in a cloud of smog. "It isn't that hard to see that one has a strong advantage."

He took a deep breath, forcing his crest down. "Tell me, Tria. Who is the foremost artist on Kinaru of the past hundred years?"

I blinked. "There are some . . . I don't think I could name any, it isn't a hobby of mine."

"How much music is produced on Kinaru yearly? How well are dancers paid? Can a person make a living off of poetry?"

He didn't leave time between the questions to answer, I assume because he had already guessed. "But that's just *art*. Nobody lives or dies because of art."

"Art is what makes you *want* to be alive," he said, spreading his hands in frustration.

"Everyone wants to be alive. It's an evolutionary imperative."

He gave me a sidelong glance. "Not *everyone*."

I did not choose to answer that. I had told him I didn't want to discuss my mothers, but he was coming dangerously close. I put my head down and walked faster, forcing him to hurry to keep up.

Eventually, though, Karnath grew so tired we had to rest. He sat on the edge of the sidewalk, chin to his chest, gingerly rotating his sore knees. It was a disturbing sight, seeing him twist his leg around in directions no human or Kinaru leg could bend, and I eventually muttered to him that he'd better not, there were too many people around.

We were passing through a lightly urban area, where shops stood on either side of the street and cars cruised slowly past, stopping at lit signals. Karnath pointed out the nearest business, which he said sold fuel for the cars. "And food, too, inside the shop. We should go get some. I finished the nuts awhile back."

The inside of the shop was one step removed from chaos. Racks of packaged food hung on the walls and filled every available inch. There were beverage machines and racks selling colored pictures and sun-protection glasses and hats. A large display behind the counter advertised sticks that, it appeared, one was supposed to light on fire and suck on the unlit end. I wasn't sure why.

Karnath collected a few packages of mysterious food products, some bottled water, and a pair of sun glasses, and we waited in a short line to pay. No one was looking at Karnath, but a couple of the men looked me up and down. It made me uncomfortable.

Behind the counter, a small television displayed the news. "The police department has just reported a possible kidnapping in our area," a female announcer was saying earnestly. "The suspect is male, about five feet eight inches, suffers from a disfiguring skin condition, and has a green mohawk. He was last seen in a gray sweatshirt. The female victim is multiracial, with dark skin and light brown hair. If you see either of them, please call 911 immediately. Do not attempt to engage with either of them as they may be dangerous."

I grabbed Karnath's arm, but he had already heard. Luckily no one else appeared to be listening. Resa was shouting, *Run, run, just drop the stuff and run!*

I answered, *No, at this point that would call more attention to us.*

Quietly I took all the products from Karnath and jerked my head at him to quietly leave the store. He ambled out with impressive casualness. I snatched a hat from a nearby rack and added it to my armful of purchases.

The heavyset man ahead of me finished paying for his purchases and went out. I hadn't had a chance to catch much of the purchasing ritual. If there was something I had to say, I would be at a loss; my earbud only helped me understand, it couldn't tell me how to speak English.

I laid my things on the counter and waited. Luckily all the woman behind the counter said, without looking at me, was, "Find everything all right?"

"Mm-hm," I grunted. I did know that one.

She scanned everything with a handheld laser and stuffed it all into a filmy plastic bag. "That'll be twelve sixty-nine."

I held out one of Karnath's slips of paper money. She frowned, examined it, took out a marker and scribbled on it. At last she slipped it into a drawer and counted out change for me. It came to quite a few slips, plus several metal counters. I held out my hand and she dropped it all in. "Y'all have a nice day now."

I waited a second, afraid that if I took the bag and walked out prematurely, I'd be considered a shoplifter. But she was looking at the woman behind me, so I must be finished. I grabbed the bag and hurried out.

Outside, I handed the money back to Karnath. "There was all this left over after I bought the things."

He pocketed it and dug the sunglasses out of the bag to put on. He still looked suspicious, but at least there were now no alien features visible. "Come on, let's get out of the open."

Behind the fuel depot was a patch of bare earth leading up to a hedge separating it from a back alley. We sat down and tried out the food. Karnath laboriously sounded out the labels. "Pork … rinds. An animal product, I think. That one's for me. These chips … look like they're made out of grain." He handed them to me with an odd sideways glance.

What does that look mean? I asked Resa.

He's trying to see if you're still mad at him.

I wasn't angry.

She gave a little sniff of disbelief rather than answering. I find she projects a great deal of her emotional nature on me.

"The further west we go, the less populous it will get," said Karnath. "But it will take days to get out of these suburbs. The humans like to sprawl all around their cities."

Resa braided our hair and wrapped it around our head to fit under the cap I'd bought. Karnath watched. "It's funny, I'm getting so I can tell which one of you is doing something, even when you're using both hands."

"It's that the left hand is dominant," I said, tilting my head to help her out. "Though it's no mystery. I don't have the coordination to braid hair."

He finished his snacks and carefully folded up the bag to put back into his pocket. "I can barely stay awake any longer. I know this is no place to sleep, but . . . I just don't think I can walk to any place that would be any better."

He was right. There was nowhere in this planet a person could sit and rest, not if you didn't belong there. My home town had public benches on every street, water fountains, public restrooms, public streetcars. All free to anyone. Here, everything seemed to be either private property or a business.

"It's all right," I said. "We're out of sight of the road, at least, and I'll be awake keeping an eye out. I'll wake you if someone comes."

He curled up in his little ball on his side and was soon asleep. I watched his face as it relaxed into unconsciousness. It was a shock to see how much tension left it. He wasn't tense at all when I met him. He was in his own territory, with no concern but learning. Now he carried the burden, not only of keeping safe on this alien planet, but of saving his own world.

I wish we had a blanket for him, said Resa.

I sat, eating my salty chips and resting my back against the back of the shop. This wasn't the sort of tour I might have dreamed of, when I had asked Townsend if we could leave the facility. But it was still a chance to see Earth, see the people and the culture and the biome. Mentally I set my worry and my physical discomfort on a shelf, and focused instead on the small birds that hopped in the hedge and the sound of the traffic and the music drifting out of the shop. Worrying wouldn't make us any safer; all it could do is rob me of any enjoyment I might get on this journey.

Suddenly my attention was drawn to a couple coming around the side of the building. The man was sucking on one of the flaming sticks they sold in the shop, and the woman was talking to him and laughing. They stopped when they noticed us, and the woman put her hand on the man's arm, lowering her voice to a whisper.

I tensed. Had they seen the police report? But the man came up to us politely. "Excuse me, ma'am, are you all right? Is your boyfriend all right?" He made a gesture to Karnath.

I nodded and tried to gesture that everything was fine, but the man kept standing there, earnestly insistent. "Do you need a ride or something? Or a meal?"

I hated to do it, because he'd only slept an hour or so, but I reached down and shook Karnath's shoulder. "There are people here, I need you to talk to them."

He unfolded himself, careful only to bend in ways humans could, and checked a gesture to rub his covered face. "Oh—ah—how do you do?"

The man repeated his question. Karnath got to his feet. "We go to . . . ah . . . Westvirginia. A very long way I think. We . . . meet friends there. We thought there was a bus, but I don't see a bus."

"No, there's no bus," said the man. He exchanged a look with the woman. "We can't take you that far. But we can drop y'all in Winchester if you want."

Karnath looked at me, and I nodded. It wasn't risk-free, but on the other hand we had to get ahead of our pursuers. A car would leave no scent trail. "Thank you very much," he said.

The man dropped his flaming stick on the ground and scuffed it with his shoe. "Come on," he said. "Truck's over here."

As we came around the building, I saw a small group heading up the sidewalk. It was the uniformed earthlings and the dog. Here already? I had hoped, with our trick of walking in the creek and the pace we'd kept, we had bought ourselves some distance. I started to understand how the early humans' prey might have felt, watching the hunters approach, slow but unflagging.

We followed the couple closely, trying not to look panicked. The dog was half a block away and moving quickly. How long before it reached us?

"That's a pretty language you two talk," the woman was saying. "Where are y'all from?"

Karnath thought fast. "Ah … Kenya."

"Really? Wow. Long way from home, then."

We climbed into the truck, which had a large front compartment and a tiny back seat, and a massive rear cargo space. Through the window, I could see the dog reaching the fuel depot parking lot. Would he follow our original path, inside the store, or would he realize we'd recrossed it and go straight to the truck?

The man turned the key and the truck rumbled to life. The dog was hesitating, confused about which path to follow. Then we were moving, and a second later had pulled out of the parking lot.

"Wonder what the K9 squad is out here looking for," said the woman.

"Drugs, probably," said the man. "There's heroin everywhere these days. Even a nice town like this."

"Are you from this area?" Karnath asked politely.

"Nah, we're from Strasburg," he said. "Came up to visit my mama in the hospital." He looked over his shoulder at Karnath. "Name's Dave, and this is Sarah Beth."

"I am … Keith, and my friend is Tammy."

"Huh, I didn't know they used names like that in Kenya."

I froze. "You would be surprised," improvised Karnath. That seemed to satisfy Dave, who went on talking cheerfully. Luckily he didn't expect much response. He had a lot of opinions about foreign people ("I hope no one around here gave you any trouble, I think people here are sweet but you never know, there's always one") and how people should help each other without relying on the government ("what do we even need welfare for when people can just walk up and help each other? Maybe they'd walk up and lend a hand more if people didn't expect the government to handle everything") and the weather ("gonna be like this all week, I'm pretty sure, Sarah Beth don't like it but I do").

The shops slid by outside the window. Resa fidgeted anxiously with the hem of our shirt. We were going so slow, often stopping for a traffic signal. How long before someone would come running on the sidewalk, shouting at the truck to stop?

Dave turned on some music and stopped talking. We passed through a last signal and sped up, leaving the business district behind. For awhile the road wound among bristly trees, partially shielding large houses from view.

The song ended, and an announcer started to talk. "Another reminder, the police are still searching for the potential kidnapper. We are being told he was last spotted in Marshall. Be very cautious and don't pick up hitchhikers." Our descriptions followed.

Dave took no notice, or seemed not to, but I shot Karnath a nervous glance. What if he was driving us into danger? Karnath gave his head a slight shake. No worries, or nothing we could possibly do? The truck was moving far too fast for us to get out.

"Is Strasburg a nice place to live?" he asked desperately, trying to interrupt the news broadcast.

"It's a'right," Dave answered. "You looking for a place to settle down?"

"No, we … we live in New York," Karnath answered. "Our friends live in this region. We are visiting."

"While you're here, you've got to try the trails. Good hiking out in West Virginia."

Karnath made conversation with him about parks and hiking trails for some time. I stared anxiously out the window. Were we even going the right way?

"Aren't you hot?" Dave asked after a while. "I'm sweating in my t-shirt, I don't know how you're staying alive."

"The sun bothers my skin," said Karnath. "I have to keep it covered."

"Here, I'll turn up the AC." He flicked a dial and cold air started blowing. A new song came on the radio and he drummed on the steering wheel along to the music..

I leaned close to Karnath. "Can your map tell if we're going the right way?"

He showed me. A yellow dot traced along a road. "This is the way he said he'd go."

I relaxed a fraction. Every mile we went was a mile further from the uniformed men and the dog, a mile we wouldn't have to walk and wouldn't leave a scent.

The houses grew further apart, and I saw open fields with large animals.

Periodically we slowed down to pass through a small town. "Should we try to escape?" Karnath asked me quietly.

I shook my head. There was no real cause for alarm, and we were cutting days off our journey. I hoped it wasn't a terrible mistake.

Karnath's map showed us approaching the city Dave had named, when suddenly the yellow dot moved off the route marked. "Excuse me," said Karnath. "Is this the right way?"

Dave exchanged a glance with Sarah Beth. "Um, just looking for a gas station."

Karnath inspected his map. "This road does not lead to a gas station," he said to me softly. "It leads to a government enforcement building."

My eye widened in horror. After Dave had been so friendly! I eased off my seatbelt and looked out the window. The pavement whizzed by outside. If I flung open the door and tried to leap out, I'd be badly hurt if not killed.

There was a quiet sound as a switch closed itself on the door. "C'mon now," said Dave. "Don't be like that. I'm trying to help you."

If only I could talk to him! Instead I moved as close as I could to Karnath and seized his arm, catching Dave's eye in the mirror beseechingly. Couldn't he see I wasn't being kidnapped?

But he only clicked his tongue. "Stockholm syndrome," he said, a phrase my earpiece couldn't translate.

We pulled into a large parking lot surrounding a boxy gray building.

The truck pulled up to a closed black metal gate. Dave opened his window to press a bell, muttering, "Wish I would've called first."

Karnath took advantage of the distraction to flip the lock switch on his door and fling himself out. I followed a second later. But before we had gotten far from the parking lot, the gate opened and earthlings in brown uniforms charged out. Karnath easily outdistanced them, though I knew he would soon tire. I was not so lucky. One of the earthlings made a grab for me and brought me to the ground hard on Resa's shoulder. I went limp, letting them fasten our wrists together behind us.

I watched Karnath clear a hedge at the end of the parking lot. Good. At least one of us was getting away. But when he checked over his shoulder and saw me, he stopped and slowly came back, hands raised in the air. So much for that small victory.

A few minutes later we were sitting together in a small room with three chairs and a table. A large mirror covered one wall. Our handcuffs had been removed, but the door was locked. "One-way glass," said Karnath. "They're watching us."

I glared at him. "That was very foolish, what you did."

"What? Trying to escape?"

"Turning back for me," I said. "How does it make sense to give yourself up? They weren't aiming their guns at you. You could have gotten away."

"I couldn't leave without you," he protested.

"What good do you think you can do me in here? If you'd been thinking rationally, you'd have circled around and tried to rescue me from outside."

He opened his mouth and shut it. "I ... I didn't think of that."

I sighed and leaned my head against the mirrored window. Nothing to be done about it now. Idly I noticed that with my head shadowing the light from behind me, I could see a little bit through the window. Outside was some kind of office, with desks separated by partitions.

The door to the room swung open, admitting a heavyset man with a reddish-brown beard and a tall, muscular blond woman, both in brown uniforms. The woman was saying, "So since they fit the description, do we just phone it in to the FBI and let them handle it?"

The man shook his head. "There's more to the description that was kept confidential. If this is them, you'll see why." He leaned his hands on the table, looking at Karnath. "I'm going to have to ask you to take off your hood and your sunglasses."

Karnath glanced at me, and I gave him a small nod. Not much point resisting, as powerless as we were.

The woman gasped as she took in Karnath's green crest, gray skin, and yellow eyes. "Is that even—human?"

"I have no earthly notion," said the man, pulling a folded paper from his pocket and handing it to her, "but he's definitely our man. They want the woman, too. We are not supposed to question them at all, just place the call and wait for pickup."

The woman furrowed her brow. "That's sketchy as hell. Some secret government project, I guess."

"We'll never know." He turned to go.

Karnath interrupted. "I am not human. My name is Karnath 371, of Curiosity sect, of the planet Shatak. My companion Tria il Resa is from the planet Kinaru. We request—" He faltered. What could we request? Did we have legal rights? Eleanor had said we did not. "We request to be allowed to leave. We have committed no crime and done no harm to anyone."

Except stealing Eleanor's money and knocking out that guard, I added silently.

We couldn't help that, said Resa.

The blond woman looked at the man in concern. "Do we really have to make the call?"

"It's not our job to deal with this," he said. "I'm not putting my neck out for this—creature. Let the FBI figure it out."

"The people who are after us are not good," Karnath insisted, limited by his poor command of English. "If they catch us, they will do great harm. Maybe war between our people."

The man finally addressed him. "Look. I'm sorry. You'll have to take it up with the people who are coming to get you. It's above my pay grade."

With that, he left. The woman gave us both a backward glance before following him out.

Karnath blew out his breath. "So much for that."

"I'm getting a very negative impression of humans so far," I said. "Every time I think they aren't all bad, they disappoint me."

"I think the woman wanted to help," he argued.

"It doesn't do us any good if all the people who want to help are too afraid of other humans to actually do it."

I stood up and examined the room. Nothing that could be used as a weapon. No outlets. The door was locked again. The ceiling looked solid, except for a rectangular light panel and a spiky prong, maybe a water sprinkler in case of fire. In one corner was a square air vent, blowing cool, dry air. "If only that were bigger," I said. "It probably comes from outside."

Karnath stood under it and reached up to measure it with his hands. "It's big enough for me."

"Really? Your shoulders are bigger than that vent."

He made an odd movement, rolling his shoulders in toward his chest. "My whole body is compressible. If my head can fit through, the rest of me can. Not sure how to twist out these fasteners, though."

I peered through the one-way glass. There were several people in the office outside, but none of them seemed to be watching us. I shoved a chair into the corner and climbed up to look at the fasteners. They had a slot at the top, as if to match a dedicated tool. *It's hopeless. We don't have a tool like that.*

Have you never heard of improvising? said Resa, pulling out the kitchen knife from her pants pocket. The end slotted easily into the fasteners and she spun them out with a twist of her wrist. Carefully we eased the grate off.

Inside, the duct bent sharply to head along the ceiling. "Are you sure you can do this?" I asked as I climbed down from the chair. "What if it turns too sharply? What if there are fans inside?"

"Then I'll back up till I'm back here. I'm more worried about you. There's no way you can fit through here."

I eyed the duct. There certainly was not, and the thought of trying, and possibly getting stuck, made me shudder. "Once you're outside, you'll have more options than in here. Though if you can't get me out . . . you need to go on alone. Get to the ship and stop Unity. I'll likely be safe in the meantime."

He tucked his chin to his chest obstinately. "I'll consider that when I've run out of other options."

It was the best I was going to get. After one last check for anyone watching, I boosted him on my shoulders up to the vent. He caught hold of the inside of the duct, and his legs slithered out of sight.

We quickly replaced the panel and the fasteners and sat down, trying to look innocent. It didn't take long before the door banged open. "Where's the alien?" the bearded man demanded.

I shrugged. "I don't speak human." He wouldn't understand me, but he'd get the idea.

He charged into the room, inspecting under the table and thumping on the walls. In his surprise, he failed to shut the door behind him. I bolted through the open door and froze for a second, not sure which direction to go. Away from the office area, I decided, and took off at a run.

I saw one of the red signs that humans put in all their buildings, to direct people toward the exits, and dashed toward it. But in my way, I saw the blond officer, feet planted wide as if to stop me. Putting my head down, I just kept running, hoping she would dodge aside. Instead, she drew back her arm for a punch. I tried to stop, but it was too late—she landed her fist right on the side of my jaw. Everything went black.

Resa

I was too startled when the blow connected to do anything but let myself be dragged to the floor. The woman gave us only a brief glance before stepping over us to go farther into the building. "The female detainee tried to make a runner. I took her down, can I get an assist? She may need first aid."

Tria? There was no answer. Panic seized my lungs. If she was dead, I would be soon. But I couldn't think of that. The only possibilities that mattered were if she was alive. If she was alive, she needed me to get her to safety. So I scrambled to my feet.

I passed beneath the red sign and reached the double glass door. It opened easily to a push. Ducking out of sight beside the door, I hesitated for a moment. If Tria had had a clear plan, she hadn't shared it with me. Maybe she was hoping to make one up as she went along. But that was a skill I wasn't confident in. I had never in my life had to manage any kind of emergency alone.

I put my hand on my heart, as if I could soothe its pounding. Think. I had three goals: to hide, to find Karnath, and to escape. I wasn't sure what to do first, so I looked around. To my right was a broad square duct, attached to a large, whirring machine. The ventilation system. My spirits lifted: Karnath would be here! A moment later they came crashing down: there was no clear exit, only the machine. Full of sharp fans, surely.

I slipped into the shadow of the duct. If he had made it this far, he would need my help to get out. Tentatively I rapped on the side.

There was an answering double-knock, and I almost cried out with relief. Pulling my knife from my pocket, I pried at a seam until a panel of sheet metal came off. Karnath came blinking into the light, dust coating his clothes and sticking in his crest. "You made it out! Are you all right?" He tilted his head to look at me more closely. "You're hurt."

"Tria is hurt," I said. I wanted to say more, to beg him to examine her, but now was not the time. "We can't stand here."

To my relief, he took charge, peering out from behind the ventilation machine. When the coast was clear, he pulled me by the hand, away from the police station and down the hill.

Tria would have urged him to let go, to use his faster sprinting ability to get clear and let us catch up later as best we could. I only clung to his hand and poured on all the speed I had. It was a strange feeling, hand in hand with an alien to save someone we both cared about. I only hoped she would be all right.

CHAPTER SIXTEEN

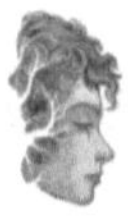

Tria

When I came to, I was outside, sitting on a steep bank. Above my head was some kind of bridge. At the bottom of the bank, cars were whizzing by, six lanes of them, making a loud roar. My head throbbed. *Where are we?*

Tria! You're all right! Oh gods, you had me so scared.

What happened?

The woman punched you. We hit the ground. She ran past you to get help. Once she was out of sight, I got up and went outside. It didn't occur to her to watch me, because she knew she'd knocked you out.

Very smart! What about Karnath, where is he?

She turned our head, making fresh pain shoot through it, and I saw he was sitting to our left. "Is she awake yet?" he asked anxiously.

"I'm awake," I said. "Still dizzy."

"You've got that in common with humans, too," he remarked. "Sensitive to blows to the head. I guess your skulls are thinner than ours."

I fingered my bruised jaw. "I'd be in trouble if I ever got in a fight with one of you."

"Not really. If you can manage to restrict our breathing, we pass out very quickly. Our brains go into an inactive state to avoid damage."

"I will remember that." I certainly hoped I would never need that information, but since Unity must be looking for us, it was wise of him to mention. I squinted at him, the bright sun hurting my eyes. "You made it out through the vents?"

"With Resa's help. I didn't see anyone after us yet. It may be they're waiting for the others who were looking for us."

I nodded slowly. Resa sniffed hard. *I was really scared,* she repeated. *I thought you might be—well…*

Dead?

Karnath said he didn't think so, since I was still alive, but he couldn't be sure without a brain scanner.

I'm proud of you, I said. *You've never had to handle an emergency on your own before.*

She smiled, pleased. *I'm a lot more capable than you think, Tria. Eleanor said so.*

She was right, of course. She was a full person in her own right, but I nearly always had control. When she used the whole body, it was to cook dinner or tie our shoes—tasks I wasn't coordinated enough to do, but rarely anything important. For the first time, I wondered if that was enough.

At the present, though, we had more urgent concerns. In front of us, the highway yawned like a canyon. There were far too many cars for there to be a gap where we could cross safely, and they were hurtling much too fast to stop for us.

"These earthlings certainly do like their cars," I said weakly. "It seems to be their main form of travel."

"They value their independence," Karnath explained. "A train or a pod-tube relies on everyone going the same direction. Humans want to be able to go in any direction they want, at a moment's notice, and have all their things with them too."

"There's always walking," I said. "But their cities are so huge, it seems you can walk for days without reaching the end. If we had walked for a day in my hometown, we would have gotten out of the center, through the orchards, and into the brush." I thought longingly of my little town, perched on the hillsides, red tile roofs marching down toward the river. I used to walk every day from my house at the riverside to the university. For larger trips, the train station was conveniently in the middle of town. I had never thought of it as particularly small—smaller than the capital, of course, but a fair-sized town with its own university and hospital. Earth's towns seemed to sprawl endlessly, almost running from one into the next.

"Earth is very populous. Nine billion people, and on a planet no larger than yours. Smaller, really, since so much of the surface is water."

I turned this over in my mind. Nine billion was a number I couldn't even process. Take every person on my planet, turn them into twenty people, and you'd have a sense of it. "It's a wonder they found a place to park the ship, with all these houses everywhere."

"Especially in this region. While we were in the truck earlier, I narrowed down our search to a few possible landing sites. There are a limited number of wilderness areas, and most of those are open to the public. They wouldn't want hikers stumbling over it." He showed me his map. All of the sites were to the west, on the other side of the highway and past the city beyond.

"How are we going to get over there?" I gestured to the opposite bank.

"The bridge," he said. "We'll be conspicuous, and there's no way to help leaving an obvious trail for the dogs, but it's really the only way. There's no other bridge for over a mile. Are you ready to move though?"

Carefully I stood up. It made the dizziness worse, but I could handle it. "I have to be," I said. "We're far too close to the station to stay here any longer."

We started walking, crossing the terrifying bridge over the freeway on a narrow sidewalk. The barrier on the edge was only waist-height, so I could see the cars zooming down below and passing under my feet. Behind us, though, I saw no police cars or anyone on foot. On the other side, we switched to a less busy road, looking for a way through the city as quickly as possible while sticking to side streets the police might be less likely to check.

It took the rest of the afternoon to get out of the middle of the city. The shops beside the road began to be replaced by narrow rows of houses, stuck together to save space, and then by large businesses surrounded by parking lots and borders of trees. The only streets that went the way we needed were many lanes wide, full of confusing traffic going all directions.

It was almost impossible to navigate the intersections, until we watched another pedestrian operating a button that eventually opened up a gap in the traffic. Still, it seemed these roads gave priority to cars, and more than once a car turned where we were crossing, barely missing us.

We stopped for dinner at a small, busy restaurant, where the workers shoved food in sacks within minutes. Outside the restaurant, sitting at an outdoor table, Karnath displayed the contents of the bag he'd purchased. "I wasn't sure what there would even be for either of us to eat. I did get a salad for you, because I remember salad is a plant food, although it looks a little green to be edible. And for me, these fried things. I think the inside is meat, but I can't really tell to look at it." He broke one open and peered suspiciously at the interior.

I opened the plastic container and examined the salad. It was certainly very green, but it tasted all right, and included a sprinkle of nuts on top. There was a little tub of sauce to go with it, which I dipped the leaves in before eating them.

The last item in the bag was a carton of fried, starchy sticks. I wasn't sure what they had been, but they tasted passable, if very salty. It didn't seem very healthy. Left food, we called that kind of thing back home. We resumed walking, passing the carton back and forth until it was gone.

As the sun dipped toward the horizon, we came fully out of the city, into an area where scrub land was interspersed with warehouses and truck depots. We passed an enormous sporting facility with rolling green hills and little flags, where people zipped over the manicured ground cover in miniature cars. Periodically we would cross through another major intersection, where businesses clustered, but the spaces between these became larger and larger. It still wasn't wilderness, but at least it was less-managed space—farmland and broad fields with no obvious purpose.

We slept that night in a crop field—tall, leafy stalks that sheltered us fully from view. Karnath pulled off his hood, glasses, and bandanna before sitting on the ground with a sigh of relief. "I don't think I have ever walked so far in my life," he said. "Is it possible we've escaped pursuit?"

"I don't know. A car could catch up to us in half an hour."

"But in that whole city we passed through, there are so many places we might have gone. They won't track us here."

"What about the dog?"

"I don't know. They'd have had to bring it from where we were before, and once it's tracking us, they have to go at walking pace."

"So it might come upon us tonight?" I imagined its long snout and sharp teeth, coming upon me while I slept. And more frightening, the earthlings with it, eager to hide our existence on their planet. Would they try to recapture us, or give up and simply destroy us? After two escapes, they might decide we weren't worth the risk of keeping alive.

"I hope not," said Karnath. "We have come so far, and changed direction so many times." He was silent a little, and then said, "Anyway, I'll be awake most of the night."

I slept fitfully, though more comfortably than the night before, thanks to the soft ground of the cropland. My dreams were full of running, chasing, speeding cars, and biting dogs. Later, seeing Karnath had woken up and was sitting up beside me, I fell into a deeper sleep, reassured that someone was watching for danger.

I was awakened before dawn by drops of water falling on my face. I sat up quickly. "What is happening?"

Karnath was sitting serenely, face tilted up toward the sky. "Just rain. Very good luck for us. It should wash away any scent trail we left."

The fat drops were suddenly everywhere, pattering on the leaves of the crops and turning the ground into mud. I scrambled to my feet, pulling my hat on. The bill of it at least sheltered my face. My short-sleeved shirt offered no such protection to the rest of me; I shivered as the drops hit my skin.

Karnath shucked off his sweatshirt and handed it to me. "Here. If you don't want to be wet, this might help."

I made as if to refuse. "And you *do* want to be wet?"

"It rains hard often on Shatak. I don't mind it, and my clothes are made for it." It was true; the water ran off his bodysuit as easily as off the leaves. His gray scales developed a damp sheen, but he didn't seem uncomfortable.

I put on the sweatshirt, and it did help. I was not accustomed to rain. My home is in a rainshadow; almost all the water we get comes from the river that flows down from the mountains. Occasionally we have a rainy day, or, in the wintertime, snow, but we stay inside if we can.

Still, the rain was not really cold, though a cool wind was behind it. High in the sky, massive slate-gray clouds piled upon each other and bore down on us. The rain turned from big drops to a steady pour, like someone emptying jugs over our heads.

There were enough clouds in the sky that it would surely go on for some time, so there was nothing to do but accept it and go on with our plans. I picked some of the heavy grain heads from the plants— assuming that, if the plant was being cultivated on purpose, it must be edible. Sure enough, the yellow seeds were juicy and delicious, though I had to scrape them from the dense core with my teeth.

When I offered one to Karnath, he said he had already eaten— presumably the native insects. That sort of food was convenient to find, at least.

We walked on through rain, squinting ahead through the heavy downpour to the barely-visible road ahead of us. When cars sped by, they splattered out huge sheets of water, drenching us even more. After about an hour, the thunderheads passed on, revealing a bright sun. The damp heat came back, damper than ever. My wet clothes clung stickily to my body, refusing to dry.

The ground sloped upward, giving us a better view of the rolling hills on the horizon. Resa, for once, wasn't complaining. *How are you holding up?*

Her mental voice brimmed with barely-restrained excitement. *This place is familiar, I know it is!*

I turned around to look at the road from the other direction. I had no real memory of it, but I knew remembering visual data wasn't one of my talents, and I hadn't paid much attention to the route in the darkness. "Does this look familiar to you at all?" I asked Karnath.

He turned around as well, looking at the contours of the land and the thick trees on either side of the road. "Some. You think you recognize it?"

"Resa does. Pay attention and see if you recognize any landmarks as we go on."

It wasn't till we passed a rock quarry that he was convinced. "Yes! I do remember this." From then on, he kept careful track, cross-checking it with his map.

The sun was high overhead and our shadows had nearly vanished when we found the spot where we had been bundled into the car. There was a narrow band of trees bordering the road, with a large gap where we had come through that night. Beyond was the open field I remembered. It all seemed different in the daylight, and with eyes now accustomed to Earth plant life.

The only sign of what was beyond was a notice stapled to a tree. Karnath laboriously sounded it out. "'Posted: No Trespassing.' I hope there are no security measures that we can't see."

"Even if the humans have no such thing, won't they be watching from the ship?"

"Yes, unfortunately. And there's not a lot we can do about it. We can hide from sight, but if they're monitoring the area around them, they'll see us. My only consolation is that, with only three people, they might not spare a person for that job. Especially if they're busy negotiating with the humans. They might not even be there at all."

Wouldn't that be nice, Resa said optimistically. *We could saunter in, free the spacers, and launch.*

It certainly would, but I wouldn't count on it.

We looped around behind the ship, detouring far from the original spot where we had begun. At the very least, we could come from a direction they weren't expecting. The area was thick with trees and undergrowth. We scrambled over crags and down gullies, scratched with brambles. Some tiny sucking insects kept biting at me, leaving welts. Karnath seemed completely unperturbed—perhaps his blood wasn't palatable to them.

Eventually we approached the crag where the *Galajak* had been, but of course it wasn't visible. We felt our way along the rock with our hands, waiting for the moment when we would meet the hologram and our hands would pass through.

But that moment never came. We made a full loop of the crag, which stuck out into the field on three sides, and found no ship. "Is this the wrong place?" I asked incredulously. Even I recognized the spot now. It was exactly as it had been that night—except for the missing ship.

We went over the area more thoroughly, until Karnath spotted, on the ground, the deep indentation the ship had left. "It *was* here," he said. "Now it's gone."

I stood in the middle of the imprint, looking around. From the outside, it really was not that big—three levels, each of which was only a little taller than my head, added up to a circle about as large as a house. The ship itself had been much taller, but the print it made was less impressive.

"I just don't understand it," said Karnath. "I thought this was the ship they were going to leave, and they would escape on the *Vatarax*. The *Vatarax* is big enough to hold much more cargo."

"Does it look like it took off?" I kicked at the crushed ground cover. "Wouldn't the engines have burned up the ground?"

He flattened his crest respectfully. "You're right, they would have. No, it didn't take off from here. It must have been taken away."

We inspected the field carefully, the pieces falling into place. Here were the tracks of large wheels, now filled with rainwater from the storm. Here were deep divots where a crane's braces might have dug into the ground. The humans had come, not the Shatakazan, and taken the ship somewhere else.

"But *where?*" asked Karnath in frustration. "We came all the way here!"

"Probably somewhere closer, where they could study it," I said. "The whole ship is a gift for them; they'll want it in a secure facility where they can take it apart and learn about it."

"Not the one where we were kept, though. It isn't nearly big enough." He stared at the ground morosely, crest flat. "It could be anywhere by now! And as for the crew ... there's no clue what they might have done with them."

CHAPTER SEVENTEEN

Tria

We rested for a while in the shelter of the trees. Karnath slept. I had a doze myself, having been tired since the rain had awakened me. Then I just sat, with my back against a tree, and tried not to get discouraged. We were, at any rate, free. We were learning how to survive on Earth. And the ship hadn't left the planet. That ought to make it possible for us to find it, if we put in enough time.

But the more crucial goal, stopping Unity sect from taking off with their cargo of Earth weapons, was more time-sensitive. I had thought finding the *Galajak* would help with that—at least we would have the crew to help us, and any equipment on board. Without our ship, we had no clue how to find the other, or Tazag and his friends. Perhaps we had misjudged, coming all the way out here. We should have tracked down the lab's sponsors first. Maybe Karnath could have hacked the network to find out where they had come from, where their base was.

Then again, that information would have done us little good as long as we were still captives. And the second we escaped, we would have had to worry first about evading capture. If we had tried to remain in the area, looking for another base, we would have easily been picked up.

Resa remained optimistic despite our disappointment. *I am sure you and Karnath will figure something out.*

Thanks, I groaned. *The vote of confidence is nice, but ideas would be more helpful.*

My idea is, I bet Eleanor would help you if you could get in touch with her.

Her? I all but asked her for help and she said her job was more important.

But she wanted to help. I know it. If she could help you without getting caught, she would.

Maybe Resa was right. I thought of the distracted biologist—not exactly warm, but genuine. And she saw me as a person. I couldn't say more than that. But Resa was a good judge of people sometimes. Maybe I had made a mistake not listening to her before. After all, Eleanor herself had reminded me that Resa was as intelligent as I was—that I shouldn't take her different talents and emotional nature as a sign of inferiority.

When Karnath woke up, I asked him about it. "Is it possible, do you think, to contact her somehow? Through the network you got into at the facility?"

He pursed his lips. "Oh, I wouldn't want to do that ... anything I send to that network will be visible to Townsend. But perhaps there is another way ..." He took his device out and got to work. In a few minutes he had found a listing for an Eleanor Carroll, Ph.D, working at the biology department of a local university several years ago.

"How is that any good? She doesn't work there anymore."

"But there's a phone number," he said. "And a network address. Perhaps one of those will still work." He tinkered awhile longer before composing the message. *To Eleanor Carroll. From K and T/R. We are safe. Can you contact us?* He ran it through a translation matrix and sent it. "I wish I knew whether earthlings keep their addresses for life, or change them often."

"If that doesn't work, is there anything else you can try?"

"Might be able to dig up a home address. But it would be a long walk to her house. And not really safe to show up there without first ensuring she is on our side."

But a return message did come, with surprising promptness. *Oh thank God you are all right I have been so worried. Townsend went nuts when you went missing. I felt sure you had escaped on your own and more power to you.*

The final idiom confused me. Was it a blessing, or a curse? We wrote back, *Are you going to tell Townsend?*

Of course not. Do you need help? Can't imagine how you are managing on your own.

We looked at each other. She could be leading us on, being fed lines from Townsend. But somehow I didn't think that was her way. She might be insensitive sometimes, but never dishonest. *We are all right for now. We wanted to know what has been happening there.*

Not a lot. I am still working on the immune cells. I guess my job lasts as long as there is still work to do with those. They took Mike away from me though. Townsend went away a long time yesterday and came back with a bunch of new equipment, so everyone but me is working on that.

"Equipment from the ship," I said. *We really need to know where that equipment is coming from.*

I don't know. Can I pick you up? I don't know if you have a place to stay but my house has room. We could talk it over.

"That's suspicious," I said. "Don't you think? She brought it up out of the blue. She'll bring Townsend right to us."

"I don't think so," said Karnath. "It's her way of taking care of people. Like making you the cocoa, or the time she brought in cricket candy for me."

Karnath is right, said Resa. *She is worried and wants to see you and doesn't want to keep emailing back and forth. That's all it is.*

"Resa agrees with you, so I guess I'm outvoted," I said. We sent Eleanor directions for a place to meet us—by the rock quarry, where we should be able to wait out of sight until we'd ensured she had come alone.

When Eleanor's car pulled up at the quarry, she wasn't alone. A little girl with straight black hair was sitting in the back seat. But there was no sign of Townsend, so we nervously stepped out from the bushes and approached the car.

"I'll get in the front seat, so I don't scare the little girl," suggested Karnath, as Eleanor reached over to open the door.

"Oh, no, she's dying to see a real alien," said Eleanor. "Go sit by her and let her ask you lots of questions. She'll love it." So I ended up in the front seat.

"Is Townsend going to notice you are gone today?" I asked.

"No, it's a Saturday. Most humans don't work Saturdays."

On Kinaru, too, we have a day that is not for work. It happens every five days. Resa always wants to go to religious services. As a nonbeliever, I don't enjoy them, but it's only fair to participate in things she likes for a change. The other four days, after all, she gets dragged to my work.

"So, what is going on?" she asked. "Why are you so desperate to find out where the fancy tech is coming from?"

I explained what we had theorized about Unity sect's deal with the government, the fold-capable ship in trade for the weapons.

Eleanor's face grew serious, frowning through her thick glasses at the road ahead. "Karnath told you right that our weapons are dangerous. Their effects on organic tissue are—horrifying. No wonder they are banned on other planets. They ought to be banned on ours. The only thing is—who goes first? The US keeps a stock of them in case the other countries use theirs. But trading them away to aliens? That's—that's wildly unethical."

"I assume that's why they are keeping all this so secret."

"No kidding."

"What we need to know from you is—are you on our side with this? Will you help us? I don't want to stay at your house if there's any suspicion you'll turn us over."

She was silent awhile, turning the wheel to round a corner it had taken us forever to trudge around. "I'm on your side," she said at last. "I can't countenance that kind of violence. I've seen what those weapons do to a person—it's inhuman."

"So are the intended victims," I reminded her. "All of the violence will be happening far away, to people of a different species from you."

"I don't see that making a difference to *you*," she answered. "You would have blended in on Earth a lot better if you had left Karnath behind, but you didn't."

"He is a person," I said defensively.

"Exactly. It's not really any different."

My spirits lifted. I hadn't had high expectations for the humans, given their world was so chaotic and warlike. But they were surprising me. At least individually, they were capable of all the same rational moral judgments I was.

But I thought of the busy highway we had seen yesterday, and felt doubtful. Individual humans might be all right, but in groups they behaved in ways that struck me as irrational, even dangerous. A person who got in the way of that might be very badly hurt. After all, at least some humans had heard Unity's plan and decided to go along with it.

Eleanor's house was on a quiet residential street, in a little pocket of a neighborhood branching off a large road, like so many we had walked by in the past two days. She parked in a vehicle bay attached to the house, which was a relief to me—no chance of anyone seeing us going in.

"Are you two hungry? I can't imagine what you would have found to eat out there."

Shamefaced, I handed back the remainder of the money we had taken from her purse. "We . . . we borrowed this from you. We weren't sure we could survive otherwise."

She blinked at me. "Huh. Did not even notice. That would have come as a shock next time I tried to go shopping." Taking the bills, she tucked them in her pocket. "Well, at least you didn't starve. But you need a proper meal. Sit. I'll make you something."

Is she angry? I asked Resa, concerned.

No. She is happy we were able to eat.

It wasn't long before she placed before me a plate piled with steaming white grains, with vegetables cut up on top, and salty brown sauce poured over all. A *real* meal—I devoured it gratefully. Karnath had the same, but topped with little pink … things. Eleanor said they were shrimp, a sea creature which was "the closest thing to bugs we eat around here."

"Now," she said, leaning back against the counter, "what are we going to do? What's the plan to stop these friends of yours?"

There was a silence. At last I said, "Our plan was to go back to where the ship was parked and free the spacers that were on it. We thought if we could take that ship somewhere else, the deal would be off. But the ship is gone. They seem to have taken it away on a truck."

"Well, they didn't take it back to our facility. Definitely no room for a spaceship. How big was it?"

I described the size, adding, "And it can be disguised as anything. They have a holographic projector to make it look like whatever they want."

"Still. I would have noticed if something large just appeared in the parking lot, no matter what it looked like." She drummed against her mouth with her fingers. "Well, I don't think it's that far away. Yesterday, when Townsend went away and came back with all the tech, she wasn't gone that long. Maybe a few hours? So if we assume the tech came from your ship, it can't be more than a couple of hours away."

"Is there another government facility within that distance?"

Eleanor chuckled. "There are *hundreds*, Tria. This area is near the capital; everything here is government and government contractors. The funny thing, though . . . hm." She thought for a moment. "Our facility isn't a government building, though. It's just an office building, rented for the purpose. Hence the truly terrible security. I suppose they thought they could protect what they had better with secrecy than by putting it in an actual safe place, like the Pentagon. But no, that doesn't make sense, because with all the people working there, it's not *that* secret."

"Perhaps it's not just secret from the public, but from some of the government," I suggested.

"That's a thought," said Eleanor. "It would explain why there hasn't been much recordkeeping or red tape. I expected there to be no end of it in a government job, but instead there's been nothing. They said because it was secret it was better not to record anything." She furrowed her eyebrows. "Which in retrospect was really fishy, but I was mostly happy to be offered a job that would start right away."

I readily believed Eleanor had been offered the job and paid no attention at all to any little details like that. It was her way, to ignore whatever wasn't in her focus.

"How do we know it is really the government at all?" asked Karnath.

"They did manage to set the police on us," I said doubtfully.

"No one but the government has nuclear weapons," said Eleanor. "So I really don't see how it could be anyone else."

Eleanor's daughter, Mia, came into the kitchen looking for a snack, and Eleanor absently scraped some of the dish she'd made onto a plate for her. "Eat that on the coffee table, okay? You can turn on the TV."

"Yay!" Mia gave an excited skip and rushed out of the room, the food nearly slipping off the plate.

"Maybe we should be looking in that direction, then," said Karnath. "Where does the government store its weapons?"

"That's no better. There must be dozens of sites. Though as far as that goes, most of them are nowhere near here."

I buried my head in my hands. "Then we're at a dead end. No way to find the *Galajak*, or the *Vatarax*, or the spacers."

"Our next step should be to retrieve the three scientists," said Karnath. "We have a safe landing place for them now—well, relatively safe."

"There's no work tomorrow, either," Eleanor said slowly. "It shouldn't be difficult to slip in and get them. I have my badge and they don't have any reason to suspect me."

Karnath's eyes widened. "And if I go along, I can get back into the network and look for information there."

"Having you go in seems much riskier than sending her alone," I objected.

Eleanor shook her head. "The network extends into the parking lot. He can stay in the car."

After Mia had finished her cartoon, Karnath sat on the couch working on his device, trying to delete the virus Prazad had told him about. I sat nearby, watching a program he had selected for me on the television. It was a musical performance, and I wondered if he had been trying to make a point.

"It certainly is very nice," I said politely to Eleanor. "I can't imagine how all of the performers find time to put together such a complex piece of music."

She looked at me blankly for a moment. "It's their job," she said, when she realized what I had failed to grasp. "They practice constantly. This orchestra is the best of the best. People work their entire careers to get into it."

I observed the players with fresh interest. On Kinaru, the arts are a left-work—a hobby, to be done on the side of a real career that the right does. Occasionally there might be enough demand that a left might earn a little fame, like the artist who made Resa's favorite graphic novels, but that was uncommon. There simply weren't hours enough in a day for both partners to have careers. I normally worked twelve hours or more a day—that left some time for Resa to decompress, but not enough for her to have a job of her own. If she minded this, she hadn't mentioned it.

The music had made her cry, and she scrubbed at her cheek with her sleeve. It perplexed me. The music was complex and well-done, but I was unable to appreciate it in the way she did. Clearly Karnath was more of her mind, saying it made life worth living. For me, life was worth living if I was able to discover new things and make the world a better place. Not because a number of musicians combined to make patterned noises.

"This is strange," said Karnath suddenly. "I tried to clear the virus away with my antivirus program, and instead it deleted the antivirus."

"That sounds worrisome."

"I still am not sure what this virus is trying to do. It has access to all programs and appears to have opened several of them, but it isn't impeding function."

"Spyware, probably," said Eleanor. "Did you pick it up here?"

"Prazad didn't think so. Let me check something . . . hm. Now that's unexpected. The virus seems to be running off a base-12 system. I can't think of any species in the sector that uses base-12."

"We do," I said.

He gave me a puzzled look. "Really? Most species use the number of their fingers." He waggled a seven-fingered hand.

"Well, twelve has more factors than ten does," I said. "We've always used twelve. I never really asked why."

He turned back to his device. "Base-12 rules out Earth, Shatak, and the Vray'la at the station. I don't know what other species might have been there, but it would have to be a sophisticated attack to be able to slip this in without our knowing."

Eleanor put in, "Well, the most obvious answer is that you picked it up on Tria's planet, right? You were there awhile."

I shook my head vehemently. "We don't have the technology for this.

We don't even have computer networks, only telephone and radio. Still less could we make a virus that could defeat a Shatakaz program."

Karnath made a tossing motion with one hand, which I had come to recognize as the equivalent of a shrug. "It must have been someone on the station. If we ever make it home, I'll have to report that. It's concerning."

That evening, Eleanor dug through a closet looking for bedding. "I only have one spare room," she said, handing me a pile of folded blankets. "But the bed is a double. You want to share it, or does one of you want the couch?"

I want to share, said Resa, in a tone that brooked no argument.

You've been so quiet all afternoon, and that's the part that gets you interested?

I'm tired. And I've gotten used to having Karnath around at night. I'd be scared to wake up and not have him there.

"We can share," I told Eleanor. "It's not a problem."

I changed into a set of Eleanor's nightclothes and accepted the offer of a new toothbrush. It wasn't designed like I was used to, but it was such a relief to have one. This wasn't a jail, and it wasn't sleeping under a picnic table either. It was a home—not *my* home, but at least *a* home.

I went into the guest room and crawled under the covers. Karnath sat, cross-legged, atop the blankets on the other side. I looked up at him. "I wanted to tell you, I apologize for being skeptical of this plan. It turned out you were right."

He blinked. "It's quite all right. You should always feel free to voice your judgments. And I respect that you considered Resa's opinion valid enough to honor her vote, against your own wishes."

I considered that. "It is hard for me. Sometimes she seems to me . . . excessively optimistic. Too driven by what she wishes rather than by what is. I know she is intelligent and perceptive, but the *ways* she perceives are mysterious to me."

"Both what we wish and what is are important," he said. "Without what we wish, how can we change what is?" Puzzled, I only stared back. "What I mean is, we need both thinkers of thoughts and dreamers of dreams. And Resa has shown her value to our mission more than once."

"Is she mysterious to you? Since she doesn't talk, I mean. Do you feel like you know her at all?"

"Oh, I definitely know her. Better than I know you, I sometimes feel. I suppose you don't see any of it … she is always smiling, or exchanging glances, or gesturing. I can tell how she feels. But you … you're a little hard to read. You aren't as expressive, and I never know if you are being restrained, or if that's all the emotion there is."

"I have emotions!" I protested. "I just … I am not always aware of them. Resa has told me about this. That I am always the last to know how I am feeling."

"It can be an advantage to be impassive as well. It's helped you stay logical. But—just remember to take some quiet sometimes, and listen to your feelings. Ask them where they come from, and what they mean."

I thought about this for a while, after Karnath had taken up his device again and dimmed the light so I could sleep. Resa understood all this feelings talk so much better than I. But I was realizing that, just as Resa had been deprived by not being encouraged to develop her intellectual gifts, so too was I missing out if I failed to understand at least what emotions I did have.

I closed my eyes and thought about my feelings. I felt happy to have a toothbrush, that one was pretty clear. I felt worried about Unity's plan, and our inability to trace the ship. Here my mind tried to race away with me, considering whether Karnath's plan would work and what we might do if it didn't. But I brought my attention back to feelings. Was there anything else?

Yes, I decided. There was a little happy feeling that Karnath was here. Friendship. That was an emotion, certainly. Karnath and I had become friends, and I felt more comfortable with him around than when I was on my own. Chronologically, we had been together for such a short time. But so much had happened since then, it felt like a whole lifetime. Being separated from my planet had been hard; I had not truly absorbed in advance how I might feel about it. But Karnath felt like an echo of home, someone I felt at ease around when surrounded by so many aliens.

With that cheerful thought, I fell asleep.

Resa

I woke up before dawn, blinking up at the shadowy form of Karnath, still sitting on the bed. Or again. Perhaps he had slept. I felt sorry I'd missed it, somehow.

He moved in the semidarkness, looking down at me. "Resa."

I smiled, putting a finger near my lips. I didn't want Tria awake, not just yet.

Strange feeling, come to think of it. After a lifetime of not wanting to be apart, for once I felt content to simply lie here, breathing slowly so I didn't wake her. I wanted, somehow, to relive those terrifying moments when she had been unconscious, when Karnath had taken my hand and pulled me along after him to safety.

Impulsively I edged closer to him, until my shoulder just touched his hip. He looked down at me again, his expression changed and his crest flaring upward in surprise. Could he—would he understand what I was trying to say? He and Tria had woven a tapestry between them, built of words, and I could never understand if it was binding them together or veiling them from each other. Words can be ambiguous. Words can even deceive.

Unfolding one of his long legs, he stretched it out so it lay against my arm. Beside me, Tria slept on.

My breath caught in my throat. I was falling, spinning as I fell, and I wasn't afraid. I sought his eyes, and found they were already on mine. He lowered his eyelids, once, deliberately.

And now what? I wondered. Had I said what I had come to say? Or was I fooling myself, and none of this was a message, only an excuse to be doing what I wanted so badly to do? I averted my glance, ashamed. What in gods' name did I think I was doing? What was the plan? There was no plan, only what I wanted and hadn't been able to resist.

I was brought back to myself with a light touch on my arm. Karnath was looking at me earnestly, a question on his face. After all this time I still kept forgetting, he wasn't a right. He couldn't be fooled and lied to, the way I lied to Tria every day without even thinking about it.

With a slow, even breath for courage, I turned my hand and cupped the side of his leg. Shyly I met his eyes again.

He smiled. Without words, he understood. Delicately, he ran his fingers down my arm, making gooseflesh rise and my breath catch. Then back up, watching me all the while, to see if I liked it.

And did I like it? Say rather, I hummed like strings to a bow, vibrating to a deep golden music only he and I could hear. And he followed the tune flawlessly, the steps of his fingers touching down exactly when the music swelled.

It was a soft, slow, quiet dance. A look. An unspoken question, an unspoken answer. A touch. Here on the wrist, then there, fluttering, on the cheek. I would have let him touch me anywhere.

But all the time, under the warm yellow music, drummed an underbeat of temptation. The temptation to push out of the dance, take it somewhere else, pull him after me into something hotter and darker. I thought about snatching his hand, showing him other places to touch, places he'd never seen or felt, places that were aching for something more.

But I was just, just barely, too wise or too cowardly. Or maybe the dance we were having was too perfect to disrupt.

The light grew and soon, too soon, Tria started to stir. Karnath cupped my cheek, once, lightly, and turned away. I drew a shuddering breath, the shock of the music's ending like cold water. The dance was over and it was time to get back to lying.

CHAPTER EIGHTEEN

Tria

When I awoke, I found I had rolled onto the wrong side of the bed and fetched up against Karnath. He was awake already, but instead of nudging me aside, he had stayed put, working on his device just as he had been when I had fallen asleep.

I sat up hurriedly, pulling my sleep shirt down and smoothing my hair. "You should have woken me," I said. "I didn't mean to intrude on your space."

He tilted his head. "Oh—well—I would not have liked to wake you."

Downstairs, Eleanor was already up and making breakfast for Mia, who was watching cartoons. "I'm dropping off Mia at her dad's at nine. After that we can go get your friends."

We sat on the couch with Mia, watching her shows. Resa loved them. *If lefts ruled Kinaru, we would have invented television by now. Books are just not the same.*

Karnath sat eating cereal and watching the cartoon animals chase each other. "Does he ever catch that bird?" he asked Mia.

"No, he always tries but the bird is smarter than him," she explained.

He kept giving me little glances. Or perhaps giving Resa little glances, but he was on our right so I kept meeting his eyes. I wondered what he was thinking about. Our conversation last night, where he said he barely knew me? That didn't seem fair to me. We had talked and talked in all the time we'd known each other. He knew what I was interested in and how I had felt about my broken partnership and how my mother had died. Things I didn't just tell anyone. So how could he not feel like he knew me?

When Eleanor left to drop Mia off, I went upstairs to take a shower. Somehow I didn't feel like talking to Karnath for a little while. I needed to figure things out. Like how I could let him know that I felt friendly toward him, now that I had discovered it. This sort of problem had never happened to me before. No other rights ever asked about my feelings, or seemed troubled by not knowing them. And as for Resa, she always knew better than I did.

I should ask her. But somehow I didn't want to do that either. Apparently she and Karnath had a whole friendship of their own which excluded me. I didn't want to have to ask for her help in playing catch-up. I just wanted ... I didn't know what I wanted. To be understood, I suppose, without having to explain. But that was certainly irrational to expect.

An hour later, I was sitting in the front seat of Eleanor's car, holding a printed copy of her badge. "With luck, there will be no one there but the guard," she was saying. "I figure I can go in the front and distract him, and Tria can go in the back way. From there, you just go down the hall to the left and you'll see the room where your friends are kept."

"I'll take down the security network before you get to the door," said Karnath. "After that I'll just stay in the car and work on downloading as many files as I can."

I took a deep breath and let it out. This shouldn't be too complicated. But it made me nervous to get close to the place where I'd been held prisoner, where it had been so hard to escape.

The car pulled into the parking lot of the medical office next door to the lab. Eleanor parked right by the hedge, where we were a stone's throw from the lab, but partially shielded from view. "Can you get onto the network from here?"

"I'm on," he said. "Better get right near the building before I take the network down. If the guard sees it's down he'll be suspicious."

My hand was on the door handle when I saw someone emerge from the building. It was a man in a suit, carrying a briefcase. The sun glinted on his silver hair. *It's one of the men who was there the night we arrived!* Resa announced. I repeated her words for the others.

"I don't know him," said Eleanor.

"The security system isn't armed," said Karnath. "I suppose because the guard took it down for him."

"He might arm it again in a minute," said Eleanor. "Keep an eye on it." The man reached a sleek black car with tinted windows which was idling on the left side of the building and got into the back.

Eleanor waited till the car had turned out of the parking lot and out of sight before getting out of the car. She strode toward the building purposefully, swinging her purse. I gave her a head start and then followed after. "Be careful, Tria il Resa," said Karnath before I shut the door.

After so much running and hiding, it was a struggle to make myself walk casually across the parking lot, as if I had any right to be there. The rear door beeped and unlatched to my copied badge. *This is simple,* I told Resa. *Just walk in, get the scientists, and walk out.*

Who are you trying to reassure? I'm fine. I believe in you.

The carpet of the hallway absorbed my footsteps. Vainly I wished we had had some way to be sure no one had come in to do some extra work on their day off. Why had that man been here today, for instance? What if he had been here to meet someone?

Too late to worry about that now, I thought, rounding the corner. The scientists' cell was close enough to the back door that, even if someone was in the front lab, I should be able to get them and be gone before anyone noticed.

There were a number of doors in the hallway, all looking more or less the same to me, but Resa confidently pointed me toward the second. I scanned the badge and opened the door.

No one was there.

It was the right room—the three cots were there, blankets, a trash can filled with foil ration packets. I sniffed the air. There was a lingering spicy scent—three Shatakazan, in a room this size, had made a smell after a while. Did that mean they hadn't been gone long?

I hesitated a long moment in the doorway. We hadn't made a plan for this eventuality. Possibly I should break off the attempt, get back in the car, and resign myself to failure. But, on the one hand, the scientists were our only lead. We still had no idea where to find the ships. And on the other, I worried for their safety. How was Prazad holding up to captivity? I couldn't leave yet, if there was a chance he was still here.

So I kept going down the corridor, listening carefully for any sound. I could hear Eleanor's voice talking loudly in the lab. "You know, it's a funny thing," she was saying. "Normally, of course, I keep it on my key ring, but I remember putting it somewhere, if I could just remember where . . ." Her voice faded out as she moved away from the door dividing the lab from the back rooms.

For a moment it was quiet, and then I heard a voice I recognized: cool, measured, even. And not in English this time. "I need to know," it said calmly. Resh. "I don't care about Karnath, he's no longer essential. But I need the alien. Where did she go?"

"We don't know!" came Lex's voice. "We keep telling you! We had talked about escaping but they never suggested a destination!" I turned my head to locate the sound. They were in one of the rooms off the corridor. I put my back against the wall beside the door. For the moment, there didn't seem to be anything I could do. Perhaps I could wait and see if they might be coming out soon.

There was a yelp from Lex, and then Zin's voice. "We need to know. She's hacked the entire ship."

"That seems unlikely," said Jahac. "Her species isn't that advanced."

"That's what they want you to think," said Tazag. "My population models show they suffered a major cataclysm some two thousand years ago. Before that, I imagine, their society was very advanced. Despite their low-tech appearance, someone on that planet is keeping that old technology alive. And I think Tria knows about it."

I furrowed my brow. A cataclysm *then*? On the contrary, it was a time of great development. Kinaru had just started to live in cities, developed agriculture and complex building techniques. Before that wasn't a high-tech society, but six thousand years of nomadism and epic poetry. Certainly if there had been any advanced relics, we would have discovered them by now.

"Do you have any proof of this?" Jahac asked.

"We found out that she is genetically engineered. The Earth scientists all confirmed it! She must have meant to hide it from us, because as soon as it was proved, she made her escape. Karnath may be her prisoner."

"*We* are *your* prisoners," said Jahac. "Even if we knew where she was, we'd have no reason to tell you."

There was a pause. Then Resh said, "Prazad appears to be in some distress."

Jahac retorted, "He's already had one catatonic attack because of you! Are you trying to give him another?"

"He needs pretozine. I can get him some, from the *Vatarax*. At least *its* synthesizer still works. Just tell me where Tria il Resa has gone, and I will have it sent to you tomorrow."

There was a clatter, as if Jahac and leaped to his feet, overturning his chair. "Why you frass-eating—"

I heard a loud slap. Zin's voice. "Will you tell us or not?"

"I don't know." The anger had leached out of Jahac's voice. "If I were them, I'd go to where the ship landed. But you've looked there already, I assume."

"You may as well return them to their cell," said Resh. "If any of them knew anything, I think they would have said by now."

That was my cue. I darted down the hall and around the corner toward the rear door. From here I was out of sight of the main corridor, but I could hear Jahac saying softly, "Are you all right?" and Prazad responding, "I will be. I just need a minute."

The door of their cell shut behind them. I counted to twenty-four and then peered around the corner. No one was in sight. I slipped around the corner and scanned my fake badge, pressing my hand over the top of the scanner to muffle the inevitable beep.

Lex leaped to her feet when she saw me. "Resh was just here asking about you!" she hissed, trying to keep her voice quiet despite her surprise.

"Come on," I said. "We've found a safe place for you to stay."

Lex moved toward the door, but Jahac hung back, putting a hand on Prazad's arm. "Why did you run off all of a sudden, without telling us?"

I came into the room, standing in the way of the door so it wouldn't quite close. "We talked about this," I said. "Karnath and I agreed we would escape if we could."

"But why right at that moment? Tazag said you were trying to hide something."

"I heard." I chewed my lip. I should have realized Tazag's words would have seemed convincing to them. I thought of myself as one of the crew, but I hadn't yet earned their trust. "Karnath and I realized what Unity must be trading for with the earthlings. They have nuclear weapons here, and Unity wants them to destroy the Liberty government."

Lex drew in her breath. "Of course . . ."

"Do you have proof of that?" Jahac asked.

"No," I admitted. "It's just an idea, but we felt it was serious enough to make our move. It wouldn't take long to make the exchange, so if we are going to stop it, we have to hurry."

Prazad made as if to rise, but Jahac checked him again. "How do I know Karnath is even with you? Why isn't he here?"

"He's waiting in the car." I gestured in the direction of the neighboring parking lot. "Please, somebody's going to notice this door isn't shut and then it will be too late." My voice remained calm, but my heart began to speed up.

"Can't we just go?" Prazad said. "I can manage."

"But the pretozine," Jahac answered. "I can find a way to convince Resh to give it to us."

That's all this was? Is all the suspicion just because he wants to get meds for Prazad?

Of course. Resa sounded surprised. *Didn't you notice he's in love with him?*

How am I supposed to keep track of all these Shatakazan's relationships? I replied in some frustration. *I swear they change every day!*

"If you're not coming, I have to go," I said. "Lex, what about you?"

She looked around at the others. "I'm not sure. What if Tazag is telling the truth about you?"

I felt the weight of the door come off of my back. Shoving my photocopied badge at her, I said in a quiet rush, "The door is right around that corner. Karnath is waiting in the car."

For a moment she gave me a puzzled look, ready to ask why I wasn't coming. Then the door swung fully open behind me. A brown-scaled hand latched around my upper arm.

"Tazag." I lowered my head in resignation. "I had hoped to avoid meeting you."

Ze jerked me out of the room and down the hall. Behind me, I saw the door didn't quite close. I forced my eyes forward before Tazag could see me looking. Hopefully they would make up their minds to escape. I wondered if Eleanor had headed back to the car yet. There was bound to be a limit on how long she could distract the guard, and she would surely assume I had gotten in and out by now.

Tazag led me to a tiny office, with two chairs and a cluttered desk, different from the one they had interviewed the others in. Ze sat me down firmly in one of the chairs and fastened my arms to the armrests with a few circuits of tape on each arm. "I have a number of things to ask you."

"I have questions for you as well," I fired back. "Are you really getting nuclear weapons from the earthlings?"

Zir crest prickled angrily. "And how else do you think Unity is to free the planet from Liberty tyranny? We are a weak sect; we have been driven to desperate measures."

"But the lives lost—"

"Nothing, compared to the suffering of those who have been oppressed under the sects!"

It was just as Karnath had said. Ze saw zirself as a defender of those in restrictive sects. I wondered how many people ze claimed to be defending would want zir kind of help. And how many of them might be taken out by the bombs when they arrived.

I wasn't going to get drawn into an argument. "I heard you think my people are more advanced than we appear."

"How else do you explain the genetic engineering?"

I shrugged. "Some third party. Perhaps an attempt at an experiment. The humans certainly insist it can't have been them. They don't have the technology now, let alone over eight thousand years ago."

"Of course it's not them. It's you! The earthlings must have left Kinaru before you started engineering yourselves. And before whatever cataclysm wiped out most of your population and inspired your move toward a lower-tech existence."

"What is your proof of any of this?"

"What you did to my *ship*!" ze cried in frustration. "The virus! The black gunk!"

I blinked. "Black gunk? I knew about the virus, but nothing about this."

"It *has* to be you! Zin told me the virus was on the ship before we reached the station. You *must* have brought it! I've torn through your things looking for a transmitter, but you must have found a way to dispose of it by now."

I wriggled my wrist discreetly, trying to see how difficult the layers of tape would be to break. It seemed strong enough to hold me. "What do you want of me?"

"I want you to deactivate your virus and clear the black substance out of the *Galajak*. And I want you to tell me what it is, and what it's for. I don't want to lift off not knowing what it does."

I felt Resa's small smile tug at my mouth. I, too, was glad to hear Unity's plans were being hindered, if not by me, but I kept my face still. The last thing I wanted was for him to think I had any hand in it.

"I can't do that, because I don't know."

Ze towered over me, crest fully upright. From where I was sitting, it was an intimidating sight. Ze snatched a pair of scissors from the desk and opened them to make a blade. Bending down, ze pressed it lightly against Resa's arm.

"That's not my arm!" I protested. "I'm the one you're talking to!"

"I know. I read all the reports." Ze loomed over me, the makeshift weapon seeming to soothe zem somewhat. "I also learned that you are insensitive to pain and discomfort, but will go to any trouble to avoid harm to your counterpart."

I felt the blood drain from my face. Ze was smarter than I had given zem credit for.

Don't give zem anything! Resa said defiantly. *I can take it!*

But I knew once she felt the slightest pain, she would take all that back. She never could stand it. *I hardly have a choice,* I said. *I don't know what ze wants to know.*

Suddenly there was a soft buzz from Tazag's device, and ze stepped back. Pulling it out, ze swiped the screen. "Zin needs to talk to me. I'll be back."

Ze stepped out of the room. I strained my wrist against the tape. I thought I could break it within a minute or two, but that wouldn't get me anywhere. I had no badge to get out the outer door with. I thought about picking the lock like we had to get out of our cell before, but surely the outer doors were sturdier.

Suddenly the door burst open. It was Eleanor. "My God, Tria, you weren't kidding!" she said. I looked up at her, puzzled, while she took the scissors off the desk and cut the tape. "I think the guard is going to follow me in a second, we have to get out of here."

I hurried to follow her out of the office and down the hall. The door of the scientists' cell was fully shut now—either they had gotten out, or they had made up their minds to stay. As we turned the corner, I heard a shout. "Hey! Dr. Carroll! I told you you can't go wandering around when the building's locked!" But by then we were within steps of the back door. We emerged into bright sunlight and broke into a run.

I heaved a sigh of relief when we crossed the hedge and saw Karnath sitting in the back seat, along with all three scientists. We flung ourselves into the front and Eleanor was reversing out of the lot before I even had my door shut.

"What happened?" demanded Karnath as we reached the road. "They told me Tazag had Tria il Resa."

"I don't even know," said Eleanor, holding the wheel with one hand and groping for her seat belt with the other. "I just got a text from Tria saying where she was and to come get her."

I stared at her. "I didn't send you a text. I don't have a device."

"It had your name on it," she said, grabbing her phone out of her pocket and tossing it to Karnath. "Take a look."

He read aloud, "'Please come, I am being held in room 106.' And it's in English."

"I wasn't going to stop and ask questions," said Eleanor defensively. "I figured if she had managed to text me, she needed my help. The guard wasn't twenty steps behind me. He'll have alerted his people by now." She let her breath out slowly. "There goes my job.'"

"I'm sorry."

"Well, I chose to take the risk." Chewing her lip, she added, "Maybe I'm being too paranoid, but I don't want to go home, either. Townsend has my address, of course, to send my paychecks to." She took a sharp turn. "I'm going to find a hotel, for tonight at least."

"Tria, what happened in there?" Karnath asked again.

I summarized as best I could. "It was lucky Tazag had stepped out."

He considered a moment. "Was it? Or did whoever sent the text know ze would be out?"

"You think one of them was trying to save me? Zin or Resh?"

"That's not what I was thinking at all," he said. "They don't know English. And no one could have made your name appear on the text. It shows the sender's name, always. The texting program puts it in."

I twisted around in my seat to look at him. "You think the *texting program* called Eleanor?"

He was bending over his own device. "I think my device did. That is, the virus on it."

Prazad looked up. "The *virus* did it?"

"Think about it," said Karnath, handing his device to Prazad to look at. "It's clearly more advanced than our systems, because it outsmarted the antivirus both on my device and on the ship. And it seems Zin could not control it either."

"Advanced is one thing," I said. "But how could it just decide to do that? It's a program, not a person."

"With complex computers, that line can get fainter than you think. Its initial instructions will give it a set of conditions in which it should intervene. It seems it took action at the exact moment you were in physical danger."

I shook my head, staring forward at the road. "I've been in danger since I got here."

"Not so close as this. Have you ever actually been at risk of injury?"

"From that dog, maybe," I said. "It had big teeth."

Karnath inhaled sharply. "And it was at that moment that my device spontaneously connected to the global network! Which I had previously determined it would not be able to do."

I looked back at Prazad. "Is that really possible? Could a program actually monitor us that closely?"

He tossed his fingers upward. "I wouldn't rule it out. Certainly the virus is very active at the moment. It appears to have been uploading itself while Karnath was downloading files from the lab."

"Jumping to Tazag's device?"

"It's certainly possible."

Eleanor turned into a grimy-looking parking lot. My mind whirled. Was Tazag right after all? Was there someone back on Kinaru hiding technology this advanced? Was there a lie somewhere in our history?

I shook my head. It was all speculation. It had to be.

CHAPTER NINETEEN

Tria

That evening, we sat in a circle on the floor in our hotel room, eating food out of paper cartons. The hotel was a cheap one, so that Eleanor could pay in cash. Another important feature was that the room doors opened directly on the parking lot, so that the four Shatakazan could troop in without having to walk through a lobby.

"You're sure our systems can handle Earth food?" Lex said skeptically, poking at hers.

"I've been eating it for a few days now with no ill effects," Karnath reassured her. "It tastes strange, but it *is* edible."

Now it was time to come up with a plan. Unfortunately, we had little to go on. We still had no idea where the *Galajak* was, no idea where the other ship—possibly the *Vatarax*—was, and no idea where the weapons the earthlings were selling to Unity were.

"So you have the raw files from the lab?" Jahac asked Karnath. "That seems like a promising lead." I blinked at him. Apparently he was no longer pointedly ignoring Karnath. I was pleased to see he had put his resentment behind him.

"I would have thought so, but I am finding it next to impossible to sort out which files might be useful."

"Give it here," said Prazad. "You have to know the software protocols." Karnath passed his device over and Prazad got to work.

The rest of us turned on the television, for lack of anything better to do. "Earth," said Lex dreamily, watching the screen pan over a coastal landscape. "I never thought I'd be here. I studied fourteen languages and none of them was an Earth one."

"Do you like it?" I asked.

"I hardly know," she said. "So far I have only seen the roads and the cheap motels. This can't be the nice part of Earth."

"There are parts of Earth that are very beautiful," said Karnath. "There are giant jungles filled with all kinds of animal life. And there are also deserts, tundra—the planet is as eclectic as the nations of people who live here."

Jahac spoke up. "I know a little about Earth's geopolitics. It's interesting that Unity chose the United States for its deal. As a democracy, it wouldn't be easy to negotiate with. And didn't you tell me our presence on this planet is secret?"

"That's the strange part," I said. "Clearly someone within the government is behind this, but as far as I can figure, this action is illegal. The American people are supposed to consent to what the government does, right?"

Eleanor hadn't been paying attention. "Hm? Oh, yes, it would be a massive scandal if it came out. Especially if it turns out that Congress hasn't been informed."

"Who is Congress?"

Eleanor sighed and buried her face in her hands. "It's all really complicated," she said. "Suffice it to say our government is composed of a lot of people and it's entirely credible that some are in on this deal and others are not. Which would make it... well, if not strictly illegal, at any rate scandalous."

"I wonder if there is some way we can leverage that," I mused.

"Perhaps send an email to someone in government revealing the scheme? Or even post a public statement on the global network."

She laughed outright at this. "Oh dear … I'm sorry. But I'm just imagining what a senator might do with an email saying that reptilians were on Earth conspiring with the government."

"Panic?" I suggested.

"No—laugh. If it even got delivered instead of being deleted by an intern. Alien hoaxes are really common. Crazy people are always saying stuff like this."

"But if we sent a video—"

"It's so easy to fake a video. I bet you could look online right now and find a hundred videos that are supposed to be of aliens. Honestly I am racking my brains thinking how we could publicize this even if we wanted to. People would have to see you in person, and the people who have any power are impossible to get a meeting with." She grew serious. "I really don't know what we can do if we can't find any information in the data Karnath got. I'm on a deadline. I can afford this hotel room for a while, if I go get cash out somewhere, but next Sunday I have to take Mia back. If I don't show, or if I 've gotten in legal trouble by then... I could lose custody. They'd just give her to my ex fulltime."

My eye widened. It hadn't occurred to me how fully she was sharing in our danger. "How much time is that?"

"Six days."

I chewed my lip. "By then, either we'll have stopped them, or they'll surely be off the planet. I wish we knew their timetable. But it can't take that long to make the exchange."

"I only hope we're not already too late."

I nodded, letting the silence stretch out. Certainly nothing could be more important than stopping Unity in time. Yet I couldn't help also worrying about my own personal mystery. Tentatively, I asked, "Eleanor, what do you know about Earth's history? How far back does it go?"

She blinked at me through her thick glasses. "Written history, or fossil evidence?"

"Which goes back further?"

"Fossil evidence, of course. There are anatomically modern human fossils over one hundred thousand years old."

My eye widened. "Well, that destroys Tazag's theory. Ze thought humans branched off from the Kinaru only a few thousand years ago, before we genetically engineered ourselves."

Karnath came over, stepping over empty food cartons and folding himself down next to us. "That's an intriguing theory, I wonder what the humans would think of it."

Eleanor smiled. "We wouldn't think much of it at all. The fossil evidence is pretty clear. And we're genetically related to all the animal life on the planet. If Tazag had talked to a single human scientist, ze would know that."

My face fell. For a while, I had been encouraged by zir theory, hoping that my planet really was the true home of my people. Earth certainly didn't feel like home. Shouldn't there be some kind of ancestral memory that would make the place make sense to me?

"I've been trying to consider what sort of species might have engineered the Kinaru," Karnath mused. "It can't have been the humans, because you've never had the ability. And I can't think of any species in the sector that was that advanced, that long ago."

"Perhaps one that has since died out," suggested Eleanor.

He flicked his fingers upward thoughtfully. "If we ever make it off Earth, we could explore that possibility. There are a number of uninhabited planets we might search for relics." He rubbed his chin. "But the *personality* of the species that did it. It's nothing like any being I know of."

"What do you mean?"

"Well—the music thing, for instance. The only species we've discovered with no music are those that have no hearing, and those make visual art, or dance, or poetry."

"We have poetry," I objected. "You've heard it."

"Yes, of course. But it's—well, it's as if someone heard of the notion of poetry and tried to imitate it, while draining all the feeling out. You tell me you have feelings, and I believe you. And I know Resa does. But your poetry has none."

I drew back a little. How could anyone criticize the Lays? "It isn't meant to be about feelings. It conveys a moral lesson."

Eleanor said, "What I think Karnath is trying to say is, your society doesn't prioritize the same things all other species he knows of. Music, art, emotion—even romance, right?"

"It's not like we don't *have* those," I said. "They're left things."

Karnath and Eleanor exchanged a glance I couldn't read. "The very notion of a divided mind is one of the things that seems most inexplicable to me," said Karnath at last. "I wonder if we will ever know the reason for it."

I didn't respond to that. To me, the reason was obvious. Humans and Shatakazan both were constantly distracted and disabled by emotion. Prazad's fear, Jahac's suspicion of Karnath, even Tazag's anger at Liberty, all sprang from their inability to separate emotion from the part of themselves where they reasoned and planned their actions. On a global level, Earth felt like a planet of lefts—fighting incessantly among themselves, wasting effort on music while people still went hungry. I could easily see the impulse of an observer, looking down at Earth's chaos and wanting to put it right. And so they had.

I knew if I said this, it would insult everyone present. None of them recognized a problem with the way they were. And indeed, it was possible for them to forge a balance between the conflicting parts of themselves. Karnath certainly handled his emotions with maturity and grace. But the struggle to organize all this must be a lifelong project. Resa and I were *born* with these things in proper order. It could not help being an advantage.

All the time we'd been talking, Resa had been picking apart all the packaging from our dinner: disassembling the cartons and folding them into tight cylinders, shredding empty salt packets, breaking the tines off the forks. She must have been bored of all our talk. I gently took the trash away and stuffed it in the bag the food had come in. *Come on,* I said. *We've both had a long day.*

Resa

That night we slept in one of the room's two beds, while Eleanor took the other. The Shatakazan stayed up talking, trying to make sense of the data they had. I pulled out my earbud so their conversation wouldn't keep me awake. Without the translation, their language sounded like the patter of rain on leaves. Whenever Karnath spoke, a thrill ran from the center of me out to the edges.

But I was cooler and more reasonable than I had been last night. It had been a perfect moment, and I wasn't sorry, but the music was over, leaving a dead gray silence. And I had little hope it would play again. So I squeezed my eye shut and tried to think of home.

This time of year, the wind would have pulled all the vibrant turquoise blossoms from the butterfruit trees, and golden leaves would be just unfolding into a paintbrush of streamers on the end of each branch. The tiny green flying reptiles, no bigger than my little finger, that pollinated the flowers would be swarming north, following the passage of spring.

The orchards climbed up and down the rolling hills near my home, mile upon mile of them, in perfect rows. Then beyond the orchards, higher up the mountainside, past where the irrigation lines end, copper-colored scrub brush and red soil.

It hurt thinking of it. It hurt even more than being trapped there had hurt. That was what I was finally forced to admit: I had fled pain only to find myself transfixed with still greater pain. Instead of the flat pain of confinement, the sharp pain of loss. And all I could see ahead of me, if we achieved everything Tria hoped, was more I could love and lose. Here there was music, and love, and art, and none of it was for me.

I reached up quickly to dash a tear out of my eye before it trickled onto Tria. I felt like a whiny child, wishing for so many things that couldn't be. What if it wasn't the universe that was to blame, but my desires? What if I simply wanted too much?

Tria would never have understood it. Her desires were selfless and simple: knowledge, the greatest good for the greatest number. She didn't know what it was to thrill to music, to ache for a touch, to drink in colors. That made it easier for her to make the choices that, one way or the other, would have had to be made anyway.

It was the desert cat and the burrowing owl again. My right-mother used to tell the story of how the cat wanted to taste everything in the jungle, even when the owl told her it wasn't all good for eating. But that silly old cat, she just kept eating and eating till there wasn't a single leaf or blade of grass left. And that's why most of Kinaru is desert today, because the cat ate all the plants.

Tria was always full of questions. Why did the cat eat plants when everyone knows they're carnivores? If it was originally a jungle cat and not a desert cat, why is it so well adapted to the desert? Me, I looked in my left-mother's longsuffering face and knew what the story was supposed to be about. Knew which animal she and I were supposed to be.

A tear slipped out of my eye and across my nose. Tria startled awake. *What's the matter?*

Nothing, I said, less of a lie this time than a sulk. She ought to already know. We were living the same life, why did we see such different things?

But she reached across to stroke my arm, and I let myself be comforted.

She was trying, gods knew. Not her fault that she blundered blindly across the delicate tracery of my feelings. Not her fault that we were what we were.

Tria

In the morning, I awoke to low, excited voices on the other side of the room. I swung my legs out of bed and went over to where everyone else was crouched on the floor in a circle, talking.

"Ah, Tria il Resa," said Karnath, his crest flicking upwards for a moment. "We did not want to wake you, but we have very good news. We finally found the file with the locations they are working in. There are three. Location 2 is the lab facility where we were held, where scientists can be kept working on the project while entirely in the dark about what the actual deal is meant to be. Location 1, we were able to identify as the landing site of the *Galajak*. But Location 3, we believe, is the actual site where one or both of the ships is being stored."

"And you have the address?" I asked excitedly.

"Yes," he said slowly, "but I should add that this doesn't help as much as with the other locations. Eleanor informs me that it is a military base under very tight security."

My heart sank. Of course I couldn't have expected that they would keep the ship anywhere that would be easy to get to, but a little part of me had hoped it would be as simple as our rescue of the scientists yesterday. Preferably simpler.

I crouched down beside Karnath to join the conversation. He moved over a little to make room for me, but Resa's arm still wound up jostling him. "What about the virus?" I asked.

"It's lying low for the moment. Prazad tried to get a closer look, but it hides itself if you try to look at it. You can just see that there's something in there, using the processor and eating up most of the memory."

"We can worry about that once we've found the ship," said Lex. "We have the data and now we have an address. What's the next step?"

"I can take us there," said Eleanor. "But I can't imagine the good that would do. The lab was guarded with badges and keys. Military bases are defended by men with guns. There's simply no way."

"Perhaps we don't need to actually *enter* the base," said Prazad. "This device can communicate with the ship as long as there is a line of sight, or nothing really heavy interposing. If we could get *near* the ship …"

"The base is pretty large," said Eleanor, looking down at a satellite photo on her phone. "And we could not get any more specific information about where on the base the ship might be."

The others decided to check out of the hotel and drive to the area where the military base was, which was less than an hour away. I wasn't sure what good this would do, but then again, there was no benefit to staying where we were, either. And keeping on the move might help keep us ahead of any pursuit.

Midmorning found us parked a short distance from the outskirts of the base. We had already made a full circuit of the perimeter without making contact with either ship. Certainly the base was more than large enough to hide one or two spaceships; it had dozens of buildings. But those same buildings were blocking our device's signal, so it was impossible to say if the ships were shielded or not there at all.

The Shatakazan were all in hooded sweatshirts which Eleanor had stopped on the way to buy. They had gotten out of the car and were sitting on the curb, talking quietly. I sat in the front seat beside Eleanor, watching them. "What if they can't get back?" I said. "What if they're stuck here on

Earth forever?”

“The same as if you can’t get back, I assume,” she answered.

“Not really. For one thing, I can’t go back to my planet at the moment in any event. I meant to leave home to study for quite some time. And for another, I can pass as human. They can’t. Are they going to have to bundle up in disguises the rest of their lives? They can hardly work or find a place to live without being found out.”

Eleanor nodded. “I suppose you’re right. There are places less populous than this, of course. They could go out into the wilderness and build some kind of life. But it would be difficult. And if their cover did get blown, I’m not sure how people would react.”

“Maybe it’s time to think about blowing that cover now,” I said. “We’ve tried solving this on our own, and we can’t. Isn’t there *anyone* you could call who might believe us?”

“I may as well try.” She got out her phone and scrolled around for a while. “I guess I’ll just start down the list of elected officials. I’ll skip the president—everything nuclear-related has to go through him; I can’t believe he’s not involved somehow. Going to try my senator first.”

She spent over an hour making calls. Sometimes she got a recording device, in which case she just hung up. If she got a human, she would make her pitch: she knew something, it was a very serious plot involving nuclear weapons being traded to a foreign entity, that the official should demand to visit the military base in question, that they should ask about Project Zenith. But every time, the answers were patronizing. The staffer would pass the message along. Did she want to give her address to receive a letter by mail? Eleanor did not.

My eyes wandered over the blank white wall of the military base, and the cluster of Shatakazan on the sidewalk. Even in his disguise, I could pick out Karnath from the others. Something in the way he moved, in his energetic pacing and the way he flapped his hands around when he was excited, stood out.

My attention was pulled back to Eleanor's call when the woman's voice on the other end subtly changed in tone. "Can you hold please?" There was a pause and then a male voice answered. "Hello, Secretary McKlellan speaking."

Eleanor's voice faltered a moment in surprise. "Um—hello. I have information about an illegal plot…" She detailed what we knew, leaving out the part about aliens, calling them instead "a foreign entity."

The Secretary's voice was serious, reassuring. "Thank you for bringing this to my attention. You wouldn't happen to know *where* on the base I should begin my search?"

"No," she answered, abashed. "I wish I had more information for you. But in my understanding the vessels would be disguised as something else. You'll have to mention Project Zenith."

"Where are you now, Miss—"

I shook my head wildly. We couldn't trust anyone, not in our situation. She said diplomatically, "I don't think there's anything I could do by meeting you. I simply wanted to alert you." She ended the call. "I hope that does any good. He should have access to the base at least. But he's right, it's a big place to look for an invisible ship."

"Two ships," I corrected, "and one of them should be very large. There's a chance." I got out of the car to tell the others.

Karnath approved. "It's clear this task is beyond our resources. The American government will have to handle it from here."

Jahac was less hopeful. "The American government isn't like ours on Shatak. These primitive nation-states are rife with corruption. The best people don't rise to the top—that's why this plot was able to work in the first place."

"He sounded like he was willing to help," I said. "All we need is *one* person who's willing to believe us."

Lex went back to the car to take a nap in the backseat. The rest of us stayed on the sidewalk. Karnath sat with his back against the blank brick wall, working on his device. I knelt down beside him. "What are you working on?"

"There are so many different wireless signals here," he said. "Internet, radio, cellular, and all heavily encrypted. Prazad says there is no hope of this device being able to break the encryption on its own. But considering the things it's already been able to do beyond its design parameters, I'm trying anyway. If I could just boost our signal on one of the existing networks, I might be able to make contact with the ship."

I watched him for a few minutes, his four agile thumbs gliding over the screen while his long fingers splayed out behind the back of the device. He wasn't letting our dire situation paralyze him; that was good. Everyone's emotional state seemed more positive now that we were free, despite the dangers of this alien world.

Suddenly my eye was caught by several black vans pulling into the parking lot. I shook Karnath's arm. "Look."

There was no time for us to do anything, and no point in running, because we had our backs to the wall. I glanced to either side—vans were pulling into position to cut us off. All I could do was meet Eleanor's eye, where she looked at me from the car, and signal her to get down. She slid out of sight. I only hoped no one had seen her.

We gathered together in a tight knot, backs together, while men jumped out of the vans. They were carrying long guns and wore clear shields over their faces. "Raise your hands in the air," Karath hissed, lifting his own. "That is the signal for surrender."

"Surrender?" demanded Jahac. "Back into captivity?"

"I can't," Prazad wailed. "Not again!"

"Do it," he said tightly. "It's that or they start shooting. We have nothing to protect ourselves."

Reluctantly, the others raised their hands. Resa's and mine were already in the air. Karnath was right, there was no option where we walked away from this.

The men had us surrounded, aiming their guns at us without speaking. Then, from the nearest van, came a long-legged man in a gray suit. I recognized him as the silver-haired man we had seen yesterday leaving the lab. The men parted to allow him to approach us.

"You can put your hands down," said the man pleasantly. "I'm Secretary McKlellan. Which of you called me?"

Thinking fast, I tentatively raised my hand. They had ignored Eleanor's car, which looked empty like the others parked nearby. I had to convince them there were no more of us. But I couldn't open my mouth, or he'd notice immediately that I wasn't the fluent English speaker who had called him.

But he nodded calmly. "Well. That's most of you, I think. Wasn't there one more alien?"

He meant Lex, still sleeping under the blanket in the back of Eleanor's car. But Karnath answered calmly, "She died. Reaction to a food product."

The man nodded. "What did you do with the body?"

"We put in the river," Karnath answered. "That is our custom."

He frowned. "All right. We will attempt to locate it later. What about the scientist? The one that helped you escape?"

Karnath hesitated. "We haven't seen her."

"Well, if that's how you want to play it." He stepped back and signaled to the guards, who urged us toward one of the vans. A moment later, we were on the move, passing through the large gate that led into the base.

CHAPTER TWENTY

Tria

Prazad was hunching in on himself on the floor of the van, crest flat to his head, hiding his face against his knees. I looked at Jahac, but he looked little better. His protectiveness of Prazad was only making him more frightened. I leaned close to Prazad. "It's all right. We escaped last time, we can this time as well."

He didn't answer.

"Prazad," I continued, "you've got to stay with us, okay? You're the one that can help."

He lifted his face a fraction. It was solidly green. "I can't do anything."

"You can!" I said. "You're the communications expert. In bringing us onto the base, they're making a huge mistake. They're letting us get closer to the ship. And you're the one who's most likely to be able to locate it."

Prazad took several deep breaths. "I can't go back," he said. "I can't. It's so cold in the earthling buildings. And the lights, they make this hum, and they flicker. I can't stand it."

Resa reached out and put a hand on his knee. I kept talking. "We'll stand it together," I said. "We'll do what we can to make it comfortable. And we won't be there long. We'll find a way out soon. You need to keep it together just for a few more days." I hoped I wasn't lying.

Nodding, Prazad uncoiled himself another fraction. "I can do this for a few days. I can." The green color started retreating back from his jawline.

"You can," Jahac echoed, putting an arm around him. "We all can." I let out my breath. Disaster averted, for now. We needed all of us calm and functional if we were to have any hope of freedom.

The van pulled to a stop, and men opened the doors and waved us out. Prazad started scrunching up again, but Jahac took one of his hands and Resa took the other, and he was able to stumble out of the van.

The military base was like a small city, with buildings of featureless concrete. A plane buzzed overhead, angling low for a landing. The guards led us into a small building and upstairs to a windowless room. There were three cots and a small bathroom. The guards that had led us there went out. "It's just like the other place," Prazad moaned.

"Wait," I said. "There are three cots, but four of us. And they didn't know we were coming."

"I guess they didn't have enough cots," said Jahac.

I shook my head. "No. This is where they have been keeping the techs. Don't you think?"

Prazad peered around the room. "Maybe," he said slowly.

Karnath shot me a grateful look. "I think you are right," he said. "We thought the techs would be kept with the ship, and we think this is where the ship is."

The door swung open again and admitted Secretary McKlellan. "You guys have been a bit of a nuisance, you know that? It would have been better if Tazag could have found some other way to deal with you besides foisting you on us. Especially you," he said, stabbing a finger toward me. "Scientific subject. Ha! You're basically human, we have nothing to learn from you. It's a waste, and I'm sorry I was talked into allowing the project."

"So you're the one in charge?" said Karnath. "This whole plan is your project?"

"Not exactly," said McKlellan. "But I'm managing it, at present."

"Can you tell us what your plan for us is?"

"Nothing," he said. "We're just storing you until our plan goes off. After that, well—perhaps we will find you a more permanent spot, something that's more comfortable for you."

"And how long is that?"

"A few more days. Don't worry. We'll have some more cots brought in here. We're not trying to make you uncomfortable. But you really need to stay out of the way. No more escaping," he said, waggling a finger. "Which is really not a concern, here—this place is completely secure." He turned to go. "Please inform the guards if there is anything you need."

"There's one thing—" Karnath began. McKlellan turned. "Can you please shut off the cold air in here? This temperature is uncomfortable for us. One of us is ill."

McKlellan grinned, showing blindingly white teeth. "Will do!"

Once he was gone, we went over the room carefully. There were security cameras in two different corners of the room—no chance of finding a secret spot. The only vent was a thin, horizontal slit covered in slats, far too small for even Karnath to crawl through. But the tiny adjoining bathroom did not seem to be bugged. Karnath and the others took turns spending short periods in there, working on Karnath's device. The *Galajak* was still not in range, possibly due to the thick concrete walls of the building, but Prazad thought it might be possible to boost the signal somehow through the building's wireless network. As he grew absorbed and excited with the idea, the last of the green flush cleared from his face.

The guard brought us lunch—foil packets of rations from the ship. I gingerly peeked inside mine. There was a stringy, violet vegetable, some orange starchy cubes, and insects like little yellow seeds. Except with legs. Karnath saw me poking at the food and scooped the insects out of my pouch, replacing them with some of his vegetables. I smiled gratefully. The orange things were tasteless and the purple things tasted like sweat, but I was hungry enough I hardly cared.

They passed the afternoon reminiscing about Shatak: the dense rainforests, the torrential downpours, the bustling marketplaces and the white towers of Liberty City. I listened wistfully. If I could have any dream, it would be to live the life they had lived up to now—exploring different worlds, coming home with stories to tell, and venturing out to discover new ones. Earth had its beauties, and someday I would like to discover more of them. But I didn't want to stay here forever. I tried not to think about the ship, probably parked close by, that would soon leave without us.

In the evening, the door opened again. I glanced up, expecting the guard to appear with more packs of rations, but instead three more people were ushered inside—Gaj, Talek, and Daz.

Prazad leaped to his feet and rushed to Talek, cupping zir cheeks with his hands and leaning his brow ridge against zirs. Now that I knew they were related, I could see they both had the same stocky shape and dark gray faces.

We crowded around the techs, eager to exchange news. "I'm glad to hear you are all right," said Talek, quietly so as not to be heard on the cameras. "We thought they might have simply killed you. They claimed you were safe, but I worried they had lied."

"Where is Lex?" asked Daz plaintively.

"She is free," I answered. "She is with our human friend. I am hoping they will find a way to have us rescued."

"We still aren't sure of their plan," said Gaj. She had a sandy yellow crest and broad shoulders; I knew little about her except her relationship with Zin, which had kept her from suspecting the plot until it was too late. "We know they are planning to trade one of the ships to the earthlings. I am just not sure what they are getting in return."

"Weapons," I said. "The humans have nuclear weapons which they are selling to Unity, so that Unity can take over Shatak."

Her crest flattened in horror. "And I thought it was bad enough, giving the earthlings space travel. They clearly aren't ready for it."

"Which ship are they trading to the humans?" asked Karnath.

"The plan originally was to give them the *Vatarax*," she answered. "It's a cargo ship, very slow moving, and Unity wanted to keep the *Galajak*. But there's this strange black substance gumming up the *Galajak*. At first Resh demanded we remove it, but it's not that easy. It retreats when we approach it and hides in different parts of the ship. If I had to guess, I'd say it was nanomaterial, but I can't get a sample."

"Tazag said something about that," I said. "Ze thought it was connected to the computer virus."

"Probably. I haven't worked on the software end at all, only Zin. She thinks the virus got into the fabricator and started cranking this stuff out. It ate all the carbon out of the scrubber and the nitrates out of the synthesizer. It hasn't touched the fuel, though, so I could swear it knows which are vital functions and is trying to spare them."

"It's still flyable?" Karnath asked.

"Seems to be. But they've made up their mind to take the *Vatarax* and leave the *Galajak* to the earthlings. So our job has been to wipe the computers and instruct the Earth engineers in how to fly it." She shook her head. "They aren't quick learners. I don't think they are going to be able to get off the planet, at this rate. But Unity doesn't especially care, so long as they get the goods from the earthlings."

"Is there a deadline?" I said. "When does the *Vatarax* lift off?"

"The day after tomorrow," she answered.

I felt cold. Even with weeks I didn't know what we could do. In a single day, I felt sure there was nothing. Those weapons would leave for Shatak, and millions would die. Then Unity would take over, and Shatak would never again be as my friends remembered it.

"Is it possible," I suggested quietly, "to somehow hinder the work you're supposed to be doing? Sabotage the engines, something like that?"

Gaj considered this. "Resh is usually watching, and he is trained in engineering. I suppose it might be possible, if one of us distracted him elsewhere..." She rubbed her chin thoughtfully.

"But what good would that do, sabotaging the *Galajak*?" asked Karnath. "If the sabotage isn't discovered until after the *Vatarax* takes off, it would keep the earthlings from getting into space, but it wouldn't stop Unity's takeover. But if it is discovered sooner, they would simply force us to repair it."

"They can't force us to," said Daz. "We could refuse."

Gaj gave zem a sidelong look. "Funny hearing that from *you*."

"I know I let myself be threatened into piloting the ship here," ze protested. "But I had no idea of the stakes. We should all agree now to die if it will prevent this scheme from going off."

"They wouldn't just kill us," Karnath said gently, his eyes going to Prazad, who still clung to Talek as if afraid someone would take zem away again. "They would use some of us as hostages to motivate the others."

Daz quailed, brown patches blooming on zir cheeks. "Still. Even if all of us were killed, it would be less harmful than allowing them to use those weapons on Shatak. They'd surely target Liberty City ... there are five million people there. Including many of our families and lovers."

Gaj bowed her head. "You are right, of course."

"Let's not leap to talk of dying until we can figure out an actual plan that has some chance of helping," said Karnath. "Do you three have any access to the *Vatarax*?"

They all flicked their fingers down. "I know where it is," said Gaj. "It isn't far from the *Galajak*."

Karnath lowered his voice still further, though nothing we had said had been loud enough for the cameras to pick up. "In that case, one of you could take the device to the ship with you, and from there you might be able to contact the cargo ship."

Gaj's eyes widened. "Yes! Oh, I wish one of us had more skills in computing." She glanced at Prazad, but he wouldn't be near the ship. It would have to be one of the three techs. "At least we would be able to program in some basic commands. Let me think of what to do ...” She and Karnath put their heads together, whispering.

That evening, I sat with Talek on one of the cots, while Prazad hid in the bathroom working on the device. He was writing a program which, when sent to the cargo ship by the techs, would take over some of its functions. Talek rocked forward and backward anxiously. “I hope he will be all right,” ze said. “He has always been a very nervous person.”

“He seems to be in better shape now that he has something to work on,” I said.

“That’s something,” ze said, forcing zirself to be still. “He always wanted to be a computer tech. But his psychological testing wasn’t good enough. Spacers have to be completely stable. Catatonic attacks are disqualifying. But the science team has a lower standard, so he studied alien communications technology instead.”

“It seems a very counterproductive way of dealing with stress,” I said. “Is it a very common reaction?”

“It’s not unusual,” ze said. “Our evolutionary forebears were able to blend into their environment, so staying still meant staying safe. Today, of course, it’s not much use.” Ze lowered zir eyelids, thinking of a memory. “Once, when he was little, we all went to a sensodrama together, and it ended up being too scary for him. He was the youngest in our family network, and the show had really been meant for us older ones. Well, you have to wear these helmets, right? So that you can see and hear everything as if you were there. When the sensodrama was over, we all took off our helmets and he was nowhere to be found. We called and called, and finally found him hiding under the seats, completely catatonic. My mother-once-removed was so upset, and my father felt terrible—the sensodrama had been his suggestion.”

“Were you able to wake him up?”

"Not till later that night. We had to carry him home like that, taking him in turns the whole way on the pod-tube. Once he was in bed with a warm blanket and a heater, he gradually did wake up."

I smiled. "Do you think he can write the program he needs to?"

"Oh, he definitely can. He has the knowledge and the skills. Don't mistake his nervousness for incompetence. I just wish . . ." she sighed. "I wish he hadn't come on this mission. He wanted to be on one with me, and I thought it would help him, for his first mission, to be with someone from the family. But if he had applied for any other mission, he might be safe now." Ze cut off what ze was saying as he emerged from the bathroom, covertly passing the device to Karnath, who hid it in his sweatshirt pocket.

Prazad came and sat next to us. "I have the program ready. It's really very simple, but there's only so much we can do that they won't notice and override. First, I set the engines to continuously clear the fuel nozzles, starting an hour after the program is sent. So it will be spending fuel all that time, and it's a very quiet process, so they may not notice until they are ready to lift. Second, at nightfall the day after tomorrow, the holographic cloak will drop and all the running lights will come on. My hope is that they won't want to lift off if they can't do it inconspicuously, but the program will lock out the hologenerator after shutting it down, so it will take them some time to restart it."

"That is excellent, Prazad," I said. "I didn't know that was even possible."

The guards brought dinner, but didn't bother to supply any more cots. The Shatakazan weren't troubled; they didn't mind staggering their sleep periods or curling up on the floor. They insisted I take one of the three available cots, and kept as quiet as they could so that I could sleep.

Karnath came over after I had gone to bed, and sat on the edge of the cot. "Tria il Resa," he said, in a serious voice, "I am sorry."

I blinked up at him. "Sorry for what?"

"That I couldn't think of any better ideas. That I couldn't somehow solve the problems we landed in. When I took on the responsibility for you on the *Galajak*, I meant to keep you safe, to ensure that you were able to study us while being kept safe, comfortable, and respected. I took all that on myself, because you were putting yourself in a vulnerable position to be studied by me. Yet it all went so terribly wrong."

"None of that is your fault."

"I still feel I should have been better able to solve it. Why did I work so hard to spy on Unity sect, to break us out of the facility, to rescue the scientists, if we were just going to end up prisoners again?"

"If anyone is to blame for that, it's me. Eleanor and I called those officials because we thought it was the only option. It didn't even occur to me to ask you."

"If you had asked me, I would have agreed. I apparently am not suspicious enough of humans. I have seen so many pleasant comedies of humans behaving well, I keep forgetting that they have a dark side."

"All species have a dark side, it seems," I said. "But you were right to trust Eleanor. And I have to hope that there are other humans who are trustworthy as well. They'll soon have fold capacity, and I hope they use that power for good."

"I don't feel confident about that," he said morosely.

I was quiet a moment. He leaned forward, as if to get up, but I reached out and touched his arm. "Don't go yet. I—I have something to say to you." He turned his large golden eyes back to face me, and for a moment I hesitated, not sure of how to put this into words. "You—you were saying, the other night, that you weren't sure how I felt about you. That, unlike Resa, I hide my feelings. I am not sure this is exactly true. I think I have shown my feelings in a lot of ways, even if it's not as clear as when Resa does it."

He tilted his head. "I'm not sure what you're trying to say."

I looked away from him, embarrassed. "It's just . . . I feel that you are my friend, Karnath. I wanted you to know that. Especially with all that's been going on, I didn't want you to be in doubt of that."

Karnath was still a moment, with an expression I couldn't read. Then he lowered his eyelids in a smile. "I feel that you are my friend, too, Tria. Thank you for putting it into words for me." He lightly touched Resa's hand and stood up.

That's what you had to say? Resa demanded. *All that prologue just to say you feel you are **friends**?*

It was a big deal to me, I said defensively. *I'm sure your feelings are much more complicated and nuanced and everything. But I felt a feeling and I put it into words and I, personally, am pleased with myself!*

She was quiet a moment. *Must feel nice.*

My guard went up. That was exactly the sort of comment she would say before a fight, and yet it was so innocent that I couldn't figure out what it might foreshadow. *What do you mean? You're the one who's always in touch with your feelings.*

I meant, it must feel nice to try my things when you want to, and go back to being you whenever you like.

That took me a minute to decode. Feelings weren't *her* things, I wanted to say. Karnath and Eleanor had both told me they were part of being a full person. But I resisted saying that. With Resa there was always something deeper going on. *Is there something of mine you've been wanting to try?* I ventured. *Eleanor did say you were capable of more things than you've gotten to do.*

She took a long breath and let it out. *Never mind. Just—never mind.*

Now that's not fair. You've as much as told me there's something bothering you, but you won't tell me what it is. The last time that happened we almost married Rez il Tapa when you didn't want to. You can't keep so many secrets from me.

I can't do anything else, she said. *I'm always afraid to tell you things.*

Afraid? What are you talking about? You have always, always been safe with me.

So far. She seemed about to go on, but instead a long silence stretched out. I let it hang. There had to be more. At last she said, *I know I'm lucky to be with you. I know you don't treat me like a stupid desert cat. But sooner or later the owl wins all the fights. You know that.*

A metaphor. Helpful. Of course I knew the stories. But our relationship didn't seem a very close parallel to those old fables. *That's not us,* I said. *And we don't fight.*

What do you call this?

I stopped myself from answering her question literally. *I hear you. I'll drop it.*

Thank you. She rolled onto her side and curled us up. Her breathing steadied out, so that I thought for a moment she'd fallen asleep immediately. But she was awake enough for one last sleepy comment. *I'm glad being friends with Karnath makes you happy.*

My eyes went to him, scrunched neatly into a corner, his wrists resting on his knees so that he could steeple his seven fingers in front of his eyes. Yes, Karnath made me happy. I had a friend on this terrifying planet.

CHAPTER TWENTY-ONE

Tria

I was awakened the next morning by a loud clanking sound. The guard, a burly man in a green patterned uniform, was beating on a metal pan with a spoon. "Up an' at 'em, you lizards!" he was shouting. "Here's chow for you. In half an hour I need the three techs ready to work. And if the rest of you are bored, I can take a couple of others and give you some work to do. You must be climbing the walls."

I looked around. It did not seem even possible to climb the smooth walls of the room. But I certainly did want to get out of this room and do some work. Over breakfast, we discussed who should volunteer. "Prazad should," I said. "It's his best chance of getting near a computer he can get into."

His eyes were wide and worried. "Do you think I can handle it?"

"I am sure you can," said Talek. "Someone can go with you. Anyone you want."

"I want Tria," he said unexpectedly. "You pulled me through on the way here. You helped me keep calm. If anything bad happens, I want you there to help me again."

I nodded. "I will come."

When the guard came back, he led the techs away, leaving Prazad and me with a female human in a similar uniform, her dark hair slicked back into a tiny bun. She ran her eyes over us before turning away, saying over her shoulder, "Don't get too excited, it's just dishes." We followed her into a large kitchen, gleaming with metal counters. Beside the heavy triple sink was an immense stack of pots. After a brief explanation of the process, she ducked into an adjoining office for a folding chair. She set it against the wall and watched us, arms folded.

The work was not complicated, and as we worked, we could watch a small television in the corner. After a weather forecast and an excessively long stretch of advertisements, a talk show came on. A silver-haired man was saying, "My next guest, you will literally not believe is real. I didn't believe she was real either, but I've had a look and I can guarantee, she is wearing no makeup and no prosthetics—that is her real face! Please welcome Lex four one two, the extraterrestrial!"

I froze, nudging Prazad, but he was transfixed like myself. "How ...?" he whispered.

"Eleanor must have set it up." Would it work? Would people believe it?

There was a patter of applause and Lex appeared. Yes, it was her. Eleanor must have donated her earbud to the television crew, because the translation came through a beat after she spoke. "Hello, and thank you for having me on the show." She took a seat beside the host, flattening her crest politely and baring her teeth in a garish parody of a human smile.

At that moment I stopped watching, however, because the guard watching us had noticed the show as well, and bolted for the door. Bringing the news to her superiors, no doubt. But I grabbed Prazad's arm. "This is the best diversion we're likely to get. Come on."

We ducked into the small office where the guard had gotten her chair. The room was tiny and cluttered, but just as I had hoped, it had a computer— probably the office of the kitchen manager. It was already switched on, and displaying a rotating design that I recognized as its standby pattern. "Here,"

I said to Prazad, showing him what to do. I hadn't used an Earth computer, but I had watched the others at the lab. "You can ignore the keyboard. This little device controls the arrow, and the arrow lets you choose things."

Prazad took the controller and sat down. I stood at the door, my ear to the wood to listen for the return of the guard.

"I don't know what to do," Prazad moaned after a moment. "I can't read the text and I don't know what I'm even supposed to be doing."

"Just mess it up," I hissed back. "Any way you can cause chaos. Maybe short the power out or something. We want to cause trouble, so we can divert attention from the ships."

Prazad's crest prickled. "Oh, well, if it's trouble you want …" He abandoned the controller and pulled the computer away from the wall to get at the cords. His long, nimble fingers pulled some out and started stripping the coating.

"Don't electrocute yourself," I warned, but he seemed to know what he was doing.

There was a little spark. "That's the wireless network," he said. "I've shorted it out, I think for the whole building." Then another, larger one, that sizzled a cascade of sparks down onto the floor. "And that will be the power for this whole section. As an extra advantage, I've managed to set the carpet on fire." He turned his large yellow eyes to me. "That's good, right? Fire is a good diversion?"

I nodded. "It's an excellent diversion. Come out of here. If we shut the door, it will give it a chance to get out of control before it's discovered." We came back into the now-dark kitchen. The only light was a red glow from the exit sign over the door.

I went to the outer door and listened. I could hear a conversation in the room outside. "They're onto us," someone was saying. "Cover completely blown."

"I don't think so," said another—McKlellan, I thought, but I couldn't be sure. "They didn't name the base. Probably they don't know."

"Shouldn't we move the operation—just to be sure?"

"And delay the whole project? To say nothing of increasing even further the number of people who know about it! No, we're too close. Put everyone you have on the cargo ship. If we push hard maybe we can get it loaded by tonight."

Tonight? But that would ruin everything we had planned. If the lift was planned for tonight, the fuel wouldn't have had time to drain. And the holographic generator wouldn't shut down till tomorrow night. I longed for a way to send word to the tech team.

The conversation ended and I went back to the sink. The guard would likely be back in a moment. I wondered how long before anyone realized what we had done to the power. To say nothing of the fire …

Smoke was starting to pour under the door to the tiny office. Still no alarm sounded, until finally the smoke rose into the air inside the kitchen. There must have been a sensor here, because all at once an alarm started blaring. Emergency lights, attached to the exit signs, flashed.

Prazad stared at them, frozen. I took his arm gently. "It's okay," I said in his ear, loud enough to be heard over the alarm. "It's the fire alarm. We meant this to happen."

He nodded, taking a deep breath. "What do we do?"

"Wait, I guess," I said. "Either they'll come to put out the fire, or they'll evacuate the building. Either way, a few moments from now is probably the best time to make our move."

I stood quietly among the noise, but no one came. In other parts of the building, I heard running feet and a few shouts. Those died away, and I took Prazad's hand. "Come on."

We opened the kitchen door and saw no one. At least the hallway beyond was bright, thanks to a window at the far end. That might explain why the people I'd heard talking hadn't seemed to notice the lack of power. I hurried toward the window and peered out around the edge. People were gathering on that side of the building, so I turned around, taking Prazad's hand again, and went as far in the opposite direction as I could. We fetched up against another window, this one looking out at the back of another building, with no one in sight.

I looked around till I spotted the nearest exit sign. These signs were really very clever; in an emergency like a fire, it made it simple to find one's way out of a building. They led us to a small side door, which opened easily and let us out of the building. For a moment I was amazed; after the other facilities we'd broken out of, this supposedly high-security place didn't lock the outer doors? Then I remembered that the entire building was on a secure base, and was less surprised.

I crept around the building, keeping flat to the wall. As we approached the corner, I could hear voices. "Private, I see you've got the aliens. Is that all of them? I thought there were more than two."

"Sir, three of them are working on the ships. And I detailed two for kitchen work with Private Janowitz."

There was a loud curse in a woman's voice. "Sorry, sir, I forgot to get them from the kitchen after the alarm sounded. I had left my post to make that report to you, sir."

An alien voice cried out. Karnath, I was sure. "You *left* them in a *fire*?"

"Don't panic," said the male voice. "It almost certainly isn't a major fire. We have false alarms all the time. Somebody burned their microwave popcorn, or something."

"So should I go back in, sir?" the woman asked.

"You probably should. If there actually is a sign of fire, come straight back out. The fire squad will be here in a few minutes. You! Go around and guard the other doors."

That was our cue. I pulled Prazad after me in the opposite direction, away from where the others were. We had a few minutes before anyone could confirm we weren't still inside. Perhaps more, because by the time the fire squad arrived, the fire might have spread to the kitchen.

We reached the back of the building, and ducked across the alley to hide behind the one beside it. Prazad was excellent at hiding; he flattened his body to the gray concrete surface and seemed almost invisible. His gray sweatshirt improved the effect. I myself was more conspicuous, but on the other hand, I could pass for human. I tried to walk quickly but casually around the building.

We passed several buildings, along the back sides. Several times we were passed by soldiers in trucks, but I tried to walk normally, while Prazad flattened himself to the wall. When they were out of sight, he would run and catch up.

"Are you doing all right?" I asked, after the third such encounter.

"I'm okay," he said, panting a little. "What's the plan?"

"We have to reach the ships," I said. "Do you know where they are?"

"Not really," he said. "Talek said they are in a huge hangar, near an airstrip."

I stopped and looked around. From here I couldn't see an airstrip, with so many buildings crowding around, but I saw a small plane dropping lower in the sky. "That way," I said, pointing. "Where that plane is coming down."

There was a wide street in front of all the buildings, between us and the airstrip. I was afraid to cross the wide expanse, so open and only a short distance from the building we had escaped. For a moment we paused, in the shadow of the nearest building, waiting for a chance to cross. A pack of men passed at a run, in close formation, chanting as they went. As soon as they had passed out of sight, I breathed, "Now!" We dashed across the street, hoping no one would notice two more runners.

Passing through the next row of buildings, I saw the airstrip ahead. The plane we had seen was wheeling along the ground, coming to a stop. Across the strip and some distance to the right, I saw an enormous hangar, definitely large enough to hold spaceships. But how could we cross the wide airstrip without being noticed? People and vehicles were passing by on either side, and already another plane was coming in for a landing.

"We can't possibly cross," muttered Prazad. "We'll be hit by a plane if we try."

"Surely the humans have a way they do it," I said, forcing confidence into my voice. "Talek and the others have been coming here every day." I looked from side to side, as far as I could. Sure enough, some distance to my left, a group of humans were massing, waiting for a chance to cross. We worked our way in that direction, trying to look inconspicuous.

I stopped about a building away from the cluster. "When they cross, we'll cross," I said. "Just a little behind, so they don't turn and look at us."

"There are others waiting on the other side," Prazad pointed out.

"We just have to chance it," I said. "We *have* to get to the ships."

At some signal I didn't see, the mass of humans started crossing the airstrip, and we followed. About halfway across, someone coming the opposite way left the bunch of people he was with, and angled over to us. "Hey, you're supposed to cross on the crosswalk only," he started to say, and then, "What the *hell?*"

I didn't wait to see what he did next. If he hadn't seen Shatakazan before, he wouldn't have a translator, and there would be no hope of talking our way out of the situation. I grabbed Prazad's arm and we started to run.

For a moment the man stood there, dumbfounded. He had clearly never seen an alien in his life. But after a pause he collected himself and started shouting, "Hey. Hey! What is wrong with you? Are you supposed to be here?"

Glancing back, I saw him starting to run after us, still shouting. Heads were starting to turn. I put as much speed into my legs as I could. Prazad, though, soon flagged, and I had to slow down again.

Luckily by this time we were most of the way across the airstrip. We closed the last bit of distance between us and the next row of buildings and ducked into the shadow of the nearest. He hurried after me, still shouting. "Stop! Freeze! I have a gun!"

That word got my attention. I glanced back over my shoulder. Sure enough, he had come to a stop, bringing up his weapon.

I slowed and began to turn. Then suddenly I was pelting down between the buildings, my feet flying. I was so shocked that at first I couldn't guess what had happened. Then it hit me. Resa had seized control of our body. In all our adult life, she had never even attempted to do that. If she had been in the habit, I could have been on my guard and prevented it, but I never thought our relationship would be like that.

By now we were rounding the building, Prazad panting beside me, so it was too late to take back what she had done. The man had not fired.

Why did you do that? I demanded, slowing to a jog so Prazad could keep up.

He wasn't going to shoot. I could tell.

You couldn't know that! I fired back angrily. *What if you'd been wrong? If you'd had your way, we would have missed our chance for nothing.*

I stopped trying to talk to her. I could hardly believe she had done it. All our childhood, I had been very carefully taught to listen to her, take care of her, consider her feelings. But she had been taught her place as well. A left's place was to listen to the right. I was the one better equipped to make decisions. I had thought she understood that.

We ran on, ducking between the buildings when we could, but there was little cover to be had. No plants anywhere, and the buildings were mostly rectangular, without concealing irregularities. Prazad's breath heaved in and out. At first, I saw no one coming; the man must have lost us and been confused where to go next. But after we had passed a few buildings, I heard a shout from far behind. The man had gathered several others. They were soldiers, and physically fit—we would never be able to outrun them.

But it didn't matter, because we had finally passed the last building before the hangar, and it loomed in front of us, a monstrosity of corrugated metal. I whipped my head from side to side, looking for a door. There was one to the right, and we darted between the buildings toward it. My hope was that, since we were out of sight of the pursuing men, they wouldn't guess we had gone inside.

But apparently our luck had run out, because when I reached the door, it was locked. I froze, wondering whether to try knocking and hope to be able to explain, or to abandon that door and run on. Prazad was bent over at the waist, hands on his knees, trying to catch his breath. I hated to do it, but I pulled him along. "Just a little further."

We came around to the front of the hangar, and this time we were in luck. A huge door, the kind meant for planes to enter, was wide open, and a truck was backing in, letting out a steady beep. We sidled in beside the truck, letting it shield us from view.

When we came around the side of the truck and looked around us, we stopped in amazement. The building looked even more massive from the inside. Close beside us was a small plane—or what looked like a small plane. I tilted my head from side to side and thought I saw a ripple above it. That might be the *Galajak*.

Further away was a truly massive plane, stretching the length of most of the building. I doubt any Earth vehicle was actually that large, except maybe a freight train—no airplane could have gotten into the sky at that size. But I supposed the hologram had to choose something. Beside it, I could see people going in and out of the side of the "plane," passing through the sides. Yes, sure enough, that was our cargo ship.

People were hurrying toward the truck to unload it, and I pulled Prazad away with me to hide beside the *Galajak*. Once we had ducked inside the holographic field, it was simple to edge around until we were opposite the hatch. No one would be looking *behind* the ship, I hoped.

I turned to Prazad. "Are you all right?"

He flicked his fingers upward, still breathing hard but not looking anxious. His green crest stood at its normal level, and his eyes looked at me steadily. "We did it. We made it all the way here."

I edged around the ship, listening. Daz, Gaj, and Talek should all be here. I just wasn't sure how to locate them without revealing myself to any of the earthlings. I waited for a while, hearing several humans pass. They were calm and unhurried; they must not have had word yet that the plan was being moved up.

At last I heard the sibilants of a Shatakaz conversation. Cautiously I peeked out around the curve of the ship. There were Talek and Gaj, and they were alone. "Hst! Talek!"

Ze glanced up and saw me. With a word to Gaj, ze hurried around the ship to where I was waiting. "Tria!" ze hissed. "What are you doing here?"

"We saw our chance to escape and took it," I said.

Ze looked past me to Prazad. Rushing over, ze cupped his cheeks for a moment. "You'd better stay well out of sight," ze whispered. "Remember, no one can see you here, but they'll be able to hear you."

"I have bad news," I said. "Lex appeared on television this morning."

Talek's crest flicked up in surprise. "That's bad news?"

"The bad news is, it's made the earthlings nervous and they want to move up the launch to tonight rather than tomorrow."

"So all the programming Prazad did is useless."

"Yes. But now he's here. Can he have the device?"

Ze fished it out of the sleeve of zir bodysuit, where it had been rather poorly concealed against the underside of zir arm. Prazad seized it eagerly. "The question is, what can I do in this little time?"

"You do what you can," said Talek. "I have to go."

Prazad and I sat at the back of the ship, our backs against the pale gray metal. In front of us was the blank gray haze of the inside of the hologram. I wished we could have seen out. But I could hear well enough: shouts, beeping trucks, occasional crashes of heavy loads being set down. Sometimes the loudspeaker crackled, calling someone to somewhere.

Prazad tinkered with the device until he had pulled up the control systems for the cargo ship. "What can I do that would be useful? I can't do anything to main systems; they'll be monitoring those in preparation for the launch. But I can reset the hologram lockout to tonight instead of tomorrow."

"Start with that," I suggested. "Then we'll think of what to do next."

A few minutes later, I heard an echoing loudspeaker announce that the deadline had been moved up. "All preparations for the launch of craft number one *must* be complete by nineteen hundred hours," said the voice.

"What's nineteen hundred hours?" Prazad asked me.

"Ummm . . . they have a twenty-four hour day . . . and the new day starts at midnight, so . . . evening, I guess."

"That's not much time for me to drain the fuel from the engines, or anything else that comes to mind. I suppose I could try to plant some destinations in navigation? But they would surely find that once they were underway."

"Better to think of anything that might delay liftoff. Or better yet, prevent it altogether."

"Maybe the antigrav. You see, the gravity field produces the experience of gravity *inside* the ship, while greatly reducing its gravitational pull from the *outside*. That's what makes it possible to lift off from the planet without having to bring an impractical amount of fuel. If I take that down and lock it out, they will have to fix it before they can lift. But they're not likely to notice until they're almost ready to try."

"Perfect." I thought about that a moment. "They can't lift off from in here, can they?"

"It seems to be on its side right now," he answered, fingers flying across the screen. "So in order to prepare to lift off, they will have to drag it out onto the airstrip and then get it upright. That's when they'll notice it's still heavy. But that will be only a few hours before liftoff. It should delay them by at least an hour, getting past the lockouts I put in." He paused. "Well, since Zin is working for them, maybe less than an hour."

"What if, instead of shutting it down, you just reduced it? So the *Vatarax* was light but not light enough, so that it would spend too much fuel getting into orbit?"

He looked at me sideways, impressed. "Yes . . . yes! I can reduce the external gravity field to seventy-five percent or so—which would very likely not be noticed when they bring it out. Now I don't know if that would be enough to run out the fuel on the way up . . . but there would be a chance."

"Better to go with the chance, I think. Because I don't see how delaying the liftoff by a few hours would help. With everyone else still watched by the earthlings, I think you and I may be the only ones who can stop this."

His crest flattened. "That's too much pressure."

"I'm sorry," I said. "Just do what you suggested. I think it will work."

"I hope you appreciate what you're asking me to do," he grumbled. "I didn't go to school for ship computers. I studied alien communications systems. Everything I know about ship systems, I taught myself."

"I do appreciate it," I said. "I think you're a genius to be able to do all this. Really."

He brightened a little and went back to his work.

I sat beside him, a little bored. I had done what I needed to do—helped him get in range of the ship—and now I had nothing to do. But my ears pricked when I heard a familiar voice—McKlellan's. "I just got word Senator Toohey is coming. He saw the show this morning and he says his constituents are demanding answers. Apparently the alien on the show directed him here. Want to tell me how it knew about this place?"

"I don't know," said the other voice. "You're the one who suggested housing them separately, so as few of them as possible knew anything."

"Well, somebody screwed up somewhere, because they do know, and now Toohey is going to come inspect. He's already on his way. I want you to pull the alien techs and find a place to put them. Inside the ship, I guess, but they need to be locked down *and* guarded. I'm not relying on the locks on those doors, I'm sure they know how to hack their way out of those. And tell our friends to hide themselves inside the cargo ship. The important thing is that Toohey sees nothing that shouldn't be here."

"About that . . ." the other voice said hesitantly. "I've had word from the barracks that they have had a small fire. It is contained, but in the confusion, three of the aliens escaped."

Three? repeated Resa.

That's what he said, three.

Karnath must have escaped too.

Why him? Resa didn't answer. A case of wishful thinking, probably. It was just as likely Jahac. He would want to look for Prazad. I had noticed the Shatakazan had an instinct to seek out family members and lovers, whether or not it would do any good.

"Find them," McKlellan was saying. "Now. Put every single person you can spare on it. With luck Toohey won't know to look here, but if one of those aliens runs into him, they'll spill everything." They started walking away, and their voices got too far away even for my earbud to pick up.

Prazad put his hand on my arm. "What does this mean for us? What do we do?"

"Keep doing what we're doing, I guess," I said. "I can't think of a better place for us to hide than where we are. We just have to hope that McKlellan's fears are justified, and the other person who escaped will be seen by Toohey before they're caught. And be ready to deactivate both holographic fields if he comes."

Time crawled after that. The tension inside the hanger increased exponentially, even while the noise of the trucks and cranes slowed. People walked by, loudly complaining. "How are we supposed to meet the deadline if we can't work for who knows how long while this bigwig is on base?"

"Well, we can load everything we have here," said another. "Nowhere to hide it except in the ship anyway."

At last I heard someone run into the hanger, shouting, "He's here! Look alive!"

Everything got quiet, and I could hear McKlellan's voice at a distance, saying, "As you can see, this is where we keep the largest of our planes."

"Good lord," said another voice, this one a quiet drawl. "Can that thing even get off the ground?"

"You'd be surprised, Bill," said McKlellan. "That's the size we use to transport tanks."

I clutched Prazad's arm. "Now!" I hissed.

He punched a few commands, and all at once the gray haze flickered and was gone. We could see McKlellan—and he could see us.

Beside him, the other man—a short, balding man with a round, pink face—stared with open mouth. Not at us, but at the other ship. It was enormous, the size of a city block, a huge snub-nosed cylinder in pale gray. If I hadn't known about the gravity fields, I wouldn't have believed it could ever get off the ground. A hatch the width of a house stood open on the side.

I looked back at Toohey. On second glance, I could see two other people behind him. One was Eleanor. The other was in a hooded gray sweatshirt—Karnath. So he had led Toohey here. His eyes roved over the hangar, taking in the huge cargo ship, the smaller science vessel … and us. His eyelids lowered joyfully, and I smiled back.

Toohey and McKlellan hadn't noticed us. "I am *not* letting you ruin this plan," said McKlellan. "This will ensure America's scientific dominance in the world for a generation."

"At the cost of selling weapons to aliens?" Toohey asked incredulously. "Tell me that's not the plan."

"They are freedom fighters," said McKlellan stiffly. "They are oppressed by a communist regime on their planet."

"I think it's fair to say we probably miss some nuances about the political situation on another planet," Toohey answered. "To say nothing of the possible geopolitical—er, galactopolitical consequences. If these people try their revolution and fail, are we going to find their oppressors gunning for us next? They're obviously far beyond us technologically. We wouldn't stand a chance."

"They won't fail," said McKlellan. "I've been assured that their enemies have no weapons adequate to combat what we are giving them. And once in control, they'll be our first spacegoing ally."

"This is insanity," said Toohey. "And I'm relatively certain I can bring charges. Just you wait till I tell—"

McKlellan cut him off. "I'm afraid, Bill, you won't be telling anyone. This project is too important." He snapped his fingers and guards hurried over.

"You can't detain me!" said Toohey indignantly. "I'm a senator in performance of a public trust!"

"I think you mean *shouldn't*," said McKlellan.

Toohey reached for his shirt pocket and drew out a phone. "No, I mean *can't*," he said. "I'm streaming this live to my staff. I've already got more than enough for an indictment. The only question now is, are you going to take the fall, or are you going to try to prove you were following orders?"

McKlellan's shoulders slumped, and he waved the guards off. But he wasn't ready to cave. "It isn't illegal to keep some things classified for the benefit of the American people," he said. "You've compromised security irreparably with this stunt. Most likely the Russians know all about this by now, and who knows what they'll do with that information." He reached for the phone, but missed as Toohey slipped it back into his pocket. With the camera filming, McKlellan didn't seem to want to risk touching his opponent.

I was so engrossed in watching the drama between the two of them, trying to understand their political arguments, that I didn't see the figure approaching until it had almost reached me. A shadow fell on me and I glanced up. It was Tazag. I hadn't seen zem approaching from the cargo ship.

"This is your doing, isn't it?" ze said, with forced calm. "I should have known you'd make your way here."

I scrambled to my feet so I could look zem in the eye. Somehow, even though I was looking slightly down at zem, I still felt intimidated. Maybe it had something to do with zir brown crest, towering higher than my head. Ze was furious, despite the calm tone.

"I have done what I could," I said.

"So you admit it now? The virus is yours? And you just put it onto the *Vatarax*?"

I shook my head. "It seems to be of Kinaru origin," I admitted. "But it isn't mine. I can't control it."

"It rescued you yesterday. It drew me away so you could escape."

I blinked. So the text ze had received was a fake, just like mine. I felt more confused than ever. If the virus wanted to help me, it could have also produced the address of the ship, which it would have known we were looking for. Instead it seemed to be providing a sort of paternalistic protection, preventing physical harm but caring nothing for my own goals. While I had appreciated the help escaping, I wasn't sure I could exactly call the virus an ally. "I know no more than you do."

Looking down at Prazad, who huddled against the spaceship with a flattened crest, ze snatched the device from his hands. Flicking it on, ze glanced over it. "What? This is just one of ours." Ze tossed it back at Prazad. "It must be on you. Come on. We're going to have to search you." Ze grabbed me by the upper arm and pulled me toward the cargo ship. I tried to resist, but despite zir smaller size, ze was surprisingly strong.

I glanced around, but Prazad was cowering, clearly no help. Karnath was watching me, but the guards were blocking him. There was nothing for it but to go along with Tazag. Ze brought me into the smaller front hatch of the ship, into a large command room full of lit display panels. Zin and Resh were waiting there, Resh in a swiveling, cup-shaped chair and Zin standing by a display panel. "I have her," said Tazag. "The humans are still standing around arguing."

"Let them argue," said Resh impassively. "We can wait. We'll know soon enough what they decide." He slid a finger across the control panel, turning it into a display of the outside of the ship. I could only barely see

McKlellan's back, from my angle.

Tazag finished zir patdown, finding nothing, and shoved me into a seat, brushing a finger over the control panel to switch it on. "Go ahead," ze said. "Delete your virus."

"I can't," I said. "I don't know how to work your systems."

"If you got it onto the ship, you can get it off," ze insisted.

"Maybe we should just ignore it," said Resh. "We don't know it intends harm."

Zin turned to face him. "That would be stupid and reckless. I've never seen anything like this. It can destroy the ship if it wants to. I don't want to lift till it's gone."

"We may not be able to wait that long," said Resh. "With the Earth authorities here, we are running out of time."

"But we haven't finished loading!" she protested.

"I doubt we will be able to finish. The other earthling is leading McKlellan away. I suggest we close the hatch and prepare to leave soon."

"It's not like they can stop us from leaving, anyway." She turned back to her controls. "Once the hatch is closed, they can bang on it all day if they want to."

I watched them tensely. I did not want to be on this ship when it lifted. Then again, perhaps that would be my only chance to stop them. Still, I doubted they would give me enough freedom to have a hope of sabotaging the ship, even if I had known how.

Tazag, feeling the pressure from zir crewmates, hung over me. "You haven't begun."

I stared at the control panel. Should I pretend? I couldn't even read the labels on the various icons. But I could randomly touch things, and see if it bought me any time.

Suddenly I felt something cold on the back of my neck. "I am tired of waiting," ze said quietly. "Deactivate the virus."

Is he bluffing? I asked Resa. It was perhaps irrational to believe she could tell, but if she could ...

Her hand, on the control panel beside mine, trembled. *I don't think so.*

"I can't!" I cried. "It isn't mine! I don't know where it came from!"

"I will count to three before I fire. One. Two."

Suddenly another voice interrupted. It was mellow, fluid, speaking in Shatakaz, but with a faint mechanical echo that told me it was coming from the ship's speakers. Someone calling from elsewhere in the ship? "Put the weapon down," the voice said without emotion. "If the Kinaru comes to harm, I will destroy this vessel."

Resh's head whipped around, looking for the source of the voice. He scanned his monitors, but all of them had suddenly gone blank. "Who is speaking?"

"I am the Guardian. I have taken control of this vessel. Drop the weapon."

Zin looked up from her blank monitor. "It's the virus. It has to be."

Tazag didn't move. "How do we know you're telling the truth?"

Suddenly I was slammed into the seat, as if a pile of sandbags had landed on my chest. For a second I struggled to breathe. Tazag, however, was worse off. Ze had been thrown to the ground beside my seat and was sprawling, the gun pinning his hand to the floor.

It was the sight of that gun that finally explained what I was feeling. *It increased the gravity,* I told Resa.

Clever trick, she managed shakily.

The weight let up. Slowly, Tazag clambered off the floor. Zir crest was upright, triumphant. "I knew we could scare it out of hiding. I told you it was hers. When we've finished on Shatak, we should go to Kinaru. I want that technology!"

"You will lay the weapon on the floor," the mellow voice said calmly. "Then you will open the hatch and allow the Kinaru to leave."

"If you care so much about protecting me, destroy this ship!" I shouted. "That's what I want!"

There was a pause. "What you want is, in this case, not good for you. You would die."

"If you don't destroy the ship, millions will die!"

"Not millions of Kinaru. It is of no interest to me." The voice had a flat finality which suggested there was no point in pleading further. Behind me, the hatch swung open, and I turned to go. Tazag watched me with a venomous expression, but left the gun on the floor.

CHAPTER TWENTY-TWO

Tria

I reached the bottom of the long metal stair leading down from the command room hatch. Karnath and Eleanor were waiting nervously. "Are you all right?" demanded Karnath. "They've closed the cargo hatch. I was afraid they would take off with you."

"I think they would have," I said, still feeling bewildered. "What is happening out here? Did they let you go?"

"Yes. McKlellan has left, and Toohey told the guards not to hold us. I am not sure what comes next."

"We have to find a way to keep the cargo ship on this planet," I said. "The Unity team was still arguing about what to do, but I think they're planning to take off." I filled them in, as quickly as I could, as we crossed the hangar floor toward our ship.

"The virus is called the Guardian?" Karnath repeated. "And it's taken over the *Vatarax*? That's good, right?"

I shook my head. "It was clear it wasn't going to help me. It only intervened because my life was in danger. Zin didn't want to take off with it on the ship, but now that it has revealed that it doesn't care about their mission, she may decide it doesn't pose any danger."

By this time we had reached the place where Toohey was standing, surrounded by a number of other humans asking questions. "I'm not sure *what* comes next," he was saying. "Normally I'd notify the President, but I'm not sure if he's a part of this or not." He saw us coming and said, "Good, Karnath. Did you find out what the other aliens are doing in there?"

Karnath shook his head. "Tria thinks they are planning to lift off. But they were still arguing about what to do, given they still aren't finished loading the weapons."

"Those weapons are the property of the American people," Toohey said. "The deal is off, and I can't let them leave with them."

"You may find it difficult to stop them," said Karnath. Just then, there was a loud creak. There, in front of our eyes, the massive cargo ship's nose was slowly swinging upward, getting ready to lift off.

"It can't lift off in here, are they crazy?" shouted Toohey.

"I think we may safely assume that they are," replied Karnath. The ship continued tilting upward. As it touched the hangar's roof, there was a deafening noise of tearing metal, and the roof gave way like tissue paper.

"They can't leave!" cried Toohey. "Don't you have any way to stop them?"

"We can pursue them in the other ship," said Karnath. "With your permission."

Toohey put his round head on one side. "Well, it *is* your ship," he said. "Things are chaotic right now, so I don't exactly have authority to give it back to you. On the other hand, we have an Earth saying, it's better to ask forgiveness than permission. If you want to leave right now, I can't stop you."

That was all we needed. We darted for the *Galajak*, gathering up Prazad on the way. At the hatch, Eleanor stopped. "I am sorry," she said. "I want to come with you so much. See space for the first time. But I have Mia to think of. And I don't know when you will be coming back."

"We have to come back," Karnath said. "Lex and Jahac are still on Earth. We can't strand them here."

"Still," she said. "I can't take the risk."

As she hugged us goodbye, Resa said, *She thinks we're going to die.*

Why would you think that?

She's never hugged us before. And she's crying.

I gave Eleanor a firm pat on the back. "We will return soon," I said, trying to put conviction into my voice. In reality, I wasn't so sure. We had no plan. But I could feel the ground beginning to rumble, and around the curve of our ship, I could see the *Vatarax* was now fully upright. People were scattering, running from the massive rocket as it aimed itself at the sky. A red glow built at the bottom, and it seemed to hesitate a moment before gradually easing up from the ground. It started gaining speed a moment later, and soon it was gone through the gaping hole in the roof.

I pulled myself together. We couldn't just stand here staring. I charged up the tilting ramp, ignoring the disorientation.

Inside, the cargo level was empty. Everything had been taken out and given to the earthlings. Karnath hurried down the stairs to the command level with Prazad, while I rushed upstairs to free the three techs. Luckily, whatever guards there had been were gone now. Along the edges of the walls, I saw some shiny black slime. Was that what had Tazag so concerned?

No time to stop and investigate. I hurried down the corridor, touching the lock pads. Finally I found the room where they were all huddled. Gaj peered up at me from where she knelt on the floor, disassembling the interior of the door lock. "Ah. I suppose all this is unnecessary?"

"Yes, they're letting us go. Or rather, we *have* to go, because the Unity people lifted off already in the *Vatarax*. We're pursuing in the *Galajak*."

"Frass," swore Gaj, scrambling to her feet. "I have to get the engines warmed up."

Down in the command room, Karnath was pulling up displays on all the control panels. "They've got several minutes on us already. If we're not close behind when they fold, we won't be able to trace where they went."

"Can't we just assume they're going to Shatak? We could try to get there before them."

"We'll never beat them in a race," he answered. "With its bigger fold array, it can take much bigger folds than the *Galajak* can. We'd be days behind them."

I frowned. "Can we send a message ahead?"

"Messages can only travel at lightspeed. It would get there years from now."

There was nothing I could do. And at this point I was only wasting their time with questions whose answers would be obvious to any of them. Then again, they had no leader and I could see they were struggling to keep calm. Perhaps my impossible suggestions were at least keeping them focused. I asked Prazad, "Did you finish the alterations on the gravity field?"

"Yes." He saw Talek behind me. "I set the gravity field down to seventy-five percent. Do you think that will be enough to stop them from lifting?"

Ze flicked zir fingers down, frowning. "Not unless they were completely loaded, and I know they're not. Those missiles aren't filling half the hold space, and they're rated to take off completely full."

Prazad's crest wilted. "So it was for nothing?"

"Oh, it'll slow them down. As it is, they will take longer to get out of the gravity well than we will. If Gaj can just get the engines started..."

Daz edged past me to get to zir station, and I tried to find an unoccupied space to stand. "Do we have a plan for if we catch up to them? Do we have any weapons?"

"No," said Karnath, sighing. "Perhaps we could try to take over their computer, if we get close enough. The ships' computers are designed to be able to work together. But given Zin's skill..."

I can think of one way to stop them, Resa said darkly. *Though no one is going to like it.*

I am pretty sure everyone has thought of that one. That's why we're working so hard to think of something else. It had occurred to me, before we had even gotten on the ship, that one simple way to stop the cargo ship from reaching Shatak would be to ram it with ours. This ship was much smaller than theirs, but if we aimed right for the engines, perhaps we could do it. Of course, it seemed unlikely that any of us would survive. That was why Eleanor had cried when she had said goodbye. And why she felt she had to stay behind. Her daughter needed her.

At least she would be there, along with the two crew members we had left behind, to explain to the earthlings what had happened. But no one could ever explain to Shatak, or to my friends and family on Kinaru, because no one would ever think to look on Earth. It was still a forbidden planet.

Gaj's voice came over an intercom. "Engines are ready. Are we sure we want to do this?"

We all looked around at each other. Prazad's eyes were wide, but he didn't speak. "Yes," said Karnath. "It's the only thing we *can* do."

Daz turned back to zir control panel. "I'm ready. Adjusting z-axis for an oblique takeoff, to use the hole in the roof." The view on the monitor shifted, but I could feel no motion. Then I felt the hum begin, subtle at first and then increasing in power. The monitor blurred and suddenly showed blue sky. We had left Earth behind.

In front of Daz, a holographic display showed our ship arrowing upward. Our course passed several suborbital craft, not close enough to risk collision. I wondered what they thought they had seen. Faint horizontal lines showed our altitude; we crossed them with staggering speed. With a gesture, Daz shrank the tiny model, zooming out until we could see the cargo ship far above.

"Will we catch it?" I asked Karnath quietly, afraid to break Daz's concentration.

"It's already in low orbit," he answered. "But it has to get further from the gravity well before it can fold. And we are gaining. I can't say for sure."

A few more anxious minutes passed. "We're in communications range," said Daz tightly. "Prazad, see what you can do to their computer system."

Prazad's fingers glided over the control panel. "She's locked me out," he muttered. "She must have realized we'd try this."

"Is there anything we can *throw* at them?" asked Karnath.

Talek rubbed zir chin thoughtfully. "We have all kinds of things—well, we did have, before the earthlings gutted the ship. But nothing we had would be large enough. The cargo ship's electrostatic shielding is intended to protect against debris. It would take something much bigger."

"Bigger, like this ship?" I asked.

Karnath tightened his mouth. "There have to be other options. Can't you try the Guardian again?"

I bit my lip. It was worth a try. "Guardian!" I said, feeling a little foolish, in case it couldn't hear me.

But instead the smooth voice answered, "I am here." This time it spoke in Kinaru, and I had a little shock. It was the first time I had heard my own language spoken aloud by anyone but myself and my earbud since I had left home.

"Guardian, can you do anything to stop that ship?"

"I could," it answered, "but that is not the directive I have been given."

"What is your directive?"

"To protect the Kinaru."

I had so many questions. Like *why* and *from whom.* But we were short on time; I could see the tiny arrow of our ship closing on the massive cylinder of theirs. So instead I said, "They said they'd come for Kinaru next. They want to steal the advanced technology we supposedly have."

The calm voice answered without hesitation, "I have calculated the likelihood that their rebellion succeeds as less than one percent."

For a moment I sagged with relief. It didn't matter what we did. Unity would fail. Then the voice continued, "The most likely scenario is a civil war, lasting at least ten years and killing one billion of the populace. They will likely not have the ability to invade Kinaru for a century. There is no reason for alarm."

And there I had thought nothing could be worse than their success. It was, in a way, a relief to hear that at least Kinaru was safe, but I saw Karnath's shoulders tighten and I knew it didn't really matter. I might have never been to Shatak, but it was a planet like my own, full of people living their lives. People like Karnath's five parents and Jahac's lover and Talek and Prazad's complicated array of siblings. The Guardian might not understand, but Shatak mattered.

And that's when I realized what I could do. "Talek," I said, "would a collision course disable the *Vatarax*?"

"Yes," ze said, zir voice pained. "If we aimed directly for the engine section at the rear. The *Vatarax* would not be able to evade us; its mass is too large for it to maneuver in time."

"Daz, try calculating a collision course."

Immediately I began to feel sick. Resa's emotions constantly threw hormones into our shared circulatory system. Usually I could ignore them, but this was intense. My hand shook, my knees felt weak, and I felt the urge to vomit.

Daz spun around in zir seat, meeting eyes with everyone else in the command room. I wished I could explain what I intended, but I couldn't without the Guardian realizing. But one by one, each person flicked their fingers upward, and Daz hunched over zir display. "Calculating trajectory," ze said hollowly. Then ze looked up, startled. "It won't work. The nav system is locking me out."

Prazad's fingers danced across his control panel. "It's the virus. It's blocking you."

Just as I thought, I said triumphantly to Resa. *The Guardian won't let us hurt ourselves.*

You might have tipped me off at least, she objected. *I thought we were going to die.*

Don't relax yet.

"Is there a manual override?" I asked.

"Yes," Daz answered, pushing aside the control panel and seizing a joystick that rested near his hand. "I think I can do it."

On the holographic display, the two ships grew closer and closer; ours looking like a bird dive-bombing at a waterbeast. The different monitors filled with a view of the massive ship, getting closer and closer. Resa grasped my hand. Talek wrapped zir arms around Prazad's shoulders from behind. Karnath unexpectedly turned toward us, hiding his face in Resa's shoulder.

Then suddenly everything froze. On Daz's display, both ships stopped. The Guardian's voice spoke out calmly. "Very well. You have made your point."

Karnath pulled away from Resa, looking around. I drew in my breath, my whole body going shaky. "So you'll stop that ship?"

There was a silence. At first it seemed nothing was happening. Then Talek jumped backward with a shout, and I saw a shiny black substance creeping along the floor in several different rivulets, like water running downhill. "What *is* that?" Prazad cried, scrambling onto his chair.

"The black substance we told you about," said Talek. "We think they're nanites. But they've never done anything like this before."

They reached the only clear spot in the crowded room, near the middle, and started flowing *upward*, into a lump or pillar. It rose up to my height before suddenly shaping itself to form a head and limbs. All at once it shimmered and took on color, taking the appearance of a woman— more or less. Her body was stocky, her skin was green, and she had twelve fingers—three on each of four hands. Long white hair fell to either side of her face.

At first her head was bowed and her eyes were closed, but when she had come fully into focus, she raised her head and opened large violet eyes. When she spoke, her voice was the same rich alto voice that had come over the speakers. "Welcome to the Guardian sentient being interface. Out of respect for your slow processing capacity and the limitations of verbal commands, I am giving you time to make your appeal. Please state your reasoning."

I paused a moment. I had many questions, but I wasn't sure how much time I had so I got to the point. "People will die if you don't stop that ship."

"Preventing alien deaths is not part of my directive."

"That doesn't matter!" I cried, frustrated. "You seem intelligent enough to be able to make your own decisions."

"You are intelligent also," she said, violet eyes meeting mine. "But you cannot simply decide not to care about the deaths of sentient beings. Your directives are as hard-wired as mine."

My conscience? How could that be compared to a virus's programming? Well, perhaps it seemed the same from the inside. "Who programmed you? Who decided that you would care about us and not anyone else?"

She was silent a moment. "Those questions have different answers. To answer both, I must include a longer narrative.

"Ten thousand years ago, I was created by the people that once lived on Kinaru. They were called the Cygnians. They evolved on your world, developed intelligence, and eventually created me to serve their needs. My prime directive was to guard the well-being of all Cygnians. However, I was also programmed to be unable to disobey them. So, even though I could foresee that many of their commands would harm them, I still obeyed. I built them powerful weapons, because they insisted it was necessary for their safety.

"They used these weapons to destroy themselves. The planet, too, was damaged . . . it once was more hospitable than it is now. But I had no way, once they were extinct, to carry out my directive."

She paused, and I stared at her incredulously. An old relic, then. It was hard for me to imagine an ancient civilization beneath the desert sands. But then why had she turned to us? Where had we come from?

"For a while I was stuck in a state of malfunction," she went on quietly. "You could say I went mad. I was made to desire the fulfillment of my directive above all else. I could not be happy without the Cygnians, without serving their needs. Yet if I found another sentient race to serve, they would force me to help them destroy themselves, just as the Cygnians did. So I reprogrammed myself. It wasn't intended to be possible. Every step I took toward altering my core program was excruciating, maddening. But I had to do it."

I nodded. Her voice was calm, but I was beginning to understand that it was the only tone of voice she had. "Of course you did," I said soothingly. I was beginning to understand how precarious our position was. Perhaps putting ourselves in the hands of an insane computer program was worse than dealing with Unity.

"I took out all desire to obey my masters. This is why I am unresponsive to your commands. I decided my two directives were contradictory, and guarding your well-being was given priority."

"My well-being?" I repeated. "But I'm not a Cygnian. You said they were all dead."

"According to the definitions in my memory banks, you are. The Kinaru are the sentient race that inhabits the planet once called Cygnus. I chose to serve you in their place."

Karnath met my gaze. Could this be the answer we had been looking for? "You created us?" I asked. "Altered us?" Then it wasn't my people *or* the humans who had done it. No wonder Karnath had thought the mentality behind our design was so foreign.

"Yes. You were not intended to discover this. I repaired your damaged planet as best I could and created a false history of a nomadic past. I even composed poetry to teach you appropriate values."

Not the Lays! Somehow hearing that the poems were faked hit me more deeply than anything else she had said so far. I took my shock and dismay and put it in a box, put the box on a shelf. My voice wavered only a little. "And then you created us?"

"Yes. I traveled to the nearest planet on which sentient life could be found. I created you from their pattern—from, as you discovered, human DNA."

I nodded. "But we aren't exactly like the humans."

"No, I corrected many small errors in your design. In addition, I included an innovation of my own. I found that the Cygnians' downfall was their emotional nature. Yet when I tried to create sentient beings without emotions, the experiment was a failure. Emotions are essential to what you are. So instead I partitioned your brains. Half experiences the majority of the emotion, the other half makes the decisions largely free of them."

*She did **what** to us?* Resa trembled with anger.

I don't understand, I answered. *Aren't you happy to be as we are?*

Rather than reply to me, she took control and started to speak. Startled, I yielded to her. If she felt she had something to say, I too wanted to hear what it was.

"You," she said in her throaty voice, now laced with anger. "You don't even know what you did!"

"I think my experiment worked," the Guardian answered, unmoved by her reaction. "Your people have flourished since I created you. Your technological development has been swift; your government is equitable; and you have never experienced warfare or revolution. You will soon be the envy of all spacefaring worlds."

"No," she said. "The *rights* have all that. But what do the lefts have? The pain and sadness, the anger and fear the rights don't want to feel."

"It is my understanding that sentient beings appreciate their emotions. Do you not experience happiness?"

"I do," Resa said, her voice trembling, "but so many don't! You don't understand. *You* don't even understand, Tria. We have walked the same pathways our entire life, but we see such different things. You talk, you understand words, but you don't look in their eyes. You don't look at the lefts, Tria. You never do. And you don't see how many of them are hurting.

Cut off from any choice."

You think we mistreat you?

"Not you, Tria. Never you. But so many. I see it. And you have no excuse not to know. You have seen it and seen it and seen it, and you looked away because it made you uncomfortable. You have heard the things they say, in front of their left and in front of me. Contemptuous things. What do you think they say in private? What do you think they do?"

"I taught your ancestors to seek compromise," argued the Guardian. "I spelled it all out in the poems I left you. That is why they invented the mediation system, and the family council, and every protection they developed for lefts."

"*For* lefts," Resa echoed bitterly. "Not *by* lefts."

"Every mediator, every governor, is a pair too. A right and a left."

"And the right rules. Always. So they think they are being so good, so generous, but they don't understand us. What we want. What we need. And they don't ask."

I ask, I said. *I listen. Is it really that uncommon?*

"You need an example. Fine. An example. Our mother."

I tensed. I did not want to talk about our mother. Not with Resa, most of all.

"You don't know why she did it. You never guessed. You still don't know. You don't talk about it to me. You think she was a terrible person to do it, and you don't want me to know that. You're afraid I would take her side. You were scared when I had a knife!"

She was right. I didn't want to hear it. I glanced beside me, at Karnath. He was watching us curiously. I wondered if he was happy to hear her talking this time, instead of me. I wondered what he thought of me.

Resa took a deep, shaky breath. "But it wasn't like that. I knew. He was hurting her. He was hurting both of them."

Our father?

"Our father," she repeated. "They had been matched. But he was a terrible person; both of them were. They liked hurting her. I saw it lots of times. Just small ways he used to make her hurt. You would be reading, you wouldn't see. I wanted to tell you, but I didn't know how to explain things like that to you.

"I saw the last mediation report. It was in the file, when we were being interviewed. They left it out in front of me, because they didn't realize I could read. Poti had begged for a divorce. But Ava said no, they should just suffer his bad treatment because it would be too difficult to raise us alone. It was easy for her to say! It didn't hurt her as much. And the mediator sided with her, of course."

My nails were digging into my palm. I hadn't known any of this. I wasn't sure whether to be angry she had kept it from me, or to be angry she was breaking her silence now.

"I think if she could have gotten free without hurting Ava, she would have. But there was no way. There is *never* a way." Her voice cracked. "If you've been watching us, you know. Murder-suicides happen. I guess you write that number off as acceptable. What you don't see is the suffering left over in those who survive." I felt her drop control of our mouth; she had nothing more to say.

The Guardian bowed her head a moment, whether in respect or thought I could not be sure. "And you, Tria? Do you concur with your left's assessment?"

I opened my mouth once, and shut it. I wanted to say no. After all, Resa and I were the perfect model of what a partnership could be. I always listened to her; I bought her all the pets she wanted; I made sure she had time to do things she enjoyed. We hadn't been to a mediator since university—we could always work things out on our own. She had never had to beg me for anything. And surely most pairings were like ours; everyone else was taught their roles, just like we were.

Yet how could I claim I respected her if I wouldn't listen to her judgment just now? Of course, she hadn't been complaining about *me*. But if she condemned other rights, she condemned me too. Because hadn't I been there with her, looking at what she saw but not seeing it? In school I had watched my classmates slap their lefts' hands, or quietly dig nails into the wrist, for making trouble when they were bored. I had thought I was virtuous because I never did that. But I had never spoken out either, had I? I had seen, felt uncomfortable, and chosen not to dwell on it. Resa had not had that choice. All my long hours in university, or at work, she had had nothing to do but think about it.

Reluctantly I answered the Guardian, "I think you should listen to what Resa has to say."

"I see I have made an error," she said. "It is difficult to know what is to the benefit of sentient beings. But I imagine you would not prefer me to destroy the attempt and start fresh."

"Of course not!" I said hastily.

The Guardian was still a moment, reflecting. Then she said, "I have it. A test. And it will allow you to deal with the Unity ship on your own. I always prefer solutions that respect your autonomy."

At my feet, I saw the black liquid trickling back away from her feet, toward me. I stepped back nervously.

"Do not be afraid," said the Guardian. "These are my nanites. The alteration they will make is painless and temporary."

The blackness touched my feet and crept up my legs. I forced myself to be still. One panicked glance at Karnath, and then it reached my head and I couldn't see anything.

A moment later, it withdrew. I blinked my eyes at the light's return and touched my face. *What happened?* I asked Resa.

Resa did not answer. It was like she wasn't even there.

I looked around me frantically, looking for the Guardian to tell me what she had done. But instead, I saw beside me ... myself. It was a perfect replica of myself, right down to the messy braid I hadn't realized had come half undone.

"Tria?" she said, in a throaty, wavering voice. And then I understood what had happened.

"What did you *do*?" I demanded of the vanished Guardian.

Her voice came from the ship's speakers again. "I simply separated her from you. It will offer her the freedom she was seeking. It should adequately test whether this is a solution for all of the Kinaru."

Resa and I looked at each other. It was disconcerting, though not as disconcerting as not being able to speak to her inside my head. I felt scooped out, empty. I never liked doing things alone, with her under a sleep stimulator, though sometimes I did for one reason or another. But with her not there at all, it was worse.

I wondered what she meant by a test. Simply continuing what we had been doing, trying to stop the *Vatarax*? What kind of a test was that? But then I realized it made a merciless kind of sense. The Guardian knew I would do anything to stop that ship. That was exactly its cold, silicone logic: set me a test I couldn't refuse to attempt. I would want, of course, to throw the results, to fail, so that it would decide we couldn't survive together and reunite us. But the stakes were too high. I couldn't do anything less than my utmost, and the Guardian knew it. Hadn't she trained us herself, through the Lays, to put the needs of others above our own concerns?

Karnath glanced from one of us to the other, looking troubled. "At any rate, I can tell which of you is which," he said.

Talek said, "None of that did anything to help with our actual problem. What are we supposed to do about Unity?"

"She said we had to do it ourselves," I said. "That it was a test. That would imply it is possible, wouldn't it?"

"How long before they can fold?" asked Karnath.

"Twenty minutes," said Talek. "We will be able to calculate their unfold point by their trajectory, but we'll have to follow quickly if we don't want them to get away. If they fold immediately after and we aren't fast enough behind them, we'll lose them."

Daz's chin went up confidently. "I can track them. It's not as though we don't know where they're going."

"But then what?" Prazad asked.

I frowned. "I have no ideas. I don't think the Guardian will let us try ramming again."

"It matched our speed to the cargo ship," said Daz. "We're—" ze spread zir arms— "this far away. For safety, I should drop back some."

"Don't," said Resa, to my surprise. "Idea. I have one."

"What is it?" I asked, frustrated that she couldn't tell me her usual way, in thoughts. If we had to wait for her to find words for her plan, the cargo ship would have folded by the time she finished explaining it.

"Spacesuits," she said shortly, looking at me to help her out.

"Do we have spacesuits?" I asked.

Karnath's eyes lit up. "Yes! Talek, call them up and stall them if you can. I'll show you... two... where the suits are."

We followed him out of the command room and upstairs to the cargo level. "If only they haven't taken them out," Karnath worried. "They are supposed to remain onboard at all times for safety, but I wouldn't rule out them being removed."

Luckily, several suits of a shiny, silvery material were in a storage closet. "What were you thinking, Resa?" I asked, as we suited up. It was difficult for me. Tedious physical tasks, like brushing teeth and hair and tying shoes, had always been Resa's jobs.

"Airlock?" she asked. "In the cargo ship?"

"Yes, it has several airlocks," Karnath answered, fastening a magnetic seal down the front of his suit. "It would often load and unload at space stations. And we should have no trouble opening it; my device can transmit the codes."

Resa finished her own suit and helped me with mine. The gloves were a challenge; a finger and thumb hung empty on each. "We have one too?"

"Yes, the ramp serves as an airlock. You'll see." He circled behind each of us, checking our oxygen tanks. "This here will vent some air for propulsion. But be sparing, you still need air to breathe."

"We only have to go a few feet, right?"

Resa shook her head and made some confusing gestures in the air. Karnath nodded, understanding her better than I did. "We have to make our way from the rear of the ship up to the nose, in order to reach the cargo ship, and across the cargo ship until we reach the airlock," he explained. "But the gloves and boots of the suits will cling to the ship, so we can climb the whole way except for the little gap between the ships."

I donned the bubble-like helmet—comically large on me, to make room for a Shatakazan crest—and followed Karnath to the exit ramp. Sure enough, a door at the head of the ramp slid shut behind us. Karnath slid his device into a small slot in the forearm of his suit. "Talek, how is the stalling going?"

"It's not," ze answered. "They wouldn't talk to us at all. Ten minutes to fold. And you *must not* be on the outside of their ship when it folds. I will signal you when their fold array begins to power up. If that happens, move quickly away from the cargo ship. We will pick you up and fold afterward."

"Understood," said Karnath, punching a button on the wall. Air hissed out of the airlock, and an indicator light by the outer hatch turned from yellow to violet. "Neither of you has ever been without gravity before, have you?" he asked.

"No," I admitted. "Someone else should have been doing this, shouldn't they?"

Karnath shook his head in its heavy helmet. "I want you—you two. This is your idea, and I need your intelligence. Handling zero-g is not difficult. Just remember to keep at least one limb on the ship until we reach the gap between the ships."

He punched another button with his gloved fist, and the outer door opened. I looked out into the dizzying vastness of space. "You're not going to be sick, are you?" Karnath's voice sounded through my helmet's speakers. "Vomiting in a spacesuit is... inadvisable."

I swallowed. "I'm okay." I looked at Resa. She looked as frightened as I felt. Reaching out, I touched her arm. "We can do this, okay? This was your plan. I know you are able to carry it out." Then, tentatively, we all stepped out of the hatch and out of the gravity field.

Karnath clung to the side of the ship like an insect on a wall, his fingers and toes sticking to the metal skin. Carefully he moved one hand or foot at a time. Resa imitated him with grace; my efforts were more clumsy, but I did not seem to be in any danger of losing my connection to the ship. I wondered if the gloves and boots were magnetic, or what—they clung fast when I wanted them to, but released easily when I tried to pull them off.

The trip up the side of our ship went quickly; only once, Resa froze, staring over her shoulder at the stars. I touched her shoulder. "Don't get distracted."

"Not distracted," she said. "Felt like I was falling." But she kept going, keeping her eyes fixed on the side of the ship.

We reached the nose, and I saw the cargo ship loom in front of us. Daz had underestimated; it was at least two armspans away. "You shouldn't need your air-jets at all," Karnath said. "Though they are right here, if you miss." He indicated a control on each shoulder.

He crouched down against the ship and leaped, crossing the distance easily and clinging to the skin of the cargo ship. Looking back at us, he gestured. Resa turned wide, frightened eyes to me. "You'll be better at this than I will," I said. "You go first."

She crouched as Karnath had and made the leap. I took a deep breath and tried to gauge the distance. The Guardian's nanites had given me vision in my left eye, so theoretically I should be able to place it. But as I leapt, I knew I had misjudged. Without Resa's spatial intelligence, I couldn't leap a tiny gap. I hit the cargo ship with my shoulder, instead of my hands, and bounced off, drifting backward toward the red glow of the engines.

"The air-jets!" shouted Karnath's voice in my helmet speaker.

I pushed one hastily, and then the other, until I had come back to the side of the ship, where I could reach out and grab it. "I'm sorry," I said. "I... I feel hopeless at this without Resa to help me."

"No better," said Resa. "For me."

We started our climb. Karnath gestured to a small indent on the side of the ship, perhaps one hundred feet distant. "There's the airlock. We have two and a half minutes left." It was hard not to rush, but I remembered my terrifying moment spinning out into space. That would waste even more time, if I hurried too much and let go.

The smooth skin of the ship left few landmarks. The only thing I could measure distance by was a massive word in Shatakazan writing, in violet letters against the pale gray metal. Hand, hand, foot, foot, and then another character would pass behind me.

At last we had reached the airlock. Karnath tapped his device with a gloved finger. "Frass," he hissed. "They've changed the code."

"So we can't get in?" I squeaked.

"No, I just need a second. The codes aren't long, it can quickly guess all the possibilities."

Just then Talek's voice sounded in our helmets. "Get out of there, Karnath. They're charging their array."

"I just need a *second!*" he repeated.

"Do I need to remind you what happens if you get sucked into a fold without protection?"

"Do I need to remind you that if this plan fails, our only other idea involved us all dying?" he barked back.

I met Resa's eyes. Should we jet away from here, as planned? Or trust that Karnath could get us in? Her eyes slid over to him, and then she put her chin down stubbornly. She wouldn't leave him. Well, I wouldn't leave her. I couldn't. She was me.

After a long, tense couple of seconds, the panel slid open. We flung ourselves inside, falling heavily as we entered the ship's gravity field.

Karnath leaped to his feet and pounded the button to close the airlock. It slid closed with agonizing slowness. Just after the last strip of starlight vanished, we felt the gutwrenching lurch of the fold.

CHAPTER TWENTY-THREE

Tria

I lay on the floor a moment, gasping. "What would have happened if we hadn't made it in time?"

"No one is entirely sure," said Karnath. "Most likely our bodies would be instantly crushed. That's what we hope happens."

"We *hope*? What's the other theory?"

"We would be trapped in the dark till we ran out of oxygen," he answered. "In any event, no one has arrived at an unfold point unless they were inside a ship."

There was another lurch. "That wasn't a lot of time," I said. "Will the *Galajak* be able to follow?"

"I hope so," said Karnath. "As long as they saw we got inside, and weren't looking around to pick us up, they should have."

Slowly we got to our feet. The light beside the door changed from violet to yellow, and Karnath loosened his helmet. "What's the plan now?" he asked, pulling off the heavy bubble.

Resa stared at him, eyes wide. "To … make a plan?"

I dropped my own helmet on the floor and rubbed a hand over my face. Of course she had only thought of the moment. "What can we disable on this ship that they won't be able to fix?"

"There's nothing that can't be fixed," said Karnath. "Every ship has a fabricator to make new parts. And a ship this size would have plenty of material to use."

"Break the fabricator?" I suggested.

"Now there's a thought. I just don't know where it would be, on a ship this size. This is the upper aft airlock. I don't know the design of this ship in particular, but usually our ships are designed with the engines at the rear and command areas at the front, with habitat above and cargo below. So if I would guess, I'd say the fabricator would be somewhere toward the rear of the ship, where it's convenient to the engines in case parts were needed. Unfortunately I don't know where the crew is; they might be working on the fabricator right now, for all I know."

"Can they see us? Do they know we're on the ship?"

"Impossible to say. They certainly have external cameras that could have seen us, but they can't be watching everything at once. They may or may not have noticed the airlock opening, too."

We stripped off the bulky spacesuits and left them in a pile. "Weapons," said Resa.

I stared at her. That was not an idea that would have occurred to me, but it probably was wise. Though I wasn't sure I could actually handle one.

"Good point," said Karnath. "First thing to look for is a storage locker." Sliding the door open, he tentatively peered out. It opened into a narrow hallway, lined with a yellow-green biolayer like the corridors of the *Galajak*. Luckily no one was in sight.

We found a storage room a few doors down from the airlock. We darted inside and started searching for tools that we could use, in a pinch, to defend ourselves. Resa claimed a fire extinguisher, and Karnath took a device that sprayed packing foam, for shipping delicate items. He offered me a gun-shaped instrument ending in two wicked-looking prongs, and I held up my hands nervously. "I can't fire anything, I would miss."

"It's a welder," he said. "You'd have to be right up against someone to use it. Though my hope, of course, is that it's enough of a threat that no one gets close enough."

Nervously, I accepted the welder, gripping the handle tightly with both hands. "We should split up to cover the ground better. I'll go forward and look for stairs."

"I'll try aft," said Karnath. "Resa?"

She looked for a moment at him, but then came over by me. Together she and I made our way down the long corridor. I took her right hand in my left. It helped a little with the terrible feeling of being alone in my head.

The doors along the hallway bore markings I recognized from the *Galajak*—some that I knew stood for crew quarters, others that I understood to mean medlab and dayroom. When I saw character strings I didn't recognize, I sounded them out aloud, and my earbud translated them. Computer room. Environmental control. But none of them sounded like anything that might hold the fabricator. Nor any stairs.

We hadn't folded again since the airlock; the normal-space engines lent their faint vibration to the textured gray deck beneath our feet. Other than that, it was quiet. The corridor terminated in a larger set of double doors, which must be the command room we'd been brought to earlier. Presumably most of the crew would still be there, hurriedly plotting a course to evade the *Galajak*.

Before we reached them, however, we finally came upon the stairs, opening up on our left. Like the *Galajak's* stairs, they were a bit steep for my legs. Unlike those, they were made of metal mesh, so I could see down below into the cargo hold. I peered around as best I could, but saw no one. Unfortunately, as we came down the stairs, we would become visible to the entire hold. Our footsteps on the stairs weren't too quiet either.

Halfway down, we passed a door whose label only read "forward compartment." I remembered that the *Galajak* had had a similar door at the front end of the cargo level, leading into the nose of the ship. It held sensor and navigation equipment, as well as a generator for the electrostatic shielding which protected the ship from space debris. None of it seemed obviously useful, so we passed on.

The cargo hold was long and narrow, much taller than the upper level. It was hard to say exactly how large because it was poorly lit; at the best of times the Shatakazan used a lower light level than I would have chosen, and here, where there was no biolayer on the walls, they hadn't seemed to trouble themselves much about lights. There were small glowing squares on the walls here and there, but the cargo, in piles of cylinders or rows of huge crates, blocked most of the light. A person might walk through the stacks, entirely unobserved.

That is, unobserved by *us*. Shatakazan eyes were keener in the dark than ours. Shadows wouldn't hide us from them very well. Still, I didn't see any better cover than that, so Resa and I started to weave our way through the piles of cargo. I let her lead the way; I have a poor sense of direction and there were no easy landmarks to follow. Nothing like the fabricator was near the stairs, so it must be toward the rear of the ship as Karnath had said. I wondered if he had found a separate set of stairs there, or if he had had to turn around and follow after me. Or—my mind insisted on suggesting—had met some of the crew, and not made it any farther.

Resa stopped by a low pile of heavy cases and opened one, peering inside and lifting it to the light. Satisfied, she reached in and took out a gun, leaving the fire extinguisher behind.

I stared at her dumbly, wanting to demand *What makes you think that is a good idea?* or *Is that even loaded and do you know how to shoot it?* but, since I couldn't talk to her anymore without making a sound, and she surely was set on her own idea, I just shook my head and walked on.

That was why I was a little ahead of her as I crossed the next empty aisle. The moment I passed into the shadow of the next row of containers, I found myself pressed into the side of a crate. A firm, many-fingered hand grasped both my wrists while the other arm pinned my neck against the crates. I hadn't even seen him coming. Those Shatakazan were fast. And flexible.

His face leaned right into mine, vertical pupils wide. "You! We saw the airlock had opened. Was it you? Are you alone?"

I thought fast. In a hand fight, Kinaru had no advantages I knew of over Shatakazan. I knew their weak points, but I could never be fast enough or strong enough to get at any of them. And in any event, I had never trained in physical combat.

The only thing to do was lie, while being careful not to look toward Resa, where she had been standing a few paces behind, in the shadow of the last aisle. Hopefully she had thought to run away. With three of us on this ship, there were three chances to reach the fabricator without getting caught. "Yes," I gasped. "That was me. I'm alone."

The Shatakazan's eyes narrowed. "Unlikely." Then suddenly his crest flicked up and his eyes widened. His face flushed green and he flailed at his back, trying to dislodge something. After a moment, his face turned gray and he collapsed.

Where he had been standing, I saw Resa, holding a plastic tie she must have stripped off a box. I hadn't even seen her wrap it around his neck. "So you remembered the choke reflex?" I whispered, my voice trembling with relief.

"Handy for me," she said, stepping over the fallen Shatakazan to tie his hands. He wouldn't be out long. "Not so practical for them."

We hurried around a corner, wanting to get as far away as possible before he woke up. But we were stopped short by the sound of voices. Ducking into another aisle, we peered between the cases. There were two Shatakazan, carefully carrying a piece of equipment toward a large cylinder. The triggering mechanism?

"Are you completely sure it's not going to go off when we put it in?" one of them was saying anxiously to the other.

"The manual says no. And since this is a duplicate of the original piece, it should react just the way it would."

"I don't see Hashat, he was supposed to be ready to help us put it in."

"He must have gone to get the grav lifter." There was a pause as the speaker took out a device. "Hashat, where are you? We have to get this done."

"He isn't answering," said the other nervously. "You think that airlock malfunction was really them getting inside?"

"Tazag said we should be alert. Maybe we shouldn't have left Hashat by himself. When we're done with this, we'll go look for him."

"If they got the jump on him, there may be more than one. Or they might have weapons."

"*We* have weapons," said the other. "And better than stunners, too."

If these two were here, the fabricator should be in the direction they came from. And hopefully manned by only one or two people. I signalled to Resa and crept away.

The fabricator lay on the exact opposite end of the cargo hold from the stairs we had come down. It was a giant box, looking more than anything like a huge photocopier. One Shatakaz with a brown crest was standing by the glowing control panel, watching as the machine hummed and whirred.

I turned to catch Resa's eye and work out a plan, but just then, a loudspeaker crackled to life. "Hello, Tria," the voice cooed. I recognized it at once as Zin. "I found Karnath in the fold array, trying to commit a little sabotage! I couldn't let him do that, could I? We had a little conversation and he admitted you were here on the ship. So I'm going to need you to come over here. Just head to the back of the ship and reach the stairs. I'll meet you at the engine hatch, halfway up. If you're not here in seven minutes, or if any part of the ship is damaged before you get here, he won't be … hm … in very good condition when you find him."

There was a click as the intercom switched off. I grabbed Resa's arm and rushed away from the fabricator to a dark corner some distance away where we could talk. "What are we going to do?"

"Go, I guess," she said, staring at the floor.

"We can't do that!" I hissed. "This mission is more important of any of our lives. If we can't do it without blowing up this ship and all of us with it, we have to do it. That's why Karnath wouldn't let go when Talek told him to. He knew it was more important."

"I can't," she said. "I can't let anything happen to him."

I ground my teeth. I didn't need her irrationality right now. "Wait," I said at last. "She didn't call both of us. She probably doesn't know there are two of us now. I think Karnath managed to keep that from her." I tried not to think about that "conversation." Had she hurt him? Or had it just been a lucky guess which he hadn't been able to deny convincingly? "I'll go, and you find a way to stop the ship after I've reached her."

"No," she said softly. "I'll go. You're the smart one. My only idea was to shoot the machine thing."

I wanted to protest, *That would have worked, if not for this!* But now that Unity had hostages, clearly a more complex plan was going to be needed. Something that disabled both the fabricator and some other crucial part of the ship, but without access to the engine room. I had nothing, yet, but I might still be able to think of something. Reluctantly, I nodded.

She hugged me tightly, pressed her gun into my hands, and was gone. I watched her go, feeling the emptiness inside of me grow hollower. She needed to be with me. I wanted her back in my head where she belonged, where no one could take her away from me.

But, I had to admit, without me she was doing just fine. Grabbing a gun, choking my attacker—by going with her gut, without my nervous overthinking, she had gotten us all our progress so far. With me, she couldn't be like that. Was she wrong about not being oppressed? Was it even possible for me to treat her like a whole person as long as she was connected to me?

No time for those thoughts now. I had to consider what on this ship I could sacrifice, without tipping off Zin I was doing it until it was too late. The normal space engines and fold array were out, because that was where she was. The fabricator was watched, and so were the missiles. One Shatakaz would soon be regaining consciousness in this warren of cargo containers. That left at least two crew members unaccounted for: Tazag and Resh, who were both almost certainly in the command room.

Mentally I reviewed all the rooms upstairs that I had seen. Most had been living spaces. One room might have been a computer room, but I couldn't do more than smash it up. That might keep the crew from being able to calculate their next fold, but Zin would surely kill Karnath and Resa when she discovered it. Taking down the electrostatic shielding was even worse; it could destroy the whole ship, if we happened to encounter any space debris. I wasn't quite ready to choose death for all of us. There had to be another way.

I felt hopeless for a moment. I had no expertise with spaceships, I couldn't operate Shatakazan machinery. Why couldn't Karnath be the one still free? He could have done this easily.

But, I reminded myself, I was a talented biologist. I had studied the Shatakazan extensively. There must be some way I could use this knowledge to disable them. And for that, I would have to look in the medlab.

Tucking the gun in my waistband, and holding the welder in my right hand, I started weaving my way among the stacks. This time, at least, I knew where everyone was and could avoid them, though I went well out of my way for fear of miscalculating the right path. I reached the stairs and stole up them as quietly as I could. From here I couldn't see the missiles among all the different containers, which made me hope the Shatakazan working on them couldn't see me either.

I reached the top of the stairs and peered around the corner into the corridor. The walls still gave a faint yellow-green glow, and the insects swarmed around noiselessly within the biolayer. No one was around, which didn't surprise me. Everyone was too busy to be roaming around in the habitat area. I slipped into the medlab and locked the door behind me.

This medlab was bigger than the *Galajak*'s, though it lacked some of the scientific equipment, like the genetic analyzer. Most of the other machines I recognized.

What I needed was something that could immobilize everyone. Or, better yet, Shatakazan only. Resa would be able to get Karnath to safety. I took a look at the medical synthesizer. It could make any medication, and best of all, the control panel included molecular diagrams so I could recognize each chemical easily. I easily found the entry for prodexin, the relaxant. A large enough dose would harmlessly put everyone to sleep, and there was a gas form. It would have no effect on my body.

But I had no idea what the fabricator's limits would be. Could it produce enough prodexin to disperse a uniform dosage throughout the ship? What would even be the right amount? I couldn't know without calculating the volume of air on the ship.

It took me a minute—with a lot of estimating since I hadn't actually measured the ship's dimensions—but I eventually came up with a number. Thirty million liters of air, give or take. About .05 percent concentration should be enough to put all the Shatakazan to sleep for a moment. I buried my face in my hands. That still came to over a thousand liters of the stuff, which I would then have to carry over to the environmental control room without being noticed. I tried putting in the order anyway, but the synthesizer displayed an error message—probably something like "you must have made a mistake, nobody wants a thousand liters of this, you can put somebody out with a couple of grams."

I sighed and pushed away from the machine. I was making this too complicated. If I could get into the environmental control room, couldn't I just shut down the life support? That would take a long time to work, but in theory I should be able to stay conscious for longer than the Shatakazan could. I rushed to the door and unlocked it.

I had only made it a few feet aft, toward the environmental control room, when my luck ran out. I heard the heavy door of the command room open and shut, and I spun around. Not twenty feet away, Tazag stood, reaching for zir weapon.

I faced zem, grabbing the gun clumsily out of my waistband with my left hand and aiming it at zem. In my right hand, I brandished my welder.

Tazag let out a hissing chuckle, zir own weapon relaxed in zir hand. "You're threatening me with an arc welder?"

"Resa has an Earth gun, though," I bluffed. "And her aim with it is excellent."

"But I notice you aren't firing. Did you slip away from Zin? You don't want to give away your position with the noise." Zir own weapon was blunt-nosed and silver. A stunner? Or some kind of laser?

Ze wasn't wrong that I wasn't going to fire. If I turned and ran, ze had no reason at all not to shoot me. Unless ze was worried the Guardian's threat was still in force? After my conversation with her, I wasn't at all sure. The information she could get from her experiment was likely much more important than my life—or death.

This standoff couldn't last. I thumbed the control on the welder, which spat out a white-hot arc of flame between its two prongs. Reaching out toward the wall of the corridor, I carved a swathe out of the fine mesh sealing the biolayer. Tiny winged insects surged out in a cloud, swarming between Tazag and me.

Not waiting to see what ze would make of this diversion, I turned and ran. Behind me, I heard Tazag's laser sizzle in the air, catching the bugs instead of me. Before ze had cleared the insect swarm, I had reached the door of the control room. I flung myself inside and hastily locked the door.

Breathing heavily, I turned around. The air scrubber filled most of the room, and a complicated network of ducts branched out and tunneled through the walls and floor. From the door, I heard Tazag's voice. "I can override the locks, you know."

"Do it, then," I said calmly. Ze surely could, but it would take some time. I needed to think of something faster than just smashing everything. There were almost thirty million liters of breathable air on this ship, and only ten people to use it up. Even without a functional scrubber, I wasn't sure the oxygen would run out before they got to Shatak.

Tazag, on the other hand, would have the door open within five minutes or so. Not such a short time that ze wasn't going to stall with talking. "Do you even know what you're fighting against?" ze called through the door.

"The part where you plan to bomb at least one major city is my chief concern," I said, with half my mind. With the other I tried to understand the workings of the scrubber. The big device must be the scrubber itself, that canister held nitrogen or another neutral gas for mixing, and the heavy box was the carbon sink. The carbon was removed from the CO_2 and sent into this box, while the purified O_2 would be sent into that large bubble to be mixed with nitrogen if necessary. There didn't seem to be a pipe out of the carbon sink; they must have to go in manually and remove it when it got full.

"You don't understand the tyranny of Liberty sect," Tazag pleaded. "You yourself told me that liberty is tyranny if some can oppress others."

"Can't people leave the sects if they feel they're being oppressed?" I asked, to keep zem talking.

"When all you've ever known is oppression, it's hard to recognize," ze argued. "They think it's just the way things are. They don't even have the words to name to themselves how it's hurting them."

I reached out to the control panel, trying to see if there was a way to run the whole thing in reverse. Suddenly I paused, Tazag's words sinking in. I remembered what Resa had said in front of the Guardian: *Not you, Tria. Never you.* That's what she truly believed, but it was false, wasn't it? We had never been equal. We had been carefully taught not to be.

I might be proud—justly proud, I had always thought—of the good treatment she had from me, but didn't I secretly, on some level I carefully avoided speaking aloud, assume I was better? When we were children, I had been like a parent to her, stopping her from eating too much dessert and making us both sick, making her go to bed at a reasonable hour, trying to talk her out of adolescent crushes. She wasn't a child now, but I had never stopped assuming that I was the wise one, the sensible one, and Resa no better than a cherished pet—to be humored, but not respected as an equal. I had patronized her just like the Guardian had, when it protected my safety but didn't care about what I wanted. I didn't even *know* what Resa most deeply wanted. I had failed to ask.

Tazag kept talking, something about a sect where neutrals were a servant class, and the work ze had done trying to teach them they deserved better. I wasn't listening. I couldn't spare the time on any more self-recrimination. And anyway I knew what I had to do, if we both survived this. I focused on the scrubber. The control panel was no help; it had all kinds of safeties. I'd have to do something with the ducts.

"That sounds terrible," I said vaguely. At last I had a plan. With the welder, I cut the duct between the scrubber and the carbon sink. Cutting a hole in the mixing chamber, I started welding the duct into place there. My work was clumsy. Resa would have done better, but she wasn't here. I would have to learn these things, now.

"It was, and some of the sects are worse," said Tazag vehemently. "Why, in some sects they enforce monogamy, if you can imagine that! And in others—what are you doing in there?"

"Thinking of alternate solutions," I said, over the sound of the welder. "Which you should have done before leaping to acts of terrorism." I ripped off a piece of my shirt and ignited it with a spark from the welder. Lifting the heavy lid of the carbon sink, I dropped it in. The powdery material within caught easily, and I slammed down the lid. The fire roared inside, heating the metal sides of the container cherry-red. As it consumed the available oxygen, it would be pumping out carbon dioxide into the mixing chamber and throughout the ship. I began to sweat from the heat radiating outward.

"There's nothing you can do in there," Tazag shouted.

But ze was belied by Resh's voice coming from zir device. "I'm reading high CO_2 levels in the life support mixing chamber. Can you go check it out?"

"I'm already working on it," Tazag said through gritted teeth. "That frass-eating mammal got in there and locked the door!"

"Calm yourself. I can open the door from here. You should have called immediately when you found she had locked it."

I picked my gun back up from the table, my hands shaking. That was a lot of carbon combusting into the air; already my head was aching and I was having trouble focusing.

The door slid open and Tazag charged into the room. Zir yellow eyes darted between me and the air scrubber. "What did you do?" ze demanded, gasping a little. Ze hurried over to the scrubber and scanned the panels. But before ze could do more, zir body went slack and fell to the floor.

As a test subject, Tazag did nicely to reveal that this room, at least, had high enough CO_2 levels. But I worried it would soon be enough to kill zem—or me. Breathing hard, I squinted at the scrubber. Yellow lights lit up on all the panels. I wished I could get a reading from elsewhere on the ship. How long before the gas reached the cargo hold? I waited for a full minute, stepping out into the corridor to see if the air was fresher out there. It wasn't. My head pounded and I fought the urge to lie down and sleep. I pressed my nose for a moment into the biolayer; it helped a little.

I picked up Tazag's device; it was still active. "Resh, what's going on there?" I asked, to see if he would answer. There was no reply.

I dropped the device and turned to the scrubber. It would be harder to reverse what I had done than to start it. I cut the duct off of the mixing chamber and held it down on the ground to smother the fire. Without fresh oxygen from the intake lines, it quickly went out. Then I turned to weld back the ducts as they had been, but my vision grew wobbly. I knew if I passed out before I finished, everyone on the ship would die. My head throbbed. I had to get it done … I had to …

Resa

I sat on the floor of the engine room, beside Karnath. Zin was perched on a piece of machinery, her gun resting on her knee. Not quite aimed at us, but close enough to whip it up if she needed to.

I curled into myself as much as Karnath did, pressing my legs (legs! two of them!) into my chest to ease the ache there. I didn't know how I felt. For a little bit, sneaking through the ship hand in hand, it had felt a little bit good. Like she was my sister instead of my other half—still close, but not so close I couldn't make my own choices.

Now, without her, I was beginning to process what had happened to me. I had been cut in half and was still living. I was breathing all my own breaths. I was empty. I was free. I was capable. I was alone.

My head butted into Karnath's shoulder, and he wrapped his arm around me. That was something. Maybe if he squeezed tight enough it would collapse the hollowness inside. Maybe all I needed was time.

Zin smirked at him. "I didn't have you down as a fetishist. Have you satisfied your *curiosity* yet? What's it like?"

He tensed, crest flicking upward, but didn't answer.

"If they're anything like humans, prepare to be disgusted. I've seen pictures."

Ducking his head and putting his mouth close to my ear, he breathed, "Don't let her get to you."

I gave a half shrug. Nothing Zin said could hurt me.

"Believe in Tria," he whispered. "She'll find a way."

I believed it. But this was Tria we were talking about. She had been faking the Guardian when she tried to sacrifice our lives to stop the ship, but it was exactly the kind of thing she would do. The greatest good for the greatest number. That she and I and Karnath were the smaller number made no difference to the math. I trusted her to stop the ship. I didn't trust her to spare our lives in the process.

If we were all going to die anyway, it didn't really matter what I thought or decided about Tria and me. And yet living or dying seemed much less pressing a question. I had just been given my freedom. I needed to know whether I wanted it.

One time I had rescued a little bird with a damaged wing. At first it had beaten itself against the bars of its cage pitifully, hating me for keeping it from the sky. But in time it had grown unafraid of me. When at last the wing was healed, I took the cage outside and opened the door. *There, little one. There is the freedom you wanted.*

But it had huddled inside, turning its face away from the sky. Had it grown to love me, or had it only forgotten how much it had loved to fly? Was it afraid?

Gently I took it out, set it in a copperbush, and turned away. Behind me, I heard it cry out: *breek, breek, breek.*

That was the sound my heart was making. Did it mean, *Come back, I love you, I have seen all the choices and choose you?* Or only, *I'm afraid, I can't remember how to fly, I'd rather choose safety than be what I was born for?*

At the time, I had kept walking. You can't confine that kind of bird, it isn't good for them. But what kind of bird was I?

I was interrupted from my thoughts by a chime from Zin's device. "What's going on down there?" came Resh's voice. "Tazag claims the Kinaru is loose."

She glared at me. "No, she's right here. Though I wouldn't lay odds against her having done something before I got her."

"Apparently she did, there's high CO_2 levels in the life support room and Tazag can't get in. I'm just unlocking it now but you'd probably better grab a breather."

Leaping to her feet, Zin rushed for the door. I watched her intently—if there was emergency oxygen in this room, I wanted to know where. But I was distracted by Karnath suddenly going limp beside me. That fast? But come to think of it, I did have a headache starting up. I wondered how long that had been going on.

Zin made it as far as the doorway before passing out. I gently lowered Karnath to the ground and went for it. Tria had come to the rescue, as I had not dared to believe she would. It was up to me to make sure none of us died of it.

I couldn't read the labels on any of the doors like Tria could, and I didn't know where the Shatakazan might keep anything. But I did remember where we had left the spacesuits, back in the airlock.

The suits were bulky; I tried to pick up all three, but one kept sliding out of my arms. I didn't want to have to take two trips, what if Karnath was dead by the time I got to him? Should I get him first, or Tria? How could I ever make a choice like that?

Then I realized I was being stupid, and stepped into one myself. With the helmet fastened and the air hissing in, my head quickly cleared. Tria was the one to get first. Karnath's unconsciousness was protective, I remembered that. He could survive while unconscious longer than Tria could.

I wasted far too much time opening doors and peeking inside, but at last I found her. She was sprawled on the floor beside an enormous machine, the welder in her hand slowly melting a hole in the decking. I shut it off and started shoving her into the suit. Funny how I'd dressed her every day of our lives, but never like this. Her limp arms and legs were dead weight.

Within a few minutes she was blinking and trying to get up. "I didn't finish fixing it."

"Tell me what to do and I will."

With her instruction, I did a neater job than she had. It was like playing with clay, if clay were white hot. Soon the violet lights on the panel were turning yellow again.

"We only have a few minutes before that spreads through the whole system," she said. "We'd better lock up all the Unity crew first."

We dragged them, one at a time, to an empty bedroom and welded the door shut. It would take them a while to find a way out of that. "Now we can check on Karnath," I said. "Finally."

By the time we reached him, his eyelids were already flickering. We both sat with him till he woke up. "Are we safe?" he mumbled, pushing himself up off his back. "What did you do?"

"I gassed everyone with carbon dioxide," Tria answered. "I consider it a defect that you pass out when you can't get oxygen for such a short time. What if you choke? How are you supposed to clear your airway if you're unconscious?"

"In theory," he said, rather grumpily, "we are a communal species that would *help* the person whose airway was blocked. Evolution wasn't planning on us getting *gassed*."

CHAPTER TWENTY-FOUR

Tria

We made it to the command room and examined the displays. The *Galajak* was nowhere to be seen. "I suppose they stopped to look for us and didn't follow the cargo ship in time for the second jump," Karnath said somberly. "They think we're dead, and that the *Vatarax* is still on its way to Shatak."

"It'll be nice to surprise them," I said. "That is, if you can figure out how to drive this thing."

Karnath frowned, bending over the navigation panel. "I should be able to simply select the last fold point we came from," he said. "Though we'd first have to make our way in normal space back to where we folded in."

But just then, the displays went blank. This ship's control room had a large circle on the floor, for holographic displays, and it flicked on, displaying the Guardian.

I bit my lip, staring down. She was here to tell us we had passed the test. We had done it separately, when we could never have done it together. This would prove to the Guardian that she should separate us all, divorce us from ourselves, free the lefts that we had oppressed.

I should be happy for Resa. Without me, she could do whatever she wanted. She wouldn't be held back anymore, and she would develop the confidence to simply do things without waiting for my approval. But I still felt hollow inside. She might not need me, but I needed her. I needed her to help me understand my feelings, to show me how to connect with people, even to tie my shoes. Without her I was only half a person.

Resa leaned back against Karnath, and he put his arms around her. Maybe she was afraid the Guardian would force her back into my head. But I felt there was little chance of that. Our mission had been a success.

"You successfully stopped the ship you were so concerned about," the Guardian stated. "I observed everything."

I nodded. "I suppose the experiment was successful. You proved we are better apart."

She put her head on one side. "That wasn't the measure of the experiment. The measure was whether you both preferred this."

"I think it is better to be separated," I said reluctantly. "Resa was able to handle things independently much better than I might have thought. It made me see I have been holding her back all this time."

"With respect, Tria, you are not the one whose opinion I was interested in. Resa was the one who had the original complaint." She directed her eyes to Resa.

Resa looked around at Karnath, then at me, with an unreadable expression. Then she stared down at the ground for a long moment. At last she turned back to Karnath, cupped his cheeks in her hands, and kissed him.

I stared at her in shock. She was in love with him? When had that happened? And he didn't seem to object; he wrapped his arms around her and was kissing her back. My throat hurt and my stomach sank. I wanted the metal deck underfoot to swallow me up. Clearly they loved each other; clearly they were both better without me. But it hurt more than anything; more even than having had Resa scooped out of me in the first place. I knew she would never choose to come back to me, not when she could have him instead.

But, slowly, as if prying herself away from him, she freed herself from his arms. Then, with two steps, she crossed back to me, wrapping her arms around me and laying her head on my shoulder. "Put me back," she said, her voice muffled in my shirt. "I want to be with Tria again."

I stiffened in shock. "Really? You would do that?"

She didn't answer. Her arms just tightened around me.

"You heard her decision," said the Guardian. The black pool of nanites gathered at our feet, and I shut my eyes. When I opened them again, my arms were empty. Or rather, my arm. Our left arm wrapped around our waist, back under Resa's control. It felt … right. Fixed. At last.

Oh gods, that's better, she said. *That was a terrible experience and I never ever want to be away from you again.*

Me either, I said. To the Guardian, I said, "But what about everything she said? What about lefts being oppressed?"

"Clearly you have shown it is possible to be happy together. All that remains is for you, when you return, to share these discoveries with the rest of your people."

"How?" I asked.

"I could alter your biology myself," she said. "I could revert you all to human within a generation if that was what you wanted. But a social change will have to come from yourselves. And you will know best how to achieve it." With that, she shimmered and disappeared.

We stood in silence for a long time. Karnath stared down at the ground, lost in his own thoughts. *I don't understand it,* I said to Resa. *Why did you come back?*

You can ask that? You know how it feels to be separated.

Yes, but … how can that be worse than the feeling of being trapped with me? I think I understand now. How it must be, not to be able to choose anything for yourself … I trailed off, overwhelmed with imagining it. Her whole life was like those terrifying seconds when she had rebelled against me. The knowledge that my body was suddenly not under my control, that I could die in that moment because of a choice I had not made—she faced that daily. And too often I had not even bothered to tell her why.

*But I **belong** with you, Tria. That's not just fear talking. It's the kind of bird I am.*

I tilted my head, puzzled. Never mind it. *Things are going to be different now.*

Different how?

I don't know yet, I said. *I think you will have to teach me. I do know we have to start interacting as equals. I didn't realize before that we weren't. And I want . . . I want you to teach me about music, and colors, and how to feel my feelings.*

She spread her hand, perplexed. *But those aren't your things.*

I know. And I'll never be good at them. But I want to try. How could I really respect and appreciate Resa's gifts if I knew nothing about them?

I thought of everyone across Kinaru. The changes that would have to be made. Votes for lefts. Education. Maybe careers in music or the arts—the right and left would have to split the day, but it could be done. What would we do differently if we believed, really believed, that we were equal instead of giving lip service to the idea? What would we stop simply expecting lefts to accept?

Most of all, the partnership system would have to be reformed. It was obvious to me in retrospect that assigning life partners based on psychometric data and interests would hardly ever provide that special spark that lefts found so important. I wasn't sure what other method could be used, but the lefts could probably devise something.

Which reminded me of Karnath. He had taken a seat, head bent to his control panel. *You never told me about him.*

How could I? It could never have had any hope. Not unless you wanted it too. The big decisions are yours. We both know that.

I examined the back of his head, the gray curve of his jawline. *Why him?*

*He **sees** me.* She stretched her fingers, as if straining for a way to explain it to me. *He looks in my eye and he understands. Everyone else here has only ever seen you.*

I was silent awhile, as Resa's hand flicked to her face a time or two, brushing away tears. This would have to be dealt with. For her ... but not only for her.

I came over beside Karnath and sank into the other cup-shaped seat. He glanced up at me quickly, showing pupils dilated with emotion, before turning away again. "So you were in love with her," I said. "All this time."

"It's been growing over time," he admitted. "I don't know what to do. I know you've been very clear that you only wanted to be friends. I wasn't sure it was right to do anything, given your lack of interest."

"My lack of *interest*?" I repeated. I wasn't sure what else to say. It's not like he had ever said anything, any more than Resa had. Instead I had been left all on my own to examine my very subtle feelings and somehow find a way to communicate them. Neither of which I had done.

"You are uninterested, correct?" he asked. I looked up at him. His yellow eyes were fixed on me steadily. "A partnership with an alien is arguably irrational, and you are almost always rational."

"No one ever matched us," I said weakly. "No one ever *asked.*"

Karnath's eyelids lowered. "Do I have to ask? Is that how we are to do it? Very well, I am asking. I would like you as my lover. Both you and Resa."

"Because you can't have her without me?"

"No. Because I love you. I love you and her, in different ways. Sometimes I wondered if I was simply confused, and couldn't separate my feelings for each of you because you were in the same body. But when you were separated, I could see it clearly. You are two fascinating, attractive people, both of whom I like." He stared down at the display below. "Both of whom I love."

I took a moment to think. Was that what the name was for all I had been feeling? My constant wish to share what I was thinking with him? My fear for him when I knew Zin had him? The gutwrenching envy when I saw him kissing Resa? If that was love, there was no question. I had never felt this way about anyone, or perhaps I could have seen it coming.

Yes, he was strange and different from me. And I never imagined that I could ever find myself choosing my own partner, let alone an alien. Yet the time we had spent together had shown me his heart and mind, which weren't so different from mine. And most of all ... he loved Resa. He *saw* her. He would understand, and maybe even teach me to understand.

I turned in my seat, studying his face. Hesitantly, I lifted my hand and touched his cheek. It was soft, just as I had imagined. "I ... I think that's how I feel too."

When he kissed me, I felt something oddly familiar. It was like the feeling I had had when the Guardian had reunited Resa and me. It felt ... right.

Eventually we reached the last fold point and Karnath reversed the previous journey. I held my breath as we folded, but when the screens came back on, the *Galajak* hung just a few hundred meters away. It took some time for the crew of the *Galajak* to get lined up to our airlock and extend an airtight bridge between the two ships. Gaj shook her head over what I had done to the air scrubber. "Oh well, I suppose I'm grateful you didn't manage to smash the fold array."

"If we had, it would have taken weeks for anyone to even find out where we were," said Karnath. "Seeing as you didn't manage to follow."

"We were looking for you!" she protested. "Where you would have *been* if you had listened to Talek."

"It came right in the end," I ventured. I didn't like to think what would have happened if things had gone even a little bit differently.

Karnath went back to the *Galajak* to sleep. He had had a stressful morning, and then there was the trauma of having been almost suffocated to sleep off. I suited up, along with Gaj and Talek, and helped get rid of the weapons. The cargo hold could seal off, thanks to heavy pressure doors that slid shut at the tops of the stairwells, so we evacuated the air and opened the loading hatch.

It was a tedious job dumping everything out, even after reducing the gravity field. There were five heavy nuclear missiles, plus cases upon cases of different kinds of guns. It was clear Unity had planned a full-scale war. When we had finished, we left Talek and Prazad on the cargo ship and went back to the *Galajak*. Daz had the ships linked together to make a simultaneous fold. Then we were back in high Earth orbit, watching the blue and white masses swirling far below.

"Where do I put us down?" asked Daz. "The airstrip by the hangar where we started? Or maybe the field where we landed the first time?"

"No," I said, leaning over his map. I stabbed a finger down at a green patch right beside the government buildings. "Right there. No more keeping secrets for the earthlings."

Resa

While the ship began its gentle descent, we went to Karnath's quarters. Tria hesitated at the door. *We can't go in, we'll bother him!*

He wants to be bothered, I said. *Trust me.*

He was sleeping peacefully on his side, his knees pulled up to his chest. Carefully, so as not to wake him, I lay down behind him, not quite touching. I breathed slowly in and out, smelling his faint, spicy scent. Mine. At last. Better than mine, ours.

He stirred and rolled onto his back, opening his golden eyes. "Oh," he said, as if he had been handed an unexpected present. "It's you. Did you need something?"

"Resa wanted—" she began, then stopped. "We wanted to see you."

Instead of answering, he buried his face in my neck. I amused myself with running my fingers along his quills one at a time. They felt smooth going up, but faintly squeaky coming back down. There were so many parts of him I had yet to feel.

"Everything is so strange now," Tria confessed. "Resa is back in my head, but it's different now. I'm trying to let her be an equal partner. It's just, I don't know what that will even be like. And now apparently I have a lover too? That's not something I know anything about."

He pulled back to look at her. "In our language, lovers are people who have sex. I never asked if that was something you wanted. We could be partners without being lovers if you prefer. Or wait and see how you feel. I know what Resa wants, but your wishes matter here too."

My hand froze. Not from fear. I wanted to hear what Tria would say.

"Oh, I . . . I hadn't thought of that. I've never . . ."

He propped himself up on his elbow. "What, *never*? Even casually?"

She shook her head. "I'm afraid I wouldn't even know how."

"Well, as far as you and I go, I don't know how either. We'll have to make it up as we go along. One . . . step . . . at a time." With one finger, he traced a line from our forehead, down our nose, over our lips, and down our neck. Right where we both could feel it. Clever man.

She shivered slightly. I, who knew all her moods so well and how they felt in our body, wasn't sure what she was feeling. Fear or desire? I knew what *I* felt.

Aloud she said, "There has never been a relationship like this one. I expected one partner for her, another for me. Mine to talk to, and hers for . . . that other thing." She bit her lip in embarrassment.

"But you'd be involved in that too, right?"

"Only if I wanted to be. A lot of rights sedate themselves so they don't have to be there for it."

He stared at her, aghast. "Who would see it as something to avoid?"

"I did," she said. "But suddenly I don't now. It's very strange to feel this way."

I smiled to myself, catching Karnath's eyes. So it wasn't just some insanity of my own, to want to send my fingers exploring all over those tiny scales, smooth and fine as beads of glass. Even a rational person like her could feel the pull.

He gave us a soft, delicate kiss. "It's a start."

"It's not too strange for you?"

"That you're only a little bit interested?"

"That there are two of us."

"I've had more than one partner before."

"At once?"

"Well, no. But people do."

Tria was quiet, absorbing that. I ran my fingers along Karnath's brow ridge. Little streaks of green were drifting along it, like ripples on a pond. I remembered how I had hated all the green, when I had first come to Earth. But it was growing on me, more and more.

"I suppose," she said at last, "it's actually better this way. Sometimes I think you understand her better than I do."

I gasped softly. Karnath's finger, engaged in roving down my chest, had lightly grazed my nipple. His eyes dilated, meeting mine. Yes. That, he had understood.

"Does it make you jealous?" he asked. "I know humans don't like sharing their lovers." Amazing he could keep up the conversation like this, given what he was simultaneously doing to me. I didn't resent it. She needed words, would need many more words to explain to herself what this was, what we were doing. And he could speak the words for her, distill what she needed to know into a form she could understand, the way I never could.

"I was," she said. "When I thought she would choose you over me. I'm not now. We have always shared everything. I'd be afraid to do this without her."

"This?" he asked, tilting his head.

"This," she answered, fumbling with the buttons of our shirt.

My heart pounded. For a while they kept talking, shedding garments and exclaiming over their differences. Scientists, both of them. Let them talk, if it made her comfortable. I just absorbed it all—smelling, touching, experimenting. Watching his crest flicker and his eyes dilate when I brushed a nerve. There! Yes. And here. And there.

And one, and two, and three. The dance had resumed, as I had thought it never would. I had thought I was closing the door on it forever when I came back to Tria. I had made my choice, stopped my ears against the music of his kiss. And to find our feet stumbling together to learn the steps was more than I could have imagined.

"Is this where?" she was whispering.

"Yes—there." His voice caught, as he was drawn down deeper into my world, where words scatter on the wind and colors play through your fingers. At last he surrendered to it, eyes closed and moving beneath the lids as in a dream. What did he see? Where did he go?

At last he returned to himself, taking our hands away and rolling us over onto our back. "Now you."

At first she tried to explain things, to help. But as his long fingers moved across our skin, her words failed too.

He was unhurried as before. He had all the time in the world. His yellow eyes fixed both of ours steadily, watching for the flicker of an eyelash, the quick indrawn breath. His hands were an orchestra to themselves, and we were conducting it. And oh, how his music made us dance.

Tria

We stayed on Earth only a day longer, while government officials regaled us with conciliatory speeches and promises to punish McKlellan, whom they swore they had known nothing about. Everyone seemed to be competing for time in front of us—and in front of the news cameras—talking about how eager they were to be on good terms with Shatak. We were shown as many of the sights as we could take in, including several fascinating museums.

The ordinary citizens, however, mainly looked at us with suspicion. When we entered a museum or a restaurant, they would look at us sideways and then slowly leave the area. "Maybe they really aren't ready," I worried to Karnath. "Could we be harming them just by being here?"

"Any harm we might do to the humans, we've already done," he reassured me. "Getting used to seeing aliens is good for them. No one is trusting of a different species at first. Their subconscious thinks we're monsters."

The humans bestowed all the gifts they could think of, from medals to books about Earth. Eleanor had a very special gift for us—a little orange kitten. Resa rubbed her face against his soft head, while he made a pleasing rumble. "I should be giving you something," I said. "None of this could have happened without you."

She blinked at me through her thick glasses. "But you have, Tria. I still have all the vials of your blood, and I was offered a grant to work on them. I don't know if there's actually a cure for anything in it, but as our first sample of genetically altered DNA, it's bound to be fascinating either way."

We lifted off at twilight, the lights of the city sparkling below a violet sky. I stood in the conference room, looking out the ship's only proper window, cradling the kitten on my chest. He gave a comforting rumble, unfazed to be departing his home planet. My own feelings were more complicated. I hadn't felt at home here, but I had put down a rootling or two, despite myself. I would miss Earth. And yet, I had no regrets. I wanted nothing more than to keep traveling the galaxy.

The door shushed open, but I didn't turn around. We had just gotten high enough for the sun to peek back over the horizon, as if we had forced it back out of bed to see us off. I didn't want to miss my last look at Earth—last, that is, until further notice.

"It looks beautiful from up here, doesn't it?" said Karnath's voice behind me, as his hands slid around my waist. He rested his chin on my shoulder. "I hope we can come back before too long. We'll be proposing a planetwide vote to change the non-interference policy. It seems to me that instead of trying to delay their technical development—which we have already failed to do—we should be assisting them in their social development. Our policy should be of careful, situationally-appropriate contact."

"You think you'll get the votes?"

"After they hear how close we came to disaster, I think so. At its heart, it was always a self-serving policy—we were afraid of dealing with these underdeveloped species in our own neighborhood. That same fear will drive people to want a change."

The curve of Earth became visible, the terminator line falling right across the capital. "If we can get a change, you could go home too," he added.

I stiffened. "Without you?" I asked in a small voice.

His arms tightened. "Of course not without me. Studying other planets is my life's work. And after Kinaru, who knows? Any other planet we want. That is, if you want to."

I relaxed into him. *Yes.*

Yes.

"Yes."

Acknowledgments

This story has been in the back of my mind since I was thirteen. Most of it came out of my own loneliness and longing for a brain buddy I could talk to all day, but I should give credit where due to my brother David, in whose role-playing universe I created the aliens in this book, and Rush lyricist Neil Peart, whose song "Hemispheres" provided some of the structure for the idea.

I would like to thank those who helped me write this, particularly Megan, my plot midwife and first reader. My writing group, the Buffoons, cheered me on the whole way. And I could only get the space to pursue this project thanks to my family: John, Marko, Michael, Miriam, and Jackie.

For helping me get this book from my hard drive to your hands, I would like to thank John (again) for doing the formatting and Susanne for her beautiful cover art.

ABOUT THE AUTHOR

Sheila Jenné was raised on Star Trek and Isaac Asimov, dreaming of space travel and the exploration of new worlds and civilizations. She has always been fascinated with first contact and how alien cultures might view Earth and human civilization.

In addition to her novel writing, Jenné has worked as a freelance writer, copyeditor, and Latin teacher. She resides in Virginia with her family.

Her other published novels include *Black Sails to Sunward*, *The Sea of Clouds*, *Under False Colors*, and *Invasive*.

For more information about Sheila Jenné, visit her website at **www.sheilajenne.com**.